THE BOY THE MONSTERS MADE

RONAN GRAVES

REAPERVERSE

BOOK I

Contents

Also by Ronan Graves

The Shintori Chronicles
Written as Elle Samhain

Aegis
Hemlock
Knight

CONTENT WARNINGS:
Loss of a parent
Loss of a spouse
Description of food
Descriptions of off-page episodes of delusions (paranoid)
On-page descriptions of visual, audio, and tactile hallucinations
Violence and murder
Monster horror
Blood and gore
Sleep paralysis
References to off-page domestic violence
Alcohol use
Smoking
Desecration of remains
Explicit sexual content
Ritual murder

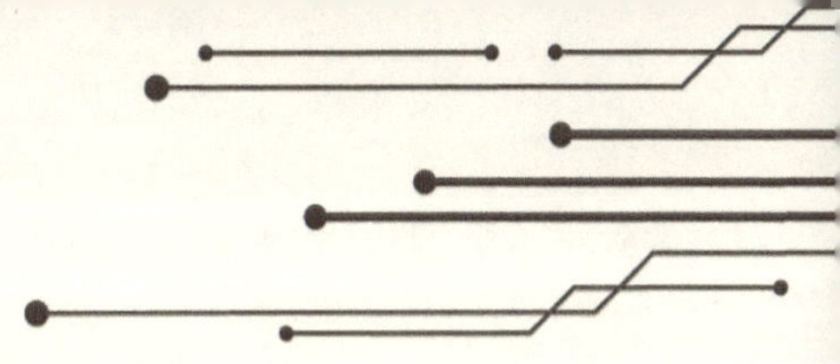

AUTHOR'S NOTE

M Y WONDERFUL READER,

There is a chance that upon beginning this adventure, you may already know of the struggles that befell me as your guide. Between the publishing of HEMLOCK and KNIGHT, I was diagnosed with schizoaffective disorder – a comorbidity of schizophrenia and a mood disorder. Writing has been a wonderful escape, a fantastical outlet, and I am so honored to be sharing with you again.

As you see the world through Griffin's eyes, I would like to note that his experience with schizophrenia is just one of many iterations. We will walk with him through hallucinations and other symptoms through a world with already blurred edges of reality. Though this condition will not be sensationalized and instead draw from my own personal experience, I understand if discussions of any kind may resonate in an uncomfortable way. If you find that this sort of content may not be best for you, I trust you will put this book back on the shelf.

Heroes must look out for themselves as they do for others.

Love & Swords,

RONAN GRAVES

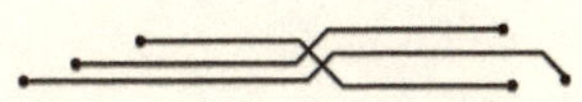

For anyone who has ever gone to bed defeated and said:

"I will try again tomorrow."

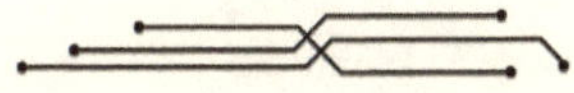

"That she loved me I should not have doubted; and I might have
been easily aware that in a bosom such as hers, love would have
regained no ordinary passion.
But in death only was I fully impressed with the strength of her
affection."

—— Edgar Allan Poe, *Ligeia*

*G*RIFFIN,

My sweet boy, it's your first day of school! I just saw you off with Jude and her mom, I wish I could have walked with you all the way to the school doors. You had already splashed in five puddles by the time you disappeared around the corner, so I hope you at least made it to school mostly dry. You were so excited to be starting and I wish I could have photographed the joy in yours and Jude's beautiful little faces. The whole world is going to open for you both and I hope you find the most wonderful magic in the knowledge.

I wonder what you will be like when you read this. I plan on giving it to you when you graduate so we can both laugh at how much you have changed and grown. What was your favorite subject? Did you like your teachers? Did you enjoy reading The Rambler and The Rook as much as your mama and Mimi did? Let's talk about what you think of that Griffin and I'll tell you why you are by far my favorite Griffin.

I love you endlessly,
Mama

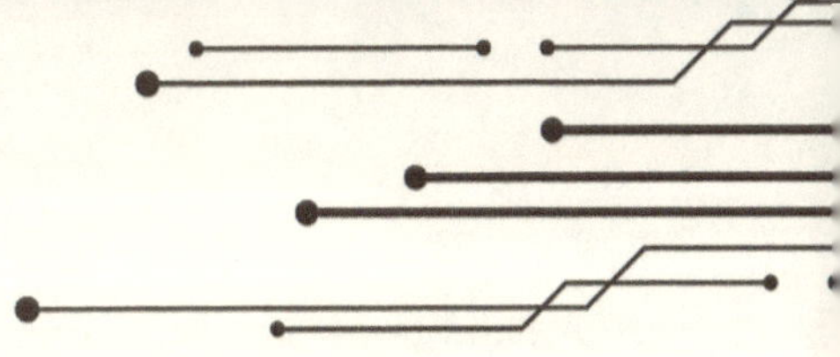

CHAPTER ONE
GRIFFIN

H E LOOKED DOWN AT the copper coins in his hands, double-checking that he had three of them, and then back up at the bronze statue. The metal woman watched him right back with a slight smile to her smart mouth. He must have seen it countless times by now. Her curls and cape were sculpted to blow in a wind he would rarely feel from behind the sarsen blockade of the Brightloch walls. A metal cat slunk around her oxidizing boots and splatter from birds dripped down the longsword she held at her side.

Sighing, he set the copper coins down at the base of the statue in a triangular formation.

"I'll be back on my way home today to clean you off, don't worry. I'll have your rocks then, too."

He received no thanks for the care he put in and he had to admit that he felt grateful for the silence. His eyes fell to the plaque:

AVERY PORTER

THE BERSERKER WITCH, SLAYER OF MONSTERS

MAY HER MEMORY BE A BLESSING

"Happy birthday to you too, Mama," he said. □

A hand firmly clapped around his left shoulder. He knew he should have flinched in startle, but he came around full circle and knew that he lost his ability to be jumpy long ago. Simply lifting his own hand to touch the fingers on his shoulder, he tested the reality of the sensation and felt satisfied when he hit rough calluses and fingernails cut to the quick. He turned his head to look at the man who had approached him.

"Hi, Dad."

The man watched him with a half-smile and he knew that his father tried to stifle down sympathy. It never worked, but at least he tried.

"I'm glad I caught up to you, Griffin," his father spoke. "You left without taking the money I left for you."

His father held out an open hand with several silver and gold coins and Griffin plucked them gingerly. He stared at them for a moment too long and he felt the concerned eyes of his father watching the top of his brown hair.

"Is it bad today?" His father asked in a low voice, knowing that the nature of the question was sensitive. It annoyed Griffin that he hadn't asked in the privacy of their own home and instead had waited until they were standing in the crowded town square.

He was all too aware of the people passing in a blur of colors around him as he frowned at the oxidizing coins in his hand. Griffin wasn't about to cry, not in the slightest, but he felt his mind skipping beats as it tried to speed ahead of him. His father waited patiently for him all the same and Griffin felt the presence of the body passing behind him as someone strode past. *Not a threat.*

"Good morning, Mr. Mosley! Happy birthday, Griffin!"

He caught the flicker of movement as his father politely raised his hand in a wave to acknowledge the friendly stranger, but he quickly turned his focus back to Griffin.

"I didn't see the spiders on the way here and she didn't say anything to me, if that's what you're asking. Why don't you ask a little louder next time," Griffin didn't bother to hide his thick agitation.

He finally looked up from the coins to his father. Griffin found the flicker of concern in his father's face too quickly for the man to change it. The eyebrow sliced by an old scar furrowed and though they were filtered by glasses, Griffin saw the glassy glaze over his green eyes. His eyes flicked over Griffin's shoulder to the bronze statue behind him.

"They jumped the gun on that one, Avery didn't die like that," his father had said when the statue was erected, unbeknownst to him. Griffin wasn't so sure. He had never seen his father quite as angry as the day he found the memorial in the town square.

Moz scratched at his short beard speckled with grey, just another one of his many tells. Griffin had memorized and categorized many of them in just eighteen years of life; it was even easier when he had one less parent to study. This particular one meant that his father was choosing his next words very carefully.

"I'm sorry, bud," Moz said. "I didn't mean to make you feel exposed by asking, I just worry."

Griffin frowned. He quietly accepted the apology but knew he had to hold a line.

"Regardless of that," his father knew Griffin's strategy well enough by now and changed the subject for him, "there's extra coin in there, why don't you pick yourself up a treat today? I've got a surprise for you later as well."

"Thanks, Dad."

Moz smiled, the aging lines of his face folding in the most familiar warmth. "Happy birthday, Griffin. Your mother and I love you so much."

Griffin let his anger melt away even when he ignored the brief hum of song he heard coming from the bronze statue behind him. He smiled up at his father before throwing his arms around him in a hug. Griffin's head grazed the bottom of Moz's chin, the margin between their tall statures seemingly shrunk by the day.

"Oof, you're going to knock me in the goggles next time! Thank gods you didn't get your mama's height."

"I love you too, Dad."

"Mistress of Nightshade, Beldam of the Veil between things living and dead! We beseech you, reach out your discerning hand to pull the flower we seek from your garden."

Griffin looked left and then right from where he laid on his back. His dark brows lifted in skepticism and his lips pursed tight as he tried to stifle back his laughs. He shifted again on the creaking floorboards of the darkened Old Library and the pair of feet pressed against the soles of his boots dropped a swift kick onto his shin;

the person they belonged to had finally had enough of his restless fidgeting.

"Fucking gods, would you sit still? This isn't going to work if you don't focus!"

Jude was wrong. It wasn't a problem that he wasn't lying in the circle of salt with the same reverence; it wasn't going to work because only one of them knew for sure that this was a fool's errand. And it certainly wasn't the one who had dropped a bulky tome of rituals on her face thrice already.

He felt the stir of her when Jude sat upright, closing the book with aggressive disappointment. She dropped it to the rotting floorboards, sending a plume of dust scattering in all directions. Jude shook her halo of black curls to rid herself of the salt she had disturbed when she came up off the ring.

A shadow flickered from between the empty book stacks and his eyes automatically followed to the late afternoon light filtering in through the dusty windowpane. He saw the vague shape of a black bird on the sill and couldn't quite tell if the bird watched him right back.

"It's there," Jude confirmed for him in a routine that had become their second nature. He didn't thank her because after about the second-hundredth time of reality checking him, she insisted that it wasn't necessary. So instead he said:

"My dad would be so pissed if he knew we were doing this."

Jude looked from the window, down to Griffin's face where he still laid on his back inside the haphazard circle of table salt. Her eyebrow arched, challenging him with a beautiful face of amber skepticism as she loosened the maroon necktie underneath the collar of her grey uniform sweater. "Then it's a good thing he'll never find out, right?"

Griffin sighed when he finally sat up.

"No, he won't," he agreed. "And I take back what I said. He would be hurt if he found out we were looking into resurrection circles. 'Your mama's not dead', he'd say. Something, something, 'time spent mourning is time spent not looking'. He's too fixated on his Suspect of the Week. Right now it's the Oracles of Neri, probably for the seventh time. It's Yumi who'd have our heads."

Jude huffed something resembling amusement. "The Queen would have our heads, for sure."

Griffin tried to imagine Mimi beaming proudly up at a study wall littered with mounted heads of people the same way hunters would collect taxidermies of prized kills. His gentle, bonus parent on one side of a coin and the stern Ink Queen on the other. It was a stupid thought and that's precisely what made him laugh.

He pulled himself up to his feet and reached down to help Jude stand. Her slender hand enveloped his with soft warmth as she rose to her feet. She let go to brush the dusting of salt off his Brightloch University sweater. Griffin looked down at Jude with the corners of his mouth turned up in just the smallest smile that he wasn't sure she would have seen in the darkness of the abandoned library if she had looked up.

"What are you doing in here?"

They both froze, looking up towards the silhouette in the door-frame. The figure stood much shorter than Griffin and Jude, with instantly recognizable cascades of light hair that caught the sunlight filtering into the hallway. Jude dropped her hands from his sweater to fold them in front of her chest, her affect falling flat so as to not betray her displeasure.

"Hi, Hanna," Griffin greeted them politely.

"Gloomy Prince," Hanna replied with saccharine sweetness. She stepped into the decaying library and her pale features came into view when she approached the circle to examine their handi-work. An eyebrow woven with carefully manicured threads of silver blonde lifted as she looked from the circle to Griffin's face, just long enough for her to make sure he was watching her before she glanced back down.

"A pull from the afterlife, huh? That's serious stuff, Gloomy. Maybe it would be best to find a Priestess to help you."

"It will be a push into the afterlife if you tell anyone," Jude bit before he could answer.

Hanna looked up from the ruined circle to Jude's face that began to falter in its neutrality. The face of the shorter student never broke its pleasantness when she obliged with, "very well. I just came in to tell whoever was in here that Grant is locking up for the night. I don't think you two were as quiet as you assumed."

"Thanks, bye now."

Hanna looked from Jude scattering the salt with her loafer to Griffin, giving him another sweet smile. "That's my cue, Gloomy. See you tomorrow."

Hanna floated through the doorway to leave in a cloud of ashen blonde and Griffin watched her back until she disappeared. When he turned his head, Jude scowled at him with her arms still folded.

"I don't understand why you suddenly get like that with her," he said.

Jude scooped up the tome from the floor, shoving it into her rucksack hastily as she mumbled "So I can't stand a nosy elf. Sue me."

"Don't be ridiculous, there's no such thing as elves."

"HA!" Jude's sarcastic bite led him out of the library and into the empty hall of the anthropology building. "Say what you will, but you'll catch on eventually!"

-Follow her-

Griffin ignored the voice and said instead, "did you still want to cram some studying tomorrow?"

Jude sighed, melodic and irritated as she bounded down the stone stairs to the darkened mezzanine. "I don't want to, but I'll be there. Have fun with your family tonight while you can, because it's going to be torture from here on out!"

"Absolutely, I'll be sure to throw back shots in front of my mom's empty grave."

Jude looked over her shoulder at him, her brown eyes widened in horror and he just grinned. Griffin made sure to throw in a dark joke about Mama every once in a while because he found it helped stave off the pity that felt far worse - some zingers landed better than others and some days if he couldn't laugh about it, he would have to cry.

She shook it off as she finished pulling on her coat and pushed through the oaken entry door into the vanishing light of the late afternoon. Griffin shuddered at the cold bite of winter after spending an hour in the dank air of the Old Library. Jude gave him a knowing look and he dropped his rucksack to pull on his own black peacoat.

"Before you go," Jude said as he threw the bag back onto his shoulder, "I have this for you."

She fished from her coat pocket a small box, wrapped in finely folded paper of cerulean and twine. Holding it out in one hand, she waited for him to take it.

-Trap-

He almost told the monotone voice to fuck off, but instead Griffin took the box from Jude's hand with reverent care as to not muss up the delicate gift wrap. Griffin looked from the small box in his hands to the waiting face of his best friend.

"Yes, for godssake open it now!"

Griffin almost felt bad for ripping into the paper, but not enough to stop him from acting on his excitement. Inside the gift was a white cardboard box, unlabelled and not giving him any clue as to its contents. He stuffed the torn paper into his pocket for later use and opened the top flap of the box to peer inside.

"It's the willow charcoal set you pointed out to me last time we were at Anne's shop," Jude explained. "I know you were having terrible luck with them being available, so I jumped on that as soon as they came back. There's a wrapped white one in there as well, I couldn't remember if you had any left."

Griffin looked up from the box to her face, softened with a smile that he felt almost certain matched his own. "This is perfect. Thank you, Jude."

"Happy birthday, Griffin. Welcome to awful, terrible adulthood!"

As if her two month head start gave her any authority to usher him into it like a wisened sage. He grimaced as he put the box of charcoals into his other pocket, with even more care than he had shown the beautiful paper it came in.

"Do you want me to walk you home?"

Jude shrugged at his offer. "I'm meeting my Pa halfway, they were in town today for something. I'll see you tomorrow!"

She shot him one more smile before she turned her back to walk alone towards the east campus gate. Griffin patted the box of charcoals in his pocket as he made his way to the northern gate, wondering what he would sketch with them first. Or rather, what he told Jude was his first sketch because there was no way he would ever tell her that he was still trying to translate her cheekbones to paper. He enjoyed art, but that was different from feeling he had a talent.

Griffin walked alone towards the castle on the hill. He hated it there; there were too many paintings of Mama on the walls and it made him far too aware that there was a chance his father was wrong. That she wouldn't be found.

As Griffin walked down the cobblestone avenue towards the bronze memorial of his mother, he felt the distinct sensation of eyes on him. The feeling was familiar, but sometimes too bothersome for him to simply ignore. Before he bent down to set the smooth rocks on the base of the statue, he looked up and his attention was immediately ensnared.

The man stood tall in the shadows of the narrow alleyway between brownstones and watched him with eyes glazed in inky black sclera and a flicker of golden irises. He waved with long, clawed fingers as Griffin stood up.

Griffin tried to blink him away but to no avail. He was too unimpressed to even be bothered by the presence of the figure - why were his hallucinations so uncreative? It would have been much better if he were a "crazy person" with a special gift or artistic affinity.

He ignored the ghastly figure and continued walking. Maybe there was still time to take up oil painting.

The doctor had called it schizophrenia. Griffin had never heard of it before, but the woman guessed that it had laid dormant in his lineage at some point. Maybe one of his mother's parents had it, or maybe his uncle Soren. Perhaps even one of his father's parents, whoever they had been. He had never met them and Moz never spoke of them. Regardless of where it originated, the doctor said that its onset was almost certainly exacerbated by the disappearance of Avery Porter two years ago.

It was more of an annoyance than anything, really. He felt grateful for his aunt Lily, Dr. Clements if you were being formal, and for all of the times she had been able to explain what was going on in that no-man's land between his ears.

His words kept getting jumbled? *"It's colloquially called 'word salad' and is completely normal. You're not any less intelligent, you just might need to start over sometimes."*

Hearing a bronze statue of his dead mother singing to him? *"Your brain is creating external stimuli and sometimes it can affect how you perceive things in the collective reality. We don't know a lot about why right now, but doctors here and in Eyon are studying it."*

Believing his father had poisoned him? *"It's called a delusion and they can be incredibly scary in the moment. It isn't something you'll be able to understand when it's happening, but he would never do anything to hurt you. You're his flesh and blood and the light in his eyes."*

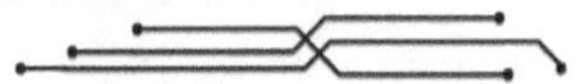

BRIGHTLOCH POLICE DEPARTMENT

SUBJECT: Sentinel William "Moz" Mosley of The Royal Sentry. Husband of Scout Avery Porter.

INTERVIEWING OFFICER: Deputy Ethan Woods

WOODS: Thank you for your time, Mosley. I understand your priority right now is being with your family, but anything you can tell us of any significance at all can make the world of a difference. It's not really standard for two officers to be on both sides of this so-

MOSLEY: Don't mistake me for one of you, I'm not a cop.

WOODS: I understand that, Mosley. Now let's not waste time splitting hairs. Can you tell me of anyone who might have wanted to harm your wife? Did she have any enemies?

MOSLEY: (*laughs*) You're shitting me, right? How long you been in town, kid? That woman collected enemies the way my son collects rocks. You'd be better off figuring out who never crossed her path. The whole town kissed the ground she walked on once she slayed the first demon, but they never really forgot about the campaign King Harthmoor spread to have her killed. Rest in shit, royal jackass.

WOODS: Interesting choice of description for the woman you married.

MOSLEY: I literally went to Od and back for Avery. We've seen each other at our absolute worst and still I loved her more than anything. You can quit sniffing here.

WOODS: It's just protocol to look into the spouses. Particularly in our line of work, you know that. But I'm on your side here.

MOSLEY: Speak for your fucking self. You going to pull this shit on the Queen, too? The only people allowed on my side are the ones I call family. Ask me your fucking questions so I can go home.

WOODS I think that's enough for today. Come back when you're ready to cooperate.

-END OF RECORDING-

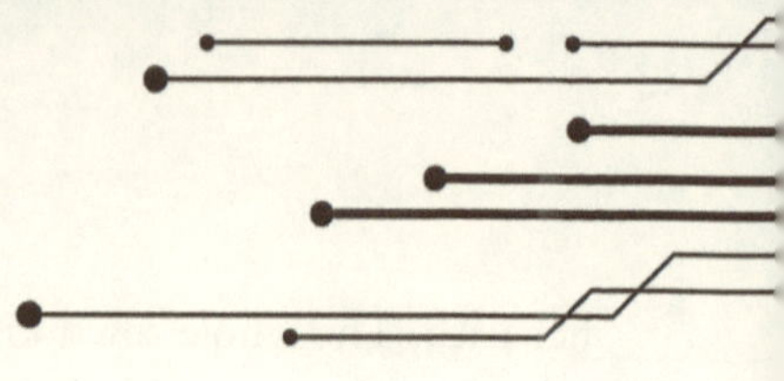

CHAPTER TWO
GRIFFIN

G RIFFIN SHOOK THE STRAY flakes of snow out of his hair and off his coat when he closed the large entry doors to Brightloch Castle behind him. The warmly lit foyer yawning before him was empty, save for voices echoing off the grey-veined marble floors and high vaulted ceilings from the last of Queen Harthmoor's advisory staff to leave for the day. A grand staircase stretched out and at the top the balcony open to the foyer, a painted portrait of his mother watched him with a slight smile.

Maybe it was because the wall wobbled and wouldn't lay flat in his vision, but he couldn't see the resemblance in their smiles that people were so eager to tell him about. He carelessly dropped his bookbag by the door just as a short woman with burning red hair strode out from the West Hall. She tugged on a black wool peacoat over her white button-down as she frowned at him.

"Please do take care with your belongings," she chided him, looking from the slumped bag to Griffin.

He picked it back up again and slung it onto his shoulder, "Sorry, Sarah."

Sarah smiled at him as she gave his shoulder a small squeeze. "Thank you. Happy Birthday, Master Griffin."

He did his best to not grimace at the honorific. *Hate it, hate it, hate it* - but the staff would rather ignore his request than his bonus mother's regal expectations.

Griffin walked down the Lower West Wing and into the Blue Study - Mimi's favorite - and found her already seated on one of the cognac leather couches. Yumi rose from her seat and met him with a tight hug after he dropped his book bag again.

"Happy birthday, Griffin," Yumi said sweetly with a small squeeze on his shoulder before she let him go. Griffin smiled down at her, just a couple inches shorter than he stood. Her topaz eyes were youthful and the lines around them made it clear to anyone that Yumi spent plenty of time smiling. She alternated between phases of thick bangs across her forehead and letting them grow out; now the dark hair streaked through with a gossamer of silver hung long and parted down the middle.

"Thanks, Mimi."

He looked down at the four wrapped boxes on the low oak table before he sank down into the couch beside her. Griffin felt guilty thinking it, but he couldn't think of anything he would want more than the small box of willow charcoal that still sat in his pocket and the smile on Jude's face that accompanied it. He wanted for nothing but had an exception of just one.

Nails clacked on the marble hallway floor just before a large dog trotted into the room. She went straight for him on the couch, seeming to know that he was the person who was supposed to be receiving her doting attention. The dog dropped her head into his lap and he petted the sides of her neck with deep strokes, her long saddle fur soft under his hands.

"Thank you, Maya," he said to the shepherd dog. Maya's tail wagged, her whole body wiggling along with it, and Griffin smiled down at her.

Shortly behind Maya came Moz, walking much slower as he balanced a large plate. Atop it was a cake, misshapen but made at home with love. His father had interests in the kitchen before, but his time there only increased after his wife's disappearance and he needed something to distract his mind in the evenings when he had no choice but to return to the case the next day.

"*Haaaaaappy birthday tooooo yooooooou,*" his parents both broke into an out-of-tune song and Griffin frowned hard. He had meant it when he specifically requested the absence of a song.

"Can we not, please?"

"*Haaaaaappy birthday tooooo yoooooooooooou,*" his father repeated but let the song end there, singing alone when Yumi fell silent immediately at her son's request.

-Fire-

The obnoxious and disembodied commentary grated on his nerves with how relevant it had been that day. He watched Moz set the cake down on the coffee table, shooing away Maya's curious nose with a playful rustle of her scruff and Griffin felt relieved to see that the most important request was heeded. No candles.

"You wanna break into those presents while I cut this?" His father asked as he carefully sliced a knife through the spongy cake, scooping the first piece and flopping it onto one of the plates Yumi had brought with her.

"Sure," he obliged.

"Not that one," Moz said in response after he licked stray frosting off his thumb when Griffin reached for the smallest box. "That one is last, pick a different one."

Griffin hovered his hands over the next biggest box, looking at his father while he waited for him to say that this one was off-limits as well.

"That one is fine."

When he picked it up, Yumi shifted in her seat and announced, "that one is from me!"

She wasn't nearly as tidy of a gift wrapper as Jude had proven to be. Tape sloppily wrapped around corners that had already torn at the vertices like she had struggled to fold the same piece over and over again before resigning. He ripped open the paper hastily.

Inside was a black box that he shook open to reveal a carefully packaged wristwatch with a black leather strap and a face of gold metal, neatly wrapped around a cushion. Griffin smiled. He liked the steady and reliable ticking of the second hand.

"Eighteen is a big deal, Griff," Yumi explained. "You deserve something nice. This will hold out for the rest of your life if you are good to it."

He looked up, still grinning. "Thank you, Mimi. I love it."

Yumi helped him put it on, gently closing the buckle as Moz dished the last slice of cake. He felt a small pang of loneliness at the number: three, not four.

After they finished eating the overly-artificial strawberry cake that his father had coated too heavily in frosting, Griffin got to work unwrapping the rest of the gifts. A leatherbound sketchbook with deckled edge pages from Aunt Lily and a tin of watercolor paints from Uncle Soren. Griffin didn't paint, but he felt grateful that his mother's somewhat distant brother was getting better in his efforts to connect since her disappearance.

Griffin unwrapped the smallest box that had first been off-limits to him and it was no larger than the size of his palm. Inside the folded tissue paper was a slip of paper, turned downward until Griffin flipped it over. On it was his father's handwriting in smudged black ink.

"*Too big to wrap, ask Dad*'," Griffin read the parchment aloud, but Moz was already out of his seat and headed out the open study door.

Yumi and Griffin waited, silent except for Maya's quiet snoring at his feet. When Moz came back, he was holding a tall, wooden staff in his hands. Griffin's eyes widened, instantly recognizing the staff as one meant to be used in martial arts. He jumped to his feet, reaching out with flexing fingers so that his father would hand it over. Moz laughed at his excitement and surrendered the thick staff to him.

Griffin turned the staff in his hand, running his awed gaze over it from end to end. It felt heavy in his unfamiliar hands, but he knew that it could easily become an extension of himself the more he handled it.

"Dad, this is amazing!"

"But wait, there's more!"

Moz held out his hand, gesturing for Griffin to hand the staff over to him.

"What? No, just tell me!"

"Please just let me show you, I don't want it to hurt you."

"Hurt me? How would it-" Griffin started, but handed over the staff anyway and cut himself off when Moz reached his fingers for the dead center of the heavy wooden staff.

Griffin had not noticed the lever before Moz flipped a finger on the small silver switch. Metal clinked and Moz rapped the staff once on the floor to shake loose three rows of pointed metal blades on each end of the staff.

"Shank outfitted it for you," Moz explained. "Flip to release, give it a good bonk to push them out of the tiny slats. And then you can pull that same lever back up to retract."

Griffin held out his hands, but Moz pulled the staff farther away from him.

"This gift does come with a safety condition."

He huffed with annoyance. "Yeah, what is that?"

"You practice. No fewer than four days a week at the university gym," Moz said sternly. "Something like this could really hurt some-one if you don't know how to use it correctly. And I know you're good as it is, but this is a weapon, bud."

He hesitated when he saw the humanoid shadow pass through the doorframe just past his father's shoulders. It stood too tall, moved too silently. *Not there.*

"I understand, Dad," he agreed when he snapped back into the moment. "I can do that."

Moz smiled warmly. "I don't think it needs to be said that you're not using this against the boys on your level. If I'm not able to meet you for practice, you call Jack or Shank, okay?"

Fight against Jude's parent? Griffin would rather eat sand.

"Will do," he said instead.

Moz clapped his hand and turned for the door. "Now that we've done the birthday 'cake before dinner', we need to have a real dinner. What would your mother say if you tried to skip vegetables?"

"'Fuck them vegetables?'"

"Your other mother."

"Oh," Griffin turned and looked at Mimi. "'Eat your vegetables or you'll shrink, just like Mama.'"

"Thatta boy," Yumi beamed. "Mama used to be six feet tall, believe it or not."

Griffin frowned. "Disbelief, easily."

They followed Moz into the kitchen. Since his mother's disappearance, it felt far too strange to eat in the dining room with her usual chair empty. Something about gathering around the butcher block kitchen island stung a little bit less with her absence.

Fragrant spice hung in the humid air of the kitchen when Moz took the glass lid off a deep-walled pan. Bubbles simmered and popped as he began plating the curried lamb shoulder atop three plates of rice. Griffin's mouth watered as he sat down at a stool opposite from Mimi.

"Did Theresa help you?" She asked Moz, her chin cradled in her hand as she watched him bring the plates over.

"Nope, all on my own this time!" He beamed as he slid a plate to Griffin, vibrant with the earthen colors of spice and roasted carrots under a blanket of parsley. Yumi hummed a small, impressed sound.

When both of Griffin's remaining parents were seated with their steaming plates of curried lamb, his father looked across to the empty space where the fourth stool had been tucked under the counter ledge. He took a sharp inhale before he looked to Griffin.

"Happy birthday, Griff," he said with a forced joy before he turned back to the empty space, "and happy birthday, Ave."

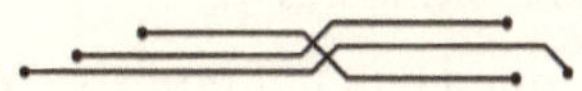

BRIGHTLOCH POLICE DEPARTMENT

SUBJECT: Scout Shank Sills (transcriber note: pronouns for Mx. Sills used hereafter are singular neutral "they" and "them") of the Brightloch Department of Forest Management

INTERVIEWING OFFICER: Deputy Ethan Woods

SILLS: One more time for the recording device, am I being detained?

WOODS: No, Sills. We just want to ask you what you witnessed so that we can paint a better picture of what happened yesterday. You are free to leave at any time, but it would help our investigation tremendously if you stayed.

WOODS: Can you please describe the events that you witnessed when Scout Avery Porter went missing?

SILLS: Certainly. We were on a team doing a routine sweep outside of the northeast wall. No subjects were found worth engaging and no evidence of possessions of an advanced stage were discovered.

WOODS: So you didn't see anyone who shouldn't have been there? Human or demon?

SILLS: No, it was just the Scouts. Avery, myself, and three others. Wilson, Gaspard, and Lind. She went back to where we parked the truck on the trail because she found a shrine in the woods she wanted to clean up before we packed out.

WOODS: Whose shrine was it?

SILLS: I never found out, but probably Malo's. She was a dedicant and it seemed he was who she cared the most for. Everyone else could have kicked rocks, in her eyes.

SILLS: She was out of sight but not far at all, the rest of us at the top ledge of the ravine nearest the wall. Avery was gone for maybe 10 minutes before we just heard her scream out. We hurried to find her and she was gone. No sign of her at all.

WOODS: What did you hear? Was there anything else before you heard her scream out?

SILLS: Nothing.

WOODS: I'd also like to make a note of your word choice. You didn't say scream, you said scream out. Did she yell anything out for help?

-NOTABLE PAUSE IN RECORDING-

WOODS: It's okay, take your time.

WOODS: What did she say, Sills?

SILLS: She screamed out a name and nothing else.

WOODS: Whose name?

SILLS: Aegis.

-END OF RECORDING-

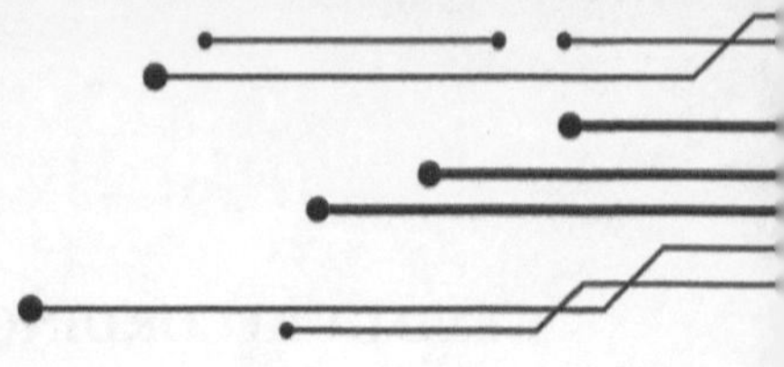

CHAPTER THREE
JUDE

"**A**WAKEN, *REAPER*," A VOICE spoke with the clarity of an alpine lake and Jude's eyelids shot open.

The command could have easily come from someone standing in the room with her, but when Jude's eyes darted across the small space of her bedroom, she found she was completely alone. She gingerly sat up and looked to the window just above where her bed pushed up against the wall. Locked and secure.

"Are you listening?"

Jude yelped at the voice and she jumped upright out of bed, her bare foot kicking the hard edges on the stack of books she left carelessly on the floor. She stumbled across the floor littered with clothing and textbooks to reach her desk where the radio sat. Grabbing it in both hands, she hastily turned it around in her fingers to figure out how she heard radio interference so clearly when the damned thing wasn't even turned on. Not a single knob was turned out of place and when she held it up against her ear, she heard nothing. Jude looked up to her closed bedroom door and wondered if it was too early in the morning to see if her parent had a radio on in another room.

A black blur fell from the ceiling and landed on the floor with a soft thud. Jude slowly set the radio back down on the desk and inched to the middle of the room to see what had fallen out of thin air. She crouched down and fumbled through the mess, struggling to make out the covers of books in what little of the sunrise light crept through the space between her curtains.

On the floor was a black notebook she had never seen before. Jude picked it up and sat on a cleared space on the hardwood floor to examine it carefully. The pebbled leather of the cover felt soft and worn in her fingers, like it had been loved for a lifetime; but when she opened it, the yellowed parchment pages were completely blank.

"*This is yours,*" the voice spoke again and Jude flinched. She had enough words to go by and decided that it was a man's voice she was hearing and she looked around once more to find its source but again came up empty-handed and confused.

"What do you mean it's mine? Who are you?"

She felt damned silly talking back to the voice but decided that she must have still been asleep. It wouldn't matter once she really did wake up.

"*In this ledger you will find names appear of those ready to approach the Crossroads,*" they ignored her questions and pushed through their disembodied monologue. "*They may be identified with a white miasma only you will see as their Reaper. To send them on their last voyage, you may set them into motion with a touch. Or kill them at your discretion.*"

"This is the dumbest fucking dream I've ever had," she answered with her head lifted up to the ceiling to make sure whoever it was heard her. Jude stood up and climbed back into bed, leaving the ledger on the floor. She shut her eyes with more force than what was natural and pulled the covers up over her nose.

Jude waited.

And then she opened one eye.

"I'll give you credit for theatrics. Perhaps there is someone else who can convince you."

A loud smack hit the window above Jude's head and she bolted upright with a scream. Her heart racing, she threw open the curtains to find the largest black bird she had ever seen flapping in a mess of inky feathers like it was trying to break through the window with brute force.

"Good luck with this one."

"Hey, kid! Let me in!"

The second voice came from a strange space in Jude's head, croaking and half-garbled from somewhere between her brain and the interior wall of her skull.

Over the desperate flapping of wings, Jude heard the sound of feet running down the creaky floorboards of the hallway. Her door burst open and her parent burst in, a wooden bat held defensively in front of them. Shank had clearly still been asleep when Jude screamed and they looked about the room frantically while they stood in cotton sweatpants. Their wide-eyed gaze fell to the black ledger on the floor. Traveled up to Jude's panicked and heaving shoulders. And beyond her to the black bird trying to break and enter.

"You have got to be fucking kidding me."

"What's happening?" Jude wanted to cry, but couldn't when she still rationally had no idea what was unfolding. She watched her parent lower the baton.

"Put on your shoes, honey," they said. "We're going to the castle."

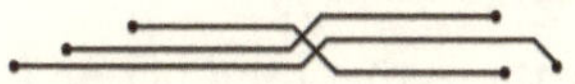

BRIGHTLOCH POLICE DEPARTMENT: Sentinel William "Moz" Mosley of The Royal Sentry. Husband of Scout Avery Porter.
INTERVIEWING OFFICER: Deputy Ethan Woods

WOODS: You ready this time, Mosley?

MOSLEY: Just ask me the questions.

WOODS: Very well. Your alibi checked out - you were vouched for at the Royal Sentry Headquarters at the time of your wife's disappearance by a number of your direct reports.

MOSLEY: Like I said.

WOODS: Do you know of anyone in particular who may have wanted to hurt her?

MOSLEY: Honestly? I can't think of anyone who might have gone through the trouble to actually go through with it. Sure, she wasn't popular with folks but we weren't exactly getting death threats either.

WOODS: Why did they not like her?

MOSLEY: They were afraid of her, maybe rightfully so. She got sucked into some bad situations and I don't think she was ever the same afterwards.

WOODS: What kind of bad situations?

-PAUSE IN RECORDING-

WOODS: Sure, you can smoke in here.

MOSLEY: Great.

-PAUSE IN RECORDING-

MOSLEY: Situations that I put her in. I was asked to bring her along to fulfill a ritual for the Oracles of Neri and then they ended up trying to kill her when it was done.

WOODS: So then they're worth looking at? What was the ritual?

MOSLEY: They're the first ones I would rake over the coals. It was to exorcise the Knights of Od.

WOODS: Did it work, who were they?

MOSLEY: No. Well, sort of. I'll give you three good guesses.

-PAUSE IN RECORDING-

WOODS: Well, shit.

MOSLEY: Yeah.

WOODS: I hope I'm not out of line by asking this, but do you regret bringing her with you? It sounds like there were some unintended consequences we're just now beginning to reap.

MOSLEY: I'm gonna fuckin' ignore that.

MOSLEY: No, that's not what I regret. Do you want to know what I really regret? I regret not waking her up that day to say "baby, let's both skip today. Instead of going to work, I'll make you chocolate pancakes and we'll fuck all day and when we need a break, I'll read you your favorite book. Because you're the sun in my sky and I would spin out of orbit if I ever lost you. And you'll be right where Griffin left you when he comes back from school - safe and sound." But I didn't.

-PAUSE IN RECORDING-

MOSLEY: She was alone and afraid and she screamed out for Aegis instead of me. Instead of Yumi. Why? How could he have protected her in a way we couldn't when he hasn't been around for years? I'll grind my fucking teeth out of my skull trying to figure out why.

WOODS: Who is Aegis? Nobody has been able to tell me.

MOSLEY: He's a real fuckin' problem, that's who.

-END OF RECORDING-

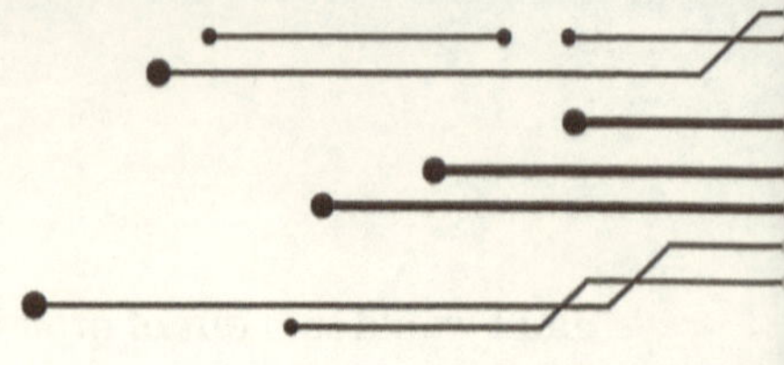

CHAPTER FOUR
GRIFFIN

G RIFFIN POKED HIS HEAD around the corner when he heard a knock at the large doorway of the main foyer. Rather than wait for an attendant to open it, his father turned around from his stride to the west hall to do it himself. Griffin frowned, looking down at the new watch that didn't quite sit on his wrist right. It was bizarrely early to be expecting guests, so he went to stand at his father's side out of curiosity.

To his surprise, it was Jude's face that greeted him. Her expression was fearful and she looked rattled with her winter coat thrown over her pajamas as though she had left home in a hurry. Beside her stood her parent, their graying locs were disheveled and they had left their wireframe glasses behind entirely.

Griffin had ignored the large black bird perched on Jude's shoulder at first, dismissing it as a rather vivid visual hallucination until it croaked and she flinched. Moz looked from the massive raven to the expressionless gaze on Shank's face.

"You're joking."

"Do I look like I am?"

Moz sighed, but stepped aside to let Jude and her parent inside.

"Dancing shoes back on, everyone," Moz grumbled. "Here we

go again."

Griffin's face twisted in confusion. "What's going on?"

"Our dear Jude has been made into a Reaper," his father answered as he closed the door behind them. "You brought the Ledger, I'm assuming?"

Shank answered only with a lift of their hand to show the small book they held, bound in worn black leather. Moz pressed his fingers hard into his own temples, sucking in a sharp breath.

"Oh fucking hell," he said on the exhale. "Is someone's name in it already?"

Shank flipped open the book with thick and yellowed parchment papers and held their thumb down to keep it from opening past the first page. "Matthew Sandoval," they read aloud.

Jude's eyes widened in horror. "What? Who's that? What does that mean?"

"It means their time is up," Shank said, closing the book and handing it out to Jude. She slowly took it from them, an absent stare on her face. "Your job is essentially to put their death into motion before they go to the Gatekeeper."

They then turned to Moz before saying "Y'know, I'm so fucking surprised that we're still doing this."

Moz shrugged. "Beats me."

"What do you mean? What are you still doing?" Griffin watched his father when both he and Shank turned their gaze to him, frozen as though they had expected he wouldn't have been listening. Shank slid their eyes towards Moz expectantly.

"Bud, your moms and I... I guess, all of us, really. Except for your

Aunt Lily and Tristan. We were all Reapers at one point, that's how we know each other."

"You *killed* people, Dad?"

Griffin might as well have punched his father in the throat with the look of hurt on his face from the accusation in his question. Moz opened his mouth like he was ready to speak, but closed it again with nothing.

"We can come back later," Shank said in a low voice, already putting their hand on Jude's shoulder to steer her back to the front door.

"Mimi too?"

Moz held up his hand. "No, you can stay. Griffin is asking the right questions and I think Jude needs to hear the answers." To Griffin, he added: "Yes, Mimi too."

The foyer was spinning. All of those times Aunt Lily assured Griffin that his father would never hurt him, and the whole time he was a Reaper? It didn't make sense. How could someone do that? How was Jude going to do that?

As if she felt his worry, she broke the silence. "Do I really have to kill them?"

"No, well, yes," Moz admitted to Jude, who looked like she could break into tears at any moment. "But not in the way that you're thinking! All you have to do is touch them when they're marked. It's more like giving them a kiss of death than killing them, if that makes any sense to you. It won't hurt unless... fuck, I wish Avery was here. She knew how to be kinder with this than I did."

"If shit goes wrong, she'll need a weapon," Shank pointed out, their tone perhaps more grim than what would have helped with Jude's panic.

"Wait right here, I'll see if we have anything I can give her," Moz said before he turned, jogged down the hallway and disappeared.

They stood in silence and Griffin felt the heaviness of Shank's gaze when it slid over to him. It picked apart his fear and Griffin felt his anxiety spike before they finally spoke:

"People change, Griff. Your dad's a good man. Nobody asks for this and there's only one way out of it."

One way out of it? *That means that Jude could be-*

"This should work!"

Moz came back. Holding a long-handled scythe out to Jude expectantly.

"A farming tool? What kind of Reaper uses a farming tool?" Jude complained.

"The armory is locked down and this is all we have to lend," Moz defended his quick decision. "We can find you something later, but it will be better than nothing."

Jude grumbled something under her breath, but reluctantly took the scythe anyway. Shank put both of their hands on her shoulders, shooing away the bird so it hopped lazily on the floor.

"We're going to walk you through the first one," they said. "You'll get the hang of it in no time, okay?"

"I would prefer to not have to get the hang of it, but it sounds like I don't have much of a choice, do I?"

Shank said nothing, but reached down to give their daughter's hand a squeeze.

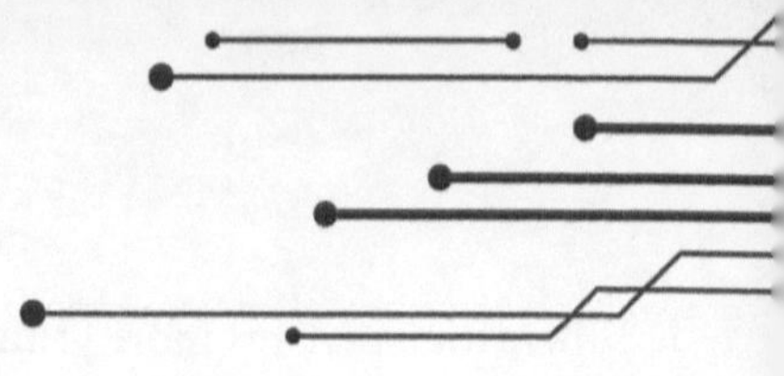

CHAPTER FIVE
JUDE

"**H**OW ARE WE SUPPOSED to find him?" Jude groaned. She was still in her pajamas when they turned yet another street corner to scour a boulevard buzzing with people on their way to start the day.

"You'll know them when you see them," her parent explained. "They'll be marked with a halo only you can see. Look for little, white orbs around someone's head. Until then, just be patient."

"*Patience? Ha!*"

Jude frowned, and turned her head up to look at the bird from his perch on her shoulder. "Piss off, Creak."

Moz huffed a laugh. "Bird Brain's name is Creak?"

"*Oh, I've heard plenty of names for you, asshole!*"

Jude's gaze slid to Moz, waiting for his snarky rebuttal, but it never came. He still walked ahead as though he would have been able to point Jude in the direction of her mark without seeing them. She frowned.

"You said I'm the only one who can see the halo," she repeated Shank's words. "Does that also mean I'm the only one who can hear Creak?"

"Not necessarily," Moz stopped. "Creak is a demon. Other familiars and demons can hear him, but not other Reapers. Consider him your incredibly annoying confidant."

Jude paused and looked back to the raven. Creak watched her with beady eyes and a small squawk bubbled in his throat.

"For the record," she said in a low voice to him, "I don't think you're any more annoying than the rest of these guys. We're good. Though do you mind being a little more careful where you're swinging those talons?"

Creak bobbed deep into his laughter, croaking loud with a garbled sound. He sounded just like any other raven Jude had encountered until he spoke clear in her head:

"I can't make any promises, first time flier!"

She rolled her eyes, but followed after her companions.

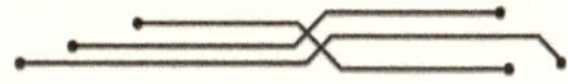

"There he is!"

Jude pointed across the avenue, forgetting that she was the only one who could see the bobbing orbs of white floating lazily around the head of the short man. He was dressed in thick layers under a wool trench coat and moving hurriedly with a steaming tumbler of coffee in his hand, looking more at the walkway below than above in order to follow the footpath of people who had trudged through the grey slush before him.

Shank took the scythe from her hands. "I don't recommend a weapon your first time. Don't let your sights off him and go touch him."

"What happens if I decide just not to do it?

She watched Shank's gaze slide to Moz and they leaned to the side towards him.

"You know...," they mumbled, "that's actually a great fucking question. What if we just... didn't do our job."

Moz frowned deep. "Trust me, I've tried. It pisses some important people off."

"The Beldam? I don't see why she would be an issue anymore."

"Nope, not her," Moz responded with a shake of his head. "Yve is the one who would throw a fit. It would throw off the balance she wanted from the Beldam in the first place. She'd probably settle the score with a tidal wave or Mount Forge blowing a lid."

"Hello?" Jude waved her arm above her head. "May I please be included in this conversation? It's me with the bird and the rusty farming tool."

Griffin, who had been observing quietly like always, ducked his head down to hide a small laugh and she couldn't help but smile a little even in her frustration. Jude knew she probably would have been suffering a much more dramatic freak-out if his grounding presence had been absent.

"Sorry," Griffin's father rushed through the apology a little too quickly for her liking, like he was stepping over it. "Think of yourself as a tool of the gods now. Going against them would be risky, wouldn't it?"

She watched her parent's expression change to a tone of solemnity and the silence weighed heavy with meaning. Moz pointed low, close to his torso to conceal his signal towards the stranger:

"You're going to lose him if you're not careful."

Jude groaned. "Fine."

She turned back in the direction she saw Matthew Sandoval walking in and caught a glimpse of the white orbs in a cluster of people moving with the flow of morning traffic. Jude took long strides, light on her feet to ensure she could catch up to him undetected. Creak flapped, flicking her in the face with iridescent feathers before he launched himself into the air to take perch on a rooftop ledge.

Finally, she was close enough to reach out and touch him. Did it matter if she touched clothing or skin? Jude wasn't sure, but knew she just had to find out through trial and error. Her fingers brushed along the wool houndstooth of his coat.

Jude thought she had been gentle enough to remain unnoticed, but the man stopped and turned abruptly to see who had just touched him. He was a serious looking man, with thick glasses and a shadow of a close shave painting the bottom half of his square face. She felt the heartbreak on her face when she realized that he was still so young; not much older than her own parents, if older at all.

Matthew Sandoval looked at Jude's face in a way that made her feel so small, despite having a good five inches of height over him. He rolled his eyes and turned away, holding up his hand in a wave when he said, "No thank you," and kept walking as though he had just turned away a solicitor on his front stoop.

Jude was bewildered— *does he not understand?*

The white orbs around his head faded, but he kept walking. Jude frowned. *Did it work or not?*

Her parent caught up to where she stood in a daze, trying to piece together what had happened and where she was to go from here. Shank put a hand on her shoulder and gave it a gentle squeeze.

"Unless you directly end their life," they spoke softly, "you'll almost never see them pass."

Jude turned to her parent and saw so much of her own face watching her with concern. In the furrow of their dark brows, the hard lines of a square jaw set in seriousness, and the crackle of a warm fire in their eyes. But the greying beard they rubbed their palm across in thought was all their own before they spoke:

"The Keeper of the Crossroads will catch up to you, no doubt. Just to make sure you are understanding your duties."

Griffin and his father caught up to them just before Shank fell quiet again.

"Balthazar should be here any minute," Moz said. He frowned as he whirled his head around to look in every direction.

The hell is he looking for? Jude scanned the crowd as well, but nothing seemed out of the ordinary. No more orbs, nothing.

"Keep doing your thing, I'll be here," Moz called out, not turning back towards them as he strode into the alleyway and ducked out of sight.

"What the hell is your dad doing," Jude muttered as she leaned towards Griffin to keep her voice low and out of earshot of his strange father.

"Fuck if I know."

They waited on the sidewalk and Jude's patience was the first to wear thin as she started kicking her boots at air and pacing in circles.

Finally, the air around them shifted. The shape of a figure stretched out from the ground and kept growing until they materialized. The man wore a suit of crushed purple velvet with coattails too long and a stovepipe hat too tall. His hair hung in dark locs and a stripe of black paint smeared across his cheekbones and over his nose.

The man grinned toothily as he held out his open hands, adorned in thick rings of gold. His voice was velveteen and whiskey-smooth when he said: "Well hello, children. I am called Balthazar."

Jude watched Griffin's father sprint out from the alley full speed. Moz leaped onto Balthazar from behind, his hands wrapping around Balthazar's face and neck. Jude flinched when Balthazar wobbled forward and Moz howled out in pain as the suited man crunched one of his tattooed fingers between his teeth.

"Yoooou son of a bitch!" Moz withdrew his hand and flapped the bleeding finger in the air.

In the moment of pause in his offensive strike, Balthazar seized him hard by the shoulders and slammed him hard into the ground. Moz groaned, laying on his back when the suited man turned back to Jude with an eerily pleasant smile across his paint-streaked face.

Griffin's father took a deep breath before he yelled, "WHERE IS MY WIFE?"

"I have a gift for you," Balthazar said, completely ignoring Moz, with his head tilted down to grin at Jude. "Would you like it?"

"NO!" Moz yelled as he picked himself up off the ground, wet from falling into the half-melted snow. "Jude, say no!"

Shank held out their hand in front of Jude to stop her as they watched Balthazar.

"Jude honey, let's be smart about this. What kind of gift are we talking about?"

"You know that I can't tell you," Balthazar answered them.

"What I am asking is if it will make my daughter safer."

Balthazar straightened up and turned his gaze to them, holding a calculated stare and the air between them grew heavy.

"I understand your fear, Shank Sills. I know what it means to be a concerned parent, particularly in these dark times we face," Balthazar said. "You have a clever kid, one I'll be sure to be careful around. I can promise you that the gift my wife has for her will make her safe. Stronger than she already is."

With their hand still held out defensively, her parent looked down at Jude.

"It's your call," they said quietly. "I know he's intimidating, but you can say no. If that's what you want."

Jude gently slid her hand over Shank's and pushed it down to step towards Balthazar. The Demon of the Crossroads watched her, looking down with delight in his charcoal eyes. When she was close enough to see the smear of black paint across the bridge of his nose and the crooked set of his grin, she stopped.

"I'll take it."

Moz swore and turned away with his hands set in frustration on his waist while Balthazar smiled wider at Jude.

"I look forward to seeing what you do with it, Daughter," Balthazar said as he lifted his hands, rolling back his cuffs with an air of showmanship and a stare that never left Jude's face.

It wasn't until then that her nervousness set in. She had expected him to reach into a pocket and pull out a small package, not whatever this was. Before she could question the act, he reached fast and closed his hands around each side of Jude's head. She tried to wriggle free before the grinding screech of metal filled her ears.

Jude shrieked, buckling at the knees when pain flooded her skull in throbbing pounds. Instead of releasing her, Balthazar bent at the waist to follow her down to a kneel. She could swear she felt her nerve endings snap and rearrange themselves into shapes they were never meant to be. Her stomach seized and acidity rose in her throat.

The shrill sound wavered, rising and falling in pulsing terror. Blood dribbled down her philtrum and she felt the copper warmth spill over her top lip. Jude quickly stopped her screaming to avoid a mouthful of her own blood.

Balthazar stumbled away from her when he was rammed from the side, but this time Griffin was the assailant. The demon staggered backwards, but Griffin stayed planted firmly in front of Jude to keep them separated.

"Of *course* you brought a guard dog with you! Because my job can never be easy, can it?"

The suited man dusted himself off, refolded his cuffs and looked past Griffin at her. Jude wiped the blood from her face with the back of her hand and looked down at the crimson smear.

"My Daughter, where would you like to go most in this world?"

"Wh...What?"

"Anywhere, you can go anywhere in the world. Where to?"

"Uh, I don't know? I'd like to see the protected wetlands in

Wrencrest, I guess," Jude said as she was picking herself up off the ground. "Why does it-"

"Too far, pick somewhere closer."

"What? I thought you said-"

"How about that lightpost across the street?"

"Why did you even ask me if you were going to decide my answer for me?"

"Think of that spot. It will work better at first if it's a place you can visualize. Eventually you won't need to, but let's start small."

Jude looked to the light post across the boulevard that Balthazar was pointing towards with one finger outfitted in three rings. She sighed.

"Okay... I would really like to be at that light post over there."

"Don't wish for it. Will it."

"I don't see what the difference is."

"You don't wish to be there," he said again. "You will be there and you defy space to make it so. Say it. That is where you will go."

Jude took a deep breath in through her nose.

"This is where I go."

In front of her, the air flickered with black streaks. She thought at first it was a trick of the light until it grew thicker and churned, taking shape into a flat black shadow. The air had undone itself and it looked as though the world had splintered with a gaping wound of darkness. Jude watched with wide eyes and felt the ice cold that emanated from the split.

"It is a portal, Daughter," Balthazar explained and she felt glad for it; she never would have come to the conclusion on her own because she had been just on the cusp of running in the opposite direction. "Now step through."

She hesitated and her uneasy gaze shifted towards her parent.

Shank nodded, "It's okay, you can go. We won't let anything happen to you."

When she looked to Griffin beside her, he exhaled that small cue through his nose that let Jude know he didn't like what was happening at all. But he nodded.

Jude slowly inched towards the swirling portal with an arm extended forward. When her fingers touched the surface, it felt like nothing more than frigid air, even in comparison to the winter around them. She sank forward and her arm disappeared into the darkness. She could still feel her fingers as she wiggled them on the other side and before she could allow herself the time to panic, Jude dove in behind it.

The pitch dark startled her with its oppressive nothingness.

"Hello? Can you hear me?"

She heard no answer and the silence tipped her over the edge of her fear. The sound of her own voice was devoured by the void. There was no way her parent would have heard her from the outside, but still her instinct was to cry out:

"HELP!"

Still no reply, but she felt the pull to step forward like a gentle thread stitched into her navel to draw her footsteps. Jude's breathing fell staggered and frightful, but she didn't know what else to do. She followed the pull from the depth of the freezing darkness.

She passed through a threshold of warmth like she had been underwater and finally breached the surface before her lungs could fail her. Light encompassed her once again and she had never before felt so grateful for it. Jude laughed in relief when she saw the cobblestone again underneath her boots and the warm glow of the bookstore basked her in golds.

Wait, the bookstore?

Confused, Jude turned around and caught the last of the portal vanishing into empty air. Behind it, she saw the others across the avenue. Balthazar simply waved to her, a pleased grin on his face.

"Holy shit," Jude said breathlessly.

The excited pitch in her breathing turned to laughter as the men and her parent crossed the street to meet her. She looked down at her hands in amazement at what they had done. Creak landed on her shoulder, pinching her skin through her clothes as he settled into position.

"How did it feel, Daughter?" Balthazar asked.

"I... it shouldn't be possible. How?"

"I think you'll find that possibility is only subjective," Balthazar said. Jude instantly knew that the words would stay with her forever. Before she could respond, Balthazar turned his head in an exaggerated swing towards Moz, glaring through Shank's head.

"And to answer your question," Balthazar said to Moz, "I do not know where your wife is."

Moz hesitated before he asked, "Did she come to your gate?"

Balthazar drew in a breath. "Do you know how many souls I send off each day? Pick a number, double it, and add three zeros. This is no knock on whether or not your wife is memorable, I just do not know."

"You do know my wife is Avery Porter, right?"

"I am unfortunately very aware."

Griffin's father frowned, but he did not fight Balthazar any longer. He shrunk away, withdrawing his request for help when he knew that he was not going to receive any.

Balthazar looked down at Jude, a small and knowing smile on his upturned face. The look sent chills down her spine and she had never before felt so small and insignificant.

"We'll be in touch, Daughter. Remember your responsibilities."

He sunk back down in a blur of amethyst velvet and disappeared into the ground. She stared at the wet cobblestone in disbelief.

"Are you okay?" Griffin asked, a frown of genuine concern cutting through the flatness his face had worn lately. His dark hair was still disheveled from sleep with the section of bleached blonde above his forehead splaying in every direction it wasn't trained to.

"Yeah," she answered him and the staggered breathing around her panicked words became detectable to her for the first time since she had woken up to the strange voice. "Yeah, yeah, I'm okay."

Griffin didn't answer with words, but pulled her into a hug. She took a deep breath to push out the fear and drew in the scent of pine and parchment before she squeezed around his middle with her arms, locking her hands behind his back. Jude felt safe wrapped in his tall frame and wiry muscles.

"Thanks, Griff."

The safety of the embrace was easily broken when her parent spoke from behind them:

"There's something else you need to know, sweetheart."

Jude let go of Griffin and turned to them, frightened fast by the grave expression on their face.

"There is another cost to all of this," Shank said. "To be a Reaper means that this was not your first go around at life, you understand that, yes?"

Jude shook her head. "I had assumed all this to be a legend... what does that mean?"

Shank inhaled sharply through their nose.

"They picked you, Jude. By hand. But they left something behind for you to find."

"Like a scavenger hunt?"

Their small laugh was mildly assuring until they answered: "In a way, I suppose. It's something you struggled with in your past life. An emotion, a very specific feeling. And you have to be a Reaper until you can find it and then you can move on. Do you understand?"

Jude's eyes widened in alarm. "Move on? Like 'die' move on?"

"No. 'Live' move on. You'll be free to carry on like this never happened. Like Mr. Mosley. Like me. You'll begin to age again and live out the rest of your natural life."

Age again? Like it never happened? She would bring people to their deaths and then act like it never happened. Jude didn't understand how such a thing could even be possible. How would one even possess the hands of a harbinger and move on from that once they reached a checkpoint - a seemingly arbitrary end goal, no less.

She frowned. If she was to do this, she must never reach such a point of apathy that she could just carry on. Jude hoped that her parent and Griffin's father had never crossed that line. It felt bordering on cruelty to her.

But she knew that she didn't know; Reaping Mr. Sandoval was only the first taste of what was to come and Jude couldn't deny the sliver of possibility of reaching such a jaded point even if she resisted with all her might. Especially if aging stopped for her and she had a wide window of time to steep to bitterness. Jude couldn't let that happen. She had to find that emotion fast before life lost meaning to her. Her hands of death must always stay warm.

"I can do it," she affirmed out loud.

She was always one to bet on herself.

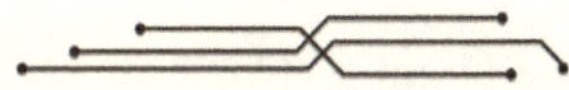

Kurosaki,

I'm sorry I haven't written to you in so long. I'm sure you get why.

I think you're the only person on the outside I talk to about this honestly. Tristan is enjoying the golden years of his life and I really can't bother him with trying to bond over dead or missing wives. He's knitting the most fabulous jumpers, I'll have him send you one sometime.

I can't tell if Yumi has suffered in her fear and grief worse. She barely ever leaves her chamber and I see her once or twice a week if I'm lucky. I think she's worried about seeing her ghost somewhere this time of year with the thinner Veil. It takes a lot less to scare her. Both her and Owen, supposedly, have said they still haven't found her spirit anywhere. And while I like to believe that Avery would rest peacefully if she had in fact died, I know my wife well enough to know she has a long list of people she would haunt the fuck out of. You're probably on that list, but only for the laughs.

I feel so angry all the time, Kuro. Like I want to rip down the world around me, burn it all down so there's nothing left that can hurt our little boy. In her love I learned mercy and in her loss I exhumed my fury. It's almost like the Thing is back again.

I think of you all the time and hope Eyon (and your new boyfriend) are treating you well. I think of Al all the time too, I know she's so proud of you.

Love,
Mozzarella

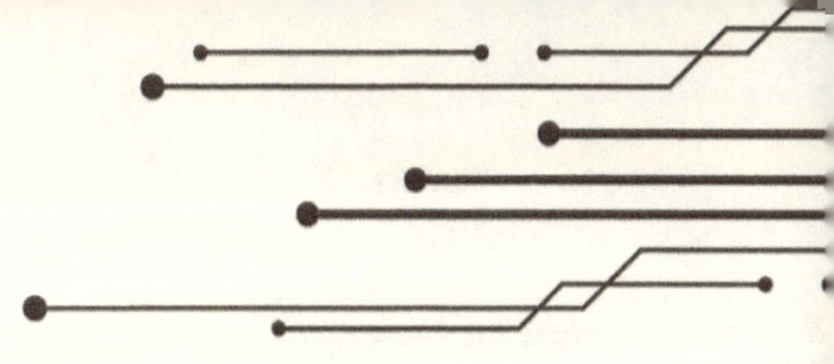

CHAPTER SIX
GRIFFIN

*D*ARKNESS TRAPPED GRIFFIN IN *an unforgiving maw. He was acutely aware of the stone floor beneath his boots and the emptiness of the hot humidity around him. What happened to the creeping cold of the coming Iverne season? Where was he?*

A faint pinprick of glowing red flickered somewhere in the distance ahead of him and Griffin assumed that the only sensible thing to do was to walk towards it. Silence blanketed him with the heaviness of a death shroud. No footfalls, no whispers of his mind manifesting around him.

Griffin drew nearer to the glow and realized that whatever it was, it came from the floor. He strained his eyes to focus and the shape sharpened. A ring of vermillion cut through the darkness and a shadow of movement floated from inside its border. Were his eyes deceiving him again? The longer he walked, the farther he felt from the eerie circle.

Metal rattled from the direction of the glow and Griffin felt the punch of fear in his gut when a band of rusted iron clamped hard around his wrist and drew blood. The band was a shackle and whatever was on the other end of the heavy chain, it pulled with an immense strength that swept Griffin's feet out from underneath him.

His face dragged fast across the uneven sarsen floor and he knew it should have shredded the skin of his cheek, but he felt nothing. When Griffin came to a stop, he looked at the ring of glowing forms on the floor before him. The shapes were linear and freckled through with small circles, but he couldn't make sense of their arrangements. Was he supposed to understand? An oppressive feeling forcing his shoulders down said that he was; that he was a fool for not deciphering them instantly.

Beyond the strange shapes, on the other side of the double rings, a pair of pale feet stood on the inside of the concentric circles. Griffin's gaze rolled past the hem of the white linen dress and up to the person who wore it.

His mother stared down at him.

No, not Mama.

A bastardization of her face, looking down at him with a grin full of too many teeth. Her neck jutted too far to one side and her eyes glowed in white, pupilless voids. Her ever-present braids were unraveled and dark waves fell down to the waist of the dress that was the dead giveaway that this was not the real Avery Porter.

The shackle on his wrist connected him to her opposite arm and when he struggled to stand up, the metal chain between them shortened and rattled when he backpedaled away from the revenant. Not Mama watched him with the fixated eyes of a ravenous predator and she began to pace within the confines of her circle like a caged animal.

Just beyond the bony shoulder of Not Mama, Griffin saw two more figures standing on the edge of light cast by the glowing ring of sigils. They were both women in the same linen dress - one with long curls of blonde, the other with blunted strands of faded rose gold. Their faces kept moving and changing, Griffin couldn't focus on them quickly enough to discern their features.

Not Mama's pacing tugged Griffin with her as the chain shortened, pulling him closer to her crowded fangs.

"The light of justice never reaches the stomach of a hungry god, *" Not Mama spoke. Griffin had expected the voice to be twisted and ugly, but it was her. And that was far worse.*

Not Mama yanked him hard and with the jolt, Griffin stood with his toes against the outside ring of the circle. He felt the hot, rotting breath of hell from Not Mama's mouth when she said:

"Lambs of sacrifice to lords of resurrection."

The floor opened underneath Griffin and swallowed him into empty air. Above him, Not Mama watched with her broken neck and empty eyes until she disappeared from the other end of the shackle that lengthened into eternity. He fell until his spine broke against the slamming impact of the ground beneath him.

Griffin opened his eyes when he felt the hard jolt and he immediately checked to ensure that he could move all his limbs. Touching his own face with sweating palms, he was satisfied, and decided that the freeze of sleep paralysis would not be an issue that night.

The grip of night terrors choked him on an almost regular basis and he had been convinced for the longest time that it was a symptom of the schizophrenia. But divulging this to his father had proved otherwise; Moz had suffered them, too. Griffin considered on several occasions to ask Yumi if she ever woke up alone in the night, frozen in place, and vividly hallucinating. But he didn't think he could bear to know that the throes of grief manifested so intensely for her. Not for sweet, gentle Mimi.

He heard the jingle of a dog collar and saw the shadow of Maya's head perk up from the end of his poster bed.

In the darkness, he exhaled sharply and said to her, "let's not share that one with Doc."

He laid on his back, knowing that there was no way he would sleep again that night, and stared at the glow in the dark stars his mother had helped him stick to the ribs of the vaulted ceiling in his bedroom when he was little. Griffin once had half a mind to take them down, but now they were precious things singing to him in the dark in her absence.

My son, my star.

My moon, my life.

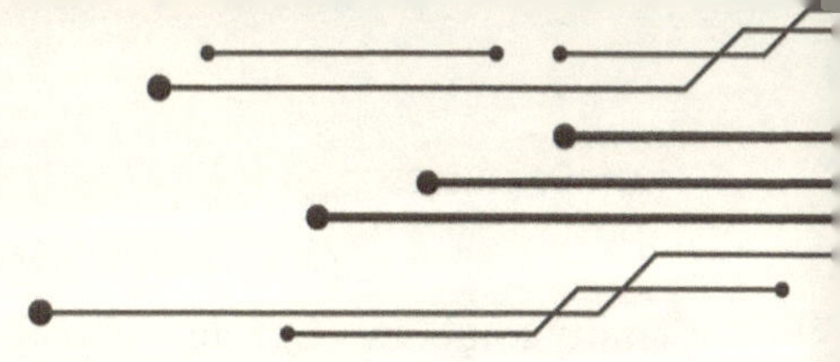

CHAPTER SEVEN
KUROSAKI

I T WAS THE MIDDLE of the night when the sleek, black motorcycle pulled onto the ice-crusted ferry and its rider cut the engine. The vehicle deck was nearly empty. Almost all travelers making the voyage between Eyon and Brightloch had the good sense to embark during the daylight hours when the sun kept the narrow roads thawed. Treacherous travel did not dissuade the rider from leaving the island in a hurry.

They clipped the key to the small silver chain at their waist and rebuttoned their long coat before starting for the narrow stairwell to the passenger deck. In the tight space, the rider had just enough room for the rifle case, overstuffed pack on their back, and the clearance for the bend of their elbows as they removed the scraped helmet. Kicking open the door with helmet in hand, Izaya Kurosaki shook out his snow-dampened hair and looked for a seat.

He had many empty rows of green vinyl benches to choose from along the starboard hall but made a determined beeline for the seating area nearest the bow. Though the Stillmaw Sea before them waited in pitch darkness, Kurosaki greatly preferred to face the direction of voyage. He slammed his pack down into one chair and gingerly set his helmet down in another before he slumped into the empty seat between them.

Kurosaki gripped both armrests with white knuckles and let his eyelids finally fall shut. The tension still would not let him go. He thought of the letter folded and addressed to him in the handwriting that felt like home, burning a hole in his interior coat pocket. The one nearest his heart. He opened his eyes to look at the back of the chair in front of him and realized he was no longer alone.

Kurosaki saw the shadow in his periphery but did not bother to turn his head. He knew this song and dance by heart.

"I'm not a fuckin' fool, 'Zay," the revenant in the chair next to him spat, but Kurosaki kept his gaze fixed on the row of seats in front of him. Anything to keep himself from the temptation to look. *This is getting old.*

"I know that every time I fucked you, you were wishing it was Will. Is that why you couldn't be bothered to pull me out of a burning car but you'll drop everything when you think you see your chance? I don't mind being the one to break it to you: he doesn't want you. Never has. Never will."

Kurosaki finally turned. Todd's half-charred face stared back at him, expressionless under the round black sunglasses that matched the pair in his own pocket. One sleeve of his leather jacket was burned and shredded to tatters, the white shirt underneath singed to almost complete black. Half of his gelled maroon hair was burned down to blistered scalp.

Of all the ghosts that could have haunted him, why this bastard? Todd's face caught the flickering light of the ferry fluorescents as though he were as solid and breathing as Kurosaki was. Under the buzzing bulbs, he heard the faint sizzling of flesh. Smelled the sickly sweet haze of spilled gasoline all over again.

"If I could do it all again," Kurosaki murmured, "I would torch that car myself."

Todd's cracked and bleeding lips turned up in a vicious smile. He ran his tongue across the bottom ridge of his top teeth and Kurosaki knew then that he had fucked up by acknowledging his presence.

"I'd pay money to see that, you little bitch."

At that, Kurosaki went back to ignoring him. This conversation had already lasted much longer than usual; he'd been too tired to cut off Todd's monologue at its start.

Kurosaki opened the buckled flap of his pack and rummaged through its contents, digging under crumpled shirts and balled up boxers until he found the notebook cushioned by the clothing. He slapped it onto his lap and pulled the pen out of the elastic on the side before flipping open to the dog-eared page he had begun at his apartment:

Moz,

Todd snorted at that. "Love letters to someone's husband? That's pathetic even for you, 'Zay."

Kurosaki would have been delighted to continue ignoring him, but unfortunately, the dead man had a point. He pinched the bridge of his nose between two fingers and let out a frustrated sigh.

"*Dear Avery's husband,*" Todd dictated in a sing-song voice that made his words all the more mocking, "*I am writing to tell you that*

I'm a pathetic bitch of a man who can't keep his fuckin' head on straight. I cry every night because I'm jealous of a woman who couldn't cut her way out of a paper bag with a longsword. Wah! P.S. Todd's dick is way bigger than yours."

"You're right," Kurosaki said, sitting up straight. "Here, you write this."

He dropped the pen into Todd's ghostly lap and it fell straight through to the linoleum floor. The revenant glowered at him.

"I hope this ship sinks and you die a slow death, you fucking dick."

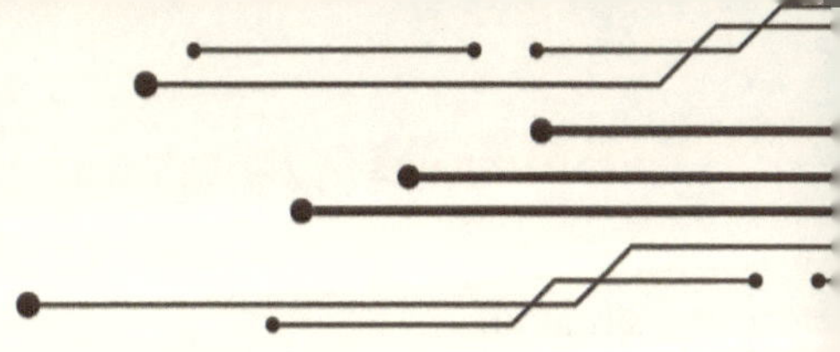

CHAPTER EIGHT
MOZ

MOZ FLOATED IN THE heavy space between sleep and wakefulness. He heard the door to his bedroom swing open and felt the feminine presence step inside. His limbs felt too heavy to roll over from his position on his stomach, so he waited with his face half-pressed into the pillow. He couldn't explain how, but he knew it was Avery.

She's back, she's home.

He felt her weight press down beside him and the following relief that she was crawling back into bed with him.

I missed you so much.

Moz wanted to tell her he loved her, that he was so happy to see her again. He might have spoken the words, but perhaps he had just thought them loud enough for her to hear. He thought he opened his eyes, but saw only darkness and heard the distant ringing of a telephone.

Her weight continued to crawl across him and he felt hands slip under his waist, fumbling for his groin. Hot blood pounded in his ears. Sex without so much as a *hello*?

No, something was wrong. He struggled to move his arms to push her off and realization struck him when he recognized the situation.

Sleep paralysis. Just wait.

The nightmare climbed onto his back and leaned its head down next to his. Phantom strings of wet hair slapped against his cheek and he saw the shadows of it envelope him in a ghastly curtain. Its mouth came close to his ear, whispering long minutes of scratched forms of words but Moz could make out none of them.

He rode out the encounter in frozen terror.

Then just as quietly as it had transpired in the darkness, it was gone again.

Moz gasped for breath, too terrified to try moving his limbs again to assure himself that it was really over. His heart rate settled back into his bones and he heaved his muscles in one fell swoop to roll himself onto his side. He curled his fingers into his palms and flexed them back out again. Everything seemed to be moving just fine.

The phone rang from the hall and Moz flinched hard. It must have actually been ringing during the sleep paralysis episode and not just an audio hallucination. He prayed again that this wasn't what his son lived through every waking day.

Moz fumbled for the glasses on his nightstand and walked into the dark hallway. It wasn't until he got halfway to the console pressed against the wall that he felt the dread that came with receiving a phone call in the dead of night. He didn't want to answer it, but it could have been about her.

He picked up the receiver and held it up to his ear. The person on the other end began before he could even speak:

"Sentinel?"

Moz blinked sleep away, only half-hearing the voice on the other end of the call through the fog of his nightmares lingering around his head.

"What's happened?" Judging by the early hour of the morning, it couldn't have been good.

"A body's been found, Sir. And I think you're going to want to come down for this."

"Why, who is it?"

"Sir, it's Tristan Díomasaigh. He was found dead in his home. We're still examining, but we can let you in at dawn."

Moz fell silent. The phone line fizzled with white noise as the officer on the other end waited for him to speak, but he couldn't. He stood in his pajamas alone in the quiet Upper East Wing hall of the castle.

Tristan.

His friend he had known the longest, who had been the first to know of his afflictions with the Knight and had done everything in his power to help Moz rid himself of it. Who cared for him all the same.

Gone.

"Sir?"

Moz hung up the phone.

He stood silent in the hallway for maybe minutes, maybe hours. However long it was, he finally trudged downstairs to the kitchen because he saw no point in climbing back into bed to wait restlessly for grey daybreak. He made coffee but stared into the black cup without drinking. The silence hung heavy around him, demanding that he not speak.

Moz gave up and went back to his room to change into his black trousers and button down shirt, throwing his long coat on top. He told no one where he was going when he left the castle; he didn't have it in him to explain that they had lost another. It could wait for when he figured out what to say.

Walking would have left him far too alone with his thoughts and so he climbed into one of the Sentry vehicles parked outside the gates. Moz turned over the ignition and pulled out in an absent-minded ritual, moving quickly because he was already desperate to be done with the day so he could climb back into his lonely bed. The black and boxy sedan bumped over the cobblestone as he drove slowly down the snow-dusted hill.

Heading southeast down the cobbled roads yet to be filled with pedestrians and the occasional vehicle, the tires slipped and slid on the slick surface. Moz didn't feel panic when his car fishtailed. He didn't feel anything at all.

It was a slow journey to the townhome and he saw the several police vehicles posted out front long before he spotted Tristan's potted plants that wintered into brittle stems on the stoop. He parked the car, shut the engine into silence, and sat with his face in his hands.

He tried to steel himself for what he was about to see, but nothing ran through his mind. Nothing could ever prepare him. If the Sentry was called to the case, the scene had to be gruesome. No quiet passing under the blanket of sleep for Brightloch's beloved high exorcist.

With his wife gone, with a beloved friend gone, Moz knew he was detaching. What else could he have done? The numbness he felt inside spread to his skin and it didn't make a difference to him whether it was the squeeze of winter or a symptom of creeping despondence.

That space in his skull was still silent and again he found himself pained by the loneliness it brought. Not even a monster for him to lean on. When the needling cold air became too much to bear, he stepped out of the car.

Moz approached the front stoop cordoned off with yellow tape. The forensics team milled about inside, passing through the foyer every now and then. He looked to the front window at the stained glass projects Griffin and Jude had made when they were little: a rose and a sailboat. Griffin had picked the rose because he wanted to make sure Tristan remembered the tattoo on the back of his father's hand and the exorcist hung both in his front window after a long day of making sure no little fingers burned on the oven-baked metal.

He took a deep breath and climbed the steps, ducking under the tape. Inside the foyer, Tristan's boots were scattered against the wall underneath an overstuffed rack of sherpa lined coats. It felt terribly sobering to think he would never be wearing them again. The air hung heavy with the earthen scent of the last dried cedar bundle Tristan had burned and Moz tried not to calculate how long it would take for the smell to fade from the walls for the last time.

Officers talked around him, but their voices were muffled in his ears and he understood nothing. When Moz saw Deputy Ethan Woods, he realized it was him who had called the castle earlier that morning. He hadn't recognized the voice through the lingering effects of sleep paralysis. A navy skullcap was pulled over his short, blonde hair and his hands were tucked into the open uniform jacket to hold at his waist. The gesture told Moz that the scene puzzled him.

"Who found him?"

"A night shift fellow was walking by when he saw the front door open and suspected a break in," Woods explained. "He's already at the station, I haven't had a chance yet to look at his full statement."

An open door didn't rule out too much for Moz. It could have been indicative of a demonic attack - depending on the shape it took - or just plain human error.

Moz took a deep breath and decided that he would never be ready to see the scene. He should just get it over with. He stepped out of the foyer and into the living room buzzing with members of the Brightloch Police Department forensics crew. Their bodies masked the worst of the scene and Moz stepped forward until he saw just enough to run his blood cold and stop him in his tracks.

Tristan laid on his back with empty eyes staring up at the ceiling and Moz flinched hard when he saw the mess of skin and gore at his ribcage. Sinew splattered across his navy tunic and into his greying beard of ale blonde. Shoulder length hair had come undone from the leather band he wore and Moz's stomach twisted when he wondered how much Tristan had struggled before his life ended so violently.

The ornate rug beneath him was stained with such a dense pool of blood that he would have no idea what the pattern originally was if he had not visited the home of the retired exorcist countless times in their years living in Brightloch. Acid bubbled in his throat and he wanted to excuse himself for a cold lashing of fresh air, but even just a moment away from the body would feel like betraying Tristan. Like leaving him behind.

"Who did this to you, Big Guy?"

The forensics officers buzzing around him either did not hear his murmur or they were trying to grant him a moment of what little mournful privacy could be afforded.

On the floorboards beneath the rug, Moz caught sight of a smear of black that didn't appear to be settled blood. He crouched down low to get a closer look.

"Hey, can I get someone over here?" He called out to no one on the forensics team in particular.

A blonde woman with a name he couldn't quite recall at the moment walked over to him, standing just behind where Moz balanced on the balls of his feet to look over his shoulder.

She didn't make any comment on whether she saw what he did, but offered, "let me get something to lift that with."

Disappearing only momentarily, she came back with a pair of long tweezers and a swab kit. When Moz turned to take them from her, he saw the badge hanging around her neck: E. Stern.

Before Moz could take the tools from Stern, she reeled them back out of his reach. "Gloves."

Right. He was off his game when it was his friend stiff on his back. So far out of his league, he wasn't even playing the correct sport. He snapped on white sterile gloves that matched hers and took the tools from Stern before she could point out any more red tape he had to cross.

Moz used the tweezers to lift up a corner of the blood-soaked rug to reveal more of the black smudges underneath. Two sweeping parallel lines rounded across the wood, disappearing farther where the full circle of them hid underneath the dead weight of Tristan's body. Closer to where he stood on his feet, Moz looked down and realized that the smaller lines wedged between them were the short and staccato shapes of sigils unfamiliar to him.

Without turning, he held the swab kit in his other hand up over his shoulder. "Can you do the swab, Stern?"

The plastic tube was taken from him and Stern crouched down beside him carefully, popping open the container and pulling out the swab. She leaned forward and carefully swiped at the black sigils closest to them. Moz made a note of how easily the material came up and stuck to the cotton.

"What do you think it is?"

"Some kind of organic material," Stern answered. "Maybe some sort of composite mixed with ash with the way it separated, if I had to be more specific. As for what *this* is, " she gestured to the rug and body with small circles of her hands before she closed the swab kit again with the sample inside, "that's your field."

He felt grateful that Stern at least recognized where jurisdiction began and ended. A human problem in the city? That was the police. City dealing with demons? Madness of that nature fell to the Queen's Royal Sentry. Anything outside the Brightloch walls was the problem of the Scouts in the Department of Forest Management.

"So then you think it was demons?"

"I can't think of any other monster who would do this to a sweet man like Tristan. He was only, what, fifty-four? Not that anyone deserves this at any age, but that's so damn young."

"Did you know him?"

"Not well," she admitted. "Spoke with him a handful of times at the Temple, but nothing terribly deep. He was always so kind and gentle, that I just can't..."

She trailed off as she stood up, packaged the sample tube in a plastic bag, and sealed it with orange tape she had kept in the pocket of her coat. Stern rolled up the excess bag around the tube to cushion it before she looked down at where Moz still crouched. "Besides, there's nothing normal about this. I think if it were just a quick and dirty murder, we wouldn't have found whatever this is."

Moz said nothing. He couldn't decide if Stern's theory made him feel better or worse. If she was correct, that meant the case that would open for Tristan would move into his jurisdiction. But it would also mean that the killer was not only at large, but a demonic entity that he had not come across before.

"I am very sorry about your friend," she added solemnly.

"Thank you," he murmured and she left.

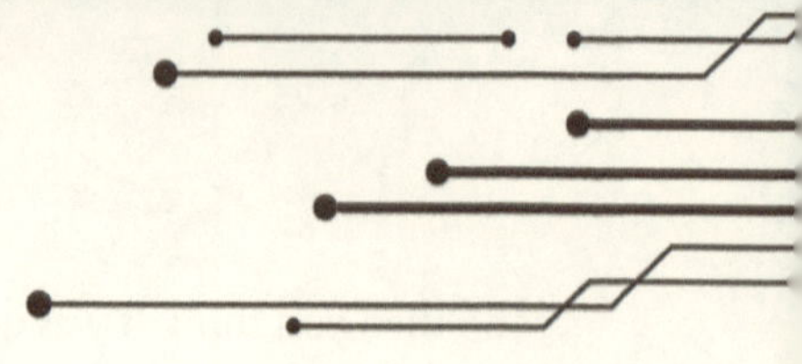

CHAPTER NINE
GRIFFIN - ONE YEAR AGO

"**A**VERY'S HUSBAND HAS PREPARED a eulogy," the celebrant said, looking up from the podium in the direction where Griffin was seated with his two remaining parents.

He felt his father freeze beside him. The woman with carefully curled brown hair and a suit of well-matched shades of black looked up from her notes expectantly, lifting her hand in what was clearly intended to be a subtle cue for his father to rise. But the gesture did not go unnoticed by those it was not meant for. People turned in their seats to stare and when Griffin felt their eyes too heavy, Moz finally rose.

He walked to the podium, too slow with a gaze that never left the coffin draped in a black funerary shroud until he finally had to turn his back. Beside Griffin, Yumi gripped his fingers tight in hers with a tense fear. Neither of them had any idea what he was going to say, but if the roiling anger they had witnessed in the months leading up to the end of the search for his wife was any indication, it wasn't going to be comfortable.

His father didn't pull out a paper from his pocket with a prepared speech; just took off his glasses before he looked up, like he didn't want to see anyone's face watching him with heavy pity.

Griffin understood the feeling.

"The first day I met Avery, she pointed a dull kitchen knife at me," Moz finally said. "And if I'm being honest with myself, I absolutely had it coming."

A faint whisper of polite chuckles rolled over the room and Moz left space for them before he continued:

"We didn't get along at first. But she has a way of bringing out the best in people, no matter what their worst might look like. She stands up for herself just as much as she stands up for others. For what is good and what is right."

Moz shifted on his feet, looking down for a moment to catch his breath like every word was a punch to the diaphragm that he had tried to withstand under stoicism. It might have looked like grief to anyone looking in on their family from the outside, but Griffin knew better. This was going to be bad.

"She has endless love in her heart and she would do anything for anyone who is lucky enough to be on the receiving end. Avery Noelle is fierce, she is gentle. There has never been a better mother than the mother she is. Griffin, our son, is her entire world. She is the best friend anyone could ever wish to have and she will hold the warmest place in her heart for you if you are lucky enough to claim that she is yours."

When he looked up, the facade crumbled. His brows furrowed and the sharp knit of his frown sunk lower.

"I bet you've noticed by now my choice in words. Not 'was', is. Not 'had', has. Because like I said before, she would do anything for the people she loves, but which of you would do anything for her?

How many of you really mean it when you say you would never give up on her?"

He pointed at the coffin behind him angrily, never taking his eyes off the crowd that had come to mourn but only a handful of them Griffin recognized. The only people that mattered to him were seated directly around him. Tristan, Jack, Uncle Soren, Aunt Lily and Aunt Maria. Jude and her parents. Everyone else could have fucked off for all he cared.

"I can count those people on just my hands," Moz's voice began to crack around the edges, "and none of them include the people who were left in charge of finding her. But that coffin is empty and you expect to shake your hands of the dirt you dug to bury it rather than dirty them by trying. She is out there. Do you really think the terrible Berserker Witch you were all so afraid of would just die?"

He let out a small, venomous laugh and dropped his hand. Like he had just realized something that tasted bitter on his tongue and couldn't believe he would have to speak to it. Even the sign language interpreter, posted on stage left on the side of the coffin where Angela Sills could see her easily, shifted uncomfortably on her feet.

"It was never about ending the search because you had to, was it? You couldn't wait to put her behind you. You wouldn't kill her yourselves, but someone else doing it was the next best thing, wasn't it?"

Moz waited for someone to speak up, looking from face to face of poorly masked apathy, but the room waited in silence. Griffin felt his anger all too well because it spoke to his own. Words had been hard for him lately, but his father knew. His whole family did.

"As my darling wife would say, and will say next time she sees you," he said and took a deep breath before adding, "you can all go fuck yourselves."

Nobody spoke when Sentinel Mosley stormed out of his wife's sham funeral.

Lily rose from her chair, awkwardly shuffling to the podium to retrieve the glasses her brother-in-law had left behind.

"He's going to want these sooner rather than later," she muttered.

The wake passed by Griffin in a blurred smear of charcoal. People milled about the east hall of the castle and talked about very few things that had anything to do with his mother. He nodded politely when people he didn't know offered him condolences, parading in a procession dressed head to toe in mismatched shades of black as they passed each member of what was left of his family.

Griffin stood wedged between Moz and Yumi, the former a stony wall of regathered stoicism merely going through the expected motions and the latter gripping his hand tight. The pinching pressure wasn't enough to hold his urge to rip out his own teeth at bay. It was hard to give a shit about anything these strangers had to offer when he knew Mama would have loathed everything about this.

Mama was laughter. She was queer vibrancy, strong kinetic energy, and firm encouragement that sometimes scared him when it dared him to push past what he believed to be the limit of his adolescent capabilities. Not *this*.

He finally gave up and decided that the kitchen was a much better place to be. Less prying eyes, and if he was lucky, Sarah would be there for company who knew him well enough to leave his grief alone and let him hide. Jude knew and even she gave him a wide berth, squeezing his hands when she stopped in the procession but said nothing. She may as well have lost a mother too.

"I heard William is accusing the Oracles of her death," the woman's voice wasn't as hushed as she had maybe assumed it was, for Griffin heard her clearly from around the corner in the Lower West Wing hallway. He froze and leaned against the wall, wanting to eavesdrop without being caught.

"Death or disappearance," a man responded with a question.

"Does it matter? The man has gone mad with grief regardless. To become a widower at such a young age is a terrible thing, but he has a family to be mindful of. Think of the boy."

"My. How old is he?"

"William or the boy?"

"The madman."

"Why, he's only forty-five! Maybe forty-six. But regardless, so young for such an awful thing."

"Indeed. I pity the boy, but I worry most for the Queen. She was thrown so abruptly onto the throne when already there were whispers of unrest. No guidance, no true descendants, and now no faithful spouse."

The last jab managed to insult every single member of Griffin's family in one fell swoop. He knew that any words he heard before or that would come after were utter bullshit, so he stormed from his hiding place through the hall. The gossipers looked at him with bewilderment as he shoved between them, not caring at all that he was being aggressive.

"You heard the man, go fuck yourselves," he echoed what his father had said at the podium before he disappeared through the archway of the kitchen.

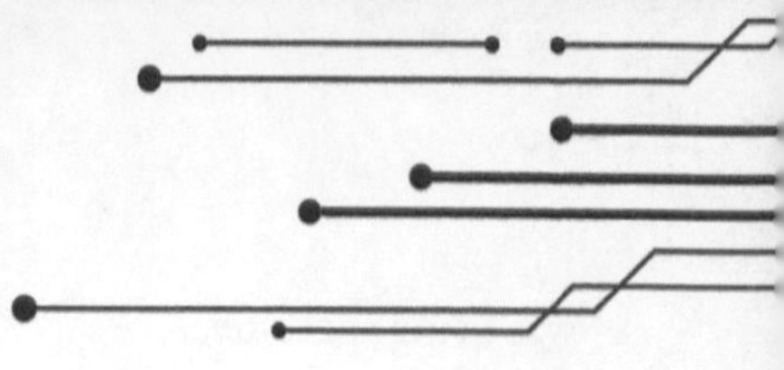

CHAPTER TEN
GRIFFIN

WHEN GRIFFIN CAME DOWN the stairs, one of Yumi's attendants, Annabel, walked from the front door with a man trailing behind her. The man stood tall and was dressed head-to-toe in black, right down to the scraped motorcycle helmet strapped to his canvas rucksack and the round sunglasses over his eyes despite the snow beginning to accumulate outside. Disheveled black hair fell around his jaw and his mouth fixed in a slight frown was framed by a short trimmed beard and mustache.

Griffin stepped down from the last stair and the man stopped his stride toward the east wing, abandoned by Annabel, who kept walking. He pushed his sunglasses up onto his forehead to see Griffin clearly before he spoke:

"Hey kid, haven't seen you in years," he said with a low warmth to his voice. "Your dad around?"

"That depends, who are you?"

"Ouch," the man feigned injury, clutching his chest with a long hand adorned in silver signet rings. "I'm Kurosaki. You wouldn't have seen me since you were a tiny thing. Now you're, well. You're definitely Moz's kid."

Kurosaki's pale face felt vaguely familiar to him with the sunglasses but for some reason Griffin wanted to assign his face to a head of bleached blonde hair. Strange things, brains were.

"How do you know my dad?"

He saw the subtle rise of Kurosaki's shoulders, taking in a brisk inhale before he could fold his sunglasses into the pocket of his long coat and answer.

"We've been friends for years. I guess in a way we, uh, worked together. You have forty-eight questions left, so use them wisely."

-Intruder-

-He's gonna kill the Queen-

Griffin mentally waved off the voices just as his father strode into the main foyer, followed by the clacking of nails on marble as Maya trotted behind him. He watched Kurosaki's face light up in such a small way that Griffin might not have noticed if he had not already been actively studying the stranger. Moz stopped just before the man who stood only a few inches shorter. Maya hurried to greet Kurosaki first with a furiously wagging tail and wedged her nose between his knees, sniffing loudly to inspect the stranger.

"Maya, leave him. Well, what a fucking surprise! Look at you, Mr. Island Life! You look good, love what you've done with your hair," Moz said, strangely jovial, just before nudging the dog out of the way so that he could hug Kurosaki.

The hug lingered and Griffin watched the slight bend of Kurosaki's fingers like he was about to ball up his father's shirt in his hand.

"What are you doing here, Kuro," his father asked when he let go of the other man. He dropped his jaw and framed Kurosaki's mouth with his hands, squishing his face the slightest when he added, "oh my gods, you have a mustache now."

"My pen ran out of ink halfway through a letter," Kurosaki said through pinched lips.

Moz dropped his hands and shoved at Kurosaki's shoulder playfully, only hard enough for the other man to lightly sway on his feet when he said, "Don't be an idiot. Let's track Jack down, he'll be happy to see you."

Moz led Kurosaki down the hall, and Griffin trailed behind as silent and unnoticed as a ghost when Moz asked, "did you just get in?"

Kurosaki nodded. "Took the overnight ferry."

"How was it? I haven't actually taken it yet."

"It was, uh, something. That's for sure."

Griffin knew his father to be an outwardly friendly person unless pushed in the wrong direction, but something about standing next to this stranger made him feel even warmer. His toothy smile looked a little wider.

The first place anyone looked for Uncle Jack was always in the armory and the validity of this remained unchallenged when they found him there, standing over the metal table in the center of the room with an array of knives rolled out for sharpening. When they stepped through the door, he caught sight of them in his periphery and looked up, dropping the knife when his gaze fell on Kurosaki.

Griffin watched Kurosaki and Jack hug in a long, tight embrace. When they parted, Kurosaki held a palm against Jack's cheek and gave him a sharp nod. He patted Jack's face before letting him go entirely. There was a silent meaning in the gesture that Griffin didn't fully understand, but he decided he wanted the story behind it.

"It's good to see you, Twin," Jack said.

Griffin looked at them puzzled - they looked absolutely nothing alike. Where Kurosaki had black hair that nearly grazed his shoulders and brown eyes, Jack's blonde hair was shaved close to the scalp and he looked at his friend with bright irises of gold.

"You too, Rat Boy."

At that, he gave up on trying to figure them out.

The joyous reunion was broken by his father's somber words: "I am glad to see you, Kuro. But I'm afraid that you've arrived just in time to hear terrible news."

Griffin's stomach dropped. "What's going on?"

He had mostly expected his father to shoo him out of the room so the older men could speak privately, but he didn't. Moz stood with his fists shoved deep into his trouser pockets and a darkened expression when he said:

"Someone, or something, murdered Tristan."

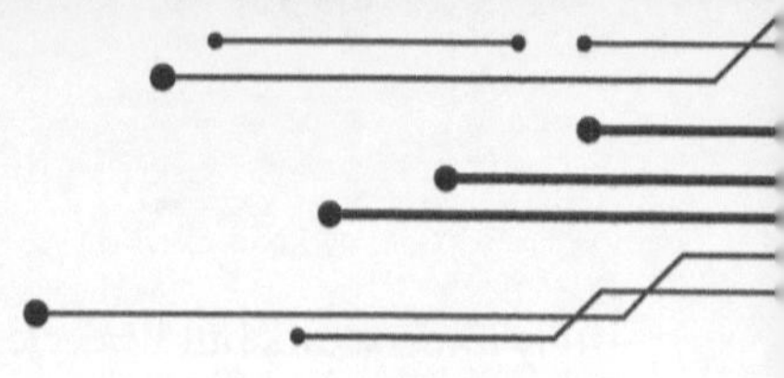

CHAPTER ELEVEN
MOZ

MOZ SAT ACROSS FROM Jack and Kurosaki at the kitchen table after he had shooed his son away on to class, steaming mugs of tea in front of each of them. Though he was excited one of his favorite people in the world had returned after years away, Jack's expression was grim. His frown was cast in grey light from the lancet windows above the sink behind Moz. The sun hung too low in the sky to cast the butcher block island they sat around on backless stools in hues of blue and gold from their stained pieces at their crown. Cherry hardwood floors creaked under the weight of Moz shifting uncomfortably.

"There was a large circle drawn on the floor beneath him," Moz continued his debrief on what had happened that morning. "Hidden underneath the rug. Two concentric circles, actually, with sigils in the space between. Nobody has been able to identify what they are yet. Whoever did it, they were in Tristan's home prior to the murder. It was someone he either knew well enough to let inside or someone who feigned well enough for him to lend his trust."

He watched Kurosaki lean back in his chair as he considered this. The familiarity of the mannerism made Moz smile, fleeting fast as they broached the grave topic.

"To be frank, that doesn't rule much out. The Big Guy would have let anyone in if he thought they needed help from an exorcist."

With those words, Moz could pinpoint the exact moment his grief shifted into rage. The killer could have picked anyone in Brightloch, but chose to slaughter Centralia's gentle giant. *Why?*

"We need to find who did this," Moz murmured.

"We will."

Jack looked from Kurosaki, back to Moz, and stood up.

"I should, uh, get going. I'll be back in the armory if you need anything," Jack said. Before Moz could question his departure, he had already vanished and left his half-empty cup behind. He sighed and stood up to take the cup over to the sink.

"He's sure mellowed out a lot," Kurosaki noted.

Before Moz circled the table, he peered into Kurosaki's cup to find it empty. He moved his hand too fast to take the teacup and Kurosaki flinched. He might have missed the small flicker of movement had he not spent so long studying his youngest emotion: fear.

Moz slowly lowered it, keeping his eyes on the other man who couldn't even look at him.

"Izaya," he murmured the seldom used first name.

Kurosaki didn't answer. That was enough to give Moz the answer he had been looking for.

"What did he do to you?"

He knew Kurosaki well enough to recognize his mask of collected calm and to listen for the broken edges in his voice instead of looking at the blank stare on his face when he answered, "nothing that matters now. Ghosts can't leave a black eye."

The word shocked him; Kurosaki had never spoken of ghosts before, despite everything they had seen together. Despite seeing his best friend possess the Knight of Spirit to speak to him.

"What do you mean by that?"

Kurosaki finally turned to him. If Moz hadn't been so practiced with his son to catch the physical cues, he might have missed the small flick of Kurosaki's gaze to land somewhere beyond his shoulder. Too fast to be avoidant, like he wanted to assess before Moz could notice and ask questions.

Something was there.

But he kept his focus forward so as to not let Kurosaki know that he suspected anything was wrong.

"I don't mean anything by it, it was just a turn of phrase."

He saw the twitch in Kurosaki's mouth. Right at the corner of his bottom lip. *A lie*. But Moz knew better than to push Kurosaki, so he let it go.

"I'm going to the university later today," he said instead. "Thought their library might have useful information on the sigils or any leads to what they might be for. You're more than welcome to join me, if you like."

Kurosaki planted his hands on the table before he stood up. "Well, I came to help."

"While I'm there, I'm meeting Griffin for a martial arts practice. Shank outfitted a staff for him that I can't let him swing wildly around. You're welcome to sit in on that as well if you haven't got anything else to do, Yumi's not finished with her day until much later."

"Is he any good?"

"In my completely biased opinion as his father? Yeah, he's good. Completely objective? Kid's a fuckin' prodigy."

Moz finished washing up the cups and set them to dry in the wire rack on the counter. He turned to see the amused grin on Kurosaki's face; a handsome smile that he suddenly realized he had remembered with complete clarity.

"The prodigious son of a Knight of Od and the Berserker Witch? Wouldn't miss it."

Kurosaki followed Moz outside to the sedan and by default headed to the driver door. Moz jingled the key in his hand and shook his head.

"I don't think so, short stack."

Kurosaki frowned, but shrugged in acceptance as he rounded the car to get into the passenger seat.

"Sure, what's a couple more bodies?"

Moz grimaced as he ducked into the driver's seat. The jab was made in definitively bad taste, but it meant he was working through coping. Moz couldn't fault him. Tristan had been his friend too.

He felt Kurosaki's eyes watching him as he turned the engine over and waited for the man to correct him or offer snide commentary, but Kurosaki said nothing as they started down the hill into town.

"I'm impressed," Kurosaki finally said as he dropped his ringed hand from the frame of the door, like he realized he wasn't going to have to sit passenger with his knuckles whitened in terror.

"Ha," Moz bit the laugh with sarcasm, but he smiled.

As he drove them across Brightloch to the university cam-pus, Moz's gaze slid several times over to the passenger seat where Kurosaki was turned to look out the fogged window. It felt strange seeing him there from this vantage; even stranger that he wasn't yelling at Moz to get his feet off the dashboard because *fuckin' Idiot, I just detailed!*

He'd happily take it either way.

The car struggled up the hill to the university campus on the southwestern quadrant of Brightloch. Its architecture resembled that of the castle: a stone perimeter wall with iron gates, daunting structures of sarsen with looming flying buttresses, and lancet win-dows– though these ones were unornamented with stained glass art and were purely utilitarian.

Moz parked the car in the small lot at the north end of campus. It was almost entirely empty save for a few groundskeeping vehicles and other sedans presumably belonging to staff and students who lived just outside of a reasonable walking distance.

Kurosaki trailed after him, looking up in wonder at the towering walls around them. Moz remained undazzled by the campus - he had utilized its resources a number of times for research and the novelty had worn off long before his son had become a student of the university.

"What does Griffin study?"

Kurosaki asked the question as their strides lengthened to climb the hill and a snap of guilt struck Moz when he realized the likely possibility he had failed to mention it in any of their written corre-spondences.

Griffin had the impression at a young age that Moz worked within the police department – guns and badges all look the same to an easily excitable toddler. For the longest time, Moz let the misunderstanding go for the sake of keeping his son engaged with the ideas of careers when he seemed to be developing an interest in justice as a concept; particularly in games of imagination as a detective duo alongside Jude on the sticky summer afternoons buzzing with cicadas. Was he just supposed to explain it was all a sham?

Somewhere in his mid-teen years, Griffin had discerned the Sentry from the Brightloch Police Department on his own and pried his aspirations in an auxiliary path. *"I'll find what turns people into monsters so we can stop it. All of the bad feelings that the weird things think are so tasty."*

He climbed the stone steps to the Main Library and held open the heavy wood door for Kurosaki as he answered:

"Forensic psychology."

"Impressive," Kurosaki muttered, but he had been looking up at the low-relief sculptures of philosophers and scientists carved into the pointed tympanum above their heads.

Moz followed him inside and was embraced in the warmth of the sanctuary. Immediately he wanted to shed his coat and take his time. To drink up every drop of information he could get his hands on. A part of him felt jealous of the students who had every excuse and more to spend all day in a place like the library. As far as he was aware, Avery had never been inside and he resented that fact every time he visited. *She'd adore it.*

He stepped past Kurosaki and led him further inside, down the nave and its altars of knowledge in the form of countless bookstacks. At its midpoint, a rounded desk straddled the aisle. As Moz began taking off his coat, he turned to Kurosaki; he looked around in wonder in every direction but his.

"I'm not entirely sure where we're looking for, so hang tight a second," he explained before he approached the desk.

"Pardon. Where's social sciences?" Moz asked the young woman seated behind the information counter. He was used to automatically detouring towards the books on demonology tucked into the rear enclave of the library, but it didn't feel right to start there.

The young blonde turned in her chair and pointed towards the back of the library.

"Second row from the back! It should be at the far end on your left."

Moz thanked her before he hurried to follow the directions. When he finally found the Social Sciences section, it dawned on him that he really had no clue what he was supposed to be searching for. Immediately, he felt mistaken.

"Stumped already?" Kurosaki teased him.

"Maybe this wasn't it," Moz mumbled and started for the section on demonology, already well acquainted with how to get to it no matter his starting point in the library. Kurosaki followed without further comment. Moz felt infinitely more at home in Demonology, despite the constant expectation for The Thing to give unwelcome commentary and always coming up silent.

He ran his fingers along the spines. Most of the titles he had already read cover to cover and he frowned. Instincts were the only thing he had to go on and nothing struck him. Until he stopped on one:

Daemons: Behavioral Studies, Hierarchies, and Zoological Applications.

As he stared at the worn book spine, he thought of a sharp pain in his ass roughly the size and shape of a domestic cat. The last time Aegis showed his face, he sat on the other side of a two way mirror while Ethan Woods interviewed the demon. Woods had rejected Moz's request to throttle his interrogation subject. His eyes lit up in realization and Kurosaki turned closer to him to investigate why.

"Hello, Mr. Mosley."

Moz flinched at Jude's voice and looked up. She watched him with an arm full of textbooks and a skeptical raise of her brow; she looked so much like her parents in that way.

"Hey, Kiddo. Where's Griff?"

"He's in Psych 205 right now," Jude answered. "He was just going to meet you at the gym right after."

"Great, I'll meet you all there."

Kurosaki frowned, "Why? Where are you going?"

"The police department," he answered as he began putting his coat back on. "I want to look at one of the transcripts we took for Avery's case. I think something Aegis said might be helpful here."

"What did he say?"

"I don't remember for sure, so hold that thought."

Moz hurried out of the library before Kurosaki could finish his next question. Undoubtedly something along the lines of: *what the hell is wrong with you?* He felt his eyes on his back until the very last moment when the heavy wood doors shut behind him and the bitter cold swallowed him once more.

He left the car where it sat accumulating fluffy snowflakes; the police station was well within walking distance from the north end of campus.

The police station was a needlessly gaudy building with deep marble steps, ridged columns, and a pediment relief sculpted with some bullshit visual allegory about justice. Though Moz had to admit, he found humor in the resemblance it shared with the facade of the elslith's chamber in Od.

He took long strides to climb the steps and pushed through the heavy double doors. The central heating of the department was cranked far too high and after Moz was slapped by the initial burn of hellfire, his face pricked with needles after the drastic temperature change.

He walked down the long hall illuminated by cold, buzzing overheads. Moz brushed against several uniforms as he passed the central bullpen. Discomfort rolled up his spine in waves and he swallowed hard. He hated being there. It didn't matter that this was an entirely different city from where Morgana's Legion had taken root and leaked noxious poison; he could die happy if he never saw a police uniform ever again.

Moz knocked on the door of the Deputy's office just before he cracked it open.

"Woods? Hey, it's me. I need to take a look at..."

He trailed off when the figure at the desk looked up and it wasn't Ethan Woods at all. This man had white-blonde hair smoothed back with gel and light brows that had half-arched in amusement when Moz let himself in. He lowered the fountain pen he had balanced in his hand and leaned back in his leather chair, almost knocking into the towering bookcases behind him.

"Where's Woods?"

"My name is Cain," the man explained, his pale hands folded neatly on the table in front of him. "I am taking over for Ethan Woods."

Moz lifted the marred eyebrow. "Taking over," he repeated. "Why? Where's Woods?"

"Internal reasons."

"Internal reasons," Moz echoed back, a skeptical murmur. "Right then."

He pulled up the chair on the side of Woods' -*Cain's?*- desk and sat down. If it was just a simple changing in leadership on the case, why was Cain in his office? Moz didn't think he would get anywhere with such direct questions and he didn't feel like hearing "internal reasons" again.

"In the file for Avery Porter, there's a few transcripts. I really need to review the interview with Aegis again," Moz explained. "I think he might have said something that would help me with the Díomasaigh case."

"That is evidence under the jurisdiction of the police and I am afraid that I cannot surrender that to the Sentry."

Moz froze. "Are you fuckin' serious? That is my *wife's* case."

"I don't see why I would make a joke of this, Mosley."

Moz almost flinched at his own name, realizing that Cain had known him before Moz had known *him*. He slammed both palms onto the desk, rattling Cain's cups and dislodging papers from their neat stacks.

"Are you really going to make me send my superior down to make you do it? Because I hardly think that would amuse the Queen."

"Be my guest, Mosley."

Moz stood up from the chair, nearly knocking it over with his violent anger. "Fuck off."

"You came into *my* office," Cain answered as Moz turned his back to leave.

He grimaced as he slammed the door shut behind him and decided he would have fun being a thorn in this bastard's side.

Ave,

I've stared at this page for a very, very long time and I'm still not even sure that I know what I want to say to you. Because that's the thing, it's not to you. You're not here. Not even in the ground. But the family therapist we've been seeing suggested writing down things like this and I have to set a good example for Griffin.

I don't know how you vanished without a single trace. Just a name and you were gone. That stupid fucking cat. I'll never speak ill of him ever again if you just come back.

Every day that passes, I feel a day closer to when they find you. But not the way that we want you to be found. You are very much human, and I see it on the lines your smile has left and in those silver glitters in your hair.

That human transience is what we thought we wanted, isn't it? But now it is here and I would take up the monstrous mantle again if it meant there was no death that could lay hands on you. I'd undo everything we did and I would do it with relief. I don't dare say that to anyone but you.

We were supposed to have another thirty years together.

I love you,
Moz

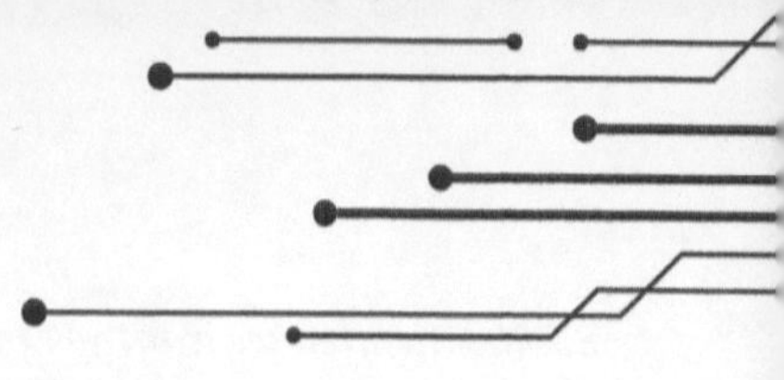

CHAPTER TWELVE
KUROSAKI

KUROSAKI AND JUDE WALKED into the university gym just as Griffin took to the mat. He had changed into black sweatpants and a grey t-shirt, the long sleeves of a black compression shirt showing from underneath. Moz was at a bench on the opposite side of the mats from the entry doors, folding his coat, and setting down his glasses.

"How long can you hold it now?"

It wasn't a question for Griffin, it was a challenge. Without answering verbally, Griffin threw his arms above his head and leaned downard, setting himself into a handstand with a practiced posture. He flexed his palms on the floor, adjusting comfortably into the stance.

"Holy shit," Kurosaki marveled; he made it look easy.

"He does this all the time," Jude explained as she shrugged off her bookbag and dropped it on the floor next to the nearest bench, pushed against the wall underneath a bulletin board of try-out schedules and competition dates. "Claims it's *fun*."

Beyond Griffin's freakishly balanced handstand, Moz unbuttoned the last of the closures on his pressed shirt and he tossed it onto the bench beside his coat. He stretched his arms as he rounded the bench, crossing one over the other and Kurosaki flushed across the cheeks when he saw the muscled arm of ink. *You're fucking joking.*

The planes of muscle across his chest and down his stomach that Kurosaki could recall fondly under his fingers looked stronger than ever, even if the dark tufts of hair were somewhat new. *No one should be allowed to look like that at this age.*

Just when he thought it couldn't get any worse, Moz turned and Kurosaki saw the shapes of new tattoos spanning across the broad surface of his back from shoulders to lumbar. He was too far away to make out specific details, but the black and grey shadows reminded him of the stained glass windows in the Centralia temple depicting creation stories. After everything the gods had put him through, Moz's devotion never faltered.

Kurosaki narrowly avoided swearing out loud. Coming here had been a mistake– whether it was the gym or Brightloch altogether, he was not yet sure. Moz kicked off his boots and socks, taking two wooden sparring staffs from a nearby rack before he met Griffin on the mat. He came down from his handstand with a careless drop of his legs just before his father held one of the staffs out to him.

"Great job!" Moz said. "You've gotten steadier, for sure. You ready?"

Griffin took the staff from him. "Are *you* ready, old man?"

Moz grimaced before he took his stance on the mat across from Griffin. "You're on, buckaroo."

They clacked sticks with a hard *whack* before the sparring began. Kurosaki's jaw nearly dropped; he knew Griffin would be good, but this was something else entirely. He met Moz's strikes with complete ease, spinning his own staff in wide circles to make good use of each end. Griffin sparred with his whole frame, turning with his opponent.

When Moz suddenly switched his attack to come in at Griffin's opposite side, Griffin rolled the staff with one hand up his shoulder and behind his neck, catching it again in his opposite hand to block the strike.

"Holy shit,that was cool," Kurosaki marveled just as he sank down onto the bench to watch. "Is he ambidextrous?"

"Huh, I guess he is." Jude was either unimpressed or watched too often to be phased by the trick. Her nose was deeply buried in the pages of an overstuffed notebook and she didn't look up when she answered him.

Kurosaki leaned back when he decided that there was nothing wrong with his eyes falling on Moz. He was amazed that his footwork hadn't faltered even in his middle age and it was no wonder to Kurosaki how Moz had managed to raise an apparent martial arts prodigy. Without lifting his enthralled gaze, Kurosaki fished into his coat pocket for the lighter and metal tin. Popping open the aluminum case, he pulled out a cigarette.

"Are you seriously trying to smoke in here?"

Jude looked up from her notebook with a raised brow. He didn't complain, just smiled and put the cigarette back in the case before he tucked the metal container into his coat pocket.

"You're right," he responded.

Kurosaki saw the movement of faces peering in through the windows of the doors. Clearly, young women still wandering the hall heard the clatter of sparring sticks and wanted to investigate the source, but their stares lingered a little long on Griffin and Moz. He rolled his eyes and turned his attention back forward.

Jude wasn't as easily re-directed and she huffed, standing up fast to storm towards the gym doors. She yanked down the paper blind mounted to the top of the door so that the narrow window was blocked and did the same with the opposite door. Her movement swung with anger when she turned around with a frown on her face and she plopped back down onto the bench.

"Mosley men," Kurosaki mumbled as he watched her, knowing Jude would know exactly what he meant. Her lack of an answer when she folded her arms and leaned back against the wall told him all he needed to know. Falling for a friend was a concept far too familiar for him.

He looked back at Moz and Griffin sparring on the mat. Griffin moved with fast fluidity, keeping up with Moz's strikes with im-pressive speed. He had the advantage of agility over his father and he leaned into his shorter frame, ducking and dodging easily when Moz could not.

"What does your Pa think about all of this?" Kurosaki asked Jude without turning his gaze away from the sparring match.

"About fighting?"

"No, Avery's case."

Jude was silent for a long moment as she considered, hiding under the boisterous cracking wood as she thought.

"They're sad, of course," she finally said. "Sad and frustrated. I mean, you know them, right? They look at it like it's one giant puzzle to crack but the problem is, they can't sit down to take the time to solve it. It's hands-off. Someone else's to solve. I think that hurts because they were there when it happened. The answer is so close, but so far away at the same time."

Kurosaki nodded slowly. *Insightful one, that Sills kid.* "Do you think she's out there?"

"I mean yeah, Griffin said-"

"I didn't ask what Griffin thinks," he cut her off gently, turning to look at her with a raised brow. "I asked what *you* think. You're a smart kid. I want to know."

Jude pursed her lips, careful with her next words.

"It's been two years," she answered in a hushed murmur, cloaking her words under the racket of sparring staffs. "Two cruel winters and two unforgiving summers. Would anyone be strong enough to survive that alone in the wilderness, at the mercy of monsters and elements, but not strong enough to just come home?"

Her words chilled him and Kurosaki pried his gaze away, staring blankly at the floor. It struck bone when he thought of just how airtight her logic sounded.

"Please don't say that to Griffin."

"I would never."

Kurosaki nodded once in a silent approval before he turned back towards the mat, where Moz laid on his back with a victorious Griffin standing over him. Moz's staff had rolled out of his hands and Griffin's pointed his own towards his father's sternum.

"Match," he announced to his father.

Moz laughed, tapping the bottom of Griffin's staff twice with his palm to gesture acceptance with the outcome. Griffin eased off and his father rose back to his feet. He strode over to pick up his fallen staff and just as easily as he had met defeat, they clacked staffs and started again.

They sparred this way for just shy of an hour, with Moz's wins taking only a marginal lead over Griffin's before their movements had slowed and exhaustion finally set in.

"Alright... I'm calling it," Moz huffed with heaving shoulders. "Good job, bud."

Jude began repacking her bag when they racked their staffs and dressed back into their street clothes. Kurosaki mentally shook off his undoubtedly awed look when Moz began walking towards their bench, straightening the collar of his shirt.

"That boy is a carbon copy of you. But with Avery's demeanor. And Yumi's good sense because hell knows he wasn't going to get it from either of you," Kurosaki said.

"Ohoho, don't clear Yumi just yet," Moz joked. "She's a willing participant in this circus."

Kurosaki let himself smile when he stood up to follow Jude and Griffin out the gym doors. He couldn't even jokingly blame Yumi for it; it had not been long since he had arrived in Brightloch and already he felt the charm of the small family even in Avery's absence. Kurosaki would have gladly nestled his way into it if there was a space for him. It felt easy to imagine for just a moment when Moz's footsteps fell into line with his own.

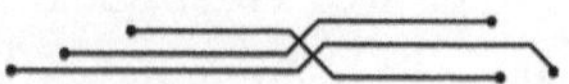

When Kurosaki crossed the foyer in front of the grand staircase, he felt eyes following his back. He stopped and looked up at the landing to find the steel eyes of a young Avery Porter watching him. She wore a fine navy suit with embroidered stars of gold emblazoned on the lapel, her dark hair pulled back and adorned with celestial hairpins. Her mouth turned in just the slightest smile and he remembered that on hers and Yumi's wedding day, she had argued with the photographer who took the tintype the painting referenced. He had no doubts that this was the same smile that came from a quick-witted remark that cut egos with the same brutality the Berserker Witch had cut arteries with.

"Where did you go, Ave?" Kurosaki murmured to the painting of his missing friend. She didn't answer, of course, but he would have appreciated a hint.

As he continued down the hall, a faint echo of music floated from somewhere deeper in the castle. He followed the sound, stumbling into several quiet rooms before he finally found the source in one of the countless studies.

The room glowed with a dim warmth from the oil lamp on the desk. It sat beside a small radio crackling with small pops of static that speckled a jazz melody. Bookcases lined each wall of the green study, filled with as many seemingly random sculptures and mounted insect specimens as there were leather bound tomes.

Opposite the open door was a sofa of worn cognac leather and the person sprawled across it was much too tall to be laying down, for their feet draped off the squished arm. Their face was covered by an open book, carelessly dropped as they had fallen asleep in the middle of reading.

Fatherhood suited William Mosley quite well.

Kurosaki stepped into the room, setting his whiskey glass on the coffee table before the sofa. He looked at the full ashtray and open carton of rolled tobacco beside it. Kurosaki frowned, knowing that he would smell cloves if he picked them up to investigate, and he looked down at his book-faced friend with concern.

It's like The Thing is back Moz's last letter had read before Kurosaki took the next available ferry from Eyon. He hadn't realized just how strong Moz's worry had been until seeing his instruments of self-inflicted exorcism for the first time in years.

Kurosaki crouched next to the sofa before he carefully lifted his silver-ringed fingers and plucked the book from his face, shifting Moz's glasses too far down his nose. He set the worn tome down carefully on the table, looking at the title. *Necromantic Cults of the Stillmaw Basin: An Annotated History*. Kurosaki huffed a small laugh.

"Nice bedtime story," he whispered. When he turned back from the table, he froze.

It felt strange to look at Moz in the warm lamp light, especially when Kurosaki knew he wasn't going to be jabbed with the lingering vitriol from when they were young. There was no expectation that he would look away when he studied the greying in Moz's beard trimmed close to his jaw. He had accumulated even more freckles dotting the bridge of his nose and under his eyes in the ten years since Kurosaki had seen him last. Avery's husband was a thing of beauty and Kurosaki would have hated her for it if he hadn't treasured her friendship beyond measure.

The years had softened Kurosaki as much as they had for Moz, maybe even more when he felt the sharp yank on his heart just from seeing him so vulnerable. How different would things have been if he hadn't wasted so much time on people who had no interest in loving him? If he hadn't spent so many nights in screaming matches with Todd and feeling indifferent to leaving Andrew behind without so much as a *goodbye*? Everything had been going so well but when Moz called, he came running. Maybe it was happening again.

For his own sake, Kurosaki decided that it wouldn't have mattered one way or another. That he was simply looking too hard at everything that had happened that day. He was just a friend doing what friends were expected to do.

He reached again and carefully took the glasses from Moz's face, folding them neatly and setting them on top of the book. Standing up, he shut off the radio, and took one more look at Moz's unguarded face before he dimmed the lamp.

Kurosaki stumbled through the dark alone and wondered how well it would be received if he had simply stayed. He shoved his fists in his pockets, hurrying through the hall past Avery's chiaroscuro gaze without looking back at her.

"Don't fucking look at me like that."

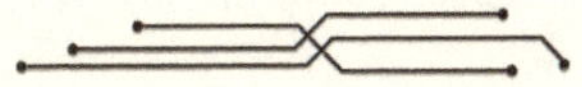

Kuro,

Wow, my handwriting is terrible. I'm sorry if you can't read this very well, I've been practicing but evidently not enough. Right now I have to use my left hand because a demon ate my fingers.

No, I'm not kidding.

(Transcriber's note: Avery has given up)

It took the pinky and ring fingers off and took Yumi's wedding ring right with it. Moz dug around in the cadaver when we finally got it back to the Sentry, gave it a good clean for sure after he found it in the esophagus. (Transcriber note: It was super gross. She asked if Maria could just reattach a half-digested finger. I am telling myself Avery only said this in a state of shock for the sake of my own sanity.) We'll just plop it onto the next finger when the swelling finally goes down.

Poor Griff was screaming, he was so freaked. I lied and told him it was from a hunting accident, he's way too young to be worrying about things like demon aggression. Shank said they're going to make me a leather cap to go over the stumps. Oh gods, I hate that it Moz (Transcriber note: I wasn't supposed to write that)

Love you always, Kuro. Count all your fingers and toes for me,
Ave

Love,
Moz (Avery's Right Hand Man)

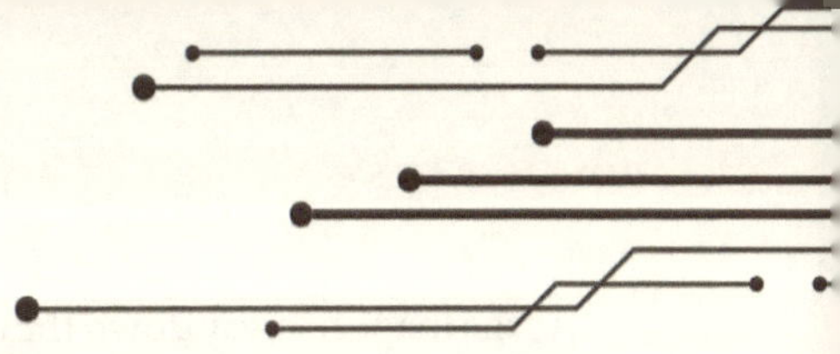

CHAPTER THIRTEEN
YUMI

Y UMI SHUT THE DOOR behind her when she stepped out of the Blue Study, careful to wait for the soft click of the latch into the strike plate. It would make it far more difficult for Maya to bully her way in and stretch across the sofa with dirty paws. She hadn't been caught chewing on books since she was a puppy, but the possibility of walking in on a flurry of ripped paper again frightened Yumi.

Night had fallen and settled the castle into thick silence. She had meant to retire to her chambers before the darkness could seep into the veins, as usual, but had failed this time. Her footsteps fell with hesitance as she assessed her surroundings with care.

She caught a flicker of someone passing through a corner between perpendicular doors, but the gold head of curls was a familiar sight. Yumi didn't know how Owen occupied his time when her ability to interact with him waxed and waned with Ara's moon; but she didn't know where else he would have gone, either.

Her fingers gently trailed up the stone banister as she climbed the steps to the upper wings. The rest of her family had curled safe into their beds hours ago. A shadow flicked in her periphery from the Upper East wing but she paid it no mind.

As she made her way down the opposite wing, a hushed voice fell on her ears from something out of sight. Sound without discernible words. Yumi froze and waited for it again. A long moment passed before she heard it, clearer:

"Yumes?"

Blood drained from her face. She knew that voice.

"Yumi, baby, what are you doing?"

The unmistakable tenor of her wife's voice came from behind one of the doors farther down the hall - a top floor entry to the armory locked within the heart of the castle. Yumi watched the counter-clockwise turn of the doorknob, and then its sharp reversal. Only three people had the key to that door; none of them were Avery.

"Yumes, can you please let me in?"

Possibility would not allow this to truly be Avery, no matter how Yumi rationalized it. If Avery was truly dead — Ara forbid — there was nothing to anchor her to the armory specifically. Why, of all places? This thing speaking did not live in flesh and bone; but nor was it from the aftershock of her death.

When she approached the door, the spirit mimicking her wife rattled the handle harder; like that would have coaxed her into opening the barrier between them. Though Yumi felt her heart pounding in the divide between her collarbones, a bizarre fascination came over her and she cocked her chin curiously.

How is this possible?

The Mimic pleaded with her, as though beginning to cry: "Yumi... Yumi, please. It's so dark in here. I'm so cold... I don't wanna die, baby please let me in."

Vertigo swung her skull and Yumi stumbled backwards. Her lip trembled and she bit down too hard when she jolted into a table and vase behind her. The manipulation threw her hard and she tried not to envision Avery's face as the spirit begged her to grant it entrance. Yumi wasn't powerless. She knew she could swing even harder:

"What is her name," she asked the Mimic.

The doorknob stopped. With a voice that sounded less like her sweet wife and more like a corvid who had only just encountered humans for the first time and could not replicate their voices without mechanical uncanniness, it spoke once more:

"*Nora*."

Yumi bolted down the hall, heaving frantic breaths until she could slam the safety of her chamber door shut. She slid the latch lock and backed away. Her foot grazed the lip of a low altar table and she stumbled into the post of her bedframe.

Brightloch Castle was never dormant, but most often quiet enough that Yumi could simply pretend to not notice the specters that took up residence in its stone ribs. They came, they went, and sometimes greeted her in between. But never before had they tried to manipulate her— and with her wife, no less.

Yumi knew in that moment she was not Queen. She was a frightened little girl again, flinching at the things that bumped in the night when her mother couldn't explain them away. What would she say about the Mimic?

"*Playful beasts often do not understand our fright,*" Yumi imagined as she laid on her back and mother's voice was only a skeletal memory of how clearly she once could summon it. *"A beast's roar is a puppy's bark if you are the wolf."*

The thought helped until Yumi remembered her mother never saw spirits. Sleep did not come for Queen Yumi Harthmoor of Brightloch that night.

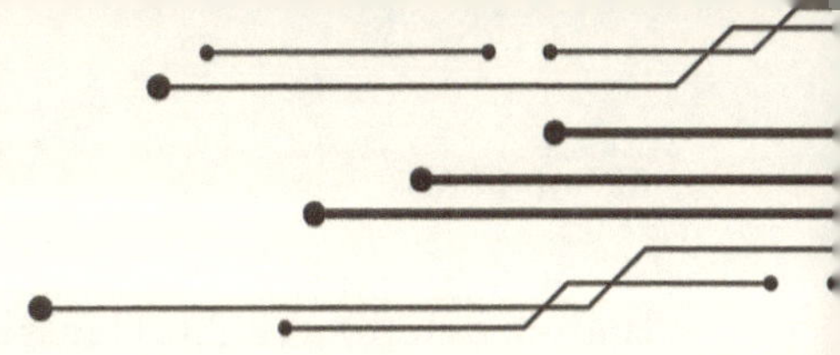

CHAPTER FOURTEEN
KUROSAKI

KUROSAKI STRODE INTO THE large sunlit kitchen and was surprised to find that he was not the first early-riser. Across the butcher-block island from the archway entry, Griffin sat atop a stool with a full mouth and a half eaten, half syrup submerged plate of pancakes before him. The boy waved at Kurosaki with his hand that did not carefully balance a fork.

"Good morning," Kurosaki responded, his voice gravelly with the remnants of sleep lodged in his throat and he remembered being Griffin's age when such a thing would have thrilled him.

Behind Griffin, Moz's tall frame stood in front of a gas stove with his back to the door. He wore a forest green shirt with the long sleeves folded up to the elbow as he worked, the lowest section of his arm revealing the tattooed pits of the ocean and part of the churning surface above it. A white linen towel was thrown over his left shoulder for easy access while he flipped the next pancake on the griddle.

"Morning, Kuro," he said without turning. "Still take pancakes in batches of three?"

"That would be perfect, thank you."

Kurosaki pulled out a stool and took a seat on the side of the island opposite from Griffin. He felt like an intruder as he watched the effortless morning ritual between father and son, but he reminded himself that intruders never got Moz's fluffy pancakes.

He would have loved to feel at home in a kitchen like this one. Stained glass pictures of the changing night sky adorned the top arches of three lancet windows stretching all the way from the sink counter to the ceiling before it vaulted with black beams. Potted ferns and schefflera sat on empty corners of the marble countertops, thriving despite the dusting of snow outside just beyond. With the way Moz moved with ease, it was clear that though it was not in name, it was his kitchen.

As Moz plated the pancakes, Griffin's head shot up and he fixed his ivy green gaze on a point somewhere beyond Kurosaki's shoulder. Before he could turn around to see what had captured his startled attention, Moz was already walking with the plate towards Kurosaki and his mossy eyes flickered once to the point and back down again.

"Nothing, bud," he said simply to Griffin as he set the plate down in front of Kurosaki.

Griffin frowned, but said nothing. Kurosaki finally looked over his shoulder to find a rack of pots, pans, and a shelf lined with cookbooks behind the round dinner table on the opposite end of the long kitchen. Nothing looked out of place, as far as he could tell.

"What is nothing?" His words felt clunky when he turned back around to Griffin and Moz's back was to him again as he finished up the last batch of pancakes.

"Griff, bud," Moz said. "Me to explain, you to explain, or no one to explain?"

Griffin threw back the remainder of his orange juice before he wiped his mouth with the back of his hand and said, "you can. I have to leave to meet Jude."

He got up and set his sticky plate and empty glass in the deep steel sink. Moz looked over his shoulder at Griffin with an eyebrow raised just as the boy was ready to walk away. Without so much as an annoyed huff, Griffin started washing his dishes.

"It's just something we need to do sometimes," Moz said to Kurosaki without turning away from the stove. "Sometimes Griffin will see or hear something that catches him off guard and it's pretty easy to tell when something throws him, so we'll just confirm for him one way or another. The trick is not to investigate further and just move on. If he wants to talk about a hallucination, he will."

Kurosaki nodded with a mouth full of the fluffiest pancakes he could ever recall having. After he swallowed it down, he said, "that's genius, really."

Moz plated the last pancakes and turned around just as Griffin was headed to the door, cleaned plates shelved away.

"Thanks, Griff," Moz said. "I'll see you later."

"Bye Dad, bye Kurosaki."

Griffin left in a hurry without giving time for Kurosaki to answer. Moz pulled up the stool on the left side of the island and Kurosaki made an effort to not read into why he had chosen the stool next to him and not the one Griffin had previously occupied.

Instead he said, "Griffin's a good kid."

Moz chuckled, dashing a splash of maple syrup across his pancakes. "Yeah, he gets it from his moms."

"And you too," Kurosaki said. He wasn't going to let Moz dismiss himself so easily anymore. "You've always been good at heart. Even when you thought you had fallen past the point of no return, you always had nothing but others in mind."

Moz stabbed his pancake with a fork, his face turned down but Kurosaki saw the sheepish smile he had been trying to hide. "Well damn, good morning to you too."

"I mean it," Kurosaki said and he debated his next words when he saw Moz freeze. "And I was a fool to not see it sooner."

Moz looked at him finally and they held a locked stare. He still wasn't used to seeing the forest in his eyes through glass but the discerning look burned all the same. The silence felt too heavy and Kurosaki watched Moz's throat bob. The man's mouth opened just the slightest and closed again, like he had been about to speak but thought better of it. Instead, he lifted a forkful of pancake up to his face before he finally responded:

"That was good, almost makes me forgive you for shooting me in the head."

Kurosaki grinned and he felt delighted when Moz smirked back at him. A beaming thing of his yearning dreams made real again. He tried to ignore the intrusive desire to part the smart grin with his tongue and instead grumbled with a half-smile, "Idiot."

Moz laughed with him before he finished the plate of pancakes in front of him and he took Kurosaki's empty plate to the sink.

"Fuckin' amazing, as always," Kurosaki said about the pancakes, but could have meant any number of things. Like the way Moz stood with his back to him at the kitchen faucet but flourished two fingers in a spiraled wave as though to bow at the compliment.

"Thank you, thank you," he said as he began to dry. "Would you care to go with me to the Sentry today?"

"Am I allowed?"

"You are when I'm in charge and I say you're allowed."

"Well, I don't have a hot date to get me out of it, so I guess I'll go with you kicking and screaming," Kurosaki said with a drip of sarcasm before he had a chance to realize that the words were meant to distance himself and tame the warmth that had pooled in the pit of his stomach. Moz looked at him over his shoulder with his marred brow raised as he draped the linen towel across a hanger.

"Perfect," Moz said instead of addressing the gnaw of Kurosaki's words and he felt grateful for it. "Jack is going to come with us, too. He's got good perspective and I'd like it all on the record."

"Oh boy, here we go. I'm sure we'll get the rundown of every fleeting thought."

He rose from his seat and followed Moz out of the kitchen, ignoring the revenant with maroon hair and round sunglasses that watched them from the corner.

"Pass a message onto the kid for me, will you 'Zaya," Todd jeered. "I'll be waiting for him on the other side. I owe him one."

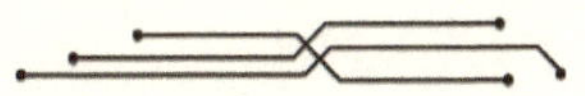

Hi Kuro,

Jack just left for Eyon, but you might not get this until after he's already left again. He says he's going to meet with one of his clients but the bag he packed looked awfully big. I know he's coming to check on you and I wish I could go with him.

I know you don't like us in your business but I need you to know that we all love you so much. And if you ever need a place to go, you always have a home at the castle. You don't even need to ask, don't even need to warn us that you're coming. Probably still announce yourself at the gate though if you've got the big guns.

Love you always,

Ave

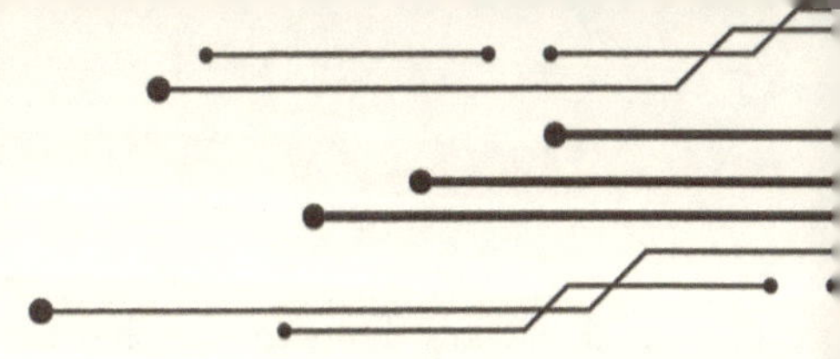

CHAPTER FIFTEEN
GRIFFIN

A WADDED BALL OF paper whacked Griffin on the left cheek before it hit his fold-out desk. He frowned, looking up over his shoulder. Higher up in the amphitheater lecture hall, Hanna met his gaze. Her slender arms were folded at her chest and she watched Griffin over her nose from her higher perch. The boys who flanked her, Marcus and Ian, stifled back snickers. Her small smile was soft but her pale face in a sea of dark uniforms that made up his morning psychology class made Griffin feel he stared directly into the sun. Her look didn't offer any explanation as to why her friends had thrown the paper, so he let it go and turned around.

Annoyances at worst.

Griffin looked down at his notes on social cognition. He got about halfway down the page to where "social schemas" was under-lined five too many times before his pencil had snapped and he was too embarrassed to rustle around in his backpack for another one and risk drawing attention to himself. Professor Zima was not kind about interruptions and already his impression of Griffin seemed unfavorable when he had been caught looking about at flashing lights on the walls that only he saw. It was grim fate that he was exactly the professor Griffin needed to be taking a mentorship from if he had any desire to complete his forensic psychology studies.

The ninety minute lecture ended and Professor Zima dismissed the students, clearing out the musty amphitheater of seats and fold-down desks quickly. Buzzing bodies spilled out into the mezzanine for their next block and Griffin looked around, easily taller than most of his peers.

"Hi, Gloomy," he heard behind him.

Griffin kept his sigh as small and close to his chest as he could before he turned around.

"Hi Hanna," he replied. "Why were you throwing shit at me?"

"Sorry, that was actually Ian. We haven't seen you in class in quite a while, have you been skipping?"

Griffin frowned. "You a rat, now?"

Hanna laughed a melodic sound as she adjusted her hold on the small stack of textbooks and leather notebooks against her chest. She shrugged the strap of her bookbag higher up on her shoulder.

"No, but we wanted you to come hang out with us. We're going to the cafe on Alder Street. Will you join us?"

The question came just as Marcus and Ian approached from behind her. They were identical twins, brown eyes just as the same as their bulbous cuts of dark curls were, and still they found ways to see who could grind on Griffin's nerves the hardest. Almost a full semester in and Griffin still couldn't tell them apart, so he had taken to calling them Bulbhead One and Bulbhead Two. Whoever stood on the left was Bulbhead One.

"I actually have to meet Jude to study," Griffin answered. "Maybe another time."

"Awww c'mon, Porter," Bulbhead Two groaned, leaning an elbow on Hanna's shoulder. "You can study another time!"

"Just as I can get coffee another time," when Griffin responded, he wasn't aware of how flat his affect laid until Bulbhead One flinched. As though Griffin was being deliberately cold; but he didn't try to correct himself, so maybe he was.

Hanna just smiled, closed-lipped. "Another time then, Gloomy."

Griffin gave her a polite nod before he turned for the door of the social sciences department, easier to navigate now that other students had already hurried out to begin their treks through the snow. He walked alone towards the Main Library, hands shoved deep in his coat pockets.

Stepping inside, he found Jude fast. She sat at a table alone with a menagerie of open textbooks spread in front of her. A pencil bounced on her temple as she fidgeted in thought, the curve of her mouth pulled in a frown. He was careful not to interrupt her as he sat down across the long communal tabletop from her.

"Hi," she greeted him, not looking up.

"Hi," he kept his answer short and her focus turned back completely to her notes that were utterly indecipherable to him.

He pulled out his own notes and frowned, frustrated that he didn't just let himself be a nuisance and fish out a pencil to complete his page on Professor Zima's lecture.

Gods forbid you ever let yourself take up space, Jude had once said to him in a huff of annoyance at something he had done. Or maybe failed to do.

Griffin looked up at Jude across the table. A faint hum of voices from other students cramming for midterms floated on the air of the Main Library, but she sat silent with a fixed frown of determination as she furiously scribbled her physics notes into an overstuffed notebook.

Something about watching her work felt relaxing to Griffin; the faint whisper of reading her notes aloud to herself as she drilled formulas and theorems into her brain, the sound of her fingers carefully turning the pages of her textbook. He watched as she yanked at the necktie beneath her sweater, loosening as much as she could without breaking uniform, and she crossed out an entire line of her notes with an angry scratch.

Without looking up, she chided him, "decided you're done with school?"

Griffin leaned back in his chair, slapping his pen down onto his half-empty notebook page a little louder than he had meant to before he sighed. "Kind of hard to give a shit about it right now, Jude."

Forensic psychology - *a fucking joke*. What good was psychology when he was crazy? Or its application to the purpose of justice when a cold case was going to hang over his head for the rest of his life?

She closed her notebook pointedly.

"And what would you like to do about it?" Her tone burned with annoyance and Griffin felt the same fleck of panic that came whenever it was directed at him. "I hardly think sitting and letting yourself suffer is the best course of action. So what are you going to do?"

"I hardly think I have just half the mind to even *think* about coming near a murder case."

"I hate when you do that," she mumbled before she looked back down at her notebook, dismissing whatever rebuttal he could have given before he even tried.

"When I do what?"

"Let everyone convince you that your mind is no good," she answered when she looked up again, evidently not done with him after all. "You included."

They stared at each other across the table of scattered papers and open textbooks. Jude was discerning and he felt ensnared in her look, a soft intimidation that he knew she hadn't even meant to strike him fearful. But she was right. Nobody was ever quicker to discount Griffin than he was.

He sucked in a sharp inhale.

"Okay. Fine. Let's find out who killed Uncle Tristan."

Jude nodded once. "Atta boy."

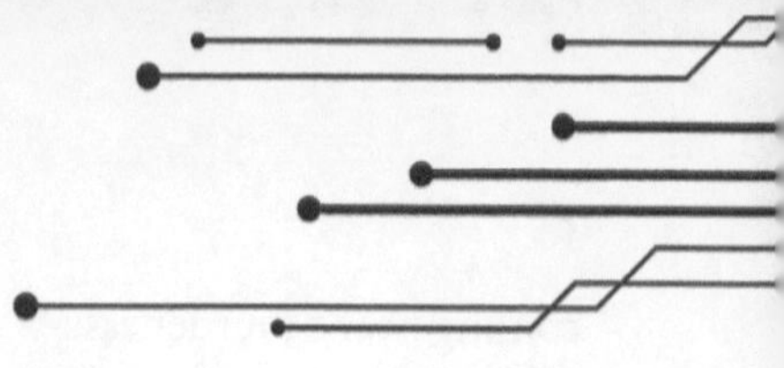

CHAPTER SIXTEEN
MOZ

"**J**ACK MOSLEY," THE LOWER ranking officer sitting at the table read from the paper held in front of his face just as Moz approached. "No chance there's a relation to a William Mosley, is th—"

The Sentry officer flinched when he lowered the paper and saw that Moz towered over him with his arms folded. He undoubtedly had something to say about Jack's possible relation to his superior and Moz did not feel bad at all for failing to hide his displeasure.

"There sure is! He's my brother," Jack answered.

The officer looked nervously between the two of them, and then again when he clearly became confused.

"My ma was the pretty one," Moz lied flatly while never shifting his unamused gaze from the officer and Jack snickered.

"Sentinel, I apologize. It's just that this guy looks so young and I—"

"Young?" Jack slammed his palms on the table, staring hard at the officer who reeled back in his chair at the sound. He stared hard at the officer with his eyebrows furrowed and the other man looked around trying to find another point in the room to look at other than Jack's eyes fixed on him. Like the hypnosis was failing.

"Goddamnit Jack, when was the last time you could do that?"

Jack straightened up and sighed wistfully. "Not since I was but a wee boy of the Beldam."

"We'll get him squared away and debriefed on the Díomasaigh case," the officer pushed on after he cleared his throat and looked back down at the paper, avoidant of Moz's stare.

As Moz had been about to speak, he stopped when he saw Cain stride into the office. The expression on his pale face was grim and in his hands he held the cap of his uniform. He strode directly to Moz and stopped close so that he could speak in hushed tones with his back to the lower officer.

"Mosley, a body has been found in the woods. Near the northeast wall," Cain informed him in a low voice, careful not to let himself be heard by anyone else.

Moz froze. The northeast wall. *That could mean...*

"Bring me there. Now."

Cain nodded before his gaze slid from Moz to Jack and Kurosaki.

Moz added, "They're coming, too."

They followed Cain and piled into one of the police department's trucks parked outside. Moz sat in the passenger seat in silence, his elbow propped on the window ledge so he could hold his head in one hand. Behind him, Kurosaki held a hand on his shoulder and though Moz felt the fear inside roll in churning waves, he welcomed the anchor of his warm touch.

None of the men spoke a word even as they passed through the east Brighloch gate and the forest beyond spilled in front of them just on the other side of the dirt road winding down the hill. Moz had traveled this road countless times since the day he was called out for the initial investigation of his wife's disappearance. But this was different and the feeling of finality settled like stones in the pit of his stomach.

This couldn't be it.

They pulled up next to the several Department of Forest Management trucks and two police sedans just as they were finishing off their cordoning tape; as though anyone was out there to stumble onto the scene by accident.

"Follow me down," Cain said as they stepped out of the truck and he slammed the driver's door shut. "Watch your step, too. It's not far, but it's tricky."

He ducked under the yellow tape and led them to the gaping mouth of the ravine. The steep decline was blanketed in thick combs of fern and cut through with jagged rocks. Tough, but doable with patience. Moz followed Cain's methodical descent, repeating each calculated step and careful turn of the feet to avoid sliding in the thin dusting of snow. When the land leveled out, Moz pulled his gun from his holster to hold at his side, ready should he need it. None of the cops seemed terribly concerned with staying at the ready, but then again they weren't demon host turned demon hunter.

He saw the cluster of officers congregating just on the other side of a thick oak trunk and Moz hesitated. Even with his gun and his wit, nothing could ever make him feel sufficiently prepared for what he would find at their feet.

To call it a body was generous. She was bones and tattered clothes washed in rain and coated in months of muck that had melted and refrozen. Moz's stomach dropped and he sank to the balls of his feet, setting the gun on the ground.

There was nothing he could immediately tie to Avery in this corpse. And nothing to say with absolute certainty that it wasn't her, either.

He felt Jack's hand on his shoulder when Cain spoke, "We're about to take her to the medical examiner after combing the scene. We thought it would be useful first if you could assess whether this was a demonic or human attack. And if you recognize the clothes... well, this isn't how we like to do things but we needed you, Mosley."

They thought he would be *useful*? Moz threw Jack's hand off him and stood up, turning to face Cain.

"No, dipshit. I don't recognize these threadbare clothes. It would have been really fucking *useful* if you idiots had found her sooner. Maybe then we'd have more to go on than this," he jabbed a pointed finger into Cain's chest. "I don't know why the fuck they put you in charge or where Woods went, but this has been utter fucking bullshit. What kind of fucking idiot asks someone to identify their wife's body and assess the scene in the same fucking go?"

Cain stepped back. "Don't touch me, Mosley. You don't want to go down that road with me."

Bold. Real fuckin' bold. Moz's face twisted into a grin and he recognized the look of fear in the corner of his vision when the color drained from Kurosaki's face.

"I paved that road, you son of a bitch."

Cain turned from him, "Cool down and just look at the scene

before we take her."

The police captain headed back toward the face of the ravine and the parked cars, leaving the trio alone with the other officers and Scouts who mostly ignored their presence as they scoured the frozen brush. Moz bent down and picked his gun off the ground. He was thankful that it had been witnessed there where the officer couldn't warp the events that played out in his report. He'd have to be careful with his temper if Cain was to keep prodding at it.

Moz turned to Jack and Kurosaki; he didn't want to look at the body again if he didn't have to. "Do either of you have any first impressions so far?"

He felt an odd warmth when he watched Kurosaki step forward to stand at his shoulder, scratching the short hair on his chin in thought as his earthen gaze flickered over the ice-logged bones. It felt infinitely better to stare at him than to consider the corpse any longer. A radiant and familiar light in the dull white of snow.

"It's oddly well intact for this stage of decay," Kurosaki finally noted. "I'm sure everyone here is going to say the same thing, but she was almost certainly moved here long after the fact. Which begs the question *why*."

"Could this possibly be the handiwork of another Reaper?"

Kurosaki shook his head at Jack's offer without turning. "I doubt a Reaper would leave this much of a mess behind."

"If it's a new Reaper, I wouldn't be surprised if they-"

A snapping branch cut Jack off. They whirled around quickly and Kurosaki drew a gun that Moz didn't even know had been on his person; though the thought of him going anywhere without one was admittedly ridiculous. To ask if Izaya Kurosaki was armed was to question whether or not the sky was blue.

Moz inched deeper into the mouth of the forest and in the direction that the sound of disturbed wilderness had come from.

"Be my eyes, Jack," he called out without turning his head. His former familiar aged, but still held better eyesight than he did on top of his remarkable attention to detail.

Moz's careful stare glossed across the white dusting of snow and grey tree trunks as he waited for something to stir. The voices of the forensics team further up the ravine had disappeared and the silence embraced him in what he knew would soon tighten into a chokehold.

"Moz, there!"

He looked quick to see the direction Jack had pointed his gun and followed it back forward. Moz almost missed the movement between the trees until the creature took an unnervingly long step.

It looked mostly humanoid, walking on two legs with arms that swung down too far to make sense. Grey flesh had lent to its ease in hiding amongst the winter wood undetected. Ten point antlers sprouted from the top of its head, splintered on end and shrouded its skull in bleeding velvet. He watched them shift as it turned its head, fixing its empty eyes on Moz. The bottom jaw dropped and viscous saliva oozed from a mouth overcrowded with fangs.

Before he could shout, the creature sprinted in their direction on ungodly fast limbs. Moz cracked shots from the gun loaded with blessed bullets, but the demon moved in quick cracks of lightning.

"Jack, guard the body!"

He heard the crunch of snow behind him when Jack stood between the corpse and the demon barrelling towards them. It darted in zig-zags amongst the trees as Moz fired blessed bullet after blessed bullet to slow it down, but none were finding their target.

Kurosaki had sidestepped away from Moz to get a different angle on the demon, but none of his shots struck flesh. With the cracks of gunfire and snaps of exploding tree bark, the officers who had been called to the scene were shouting but Moz felt too frustrated to make out whatever it was they were saying.

"DAMNIT," Moz roared in anger as another shot missed.

The antlered demon charged him fast and Moz wasn't quick enough to dodge the blow. He crashed hard into the tree behind him and the resonant sound of a thick icicle falling and splintering to a thousand pieces where he had been standing only moments ago rattled him. Moz turned around the tree to put more distance between his body and the danger of the beast and ice. The size of the sharpened ice could have drilled through his skull and killed him just as easily as the demon. His eyes widened.

Ice. Water.

"What the fuck are you doing?"

Jack cried out when Moz lowered his handgun instead of firing it again, despite the demon circling the tree to strike him again. He was looking up at the cathedral of ice above their heads, amazed that more of them hadn't fallen. A loud *thwack* sounded from somewhere in his periphery and he was almost tempted to follow the demon's investigative turn of the head. Instead, he seized the glimmer of opportunity in both hands.

He thought of that space in the back of his head where The Thing once lived. There was silence where he once heard the voice of the Knight and in it he heard his own thunder with such clarity. Rolling with him, daring him. He focused on the biggest spear of ice he could find and he pulled.

The sharpened icicle flew through the air, drilling the demon through the head. Hot blood splattered on impact, slashing Moz in black across his face. Its pained wails ended just as abruptly as they had begun and the beast slumped onto its side in the snow, leaking inky ooze. Moz let his shoulders relax as he watched the last rattles of death twitching in its limbs and he realized he was utterly freezing. He hadn't even touched the ice, but he felt all over that he had gripped it in his bare hands.

Kurosaki looked on in awe as Moz wiped blood from his face and said, "see what I meant?"

The man approached Moz and the demon, unable to speak at first. His brown eyes widened in horror as his gaze traveled from the blood, to the freakish cadaver, and to the man who had killed it without a bullet. Kurosaki stopped at its head.

"You're telling me you did that? Without a Knight?"

Moz nodded. He wished he had a better explanation to give Kurosaki, but it puzzled him just as much.

Officers with guns finally rushed to them and Moz frowned; they would have been absolutely useless if they had actually been counting on the backup. Cain stepped through the uniforms with his own gun lowering. He looked from the impaled demon to Moz for an explanation.

"Freakish luck," Moz mumbled.

"Huh," Cain huffed, looking at Moz with what he could only assume was amusement lined with irritation. "We'll have the cadaver packed up and-"

"Get your ass out of my jurisdiction," Moz warned as he put his gun back in his holster. "And off my road, bitch."

The police captain certainly wasn't amused anymore. With a flat expression he said, "Very well, Sentinel."

Cain turned to walk back to the wall of the ravine, taking his officers with him and leaving two Department of Forest Management Scouts behind. Jack huffed in annoyance as soon as the man was certainly out of earshot.

"Get off his juris-dick, son!"

Kurosaki was the only one to acknowledge Jack with a scolding frown.

Moz was tempted to ask the Scouts if either had known his wife. If they knew anything about that day. But it was hardly the time. The youngest of them, a man with a short black beard, radioed for someone to bring down a transport bag. A third Scout came down with a large, yellow bag constructed of thick tarp and together they worked to load the demon's cadaver inside.

After zipping it shut, Moz wiped black blood from his hands and onto the front of his coat with a grimace.

"Thank you for your help," he said to the Scouts. He'd rough-house with the police left and right, but he had no issues with the people Avery had worked with for a cause she cared so much about. They cared for keeping the woods safe; and keeping people safe from the woods itself.

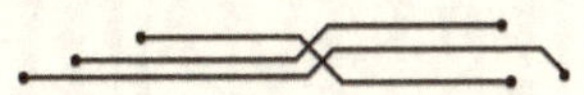

My Beloved,

I turn hell inside out looking for you. Each day when I rise, each evening when I drift. I beseech the gods in every tongue I know and wonder why still I am left in silence. Why am I left in silence?

Owen and I turn the clocks this way — when he is searching, I am grieving. When I am diving, he is untethered. We will never cease this search. Not until I hold your bones in my hands or our son is holding mine.

You haunt me and I beg for your spirit to stay forever in this home. I love you forever, I love you isn't enough.

Yours,

Yumi

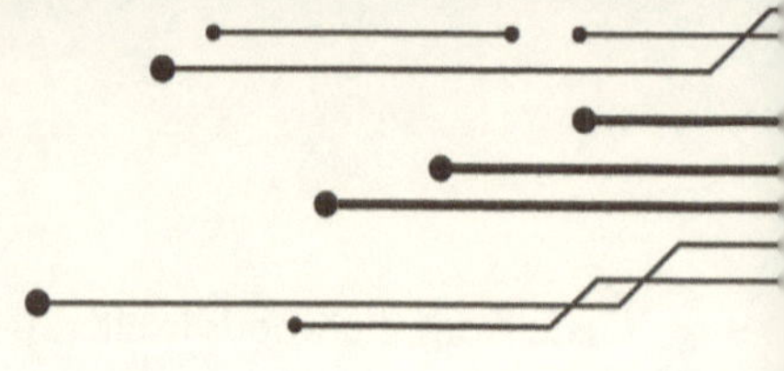

CHAPTER SEVENTEEN
GRIFFIN

WHEN GRIFFIN WALKED INTO the kitchen, his father was sitting alone on an island stool with his glasses off. His father lifted his head slightly when he heard him walk in and waved for him to take a seat. Griffin hesitated before he edged for the chair across from him. He sank down into the seat slowly, already hating how wrong this situation felt.

"Dad, what's wrong?"

Moz took a sharp inhale and folded his hands two times before finally letting them settle flat on the table. He looked up at Griffin and though he tried to mask it, the pain was evident.

"Griff, bud... I don't know how to say this. They don't know if it's your Mama for sure... but they found a body. Near the wall."

For the first time in a long time, Griffin sat in silence. No voices, no whistles, no hums. A heavy nothing.

"What do you mean they don't know?"

"They took the...remains, over to the medical examiner. The police had us come down to take a look to see if we could identify them. We couldn't say one way or another, so they're looking harder."

Griffin's eyes widened. "They had you come to the scene?"

Moz threw up his hands and leaned back before putting them

behind his head, clearly still dumbfounded by whatever events had unfolded for him that day. "That's exactly what I said, bud."

"I'm sorry, Dad."

"Me too. But better it's me than you or Mimi."

He thought of his conversation with Jude in the library. If they were going to solve anything together, it was time to start asking questions.

"Do you think it's related to Uncle Tristan?"

His father narrowed his eyes, watching Griffin like the explanation for his curiosity was scrawled somewhere on his face. Griffin touched his cheeks, then his forehead when the possibility struck him and quickly dropped his hands when he caught his own bizarre behavior.

"I don't think so, bud," Moz finally answered. The honesty was a dreadful thing in his ears. "We'll know once we get the autopsy report."

"How long could that take?"

Moz frowned. "A couple days maybe, why the interest all of a sudden?"

"Academic interest," Griffin answered; it was only a half-lie.

His father frowned. "What could possibly be relevant about a-"

He stopped abruptly when a humanoid shadow passed the open kitchen doors. Griffin's heart pounded - he was seeing it so clearly.

Moz watched the empty space as well.

"I saw it, too," he said quietly.

Griffin froze at the admission. It felt far more unsettling to realize that it had not been a hallucination for only his eyes.

"Dad, what was that?"

He looked from the doorway to his father's face as he watched the space. Griffin waited for an answer and the longer the silence, the more he squirmed in his chair. Moz finally turned to him.

"Griff," his expression was stern and he folded his hands on the table in front of him, "your moms and I... we did everything we could to keep the things in Od where they are meant to be, you know this, right?"

Griffin nodded. He was never given the specifics, just that they helped stop whatever the Knights of Od were. His peers called it mythology and he was inclined to believe the same. *Skeletal dragon demons? Hardly.*

"We helped, but it could never be perfect," Moz continued. "And sometimes, spirits leak out in addition to the demons. They can't hurt you, but it might be a bit frightening if you aren't expecting it."

"How will I know if it's a hallucination or a spirit?"

"I wish I could answer that for you. I wish I could give you all the answers, but I just don't know, bud. The next best thing I can do is tell you everything I know and hope it's enough for you to navigate this world confidently."

"I think usually it's pretty easy to tell when they get a little too bizarre to be real," Griffin admitted. "But when there's not much to it, it gets hard. Seeing a dude with black eyes and long claws is pretty easy to write off as not real, but when-"

"Sorry, I'm sorry I'm interrupting, but rewind for a second. *What* did you see?"

Griffin frowned. "A guy? Probably a little taller than you? Brown skin, black eyes, like all of the eye. And claws. Why?"

Moz stood up from his stool, knotting his fingers in his hair as he groaned in frustration. "I am gonna SKIN that cat!"

He turned back to Griffin. "Where did you see him and when?"

"Couple of days ago? By Mama's statue?"

His father put his head in his hands, rubbing his face underneath the wire frame of his glasses. Moz took in a sharp inhale.

"It never fucking ends," he muttered. He dropped his hands before he added, "you come find me if you see him again, alright?"

"Sure thing, Coach."

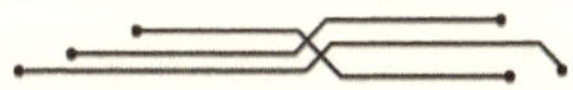

Mama,

I miss you every day. I can tell Maya misses you, too. Sometimes she waits for you at the bottom of your tower and I think she would want me to tell you that.

I graduate today. I didn't read Rambler and the Rook for class but I found Mimi's copy you gave her and read it on my own. I don't understand why Griffin needed to be transformed into a rook too to appreciate the woods, but I think I get why you liked the story. I know you love the woods.

I think I see you sometimes. I know it's not. Dad gave me your letter.

Griffin

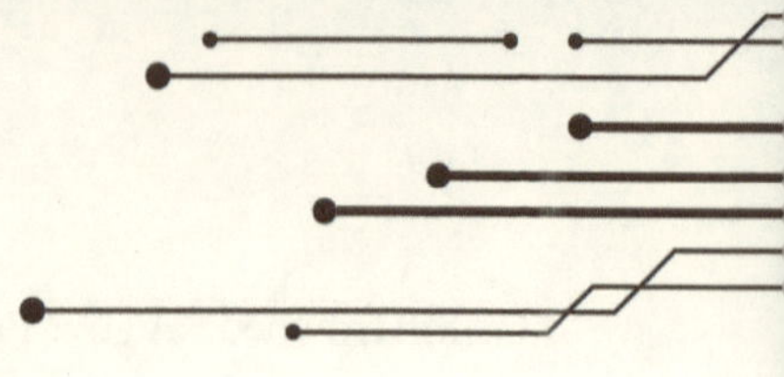

CHAPTER EIGHTEEN
MOZ

MOZ HAD BEEN TO the coroner's office countless times. But it had always been on matters for the head of the Royal Sentry to investigate, never as a loved one receiving news about a body. His stomach turned despite the warm and familiar face sitting down at the desk when he quietly shut the glass paned door behind him.

"It's okay, Moz," Maria Clements said. Her voice was kind as ever and he knew her well enough to know she was struggling to straddle the line between friend and colleague as the forensic pathologist. Yumi was right; this was too personal. "You can take a seat."

Oh gods. Isn't that always what they said when the news was bad? Was that why Maria had called him in so quickly? Identification on the same day was unheard of. He stood frozen until she quietly gestured with her hand to sit down across from her. Moz sank and Maria opened the folder before her.

"It's not her, Moz."

"Fucking hell, Maria," he took off his glasses and held his face in his hand, pinching the bridge of his nose the slightest. "You couldn't have fucking led with that?"

"The dental profile wasn't a match," Maria continued and her less-than subtle push to carry on with the information concerned him as he put his glasses back on. "And this skeletal system indicates the victim was about an inch taller than Ave. The good news is she's still out there, with a favorable probability that she is alive from what Yumi and Owen have told us."

"And the bad news?"

"The bad news is that we possibly have multiple murders on our hands. Can you handle serial homicide, Sentinel Mosley?"

Moz put his elbows on the desk, letting his head fall back into his palms. His glasses dug into his brow bone and he didn't care to fix the pinching metal on skin.

"No, I can't, Maria. I can't handle this on top of Avery's case. And I don't think it's the same killer as Tristan's. How many people are fucking out there?"

"Be mindful that I have not finished determining the cause of death," Maria reminded him. "I did a courtesy ruling out her identity first. For you as a friend."

He lifted his head, wiping his hand down his mouth before holding his hands in his lap to shrug off his air of desperation. "Thank you. I don't tell you enough that I appreciate you."

"No, you don't," she said with a warm smile, the lines around her mouth dimpling with warmth.

"I appreciate you, Maria. Lily, too."

"Thank you. Oh, and Moz?"

"Hm?"

"Next time you're worried about an unidentified body potentially being hers, check the fingers. This woman had all ten."

Moz felt his face fall. He rubbed his palm down his face and took a deep exhale. "For fucks sake, I'm an idiot."

"Well, I wasn't going to say it."

He put his folded hands under his chin as he sighed. "I would have fucking noticed it if we hadn't been ambushed by a demon. I can't believe I fucking missed that. I can't belive *Jack* fucking missed that."

"Kid's good, but he's not flawless," Maria pointed out, shrugging as she leaned back into her grey upholstered desk chair. "Either way, it's okay. Because it's not her."

"It's not her," he echoed.

They sat in silence. Moz didn't want to get up yet. Didn't want to say anything to follow up the agreed-upon fact that the body did not belong to his wife. Maria was a safe friend and he knew he could trust her always.

Finally, he did speak:

"Aegis was here."

Maria lifted her brows high on her face. "No shit?"

He nodded. "He's been hiding from me but he showed himself to Griffin near her statue. Sans fuzzy kitty body."

"Doesn't that mean he doesn't have a Reaper? Why is he here?"

"Wish I knew, but I'm gonna gut him when I find him."

"Do you think Avery would be upset with you if you did?"

Moz smiled.

"Probably. But I'll gladly take her ire if it means she's home."

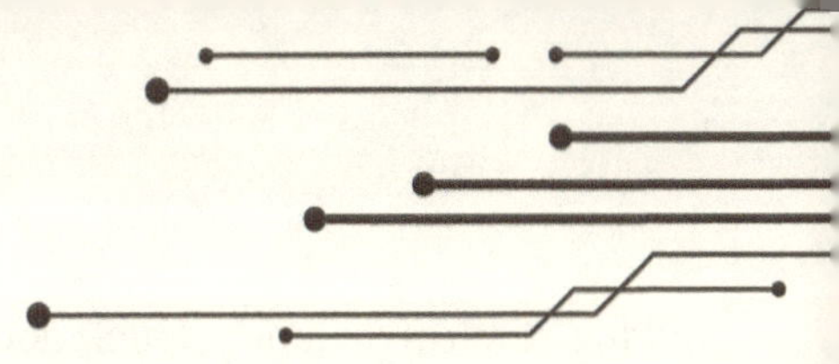

CHAPTER NINETEEN
GRIFFIN

T HE TEXTBOOK SLIPPED OUT of his lap, slammed to the floor, and Griffin shot awake. He was sideways on the cognac leather couch of the Green Study and failed to remember at which point in the evening he had fallen asleep. As he bent forward and gathered up his fallen book and stray papers, he heard the squeak of wet soles on the marble floor of the hallway.

There was a heavy and exhausted cadence to the footsteps and Griffin froze when he realized that it had to have been his father coming home. What news was he bringing?

The open door frame was filled by the tall man and Griffin held his breath when his father pulled his gaze, standing in the doorway of the study. He sucked in a sharp inhale and Griffin's stomach turned, knotting fat tangles of fear.

"It's not your mama," his father finally said and Griffin shot up, hurrying to hug him. He wanted to jab him for the unnecessary dramatics when the news was good, but he felt too relieved.

"We need to go check on Mimi," his father said, squeezing his middle tight. "I'm sure she heard the news first, but it's odd that she hasn't come out to speak to you yet about it."

He followed his father up the staircase and down the upper west wing, towards the lonely double doors of the Queen's chamber. Moz rapped on the oak with tattooed knuckles and they were left with no answer. Where else could she have vanished to? Griffin was shocked when the door finally opened and on the other side stood Yumi, her face streaked red with tears.

"Yumes, what's wrong?"

His dad pushed his way into the doorframe, pulling her into a hug with his arms wrapped around her head.

"It wasn't her," she sobbed. "I was so worried I was wrong and it wasn't her! What if it is next time?"

"It's not going to be, Mimi," Griffin said softly and took the hand she had rested on Moz's back into his own.

"I don't want to be alone right now," she said through tears, squeezing Griffin's hand before Moz let her go and broke their hold inadvertently.

"What would you like us to do? Would you like company here?"

"If you don't mind," Yumi said, wiping her face with the back of her hand. "Remember how we used to cuddle? With her?"

Moz nodded, seeming to immediately know what she was referring to.

"C'mon bud, we need you for this. If you don't like it, you don't have to but I think Mimi would appreciate you trying," he said to Griffin and moved past Yumi into her chamber.

He followed his father and bonus parent into the chamber of merlot reds and a large canopy bed. Bookshelves flanked all walls of the room, except for where the space had been made for a private altar tucked away and littered with spent incense cones and copper bells. Griffin froze when he saw the Scout's uniform coat still hanging on the wooden stand in the corner. His mother's item called to him and he watched the sleeve flap in a light breeze he did not feel on his skin. He stepped towards it, ghosting two fingers across the seam of the shoulder and down to the rectangular patch of black that read PORTER in dirtied white embroidery.

When he turned around, his father watched him but was quick to turn his concerned frown back to the Queen. Yumi climbed onto the bed above the brocade duvet, laying on her side directly in the middle.

"Climb on and face Mimi," Moz said as he sat down on the side farthest from Griffin. "We're family sandwiching until this hurts a little less."

Griffin did as instructed and it began to feel very familiar. His mother and father had done this with him when he was younger and the very early symptoms of his schizophrenia were presenting as melancholy. He remembered that while he still felt sorrow, he was safe and tucked in between two of the people who loved him the most. Griffin wanted that for Yumi and took the hand of his gentle bonus parent.

"We used to cuddle like this after you were born," Yumi said with a soft voice as she nestled into the space between them, holding Griffin's hand. "Mama had postpartum depression quite awfully and wanted as much company as we could stand. Of course, your daddy and I weren't getting along quite as well then, so she'd be stuck in an argument sandwich when we were there for too long."

"What a time that was," Moz said with a small laugh. "I think it helped Avery a lot through that, though. I love you, Yumes."

"I love you too, Moz."

When Griffin was young he had heard his mother say it to both his father and his bonus parent and grew frustrated trying to understand why it wasn't said between the two of Avery's spouses. He would throw tantrums until they said it to each other and eventually it became second nature. Even before then, he couldn't imagine what Yumi could have possibly meant about not getting along.

As Moz still sat upright on the other side of Yumi, he held a grounding hand on her shoulder like he meant to keep her aware of the fact that he was there for her.

"I'm scared, too," he admitted, as though finishing Yumi's thought that she hadn't voiced at all. "It's been such a long time and I hate how much everyone has wanted to call her dead and gone so that life can move on. But I know her and you both do, too. She'll come back from wherever she is soon and we'll have a good laugh about the whole thing while she gives us what I'm sure is a very good explanation."

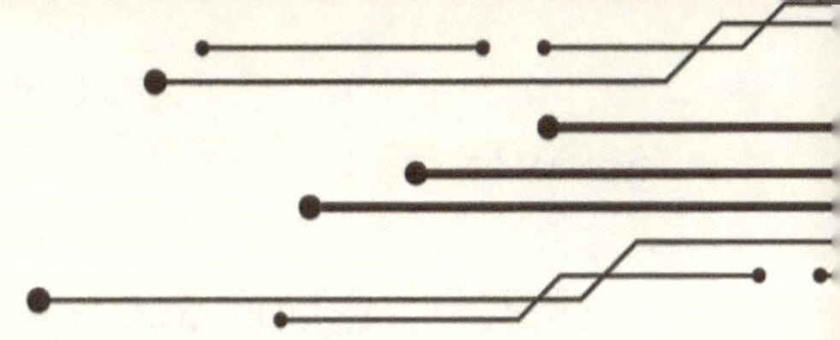

CHAPTER TWENTY
AVERY - TWO YEARS AGO

AVERY APPROACHED THE SHRINE, stepping carefully through the thick combs of sword ferns to avoid trampling any under her hiking boots. The forest should never know she had been there. She was an insignificant speck in a sea of conifers, but she felt a sublime peace in being swallowed whole.

The antlered stag skull sat in the middle of the leveled sarsen stone, ringed by pillars of quartz and the hardened puddles of white candle wax. A recent wind storm that swept through the area had dropped fallen branches into the sacred circle, tangling in the stag's antlers and shattering fallen quartz into glitter at the foot of the wet stone altar.

She lifted the strap of her rifle higher on her shoulder before she knelt down and began carefully plucking errant twigs from the stag's skull.

"Hello, Father," Avery spoke to it, quiet with love. She couldn't remember the last time she had seen the God of the Wood but wanted to make sure He knew that she still cared just as much as she ever had.

She scooped up broken crystals and placed them back in the empty spaces of the ring the best she could. It wouldn't be as perfect as it had been originally made by whatever Priestess had constructed it, but it would have to do until she could go to the Brightloch Temple later that day and ask for help to bless the space again.

A twig snapped behind her and Avery whirled around. Her hand flew to the rifle out of reflex and her heart pounded in loud raps against her sternum. Eyes watched her from the thick underbrush and Avery relaxed when she saw the golden head of the coyote watching her back. Its canine ears flicked outward and then moved on from her far too quickly for her to think that it had been just an ordinary coyote.

She missed that dumb cat all the time.

Avery turned back toward Malo's small shrine and when she leaned across it to tidy the back end of the ring, she saw the figure in black watching her from just beyond the other side. They stood, brazenly letting her see them as they watched her through the eyes of a misshapen mask of a white rabbit. In their left hand they wielded a serrated hunting machete and she wasted no time in realizing they had not been there for game. She yelped, falling backwards on the balls of her feet and fumbled for her rifle.

They lurched at her fast, leaping onto the stone altar and kicking aside the stag skull. It splintered into pieces when it crashed to a lower rock and the sound pained every reverent bone Avery had in her body. She scrambled backwards to get to her feet but the distance between her and the Rabbit Man was closing far too quickly for her to ready her weapon. She didn't know who to summon for help, if anyone would even hear her from the bottom of the ravine.

Avery screamed the first name to cross her mind, "AEGIS!"

A pair of hands closed around her biceps from behind and yanked her hard. She didn't have time to scream before she was surrounded by a warm darkness, floating in nothing. *Fuck - am I dead again?*

The darkness spat her out when she tasted all wrong and Avery stumbled back into the forest, the surface under her feet flatter than it had been at the base of the ravine. She quickly readied her rifle, whirling around until her eyes landed on the figure standing a healthy distance away from her.

"Put that down, you're embarrassing yourself," their voice ran velvet smooth and the patient way they stood with their hands folded at their waist earned them her foolish trust. Avery lowered her gun.

"What's going on? Where are we?"

"Approximately two hundred yards down from the ravine. That was not a true shrine of the god Malo."

Avery looked up the gentle slope of the hill, the jagged ravine they had fled from long buried under the thick blankets of pine trees. When she turned back to the figure, they were watching her with the assessing gaze of a cat that she felt all too familiar with.

Their dark hair was buzzed short against their scalp and the sharp cut of their bronze cheekbones glimmered with mist that hung low to the forest floor. They shoved their fists into the pockets of a black denim coat patched in places with red fabric. If Avery had to guess, they were about the age of her son; somewhere in the late teen years.

"Then what are you suggesting? Why would there be a false shrine?"

"Whoever has made an attempt on your life knows you. They studied your Scouting routines and knew that your love for Malo would not allow you to leave a place of his worship in shambles. This was calculated."

"And how do you know this?"

"I am Mercy, the son of Balthazar and the daughter of Mona," they spoke in a smooth voice that commanded silence from the forest around them. But Avery didn't mind breaking it.

"I'll be damned. That would do it."

The corner of Mercy's mouth turned up in just the slightest amused grin before they set back into authoritative neutrality. "It pains me to say this and I am certain it will pain you to hear it, but I strongly advise against returning home. Whoever they were, they'll be back to finish the job."

"Ohhhh no, no, no! No! I can't do that," Avery's denial had a panicked laughter flecked around the edges. "I have a son I need to take care of! And a husband and wife, I can't just *not* come back!. What if whoever they were goes for them too?"

"I highly doubt that is true if they lured you out here to separate them from you instead of striking from within the walls when you were unarmed and unsuspecting. You were the only target. No one can know you are still alive and out here. Not even the gods."

Avery paused. It made sense and that pissed her off.

"Where am I supposed to go," she murmured, looking around. Nothing but trees.

"There's the Reaper outpost not far from here. If you tell them you are a Saved, they are sure to at least provide you shelter while you figure this out."

"While I figure it out?"

"I'm no fool, Avery Porter. My father warned me about you and that you don't just take shit lying down. So are you going to take shit lying down, or are you going to figure out who did this so you can see your son?"

My son.

For her son, she would burn the world to ashes. Take on any god, slay any monster; nothing was off the table when it came to Griffin. She saw her husband in their son's wide eyes of evergreen wonder and heard her wife's joy in his bubbling fits of laughter.

Anything for family.

Avery sighed and begrudgingly swung her rifle strap back onto her shoulder. "C'mon, let's go. Before I get too old for this shit."

BRIGHTLOCH POLICE DEPARTMENT

SUBJECT: Aegis (Transcriber Note: No surname provided). Former familiar of Scout Avery Porter.

INTERVIEWING OFFICER: Deputy Ethan Woods

WOODS: Do you know of anyone who might have wanted to hurt Avery?

AEGIS: I know plenty of people who wanted to, but never had the balls to try it.

WOODS: Like who?

AEGIS: The officers from Ardua, Sera and Peter. Don't know their last names.

WOODS: If I'm thinking of the same people, Sera is the same one who was charged with the murder of the High Priestess of Centralia, no?

AEGIS: That's the one.

WOODS: Okay, good to know. I haven't heard anything about a Peter.

AEGIS: No one's seen him, no one's heard from him. I wouldn't be surprised if he turned up dead somewhere.

-PAUSE IN RECORDING-

WOODS: Sorry, just jotting that down. So then you don't think he did it? What did he have against Avery?

AEGIS: The fact that she killed his captain is probably a good start. He lost everything after that. But despite that, I don't think he did that. He wasn't the type to ever stand on his own for anything. I'd be genuinely surprised if he ever tied his own shoes without Morgana.

WOODS: Square one then. Anyone else you can think of?

AEGIS: No one in particular stands out to me. People hated Avery like it was their job. They bought into the cultish behavior without hesitation because the King endorsed it. Did you know people made charms for their stoops to drive her away? Like she would ever be going next door for a cup of sugar only to say 'well damn, these three rocks and braided twine sure showed me'. Fools, all of them.

WOODS: Who were you to her, anyway?

AEGIS: I was her familiar. Do you need that introductory speech again?

WOODS: No, I am up to speed on that part. You left her then?

AEGIS: I suppose I did. She didn't need me anymore. I mean, look what she built without me. Have you seen her kid? Brilliant thing, that one.

WOODS: Are you stalking her family?

AEGIS: What? No, don't be ridiculous. I just wanted to see what her life looks like now.

WOODS: The intent behind the action and the impact it causes are two entirely separate things.

AEGIS: Well, it sounds bad when you put it that way.

WOODS: It sounds bad when you do it that way.

AEGIS: Don't you have more questions for me? You know, ones that will help you find her?

WOODS: Right. Where were you in the morning the day she disappeared? Approximately three hours after dawn.

AEGIS: Where all the fuzzy house critters go. Od.

WOODS: Can anyone verify that on your behalf?

AEGIS: Sure, I can take you right now.

-PAUSE IN RECORDING-

WOODS: That won't be necessary.

WOODS: What are you doing here, why now?

AEGIS: I'm going to find whoever did this. And you can bet your ass I'll do it before you.

WOODS: (laughs) Now that's a challenge I can get behind. I

hope you do.
-END OF RECORDING-

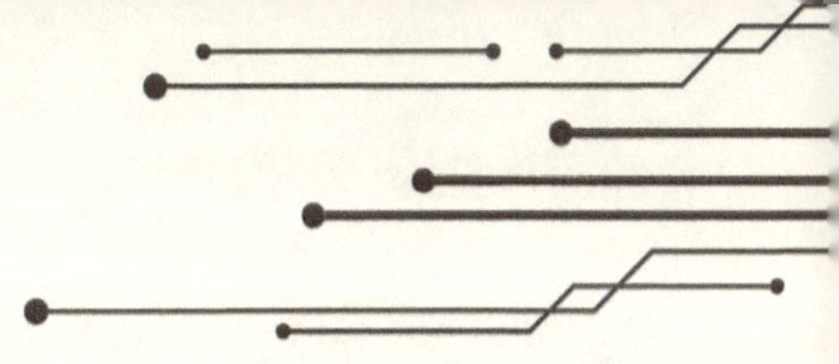

CHAPTER TWENTY-ONE
GRIFFIN

GRIFFIN PRESSED HIMSELF UP against the wall, listening to his father's side of the conversation on the phone. The long pauses and low, serious timbre of his father's voice intrigued and alarmed him.

"North of the harbor? That's a pretty significant jump from the last one.... The first name is familiar, but I never learned her surname..... Fuckin' hell......Yeah, I'll come down. Make sure forensics gets the sample quickly, we're supposed to be getting more snow this morning. Bye."

He heard his father slam the phone back into its cradle, the exasperated sigh that followed, and knew he was doing that thing with the bridge of his nose that he always did when he felt frustrated. The wall above Griffin's head pounded under the slap of invisible hands and he frowned. He stepped quietly down the hall to make sure he remained out of sight when Moz began walking away.

Assuming he meant just the beach north of the harbor, it wouldn't be all that difficult to swing by Jude's house on the way up to investigate. The location he overheard wasn't terribly specific, but if there was a whole forensics team on scene, he figured it wouldn't be hard to miss a swarm of uniforms around a dead body.

Griffin hurried to his bedroom for his coat and thundered back down the stairs, barreling out the door to make his way to the Sills household.

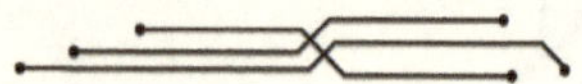

"Jude!"

He didn't want to risk getting caught climbing to her window in the daylight, so he threw another small pebble. The window remained closed and Griffin frowned harder.

"Juuuuude," he hissed again with another stone.

Finally, he saw the curtains behind the water-stained windows rustle and the glass swung open. Jude sat in the open frame.

"What?"

"I think another body's been found. My dad and his team are going to the beach just past the harbor."

"Give me two minutes, I'll be down."

Before she could close the window, Creak flew through the space and soared downward. He landed atop Griffin's head with scraping talons and Griffin frowned, trying to swat the bird off but Creak dodged his hands in feathery bows. The bird hopped down onto his left shoulder, pinching him again.

"*Well look at you, Boy Detective! What do you think you'll solve by snooping?*"

"I don't know, but I think my dad needs help."

Creak laughed, a warbled sound that sounded like he had dozens of marbles loose in his beak. It was the first time Jude's familiar had addressed him directly and he felt strange answering back. He had just begun to suspect that Creak did not want anyone catching them talking.

"Ha! He does, but not the kind you can provide!"

"Man, fuck you."

The raven laughed even harder before launching from Griffin's shoulder with a sharp shove, circling to the front stoop of the Sills' house just as the front door closed. Jude stomped down the stairs as she finished buttoning her burgundy peacoat.

So much for talking in front of her.

Griffin realized then that it had been a hallucination to begin with. Maybe a seed was planted by the mere suggestion that Jude could hold private conversations with Creak as her familiar. After all, why would he hear a birdtalking to him in his head? Even his audio figments didn't sound like they were hooked up to a speaker in the space between his brain and the inner wall of his skull.

"Let's do this," she said. "You okay with trying a portal?"

Griffin sucked in a breath. He had not yet ventured through one of Jude's portals, but he knew he couldn't put off the experience much longer. It certainly would make running around town from murder scene to murder scene much easier if they were to keep cropping up.

"Yeah, yeah, let's go," he finally agreed.

His muscles tensed up as Jude opened a black wound in the air, biting him with a cold far more brutal than the sting of winter. He hesitated as he watched her disappear into the void before he swallowed hard and followed.

Empty darkness devoured him. The sound of his footsteps falling on the nothingness was muffled by whatever split in space he had trailed Jude into. She walked forward with purpose into space and for a moment, Griffin felt unsure if he was simply dreaming again. Maybe he would stumble upon Not Mama again here and he couldn't decide if he would be frightened or relieved to see something even just remotely resembling her face again.

His teeth chattered and he shook hard; Griffin had never experienced this kind of cold before. He wanted to call out and ask Jude how she knew where they were going, but he couldn't say with complete certainty that they were alone in that void. That nothing else would hear him.

Jude reached backwards with an open hand for him without turning and Griffin gripped her fingers tight. Suddenly they passed through a threshold of warmth and were standing on a cobblestone road again, bathed in light. Griffin winced at the sudden brightness and he dropped Jude's hand to shield his eyes until they adjusted.

"Really fuckin' hated that," he told her honestly.

"I'm not sorry to hear you say that," she answered. "That shit exhausts me."

"I never said that I don't want to use it, just that I hate it," he gave her a playful nudge of the shoulder before she smacked his with the back of her hand. "That's going to come in handy."

"Oh good, then maybe you'll decide to keep me around," Jude teased and he grinned at her. *Maybe.*

They walked the street that wound up the hillside above the

beach before Griffin caught sight of a swarm of uniforms and splashes of yellow tape on the shoreline.

"Holy shit," Griffin said breathlessly, grabbing Jude's arm and ducking down behind the brambled sea brush so they could peer down at the scene without being spotted so easily.

Nothing could have prepared him for the gruesome sight on the sand. From where he and Jude watched from the cliff above, he saw a body splayed in two rings of black. Around the interior ring, unreadable symbols looped all the way around and were enclosed with the outermost ring of black. Long lines cut through the center and were freckled with small circles. He was close enough to tell that it was a woman and the ashen blonde curls of her hair made his stomach drop when he realized he had seen it all before.

"Jude, I've seen her."

"What, you know her?"

"No, I don't know her, but I've seen her before. It was in a dream, but it would be hard to miss her with that hair and the ring with the same weird writing that-"

"Wait, so not only have you seen this woman before, but you've seen that circle before? We gotta tell somebody."

"Who would we tell?"

"I'm not terribly sure," Jude said. "My closest bet is probably Yumi. She'd have a better idea of what it means before we go freaking your dad out. In the meantime, we can probably do some research to find out what those symbols mean. I don't have a class this morning, so I can get into Tristan's house and see if he had anything that might help us. Do you think you can scout the university library after your class?"

Griffin nodded. "Sure. Do you need this?"

He fished through his pockets and found the sketch of the circle he had drawn while ignoring a lecture the morning after his dream of Not Mama. It was a hasty rendering but could help her more than it served him when the mental image of the glowing circle of red felt sharper than it had been when he first woke up with the nightmare.

"Good gods," she muttered to herself.

Her eyes scanned the paper and Griffin waited for her inevitable remark about the insanity of the situation. That he was connecting dots that had no business connecting. But she didn't. Jude looked back up at him with a determined fix of her brows above the sparkle in her eyes.

"Perfect, thank you. I'll meet you at the Old Library at noon."

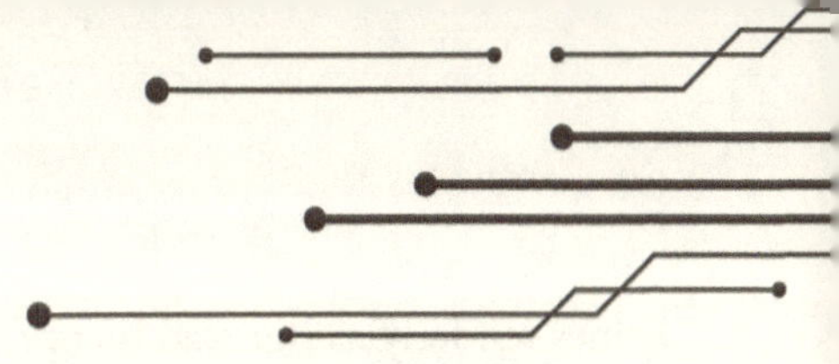

CHAPTER TWENTY-TWO
JUDE

J UDE STEPPED THROUGH THE ice cold portal, wading her way through the darkness until she crossed the threshold again. Fatigue rolled over her in a heavy wash and she blinked her eyes hard to settle her focus on the room around her.

She could pick apart little facets of who Tristan was just based on the things left behind by the forensics team. A glass cabinet filled with imperfect and subtly lopsided pottery, books that had overflowed in their case and were stacked on the hardwood floor with obvious care; like he had meant to find another bookcase that day to give them their proper home. The landscape paintings crowded on the wall, the framed photographs of people she had never met. Bronze bells and wood-carved altarpieces, spent incense ashes and candles on their last leg before snuffing out for the last time. They were all things that forensics had thought too irrelevant to package into their sterile plastic bags for observation, but big pieces of the person that her family had cared so much about. Last echoes from the person who would never speak again.

Jude's bottom lip trembled and she fought hard not to cry. She could come back to it later.

She knelt at the spilled bookcase, her finger grazing across the spines tenderly as she read them aloud to herself. Something here had to help them identify the symbols in the circles.

She settled on four books hurriedly, picking them out only based on keywords in their titles. *Dead*, *Ritual*, *Spells*, and *Sigils*. Jude knew she wouldn't have time to leaf through them before she had to go back to meet Griffin again, but she did want to take a look around first.

Jude stepped past the upholstered seats to look around the living room. She glanced down at the blood-stained rug and the freshly scrubbed hardwood floor around it. Was she standing right where he had been? How did Tristan look when the police had found him? Whatever happened, she hoped he hadn't suffered long.

Maybe this is how it looked to be given to an unkind Reaper. *You may kill at your discretion.*

Jude shoved the dark thought away and willed open another portal.

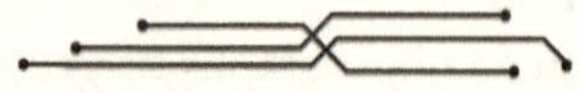

Twin,

What are you protecting him for?
Say the word and I'll fix everything.

Rat Boy

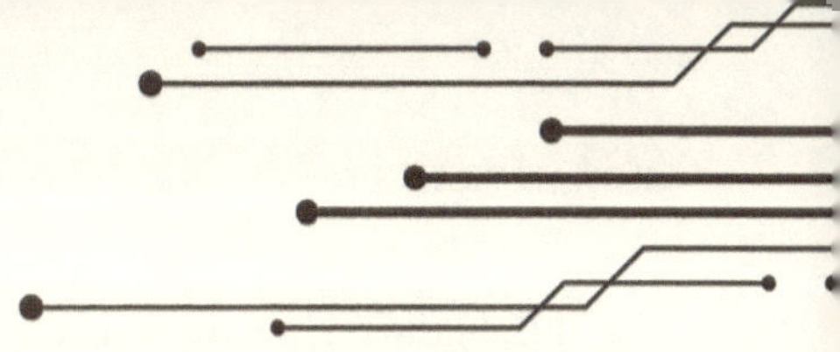

CHAPTER TWENTY-THREE
GRIFFIN

T HE MAIN LIBRARY WAS surprisingly crowded, even for winter midterms being right around the corner. Though he didn't see eyes watching him as he walked down the middle aisle of the cathedral-like building, he felt the weight of them sting on his back.

Griffin decided that he would have the best luck zeroing his focus on the sigils independent of any other component of the circle. *A written language, maybe?* He heard Mimi speak in multiple languages before and though he could identify them by sound when she was managing affairs west of Brightloch beyond Mount Forge, he had no idea what their sweeping vowels looked like on paper.

He strode to the western wing of the library, past the communal studying tables and followed the wall to peer down the labels of bookcase aisles as he passed them. When he finally came across REFERENCE - LANGUAGE, he was shocked to find how little space it took up. Despite the limited languages to choose from, he was dumbfounded as to where he should begin his search.

"I heard there was another murder."

Griffin jumped at the voice; he hadn't expected anyone to be directly behind him. He turned and looked down.

"Hi, Hanna. How do you know about that?"

She shrugged, looking up at him through blonde eyelashes when she answered, "my dad's the police captain, kind of hard to not know these things, right? You get how it is, with your dad. He's already building a profile on the guy. My dad, I mean. Not yours."

"I don't think it was just a guy," he murmured, frowning.

"What do you think it is then, Gloomy Prince?"

"Ritual killings. Nothing else makes sense."

Hanna smiled at him sweetly; so tight across perfect teeth that there was no mistaking the condescension in her lips.

"That doesn't make any sense either, Gloomy. Are you sure you're not just being paranoid?"

Griffin froze. He thought maybe for a minute he hallucinated the accusation that he knew many felt but left unvoiced. The smile still on her face told him that he had heard her correctly.

"What the fuck did you just say to me?"

"I said that maybe this is just paranoia. A ritual killing for what? What sort of ritual killing would be so brazen but leave the police and your dad scrambling to..."

She trailed off when Griffin had turned his back to storm away with blood pounding in his ears. Hanna called out his name but he didn't slow. His anger rose, thrumming in the boiling marrow of his bones when his vision flecked red at the edges. Griffin hurried desperately for the bathroom nearest the library atrium before his rage could bubble over. He didn't have room for relief when he found the door, kicked it open, and stumbled inside.

Griffin didn't care to check if he was alone before he kicked at empty air and stifled back an enraged yell by biting down hard into the back of his wrist. He reached for the basin of the nearest sink in the row, bracing himself by gripping the sides with white-knuckled fingers as he leaned forward and took deep breaths.

He heard a whistling tune - the same one he would hear alone at home. Griffin closed his eyes, counted to five, and it stopped before he could reach four.

Paranoid.

How could he be paranoid when people were turning up dead? Is it still paranoia if there's good reason to have a freak-out? What if there were no murders at all and this was all only happening in his mind?

Nope, no, lock that shit away.

If he entertained the thought longer than it took for it to cross his mind in the first place, it would linger. And lingering leads to rumination. And that's how Griffin ends up locking himself in a closet, wailing for someone to help because his father had tried to poison him.

Too many people he trusted shared his terror. It had to be real. But all that did was make Hanna's discrediting comment sting far deeper. *That bitchy fucking smile-*

Metal groaned in front of him and Griffin flicked his gaze forward as he opened his eyes. Vibrations stirred in the exposed pipes beneath the basin, traveled up the faucet, and the tap gushed as if he had turned both handles as far as they would go. Griffin jumped back in surprise when the hot water splashed him in the face.

The pipes below the several other sinks against the wall cried out as water pushed through them at full force and their faucets exploded with the same downpour.

Griffin struggled to shut off the water at the sink he had stood at, but the power of the water kept the knob from budging. Confused, he tried the other sinks but none of them would give. The water flooded faster than the sinks could drain and the basins' overflow dumped onto the floor. Griffin looked on in terror when the sensation that he wasn't alone overcame him.

He threw his head and looked into the stalls behind him with a pounding heart rate, but he found them all empty when he kicked open each door. The water pooled fast and he felt it seep into the seams of his boots when he looked down. It felt too real. No way this wasn't real. Griffin looked up again at the faucets but this time, his attention was caught by the reflection in the mirror above them.

His own face stared back at him, his green eyes widened with terror and the flush of his freckled face had drained pale. Jewels of ruby dribbled down from his nostrils, collected together in a bead, and seeped over his philtrum. He lifted a hand to touch it, fully expecting he would see a clean hand when he pulled it down.

The only thing worse than it being a hallucination would be seeing the blood, and there it was. Right there with the inches of water he stood in.

Griffin splashed through the water clumsily as he fled the bathroom, water licking like the high tide after him before the door swung shut. He hurried to wipe the blood from his face when he ran for the front door, hoping and praying that Jude would be at the Old Library already.

The cold outside stung his feet with needles inside his wet socks as he ran across campus. He slipped and stumbled in his panic and nearly collided with the ground. Griffin gripped the entry railing of the Anthropology Department like it was his lifeline and hurried through the empty mezzanine, sudden warmth stinging his freezing face.

When he stepped into the stale room of empty bookstacks, he was alone. Griffin took staggered and anxious breaths. Where was Jude? Waiting for her alone in the dark was a dreadful thought and he wasn't sure he could manage it after the vivid hallucinations he had experienced in the bathroom. That's exactly what it was; just a hallucination. *A really, really, strong one.*

-Books, books, books!-
-Two for one!-

Griffin frowned hard. *Stupid fucking voices.* Just when he thought he was going to be waiting for long, the air behind Griffin shifted ice cold and he spun around.

The black portal materialized and Jude stepped through with Creak perched lazily on her shoulder. When it closed behind her, her excited expression dropped and she recognized instantly that something was wrong. Jude set down the small pile of books she held on the book stack nearest her and she came to Griffin.

"What happened? Are you okay?"

He couldn't explain Hanna's words to Jude; that might actually have ended in bloodshed on his behalf. Instead, he reached forward and pulled Jude into a hug. Creak squawked wordlessly and flapped away before Jude returned the embrace, locking her hands together behind Griffin's back.

"Griff, what happened?" She tried again, her voice muffled where her face smashed against Griffin's collar bone.

He shook his head, wiping his face one last time before he let go of Jude.

"It's fine. Let's keep going," he said and sniffled once before he could realize he had done it. To throw her off from his unease, he asked, "Did you find anything at Tristan's?"

"Honestly, I don't know if it's anything, but I grabbed the few books I could find on rituals. It was a shot in the dark there, I think the police removed things from his home as evidence. We should take them to Yumi before we talk to your dad, we can tell her about your dream then."

Griffin nodded and he realized just how shaken he was when just the thought of pressing on with their mission exhausted him. He didn't want to go, he wanted to sit and collect his thoughts for a while. But that wasn't an option; too many bodies now.

"Yeah, let's go."

Before following him towards the door, Jude looked around with animated confusion.

"Where are your books? Did you not find anything?"

"I didn't really have the wherewithal, Jude," he said honestly. "I'll backtrack if we need to. I'm sorry I let you down."

"You didn't, c'mon," she said and hurried past him, brushing his arm with her hand. Though he wore a thick sweater under his coat, the sensation still gave him the small prick of tingles up his spine.

They hurried out of the anthropology building and trudged

their way through the biting winter air towards the castle on the hill. Jude was far too drained to rip open another portal. Griffin said nothing in complaint; he was still rattled that his vivid hallucination had run him so far off course.

Kicking off the dusting of snow they collected on the walkway through the castle garden towards the entry, Jude led the way into the grand foyer. She looked first at the doors to the west wing, and then to the doors to the east.

"Any idea where she might be?"

"Her schedule has been a little scattered, but it doesn't sound like there's a meeting happening in the east hall. Let's try her study."

They hurried down the Lower East wing towards the Blue Study, the one she favored the most because of its tucked away location that kept it safe from the noise of staff and the Queen's family. She also felt better about shutting the door to keep Maya out, claiming it was because of the sofa she wouldn't stop jumping on but Griffin knew better when she jumped in surprise every time the dog nestled her big head into Yumi's lap.

Surprisingly, the study was darkened and empty. Griffin frowned.

"Weird. Next guess is the library."

"How many rooms full of books could one person possibly need?"

"Three people, four if we're including you."

Jude smacked his arm with the back of her hand, but snorted in laughter and followed Griffin back to the foyer all the same. They rounded the staircase to speed walk down the opposite hall and he pushed open the tall doors to the library. It had a thick scent of leather and old paper; easily Griffin's favorite room other than his own.

The library was painted in hues of cobalt and gold from the stained glass lancet window that caught what little sunlight managed to break through the wintry clouds outside. Yumi was seated at a table at the opposite end of the vast room, easily spotted because unlike the freestanding bookstacks like the Old Library at the University, they were built into the walls and left the black and white checkered flooring open.

On the desk itself, the Queen was flanked by tall stacks of tomes on either side of her. She wrote furiously and the grey feathered end of a quill bobbed humorously as she copied down notes, flicking her gaze between the open book in front of her and the notebook off to the side. As they walked towards her, their footsteps echoed on the marble and he watched a brow lift on Yumi's focused face as though she were pushing to finish writing one last thought before she would be so rudely interrupted.

"Mimi, I need your advice on something," Griffin said. "Do you think you could talk us through it before you talk to Dad?"

Yumi folded her book shut and looked up from the desk, still holding the quill in her slender hand.

"Of course, what's on your mind?"

Jude stayed back when Griffin stepped forward, sinking down into the chair across from Yumi.

"I know we did something we shouldn't have," he started and Yumi's expression immediately frowned into parental concern. Before she could scold him, he continued: "but I'm glad we did because I think we found something important. How much has Dad told you about the Sentry case he's on?"

"Griffin, that's not really business that concerns-"

"Mimi, please. This is important. Has he told you anything?"

She pursed her lips and stared at him, perhaps unsure of how much information she should divulge and Griffin waited impatiently.

"He has not reported terribly much to me lately. And he doesn't have to, because he's the Sentinel and he-"

"The scene had a weird circle drawn around the body ," he forged on. "I've seen that circle before. And this new victim. The catch is though, it was in a dream."

He held his breath, waiting for her to laugh him off but his bonus parent stared at him seriously. It seemed highly likely she could easily write it off as another symptom, and if Griffin was honest with himself, he wouldn't have blamed her for it. It sounded fucking ridiculous.

"I believe you," she said and his shoulders relaxed, just the smallest tension he held shifted off and he felt much better knowing she did. "I don't know exactly what it means, I'm afraid, but stranger things have happened."

"Like what?"

She pursed her lips too carefully. "That's not a conversation for us to have without your Dad. Or Mama," she said and nodded her head towards the small stack of books in Jude's hand. "What've you got there?"

"I found these at Tristan's house. They looked like they might be helpful in figuring out what the deal is with the dreams and circles."

"You went to *Tristan's house*? Do you realize how much trouble that could get you in if anyone finds out? If your father finds out? He'll have to tell-"

"He wouldn't do that," Griffin cut her off before she could snowball her lecture any further. He took the top books off Jude's stack and set them down on the small bit of empty space on the corner of Yumi's table. "Will you help us look so that we don't have to ask him, we can just tell him?"

Yumi sighed. "Alright, what am I looking for?"

Griffin pulled the sketch from his pocket and slid it across the table to her. "This is what I saw in the dream and on the beach today."

She looked down at it, gingerly spreading it flat with her fingers, and she pursed her lips into a flat line.

"Nothing about this looks good... I'll start looking, but we *are* telling your father the minute he gets home."

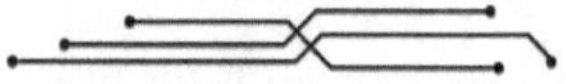

Griffin ambushed his father as soon as he heard wet boots squealing on marble. Jude followed him silently into the Library after Moz, ready to back Griffin up should he need it.

When Moz caught sight of them, he stopped. Griffin froze and Jude nearly collided into his back.

"There's been another one," Moz spoke gravely. "But I get the feeling you knew that already, didn't you?"

Griffin nodded.

"Who was it? It wasn't anyone we know, right?"

"Yes, we know this victim too," his father said quietly as he walked to the nearest desk, sinking down into the chair Yumi had only recently left. "Her name was Theirrin."

Griffin fished the paper out of his pocket and his father held it up to his face. He saw Moz's posture tense in a silent moment of studying the linework.

Then the color drained from his father's face and he looked up from the sketch.

"Where did you get this?"

"I saw it in a dream. And then again today when we saw the murder scene."

Moz held up the sketch, as though he were showing it to Griffin for the first time. He shook the paper as he said, "This is a big deal, bud. Because it wasn't just what we saw today, it was at Tristan's house too. When did you have this dream?"

"I don't know for sure. Three, maybe four nights ago?"

Moz laid the sketch flat on the desk so he could hold his face in both his hands. He muttered something under his breath and Griffin only caught "it never fucking ends."

"We talked to Yumi about it," Griffin continued. His father's head shot up.

"What? What did she say? Why did you go to her and not report it to me?"

"Because I knew you were going to be like this."

"Like what?"

"Like the Sentinel and not my Dad."

His father stared at him with a blank expression before it finally turned into a frown.

"You're right, I haven't been handling this like a parent. I forbid you from interfering with this any further, you don't know what kind of danger you could be jumping into."

"Forbid me? Who fucking taught you that word?"

"Griffin," Jude warned. She knew that he was close to saying something he might regret later, but he certainly wouldn't regret it right now.

"You have been up to your asshole in conspiracies," Griffin shouted, throwing his hands up as he began to pace angrily. "First the Oracles did it! Then Balthazar did it! I'm starting to think you just don't know shit about anything!"

"Griffin, I am your father and you will-"

"Fuck off," Griffin didn't wait to hear the rest of the argument before he stormed out of the library with heavy footsteps. He heard no reply from behind him, but caught the sound of Jude's boots on the floor a healthy distance behind him.

"Griffin, I know you're angry," she started, "but I think you should apologize to him after you've cooled do-"

"I'm going to Theirrin's house," he cut her off. "There has to be something there tying her to Tristan. Are you coming or not?"

Griffin knew she was frowning in the pause before she said "Of course I am."

On their way out the front door of the castle Griffin grabbed his modified staff that he didn't bother putting away in his room as of lately. He stopped on the front steps when realization struck him that he had absolutely no clue where he was heading.

Griffin turned on his heels and lurched back inside just as Jude was almost through the door and he narrowly avoided smacking into her.

"Where are you going?"

"I'll be right back, hang tight," he said as he began running up the stairs, taking them three at a time.

Griffin knocked on Jack's bedroom door, already pushing it open before he heard Jack's call to come inside. He was hardly worried about walking into anything inappropriate; Jack had no interest in spouses or partners in any capacity.

His room was one of the darkest in the entire castle, tucked into the north-facing wing. The poster bed sat low on the floor, with a heavy grey duvet draped far over the edges. On the opposite wall, a wide custom built desk with an oak table top stretched for the majority of the bedroom's width. Neatly organized folders sat in wire racks beneath a corkboard of maps mounted to the wall.

"What's up, Kiddo?"

Griffin had entered just as Jack was seating himself at the leather chair tucked underneath the desk.

"Can you get me the address for this victim? Theirrin?"

Jack shot up from his chair without hesitation. "Sure, I know where that is!"

His elder's lack of follow-up questions should have been concerning, but Griffin wasn't going to point it out when it was working so wonderfully in his favor. Jack plucked one of the folders from the rack and flipped through papers of scrawled writing and printed photographs of the scene at the beach. Griffin tried to peek over his shoulder, but his uncle was too fast. He flinched when Jack suddenly whirled around, holding a folded slip of paper between his fingers. When Griffin reached for it, Jack reeled it back quickly.

"Be safe," Jack warned. "But don't let them underestimate you either."

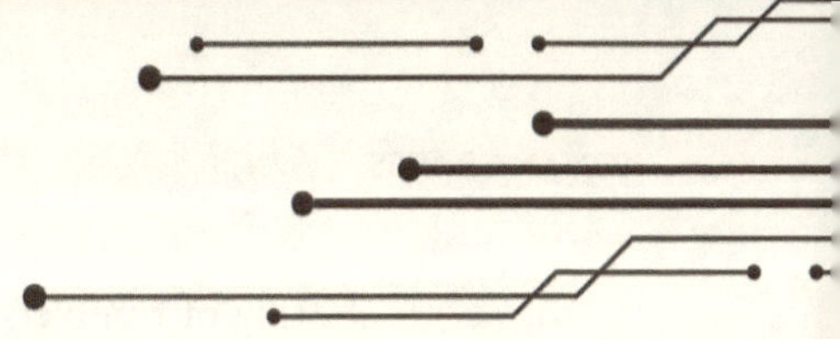

CHAPTER TWENTY-FOUR
GRIFFIN

THEIRRIN'S HOUSE WAS A modest two-story brickstone like a vast majority of the homes in downtown Brightloch. A metal pinwheel jammed into the soil of a withered potted plant on the stoop creaked and groaned in the breeze that wormed a way around the city walls.

"How do you know this is it," Jude asked quietly behind him.

"Jack got the address for me," his reply was just as low. He knew they weren't supposed to be there and it felt as if the house watched them in the dark through eyes lidded by curtains above the front door.

When he felt confident that the few people traveling down the icy sidewalks weren't watching him - *Eyes, eyes, eyes* - he took the steps in twos. Griffin fished a tool out of his pocket, a steel pick folded into a handle.

He switched it open and leaned against the door to block the door handle from the view of the street as he slid the pick into the keyhole and began working for clicks of the tumblers.

Jude kicked her feet in empty air, humming a tune bordering on obnoxious. Annoyance itched at him, but he kept working the lock.

Griffin wriggled the pick, his ear pressed against the door to listen for the subtle shifting of tumblers. He frowned hard, hearing the empty scrape of metal on metal but no give. Frustration made his careful tugs harder and the pick slid too far back, undoing all of the work he had just done. He groaned angrily, kicking the door with the toe of his boots as if his failure was the fault of the wood.

"Would you like a hint?"

Griffin turned around, ready to scold her for yelling when he had been working so hard to remain unseen. She watched him with her arms folded and a raised brow, Creak perched on her shoulder with beady eyes just as unimpressed. Then it clicked.

"Balls."

"Took you long enough."

Jude split the air just in front of the teal painted door and Griffin followed her through the portal. He walked into the dark silence after her, puzzled by the physics of how it worked when it took them just as long to cross town as it did to cross a closed door. Before he could open his mouth to speak, he burst through the threshold and stood inside Theirrin's living room.

"Oh, fucking hell."

He swore when he saw the children's toys strewn about the living room floor around the plush rug and a coffee table with corners padded by cut foam. Griffin threw his head up to look at the ceiling as he tried to persuade the tears already pricking his eyes to stay put.

"She was a mother," Jude said softly. "I don't remember anyone mentioning that."

He tried not to think about the children and how much they would miss their mother for the rest of their lives. It stung him too hard and too close. He sucked in a deep breath and centered himself.

Griffin looked around the rest of the room. A green corduroy couch with sunken cushions was draped in thickly woven blankets. A paperback book laid face down in one of the seats, open to somewhere in the middle of the novel like Theirrin had intended to come back to it when she returned home later that day. He hoped that it was a terrible book that she would not have minded leaving unfinished.

A wooden curio cabinet with smudged glass panes backed into the opposite wall. Inside were countless corked jars and open vials that sprouted infant pothos from careful propagation. Notebooks in worn leather bindings filled the bottom shelf above a drawer. Griffin propped his staff against the wall. He was interested in this fixture the most and carefully crossed the living room to avoid stepping over any of the wooden blocks and cars.

Griffin tried the drawer but it had been locked. He looked about for any key that might have been left in the room, but came up empty. Before he could ask Jude to help him look for it, she had already been sucked into the bookshelf pressed to the adjacent wall of faded yellow. He crossed the room and stood beside her, looking from her fingers to the spines of the books.

He skimmed the titles and she stepped away, her attention drawn elsewhere. A binding in a rich navy linen caught his eye and he pulled the book out of the shelf, wiggling it carefully as it had been wedged tight between the delicate copies.

"Jude, what is this?"

The parchment pages felt like they were in danger of falling apart between Griffin's careful fingertips when he flipped through. Faint sketches of celestial bodies adorned the pages, crammed in-line alongside handwriting just beyond legibility. He felt Jude's presence creep up behind him to peek over his shoulder as she returned to the bookshelf.

"It's a guide to reading the stars," she said simply.

"Seriously, you can tell?"

Jude just shrugged, looking up at the shelf he had pulled the tome from. He looked up from the pages to watch her fingers skim across the spines, mouthing the titles to herself.

She froze on one.

"Griffin, I think Theirrin might have been a witch."

The spine she stopped on was bound in worn black leather, much like the one of her own death ledger. A gilded hexagon with lines darting in and out of its sides and an arrow slashing up through the middle was the only thing that set the book apart from the others, with no title or author describing its contents. Outside Creak began to squawk and throw himself into the clerestory window above the door. *Fuckin' impatience of this idiot.*

"How do you know?"

"That's Mona's sigil."

He opened his mouth to speak, but instead of hearing his own words, he heard the groan of the front door hinges. Griffin was ready to test the reality of the noise until he felt Jude go rigid next to him in a timely enough reaction to confirm it for himself.

Griffin held a hand on her shoulder blade to silently tell her to stay put before he stepped carefully away from the shelf, leaning far around the corner to look at the front door.

It was a man dressed entirely in black, turned away from Griffin as they studied the entry hall. At his waist was a long sheathed knife and Griffin felt his eyes widen. *Abort, abort, abort, abort.*

Before he tucked himself back around the corner of the living room, he caught sight of the white mask covering the man's face and rabbit ears towering above the front of his hooded head.

Griffin reached for his staff propped against the wall and he took Jude's hand in the other. He led her further into the house to get as far from the entryway as they could; with Creak throwing a fit outside, there was no way that the intruder believed the house was empty.

As they moved in quiet, Griffin heard footsteps unsettle the floorboards of the hallway. He didn't know what direction they were headed, so he tucked himself into a corner of the kitchen and gripped Jude's wrist tight so she understood to keep still.

Griffin's options were limited when he didn't know the layout of the house. He knew where the front door was, the hallway to get to it, and the living room off to the side. His eyes widened when he realized that the book Jude had specifically called out still waited on the shelf and that her hands were empty. Of book and scythe.

His only option was to fight.

Featherlight footsteps were drawing nearer, so quiet that Griffin would have thought it didn't exist outside of his head if he had not felt the squeeze of Jude's fingers on his bicep. Outside, Creak still squawked wordlessly and flapped madly outside the door.

Griffin held his breath and squeezed his eyes shut, praying that the sound of the frantic raven would be enough to mask the small noise he had no choice but to make. His fingers slid across the smooth wood of the staff and flipped the metal switch at its midpoint. He bumped the bottom against the ground and the small *shink* of metal blades engaging hushed the footsteps. They waited. They listened.

A floorboard creaked.

Theirrin's kitchen exploded in violence when the figure rounded the corner and lurched at Griffin. He swung the bladed staff, missing the rabbit-masked intruder and punctured a hole in the wall behind their head when they dodged.

"Jude, run! Get the book!"

He yanked the staff out of the wall, rotating it into his left hand to swing again when he saw the flash of a machete crack in his direction. Jude stumbled to round the kitchen island, keeping it between herself and the Rabbit. Griffin caught the machete in time, pushing it up and away from his face with a turn of the staff. The other end bumped into the wall clumsily and he swore under his breath that he had so little room to work with.

In the narrow window the fumble created, the Rabbit barrelled toward him again. Metal swiped underneath the staff's fulcrum at just the wrong moment and Griffin felt the hot burn of a slash at his chest. He hissed; it wasn't deep, but damn did it hurt like a bitch.

"Jude, any day now," he hissed through his clenched teeth, hearing her rummaging in the living room to find the spellbook they had left behind. He turned the staff, shoving it hard into the Rabbit like a javelin.

"Sorry, I thought now was the perfect time for knitting circle to meet," she bit back sarcastically. "I'm TRYING."

The Rabbit swung their machete hard into Griffin's staff. He winced at the sound of cracking wood, but the staff did not splinter into pieces like he had feared. Griffin reared backwards, readying himself to shove the staff again as hard as he could into their direction.

But the Rabbit moved quicker this time. They lurched to their left when he had anticipated them to go right into the empty space and they shoved their feet into the wall, launching themself into his space with the fearsome flash of slashing metal.

Griffin hollered again, "JUDE! HURRY!"

"I got it, c'mon!"

Griffin threw the end of the staff as hard as he could into the Rabbit and turned, sprinting to the front door where he heard Jude's voice. She was at the end of the hall with a churning black portal at her back, sucking all of the warmth out of the room. He stumbled in his scramble to reach her and fought to keep one hand on his staff as the other caught his fall on the polished hardwood flooring.

Jude was close enough that she reached out, closed her fingers around both shoulders of his coat, and yanked him hard into the portal behind her just as a flash of metal swung behind Griffin's back. The weapon missed him by mere inches and he panicked that the Rabbit would simply follow them into the liminal space that Jude had opened.

But they stood alone, catching their breaths in frightened pants.

Griffin lowered his staff and bent forward with his hands on his knees.

"They... didn't follow us?"

"I don't know if they could," Jude answered, looking in the general space they had just come from. The void looked the same in every direction. "Maybe I'm able to close it off for people not meant to come through. If I can control the where, maybe I can control the who."

He straightened up again after he had filled his lungs with enough flushes of safe air. With his adrenaline beginning to subside, he felt the burn of a machete strike across his torso. Griffin gingerly touched his fingers to his chest where a slash had been cut through his sweater. When he pulled his fingers back, they were wet with blood and he laughed nervously. It didn't feel deep, but could he be in shock?

"Thank fuck for the portals, my ass was about to be toast. This is probably the coolest thing to ever happen to us."

Jude shot him a look, frowning hard before she snapped at him, "except it didn't happen to *us*, it's me doing their dirty work and you just get to reap the benefits."

He flinched, not expecting her anger. "I'm sorry, you're right... I didn't mean it like-"

"It's fine, let's go home and get you fixed up."

Griffin followed her one way into the darkness and trusted her to bring them home. They were quiet in the muffled nothingness until he fell into step with her and spoke as he wiped his bloody hand on his coat.

"Reap... get it? Did you do that on purpose?"

"Shut up," she said, but he saw the small turn of a grin on the corner of her mouth.

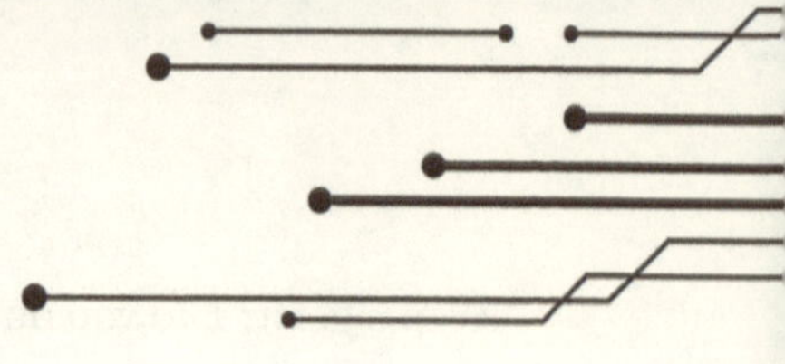

CHAPTER TWENTY-FIVE
KUROSAKI

"**T**HAT'S IT," MOZ JABBED an inked finger - "E" - at the illustration on the page. "That's the circle that's shown up twice now in a forty-eight hour window. That's not a fucking coincidence, that's a pattern."

Kurosaki took the paper from him. Thick concentric circles of black were sketched onto the page in charcoal, sealed to the parchment with fixative but still left ghosts of grey on his fingerprints. Between the circles, jagged sigils he could not recognize wound all the way around the circumference.

"Where did this come from?"

"Griffin drew it. He said he saw it in a dream," Moz said and then went quiet before he added, "he saw Avery right alongside Theirrin."

He lowered the paper and peered over the top edge at Moz's face. Water welled in his eyes, glossy beneath the glare of his glasses.

"I understand why that might be frightening," Kurosaki said softly. "But don't sign her death certificate on it."

Moz laughed a choked sound, reaching under the wire frames to wipe his eyes. "No, you're right."

Kurosaki smiled at him and carefully set the sketch back down on the table between them, forgetting about the transfer of charcoal when he gave it a single pat.

"We'll figure this out," he reassured. "We're a smart bunch, the kids included. I hope you let them continue to help in ways that are safe for them."

Moz stared at him for a long moment and Kurosaki worried that maybe he had crossed an unspoken boundary with his words when he laid his arms down on the table to lean forward, like he was posturing to yell. But he didn't. Instead, he said with great sadness:

"I never know what the right thing to do is. It shouldn't have been her."

Kurosaki's heart snapped in two at the insinuation: *I should have been the missing one.* He reached out, thinking to hold one of his hands but instead draped his fingers over his inked wrist with care. Electricity crackled in the space where skin met skin but Kurosaki knew only he was keen to it.

"No one knows the right thing to do all of the time." he said softly. "You'll both be okay."

Moz had to be, because Kurosaki would rip the world down around them if he wasn't. If he had been the one who vanished into thin air. His words still burned in Kurosaki's ears and he felt the tide of despondence and grieving love begin to overcome him. He couldn't handle this anymore.

Kurosaki gave him a small squeeze before he pulled his hand away. Moz was quiet as he stared at his own wrist where he had touched him.

"I'm going out for a smoke, I'll be back."

It was only a half-lie. He needed air that would bite his throat from the inside with cold so he could in turn burn the vicious feelings right out of him.

He watched Moz nod silently when he rose out of his stool and walked out of the room, squeezing his eyes shut as soon as his back turned.

Kurosaki stepped out of the grand entrance doors and the bitter bite of winter immediately closed around him. Iverne's maw punished him in a way he knew he deserved for what he had just done.

Snow fell in fat, fluffy flakes that melted on his shoulders. Brightloch below was silent and the night sky glowed in the freezing shades of a tintype of peace. He felt unsure of where to go, so he started for the garden paths as he shoved a cigarette into his mouth. The edges of the gravel were hard to discern under the accumulating blanket of snow and he felt only mostly sure he was following a pathway at all.

He thought he was alone in the garden as he walked until he saw a figure in the near distance sitting at a bench. They seemed to be in no hurry to get out of the cold and Kurosaki knew of only one person who would be so content to sit in the winter conditions if it meant being outside.

Kurosaki tucked the unlit cigarette away again so his company wouldn't chide him with a smile before he approached the bench where Yumi absently watched the snowfall. She turned in his direction, hearing the soft crunch under his boots with each step.

"Mind if I join you?"

"Not at all," her voice was a warm lantern in the dark and Yumi scooted to the left to afford him a seat.

He carefully brushed off the seat next to hers as best he could and sat down, careful to make sure his waterproof coat came between his pants and the cold moisture.

"We're glad you're here, Kuro," Yumi said and Kurosaki frowned at first. Was it that obvious he felt out of place? He let it relax when he remembered who he was talking to. If Yumi knew someone's insecurities, she would never use it against them. She would just kindly nudge them in the direction of realizing they were absolutely fucking wrong about them.

"Me too," he said. "Very glad. This is a sweet little family you have. I wish I was seeing it whole."

"Me too," she echoed back.

Both of their stares looked out into the frozen garden and they sat together in a comfortable silence. Any sounds they might have heard from the town below were swallowed up by the snowpack. There was a peace to the sadness and they both just let it be.

"How did it feel?" Kurosaki finally asked when he looked from the frosted topiaries of the castle gardens to Yumi beside him. "To know that Avery loved you but loved him too?"

Yumi laughed softly, fussing with the grey cowl around her neck to block out the cold bite of the air before she folded one leg on top of the other. Her laugh was a lovely sound that fell on the silence of the snow and Kurosaki immediately knew he was safe bringing this up with her.

"It's kind of like friendships. Because I am friends with you, it does not change the fact that I am also friends with Lily. They are both different, right? Different, but both precious to me in their own ways. More love shared does not mean that I am loved less. At least that's how Moz put it."

She looked at Kurosaki and saw right through his flushed ears and cheeks. Yumi's brown eyes widened and she held a slender hand over her mouth. "Oh my gods."

"What?" Still time to play dumb.

"You *love* him! You love Moz!"

"I never said that I-"

"You didn't need to. It's all over your face!"

"Don't lie to me, Yumes. Which one of your ghosts ratted me out?"

"Owen, obviously."

Kurosaki sat up straighter, looking around at the empty air around them in case there was an unseen spirit in their midst. "Owen, I know you're dead and I know you're a child but I'm still gonna throttle you for that one. You're racking up quite the tab, little buddy."

Yumi laughed. "Don't worry. Unlike some people around here, I recognize what is not my business to tell."

He grinned at her. "Thanks, Yumes."

"Are you going to tell him?"

The question hit him with the impact of a bullet and splintered his spine. What was the point in making those feelings known? He felt lucky Moz even treated him as a friend after all that he had put him through when they were younger. He carried on a balancing act with Moz and Todd for years too long and chickened out the count-less moments he had the opportunity to make the right decision. He knew it just as strongly as he did writing his last letter to Moz as he did on his wedding day; he would never speak a word of it.

"No," he said simply.

Yumi fumbled for his hand and squeezed it with tight comfort. She nodded her head, but said nothing.

A shadow shifted from behind them and Kurosaki turned his head to see who had managed to creep up on them in complete silence. It was unlike Yumi to bring a guard with her while still on castle grounds. He caught a flicker of honey blonde hair and young eyes before the face disappeared entirely. Kurosaki frowned. Exhaustion was catching up to him far too quickly nowadays.

When he turned back forward, he saw Yumi had been watching him studiously, her mouth fixed into a stern line and her eyebrows furrowed.

"Just now," she said, "did you see him?"

"Who?"

"Describe them to me."

Kurosaki held up his free hand, gesturing in bewilderment at her request. "I don't know, blonde hair? A kid? I don't see what that matters, I'm just seeing shit."

She shook her head. "Owen."

The Queen of Ink turned her chin upwards, looking up at the sky where a halo of light leaked through the thick cloud cover that masked the moon. Yumi inhaled through her nose and closed her eyes, holding the cold air in her lungs before she pushed it out again to speak:

"The moon of the Iverne solstice. It's been said the cold of the winter welcomes those embraced by the freezing grave. The draw of Ara's full moon illuminates their passageway through the Veil even clearer. The true solstice is not for another two days, and neither is the full moon. But the celestial event's impact has been felt for days now by both myself and the Priestesses. I've never seen it line up so perfectly in my lifetime; Reaper or Saved. We're going to witness such strange and beautiful things in the next few days, Kuro."

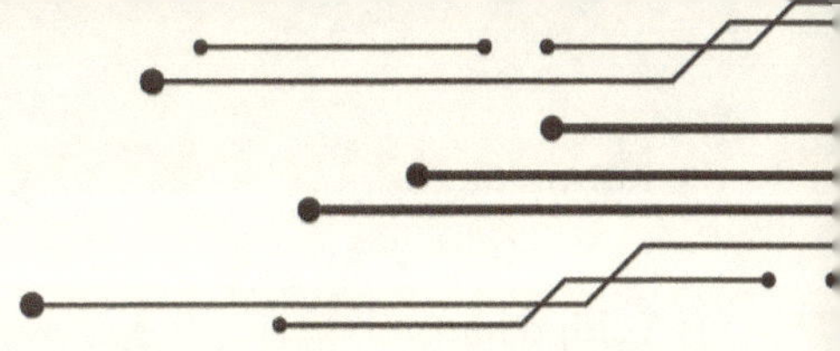

CHAPTER TWENTY-SIX
MOZ

MOZ TURNED JUST AS the children were hurrying through the open kitchen door and he dropped his wooden spoon when he saw Griffin slumped against Jude's shoulder. A slash cut through the front of his sweater and a halo of red ringed around the ruined wool.

"Fucking hell! What happened to you?"

"We went to Therrin's house," Jude explained. "She was a witch. Or at least we think she is, we found a spellbook that looks a little too authentic."

"The house didn't do this," Moz replied as he helped ease Griffin off her shoulder and into a chair. "What happened?"

"Someone else came," Griffin said between deep breaths, using willpower to redirect his mind away from the pain; just like his dad had taught him. "Real freaky guy with a rabbit mask... he didn't say a word, just started swinging his dumb little machete."

"Fuckin' hell," Moz swore. "Would you be able to sketch what you saw?"

Griffin nodded, painfully and with jerked motions. The kids must have passed Kurosaki on their way into the kitchen; he was already hurrying in with a first aid kit and Yumi trailing closely behind him.

Kurosaki set the kit on the chair next to Griffin's and popped open the lid: "alright, show me your shiner."

Griffin couldn't take off his open jacket without straining, but had just enough mobility to lift up the bottom of his blood-soaked sweater. A long, shallow gash striped across Griffin's torso just underneath the pectoral and slashed several inches across the sagittal plane, stopping just past his navel.

Kurosaki nodded. "Well, you did good! I'll count that as a stabbing and we'll add it to your Tough Guy Punch Card."

Moz frowned deeply and he felt alarmingly aware of where the skin of his wrist still buzzed with warmth.

Kurosaki poured an antiseptic on a gauze swab, swiping it carefully across the wound to mop up blood for a better scope on how bad it was. Griffin winced and hissed through his teeth at the burn on his skin, his fingers knuckling the edge of the seat to keep himself still.

"W...what did you... say?"

The pause between what Kurosaki said and Griffin's strained question was too long, and so Moz shook his head and said simply, "not us."

His son frowned. *That boy is a carbon copy of you* - Kurosaki had said. Maybe there was a sliver of truth to it, after all. He hadn't witnessed the scrap at Theirrin's house, but evidence said that Griffin held well on his own if the only wound struck shallow. Griffin wiped sweat from his face with his sleeve as best he could and the blonde streak Jude had bleached into his hair flicked astray in every direction except for the one it was meant to be.

"I didn't think she was a witch," Kurosaki finally commented as he wetted another square of gauze before he said to Griffin, "I know this hurts, my guy, but we have to keep it clean. Slap me across the face if you have to, just one more."

"The only way we'll know for sure is to ask Mona," Moz said. "Do we know where we can find one of her altars? Or any idea of who might know?"

"I've got a map on my desk, altars are marked," Kurosaki answered without looking up from the wound on Griffin's chest. His son hissed again under the burn of antiseptic but didn't take Kurosaki up on his offer to be a human punching bag. "Trifold, in the stack off to the side."

"Got it," Moz replied and before he headed for the hall, added to Griffin, "hang tight bud, you're doing good!"

He hurried through the hall, up the stairs, and into the guest room that they had lodged Kurosaki in for the duration of however long he planned on staying. Moz couldn't remember the last time he had seen the inside of the teal room; probably sometime before King Harthmoor had passed away and control of the castle fell to his only child.

"Rest in piss," he mumbled at just the mere thought of his name.

Moz rifled through the belongings on Kurosaki's desk, looking for the folded map that had been described to him. In his scattered hurry, an envelope shifted out of one of the notebooks and Moz froze when he saw his own name in familiar handwriting. He'd recognize Kurosaki's careful penmanship anywhere.

He reached for the envelope, holding it in his tattooed hand and hesitated. Should he be going through Kurosaki's things like this? Maybe it was just a scrapped envelope for one of their correspondences. Moz peered inside and found that there was a single page folded neatly and tucked inside.

Moz knew he shouldn't, but it *was* addressed to him. It couldn't be resisted. He pulled the parchment out of the envelope and began to read:

Moz,

You don't need to apologize to me for anything. Grief comes in waves. Some days you will push through the day feeling hopeful and others you can't get out of bed because a passing thought knocks the wind out of you. I can't imagine how hard it is to bounce between the two so rapidly when you know there's a chance she will come home. And she will come home - we'll all make sure of that together.

I'll ask the Big Guy about the jumpers next time I see him, I miss him. I'm actually on the ferry right now. Which means writing my response instead of just saying these things to your face is weird. So I guess this isn't going to you at all. The things you said in your letter scared me, Moz. You haven't scared me like that in years.

I'll share your feelings of emptiness for a while. I'll hold your grief for you so you can feel your rage long enough to bring her home. I should hate that she is the one who touches you and hears you say that you love her, but I don't. I hate that she is gone and that it has left you broken.

I love you, Moz. I have always loved you. I'll rot my own teeth biting back the sweet words I have held onto with you in mind.

I see you in every crash on the shoreline and hear your laugh in all of our old haunts. I look for you like metal on a magnet and I will never unlearn how to miss you. And I don't worry about how hard it will be to hold you steady long enough to piece yourself together because staying away from you has been the hardest thing I have ever done. That's what I can't do anymore. Not when you're suffering.

I'll be there in the morning.

Yours,
Kurosaki

The blood drained from his face. Moz stared hardest at only three words on the page. He couldn't imagine Kurosaki saying them to him: *I love you.* It had to have been a mistake, a forgery of some kind. But it was him.

It was Kurosaki when he followed Moz out of Eyon for the first time. It was Kurosaki standing at his side, ready for the Knights. Kurosaki who shot him, Kurosaki who rolled his eyes, Kurosaki who kissed him and tangled limbs with him only to say it was all in good fun. It was Kurosaki's writing and Moz had never before seen him so clearly.

Before he could think about the consequences of what he was doing, Moz stuffed the letter into his back pocket. He couldn't simply put it back when he knew he would want to look at the words again when he inevitably roused from his nightmares.

"Moz?"

Kurosaki's voice called out from the hall and sounded like it was drawing nearer. Moz snatched the folded map in a hurry and lurched for the door to avoid being spotted lingering near the desk longer than he should have taken.

"Yeah, I found it!" He called back as he jumped through the doorway.

His face flushed in hot embarrassment when he rounded a corner and nearly collided into Kurosaki. Moz wobbled on his heels from stopping so abruptly and he looked up at the coffered ceiling to swallow the knee-jerk reaction to swear in Kurosaki's face. Instead, he lifted the hand with the map to hold out to him and for a gut-punching fraction of a second, he panicked at the greater-than-zero possibility that he mistakenly handed over the letter he had found.

Moz held his breath when he felt the parchment taken from him.

"Oh, perfect!"

His shoulders sank in relief at Kurosaki's voice when he realized that he had handed over the correct document. Moz looked back down, watching the movement of Kurosaki's brown eyes as he read the map. He felt a creeping flush across his cheeks as he waited and realized that neither of them had bothered to take a step away from the other. *Good gods, is he making me* shy? The stolen letter in his back pocket burned him with shame. Right on the ass.

Heat pooled in his belly when it dawned on him just how easy it would have been to reach forward and close the narrow distance to steal a kiss. To shove him into the wall with his fingers threaded through his long hair and-

"There's an altar near the base of Mount Forge," Kurosaki explained. "We can go tomorrow as soon as the sun is up."

"Sounds good," Moz murmured and then instantly regretted the lowness of his voice. It felt too intimate of a volume at this close of a proximity to Kurosaki's face.

He started to walk around Kurosaki as he cleared his throat; he needed to get away from Kurosaki's room so he didn't have to think about what he had done. Or how soft his mouth had looked.

"How's Griffin? Is he okay?"

"Oh yeah, he's fine," Kurosaki said, walking shortly behind but still looking down at the map. "It was shallow. Stung like a bitch at worst. I'd still keep an eye on it for the next couple days to make sure it won't become infected. Take him to Lily if it starts looking nasty, obviously."

"Obviously," Moz echoed back, his brain still felt too much like tingly mush to form a thought of its own.

Young feelings had rushed back into his older mind and he couldn't stray his focus from the words in Kurosaki's handwriting. How long had he waited to know what they looked like? *Does he feel that way even now? Do I feel that way or is it just loneliness?*

"I'm going to have to report this, as much as I hate to say," Moz huffed as he led Kurosaki back into the kitchen. "There's no good reason why that person was there."

Jude looked up from where she had been assessing Kurosaki's handiwork with gauze bandages. "You're gonna rat on us?"

"Hey, you shouldn't have been in that house at all," Moz said, pointing first at Jude and then at Griffin before he dropped his hand. "I could have been combing the scene on my own, that's fine. But if you pull a stunt like this again, I can't guarantee I'll be able to cover for you."

"I know you're not going to like this, Moz," Kurosaki started, "but I think the kids should come with me to the altar tomorrow."

Moz raised an eyebrow, turning his head towards where Kurosaki lingered near the door with his arms folded over his chest. "Why?"

"Jude's ability to get in and out of a place is unrivaled. And I don't think Griffin is going to let me take her and leave him behind."

"Damn fuckin' straight," Griffin mumbled as he pulled his sweater back down over his bandaged chest.

"Language," Yumi warned from the table and Moz jumped, having nearly forgotten about her mothering presence.

"Sorry, damn fuckin' gay."

"Fuckin' hell, you are your mother's son," Moz said, pinching the bridge of his nose before he dropped his fingers and turned back to Kurosaki. He could feel his own exasperation painted on his face. "Take them with you, just please keep them safe, okay?"

"Their lives before anything else," Kurosaki answered. "Always."

Moz frowned as a flush crept over his earlobes. *There was literally no reason for that to have been hot. Fuck you.*

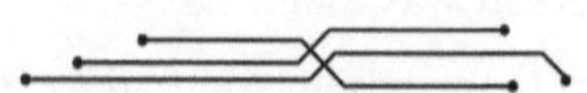

Moz awoke with frozen muscles again. He waited out the encounter until the tree limbs that stretched through his bedroom window and ensnared him in a coffin of branches had retreated. Breathing was easier once he was finally able to fling himself onto his side.

Really gotta stop sleeping on my stomach.

He thought of the experience with Malo that Avery had recounted for him once long ago; how the Lord of the Wood had entombed her in trees and refused to save Alice and the young Vinny for rejecting his blessing– the ego of a god. Moz never found it in him to point out the exclusion to his wife. Not when she had grown to cherish the King of Rot. Her fondness of a god was both precious and hard-earned and Avery didn't deserve to have it pried from her grasp.

Whenever his thoughts trailed to Alice, Kurosaki was always to follow. Moz reached for the lamp on his nightstand, flicking it on before he winced at the change in brightness. He fumbled for his glasses before he slid them onto his face and opened the top drawer to fish out the letter. Smoothing out the folds when he opened it, Moz read the letter again. Then a second time. And then a third.

I love you, Moz.

The words still didn't feel real.

What would Avery say if she could see him fawning over the stolen letter in the middle of the night? She'd probably laugh. *Definitely laugh.* Maybe do that thing where she'd then become suddenly sincere and offer encouragement after she had tried to lighten the mood. Or maybe she wouldn't care for it at all and would become angry. They'd brought up their polyamorous dynamic countless times to make sure they were on the same page. Suddenly they weren't and Moz knew there was nothing he could do about it until she returned.

If she returned.

Moz rose from his lonely bed, taking the matchbook on the nightstand with him, and floated down the hall on quiet feet. On muscle memory built over twenty years, he walked down the darkened wing through beams of painted moonlight until he reached the lone door at the end that led up the spiral staircase of the southern tower.

He struck a match for light and walked up until it was spent, then lit another for the rest of the climb. Moz opened the door that once led to Yumi's chamber, but was now Avery's hideaway. He wasn't supposed to be there - none of them were - but he climbed the stairs whenever his ache for her burned too strongly for him to resist. She kept the room so secluded that it had become more of a tomb than the one containing her empty coffin. Even the smell of her lingered on every surface and the snap of cedar and bite of dark coffee washed over him the moment he stepped through the door.

The sepulchral room was bathed in moonlight spilling across the patterned rug and stretching on the leather chair like a curled cat. Books covered every custom crafted shelf that flanked each wall and Moz felt a visceral jolt remembering how excited Tristan had been to help her with the project.

If Avery really was gone, he hoped they were at least together.

In the corner of the room, a cello waited propped on a stand. He had no doubt that it had fallen out of tune long ago without her reverent hands to tend to it, but it was still the most precious thing in the room to him. Moz sank to the floor before it and folded his legs in front of him, his back to the moon.

He had saved up for months to give the cello to her. Avery of course had no idea it was happening until he presented it to her and her face lit up in the warmest sunrise before the first excited tears fell. She took the beloved instrument into her embrace and played for him, getting a full two minutes into a sonata with a name he could not recall before she noticed the gold ring tied to the highest tuning peg.

On his knee, Moz asked Avery to marry him. She nearly dropped the brand new cello and swore at him, before she cried and said yes. And definitely swore at him again. Only a month after, they stood on the beach with a handful of their closest friends and vowed to be a beloved thorn in the other's side for the rest of time.

One person had been noticeably absent from the ceremony.

"I wish I had known sooner, Ave," he said to Avery's cello in her stead. "I know that he loves you and that you love him. I just hope you can love that I love him, too... I guess comparing them, it's more like *in* love. I know you know the difference."

Moz paused.

The yearning had never left him. It wasn't a thing to come and go, out of sight and out of mind. Space he had left for Kurosaki in the deepest part of his ribs was a burning comet, streaking through his sky first as a faint light until time brought him back into orbit and became the centerpoint of his heavens. He had always been there; the object of Moz's boyish affection grown into a man. Warm, radiant Kurosaki filled his sky.

"Yeah, I'm in love with him."

He ran his fingers down a length of the lowest string and listened for the resonant ring to fill the silence that answered him. Sitting alone, he felt the heaviness of the words. It was their secret — his and the hideaway's. Ice cold guilt leaked into his sinew and he prayed his wife would one day warm him again.

"I love you, Avery," he whispered to the sound. "We promised each other we would talk about these things. You have to come home."

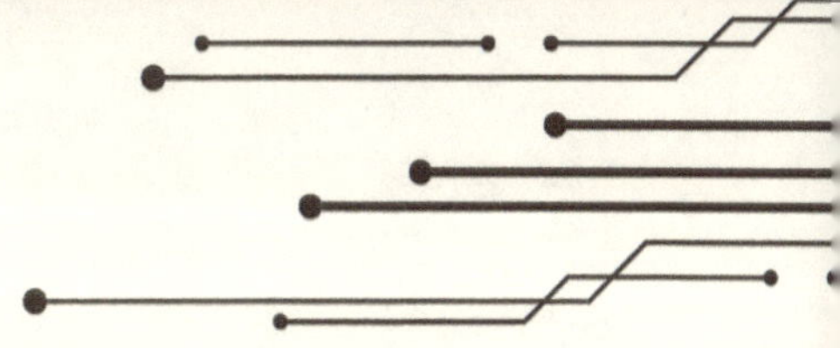

CHAPTER TWENTY-SEVEN
GRIFFIN

"**A**LRIGHT, WE READY TO go?" Kurosaki asked as Griffin and Jude approached him at the foyer.

Griffin looked from the staff in his own hand to Jude beside him, scythe in her right hand and Creak on her left shoulder. The feathers on the bird wavered and shifted colors, twisting in the kaleidoscope of Griffin's private perception. The mildest hallucination on the bird would have delighted him if he had not been nervous about their strange mission.

"Let's do this," Jude said, her face fixed in firm determination when the air iced over and the air splintered black with the materialization of the portal.

"Damn, that's cool," Kurosaki marveled.

Jude led the way through her portal, and Griffin followed close behind her. Kurosaki trailed them into the cold blackness, whirling around trying to readjust his sense of direction.

"There's absolutely nothing in here, how do you know where to go?"

The sound was dampened, with nothing to echo Kurosaki's voice around them. The surface of the ground beneath their feet was cloud-thin, but Griffin had come to trust its stability as he followed

Jude forward.

"It tells me," she answered simply.

She disappeared through a wavering threshold before Griffin could grasp her hand in his.

"Wait, let me out first so-"

Griffin didn't hear the rest of Kurosaki's words before he passed through the warm surface and he stood on the snowy face of Mount Forge.

The trail ahead of them hid under a thick snowpack and Griffin felt the wet coldness seep into the seams of his boots around the tongue. He shuddered, gripping the staff tighter in his gloved hands.

Jude pressed forward first, just as Kurosaki emerged from the portal before it vanished. Snow crunched underneath her boots and Creak perched on the back of her shoulder blades, swiveling his head to look about with beady eyes.

"There it is!"

Before Griffin could respond, Jude pointed out what her familiar was referring to. Higher on the steady incline of the mountain trail, a level surface pulled off and out of the way of where foot traffic would pass to climb higher to the peak.

The small structure was built with stone bricks and wood shingles protecting the open porch from the rain and snow. As they approached, Griffin realized the small shrine stood no taller than his waist. Inside, a small stone fountain bubbled with flowing water from a round vase. He couldn't figure out how the basin refilled or how it hadn't frozen over, but it seemed to be the least of his concerns with the way he was beginning to understand magic.

From the roof of the shrine, wooden tags hung with varying shades and colors of twine. On each of them, sigils were carved. Each had different shapes of the same lines, like they were all crafted by someone different.

"They're messages," Kurosaki explained, his voice soft on the snowfall around them. "I was expecting Mona's altar to be bigger. But that was foolish of me. Her altars are anywhere people need her."

"So what do we do now?"

Kurosaki didn't answer Griffin as he pulled out his own tab of wood and a pocket knife. Griffin watched him wedge the blade into the soft flesh of maple and work it into shapes.

"This is gonna take a minute, hang tight," Kurosaki mumbled.

As Griffin and Jude watched him, he realized that the shape he created was the very same sigil that Jude had pointed out on the book in Theirrin's home. Mona's sigil.

"Is that her calling card then, so to speak?"

"I guess you could say that," Kurosaki answered.

They stood, waiting rather impatiently, until Kurosaki finished and pocketed the knife again. He crouched down onto the balls of his feet and tucked the sigil tag into the small earthen shrine, on the muddy ground next to the fountain because of the lack of hanging twine.

When he stood up straight again, he looked around the forest around them. Griffin looked too, unsure of what he was supposed find. The forest was a painting of white and black with the eyes of alders watching them back from between the thick combs of pine trees. There wasn't a single sound for him to pick out; collective reality or his own. He might have felt peaceful if he hadn't been on edge with the uncertainty of how this would play out.

"Queen Mona," Kurosaki said, softer than a call that Griffin might have expected from someone trying to command attention from the woods. "We are asking for your help. Please."

The words weren't as graceful as the pleas Griffin heard coming from his bonus parent. Intention must have been the only thing that mattered, he decided, when they felt the whisper of a zephyr whip up stray flakes of snow from the ground.

She emerged from behind the shrine, stretching up in a tall cascade of lilac gowns. The bronze cut of her cheekbones and halo of black curls adorned in flowers was a warm sight to behold in the dead of winter. They looked upon Mona in awestruck silence, but she did not speak first as she watched down on them from her tall height.

"Queen Mona," Kurosaki said again, his voice softened. Mona's gaze slid from him to Griffin and he reflexively loosened his grip on his staff; this wasn't at all a goddess he wanted to threaten. "We believe one of your daughters may have been struck down by a great injustice and we wish to do right by her. Will you identify her for us?"

Mona looked back to Kurosaki when she said simply, "Theirrin Marshall."

Griffin looked over his shoulder to Jude; her perfect mouth parted in sublime awe. Her eyes flickered fast, drinking in as much of the scene as she could. He could take a well-placed guess at her feelings; none of this fit into her careful world of numbers and balanced equations. A *goddess* stood before her.

"I knew Theirrin very briefly and I grieve your loss," Kurosaki continued. "Do you know anything that might help us?"

Mona's square chin lifted, studying them from above with half-lidded eyes.

"We are flawed beings, not omnipotent," she reminded him, "and I am no Oracle. Miss Marshall vanished from my sight. Here and then gone again."

"Vanished from your sight," Kurosaki echoed, turning her words over carefully in his thoughts. "And when you say that…"

"Where's Avery Porter," Griffin was the one who interrupted. He knew exactly what Kurosaki had intended to ask.

Mona's stare slid to him again and Griffin's blood ran ice cold. He saw the shifting of humanoid shapes in the woods behind her, darting between the oaks but he was determined to not flinch. Silence hung heavy and the weight of each snowflake settled on Griffin's jacket like stones.

"Queen Mona, where is she?"

She turned back to Kurosaki. "I do not see her."

Griffin's knees buckled underneath him and he dropped the staff. He crouched down onto the balls of his feet, holding his head in his hands as it pounded.

"She's—"

"That is not what I said," Mona said firmly. "There are many reasons a Daughter may slip out of my vision. Death is one of them, but it is not the only one."

He hardly heard her over the whispering floating past his ears. The fingers running up his back made him twitch in revulsion. Jude crouched into the snow next to him, a gentle hand on his shoulder that normally would have soothed him but now made his heart rate spike in anxiety. He silently waved her away and she asked no questions.

"We thank you for your help," Kurosaki pressed on through the encounter so that they could recover from the distressing turn of fortune. "Please allow us to serve you in any way you see fit."

Mona's chin lifted again, just shy of an upturned sneer at Kurosaki's flattery. Instead of answering him, her brown eyes shifted to Jude at her feet.

"Thank you, Daughter," Queen Mona said to her. "We see you, Little Reaper."

Before Jude could answer, the air cracked in violet light and a gust of hot air whipped Griffin in his face, stinging him against the contrast of the ice cold. When he looked up, Mona was gone.

"Hey, Griff," Jude's voice called softly next to him. "Hey, it's okay. She said so herself, that's not necessarily what it means."

The fingers running down his back slowed to a stop, flicking across his tailbone before they were gone. Griffin took shallow breaths and the air became harder and harder to fight for. Some small part of him had tried to keep his composure in the presence of a goddess, but now there was nothing to keep him motivated to maintain what little facade of calm he held. The world around him quaked and his vision flecked dark at the edges.

He saw the vague shape of Kurosaki bend down in front of him, one knee in the snow.

"Hey, my guy," Kurosaki's voice sounded muffled in his ears.

"I'm gonna walk you through this, okay?"

Griffin didn't answer; he was focused on the whispering in the trees.

-Simmer down-

-Hello?-

He tried to strain his ears to sharpen his hearing somehow, like that would have made it easier to write off the voices. Of course, he couldn't.

"I want you to inhale through your nose for three seconds, hold it for three, and then push it out for three more. Can you do that for me?"

"Piss off."

He saw the vague movement in his periphery of Jude pulling Kurosaki backwards and away from Griffin.

"This isn't an anxiety attack," she explained. Her voice sounded warbled and wrong in Griffin's ears, like she was suddenly half-raven. "We just need to keep him safe and get him home."

"We'll keep you safe," Kurosaki called out to him instead of answering Jude. "Me and Jude."

Slender hands spread in front of him palms-up and Griffin watched the wavering lines etched into warm skin.

"Griffin," she said his name softly, the last of the raven's marbles falling from her sweet voice. "Can I take you home?"

He recognized the hands enough. Griffin nodded.

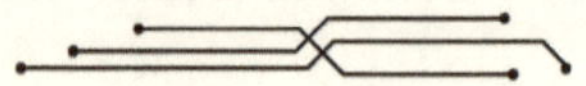

Dearest Kuro,

I am so sorry, I seem to have misplaced the last letter I received from you and I don't quite remember what it was you had said! Forgive me for rambling on anyway.

Griffin did the funniest thing in his martial arts training today. The other kid lost some of the padding on his head and while Griffin was literally still on top of him, pinning him down, he goes "hey are you okay? Do you want me to stop?" Still sitting on him!! I had to excuse myself, I was laughing so hard and I think you would have too. He's grown up so much since you last saw him and I hope you come visit again soon. I think you would both be great friends.

Love you to the moon and back + some pocket change,

Ave

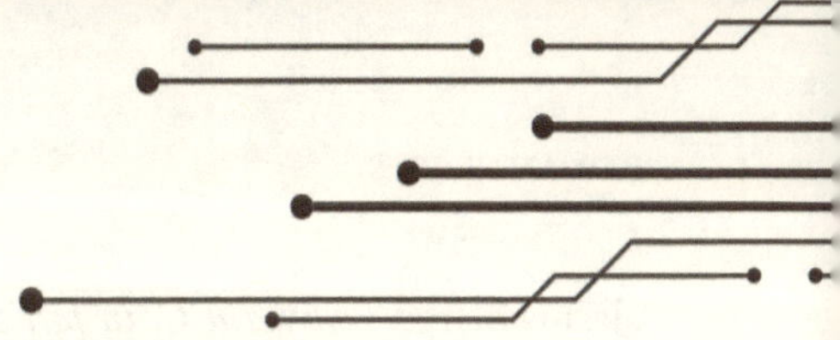

CHAPTER TWENTY-EIGHT
MOZ

M OZ FOUND HIMSELF IN the hallways of the police department much more frequently than he would have cared to lately. This time, a lower ranking officer sat at a desk in the central bullpen that branched off into the closed office doors.

He read the name on the badge: Trevor Pence. Moz found the presence of a full name strange, but he was in too much of a hurry to question it.

"Is Woods in?"

Trevor looked up and the blood drained from his freckled face. His gaze flickered to both sides of the bullpen but failed to find anyone else to push Moz onto.

"Uh, no, but you can talk to Captain Cain—"

"Damnit, I don't want to talk to Cain, I want Woods."

"No one has been able to get a hold of Woods since he left the Díomasaigh house," Trevor leaned forward with his voice lowered, his expression grave.

"What are you talking about? Where is he?"

"Ethan is missing."

Blood pounded in Moz's ears and his stomach dropped to his feet. The edges of his vision blurred and the sharp song of his internal alarms blared - *why did Cain fail to mention this?* The man to last handle his wife's cold case and in charge of the murders now happening. Vanished. Undoubtedly he would hear *"internal reasons"* if he asked Cain directly.

"The second victim's house needs to be secured," he said to Trevor. He would much rather burden the message to someone else than to waste time running in circles with Cain again. "Someone broke in while I was there yesterday. Make sure he gets that message, okay?"

Trevor's eyes widened at his lie. "While you were there? What were you doing there? Sentinel—"

Moz didn't have a good excuse prepared for why he was there to cover for the kids, so he turned on his heel sharply to leave. He passed along what he needed to; hopefully it was enough to get the Brightloch Police moving.

Unlikely.

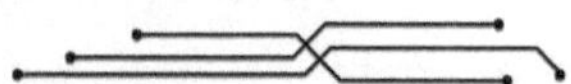

Dinner had been a quiet affair after Jude came down the steps from the upper wings of the castle, having never entered through the front doors. When she found Moz, she explained Griffin's heightened symptoms on the mountain trail.

"Not a full-blown episode," she had clarified, "but he still should rest and stay bundled."

He had given her a hug, with a "thanks, Kiddo", before she

disappeared through her portal.

Moz picked his fork absently at a chopped salad and his worry turned his stomach far too violently to entertain the idea of really eating. He knew he should have been there on the mountain. Jude was gentle with Griffin when things got bad, but Moz worried how much she would have been able to handle if he got particularly worse.

Looking at the bowl of leafy greens, he thought of the most recent flare during which Griffin's mind had convinced him that Moz was trying to poison him. Griffin had locked himself in an upstairs closet and wailed until one of Yumi's staff found him. Sarah had called for help and with a masterkey in hand, he had opened the door to soothe his son.

He hadn't soothed him at all. Griffin backed against the farthest corner and kicked until Moz had no choice but to step back and wait it out. It was cruel to witness and far worse to experience firsthand, he imagined. Yumi eventually came and talked him down as best she could, but Griffin was still wary of him for days after.

They never ate beets again.

Kurosaki had finished his own dinner much quicker and when Moz finally gave up, he cleaned out both ceramic bowls in the deep sink.

"What did Mona say?"

"Just what Jude suspected," Kurosaki answered. "Theirrin was a witch."

Moz didn't know how to answer him. He took a sharp inhale and refolded the white linen towel after he finished drying.

"Can I get you a drink?"

"Yes, please," Kurosaki said softly.

Moz turned to the cabinet, pulling out two crystal glasses. He poured two fingers of Centralian whiskey into each before he set one on the island in front of Kurosaki. Kurosaki sat with his arms folded, hunched over with his chin on his hands as he watched Moz. Without lifting his head, he reached forward, and pulled the glass towards him.

Moz smiled, small and tired, before he asked, "Come sit with me?"

Kurosaki hummed an agreement as he stood up with the crystal in hand. Moz felt his anchoring presence behind him, following into the Green Study. He let him sink first into the cognac leather sofa and Moz seated opposite the low table from him in the matching loveseat.

They sat in silence for long minutes but nothing about it felt uncomfortable. It was processing the day like they had long ago done in Kurosaki's apartment during the periods Moz lived with him in Eyon.

When Moz would meet his eyes by mistake, bashfulness crept over his cheeks and he would take sudden great interest in swirling the whiskey around in his crystal glass. He tried not to think about the subtle swoops in his handwriting and the words they had shaped.

"Mona doesn't know anything about Avery," Kurosaki finally said. His voice hung low like he was trying to soften the blow of the words.

Moz took a deep breath, his shoulders raising high before he let out the exhale. He took a sip of the whiskey, appreciating the burn that ran down his throat.

"I had a feeling. I would hope she or Balthazar would say something if they did... He already said no. So I suppose it makes sense."

"I'm sorry, Moz."

He took a bigger swig to sear the softness out of his chest. To burn his throat and offset the heat beginning to glow in his groin. Moz balanced the glass on his knee, looking down at the lamp light thrown in the cuts of the crystal.

"I don't know what it is, but I feel like I'm closing in on something. Ethan Woods is missing."

"Is that the guy who was on Avery's case?"

Moz nodded slowly.

"Shit."

"I don't know why," Moz said. "He hasn't turned up anywhere with the macabre showmanship of Tristan and Theirrin's cases. But something still feels wrong. And I fear soon a knife in my own back."

"Hey," Kurosaki said, ducking his head to meet Moz's downturned stare. *Gods*— there was a softness in his concern, fixed on his perfect mouth in the smallest smile. "Don't let fear stop you from doing right by them. I'll look out for you."

"Like metal on a magnet," Moz answered and immediately recognized his blunder when the man across from him froze.

"You read my fucking letters."

"Letters? Plural? There are more of them? Why would-"

"*Will*," Kurosaki warned and that shut him up fast. When Moz said nothing about the near-forbidden use of his first name, he straightened in his seat and continued. "You weren't supposed to see any of that. Invasion of privacy aside, what right would I have to say any of that to you? With what I've done? I batted you around like a cat toy and I recognized that mistake. I'm sorry and I will never stop being sorry. This was never supposed to be brought to the table."

"I would be a liar if I said it didn't hurt," Moz admitted, all but flinching at the memorized sound of a steel shovel on grave dirt and the smile of a beloathed Grim. "But I forgave you a long time ago. We aren't those same boys anymore and we haven't been for years."

The words left unspoken for far too long hung heavy between them. He took another sip from his drink, unsure of what to do with his hands as Kurosaki scratched at his short beard. Studying him. Moz was still getting used to how the past decade looked on him and the rich black of his hair that he couldn't remember ever seeing before. The years had been kind to Kurosaki's handsome face. He was perfect; made in his own gilded image far better than anything the gods could ever dare to sculpt.

"You may have forgiven me," Kurosaki finally said, the low pitch of his voice matching well with the warm light from the oil lamp when the flecks of anger on its edges faded, "but forgiveness and responsibility are two very different animals with two very different appetites."

"So are responsibility and beating yourself up over something that can be changed," the words came from Moz too quickly.

"Don't you mean something that *can't* be changed?"

"I do not."

Once again Moz found himself sitting with the consequence of his mouth moving faster than his mind when Kurosaki dropped his fingers from his jaw to stare.

It's been twenty years.

The last time he had kissed Kurosaki, it was a kiss goodbye. *Be good. I'll see you later.*

Twenty years since he had kissed the mouth of the man who understood what it meant to carry sin. What it meant to sit in the foul darkness and let your eyes adjust without panicking. And he had just shown up at the front gate like those years of distance hadn't meant a fucking thing and *goodbye* was just a word people sometimes said but rarely ever meant.

He knew Avery would understand when she finally reappeared.

She had to reappear.

Moz calmly set his glass back on the table between them, off to the side so it could not be knocked over so easily. He planted his elbows down on the wood and bent forward to hold Kurosaki's face in his hands. His thumb brushed tenderly across Kurosaki's cheek as he studied him. The subtle lilac of sleeplessness under his eyes, the soft flicks of his eyelashes, and the small divide between his parted lips.

With the pause, he waited for protest but protest never came. The man only watched him with flitting and widened brown eyes before Moz kissed him.

Twenty fucking years.

Kurosaki's aura still smelled of halcyon days: eucalyptus and the perpetual scent of the crisp, leather interiors in every car he had come home with to baby back into perfect condition. The kiss was gentle in spite of the eagerness Moz held back and he tasted the spearmint-spiked hesitation in the soft curves of the other man's mouth.

Moz pulled quickly away from him when he realized that maybe the kiss wasn't as welcomed as he had been hoping. The room around him shook and he couldn't tell if it was a side effect of the golden liquor or a symptom of the crashing fear that his act had been far too brazen.

Fuck, what did I do?

Kurosaki's awed brown eyes scanned his face when he reached up his ringed fingers and gingerly pulled Moz's fogging glasses away from his face. He held Moz in a familiar stare; the longing glow of campfire in a monstrous dusk that brought a weary scout the same relief no matter which direction it was approached from. His heart ran like an ensnared animal— full speed with nowhere to go. Kurosaki's gaze fell to his mouth.

"You haven't lost the taste of hell," he murmured. He folded the glasses neatly, set them on the table, and pulled Moz back in by the neck of his sweater.

Kurosaki kept the wool locked around his knuckles and gently guided Moz back into his chair. He was careful to not break the hungry kiss when he followed and stood with one foot planted on the floor and his opposite leg knelt on the other side of Moz to straddle him. Kurosaki held him there, quiet and commanding while Moz all but melted in his grip, stiffening under his trousers. Memories of younger days spent inside during summer thunderstorms and the slow grind of Kurosaki's hips into his lap hit Moz like a bullet to the chest. He held onto the back of Kurosaki's thigh with one hand, the other crumpled the waist of his buttoned shirt between his fingers.

The only thing he could focus on was the scrape of Kurosaki's teeth on his bottom lip and the scorching body heat in his lap. Avery was an alpine river that soothed his hellfire, but him? Kurosaki burned him right back and the ache he had been ignorant of became roaringly clear. Their bones could have melded into the same marrow and still Moz wouldn't feel close enough.

He pried his mouth away just far enough to speak, ragged and breathy: "Did you mean what you said?"

Kurosaki regarded him with a darkened gaze and the fingers that held the collar of his undoubtedly warped sweater snaked up his neck to cradle his chin. "You mean the things I believed I was writing in complete privacy? Of course I did."

There was a familiar bite to his words and they were young Reapers again. Moz pulled him back into his atmosphere by the back of his neck and the only two things he knew were the feeling of Kurosaki's parted lips against his tongue and the ravenous buzzing of his name in the corner of his brain once left dormant.

Kurosaki. Kurosaki. Izaya fucking Kurosaki.

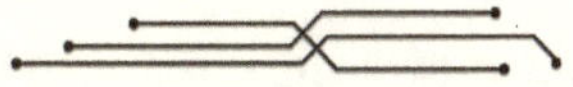

When Moz awoke, the blurry room around him wasn't the field of deep red in his chamber, but rather the teal blues of a room they kept reserved for guests in the castle. He was then aware of the warm sensation on his chest of bare skin touching him; something he hadn't felt in two years before Avery was declared missing. His instinct was to panic - *what have I done?*

Moz fumbled for his glasses on the nightstand and slid them onto his face. To his horror, it was definitely the gilded ceiling of Kurosaki's guest chamber that he stared at.

"You gotta be fucking kidding me," Moz whispered to himself. Sobriety was beginning to sound pretty appealing.

Moz looked down to find that Kurosaki's arm had been draped across his bare chest and his face nestled into his ribs where he had fallen asleep - also sans shirt. Moz's arm draped higher on the pillow to rest just above Kurosaki's mess of black hair and the other man had buried himself in the space.

He couldn't recall ever seeing Izaya Kurosaki in such a soft demeanor and while it made his heart leap, his anger flared because he knew the rough edges had been beaten out of him not by his gentle hand. They had bickered. They had fought. But neither had ever swung out of cruelty.

Rest in piss, Todd.

He felt Kurosaki stir and Moz looked down to see him rubbing sleep from his eyes as he rolled onto his side. With clearer vision, Moz's gaze rolled down from Kurosaki's face and to the two necklaces normally hidden by a shirt: a silver chain with a preserved raccoon tooth and another with a bullet casing. Both reminders on his sternum of people he had lost; a familiar and a friend.

"G'morning," Kurosaki mumbled sleepily, scratching a hand across his chest. Years of healing skin and the shadows of muscles hid the ghosts of the scars running laterally beneath his pectoral muscles and Moz felt glad knowing how much this elated Kurosaki.

"Did we uh, you know," Moz was too fearful of the answer to finish the question.

Kurosaki rubbed his eyes. "No, we did not. First of all, you were a little more drunk than you should be for that. And then you babbled on insisting that it didn't happen until Avery came back, which although it is quite the boner-killer, it's also disgustingly honorable."

Moz took a sharp inhale through his nose before he looked up to the ceiling and said, "I am so fucking sorry."

"Don't be. Thank you for caring enough to set a boundary."

He looked at Kurosaki incredulously. "Damn shorty, you go to *therapy*."

The back of Kurosaki's hand draped over his eyes, but he smiled with a sweet tiredness. Kurosaki dropped his hand and turned on his side to face Moz, nestled still under the crook of his tattooed arm. They stared in a comfortable silence and the ghosts from the night before tiptoed into Moz's memory. He saw them in the grey shadow that bloomed on the base of Kurosaki's neck, felt them in the ruby tracks raked through ink down his own back. Moz held fire in his mouth but never swallowed. Somehow he burned even more for him.

"If you'd let me," Kurosaki was the one who broke the silence with a whisper, "I'd really like to love you right this time."

Moz studied his face. Red imprints from the folds in the sheets were stamped on Kurosaki's cheek and his dark hair was disheveled around his head like a hung-over halo. The gentlest form of undone.

"All I ask of you is for time," Moz answered with a voice that felt too low in his throat. "Give me time to put my family back together. They would never cast you out, but it is far too tense right now to be changing the dynamic."

"Are you asking to keep this a secret? Because that's what it sounds like. It already feels pretty shitty that I'm going behind Avery's back."

That last remark slashed him like a cello's bow across exposed tendon. Sour guilt racked him again and he felt raw knowing that Kurosaki shared it.

Moz gently put his hand on Kurosaki's head, threading his fingers through his hair. He watched his expression shift with a tint of hurt that he would not have recognized if he hadn't known Kurosaki for as long as he had.

"I don't want to be asking this, but yes. I am asking you to keep this between us for now. I have nothing to gain from secrecy, but I do have to put Griffin first. He's taken the worst beatings since Avery vanished and I can't cause him any more undue stress. It's not good for his health. That's my boy and he always comes before anything else. You're not going behind her back. It's my responsibility to tackle that with her, not yours. Please believe me when I say that when everything is right again, everything is transparent. That's our normal."

Kurosaki paused thoughtfully before he responded, "I'd make for an awful sniper if I lacked patience, wouldn't I?"

Moz smiled before he ruffled Kurosaki's hair in his hand and sat up. "Though I wouldn't mind a slow morning for once, we gotta get up."

He rose from the covers and pulled his sweater back on over his head just as Kurosaki wrestled himself free from the quilt that had ensnared his long legs.

Kurosaki moved to button up his black shirt, but Moz gently stopped him by brushing his hands aside. Instead, he began buttoning them up for him as he spoke:

"You embody everything that being a good man means to me," Moz murmured and he felt Kurosaki's eyes watching him as he buttoned up the shirt. "You protect the people you love and you tell them that you love them. You apologize for your mistakes and you take responsibility. You are rough around some edges but you do not let that stop you from being soft. You love harder when you are hurt and you have told your fists long ago that it is time to forget what it feels like to take a swing. You are proud of you, and I am too."

After the last button, Moz straightened and fussed with the collar on Kurosaki's shirt. He ran his hands over his shoulders to smooth out the wrinkles and held them when he looked at Kurosaki's face. He watched Moz with glassy eyes and a mouth parted just enough for him to wait patiently for the words to follow.

"You have changed, so much," Kurosaki's voice wavered just above a whisper. "You are a far cry from that weird, weird man I met on a rainy street corner. Don't get me wrong, you're still pretty fuckin' weird."

Moz laughed with him when Kurosaki wiped the tear that had broken free, but he did not interrupt.

"I am sorry that you had no choice but to be cruel," he continued and Moz's laugh silenced fast. "I am sorry you had to break every bone in your body so you could reset them one by one. But I see you now, and you stand taller and stronger than ever. Kinder than ever. I see it in the way you treat others. You treat them with love and you are infinitely loved in return. I'm proud of you too, Moz."

Moz clutched Kurosaki's face in his hands and kissed him deeply. They weren't those same three words from Kurosaki's letter, but he knew the meaning was the same and that he would hang onto them just as tightly. Kurosaki had a strange way of knitting his words in curious patterns, like his fingers through Moz's untamed hair. He tilted his chin down and away from his face so he could stare at Moz's mouth when he murmured:

"But I'm not sorry I shot you. I think that might have done you some real fuckin' good."

Moz grinned toothily. "Idiot."

Kurosaki smiled - a radiant and lovely fix of the mouth - before he kissed Moz again and untangled his fingers from his hair. He let go of his face as Kurosaki stepped away, towards the bureau of polished cherry wood pushed against the wall. His black backpack sat on top, the buckled flap open and several shirts and pants were half-tumbling out of the opening. Moz watched Kurosaki dig through his backpack and frowned.

"Don't feel the need to unpack?"

Kurosaki set down the small protective case that stored his hormones and sharps. He turned, looking back at Moz with a raised eyebrow.

"Up until last night, I thought I would be going home and

business as usual after we found her."

"I can't give you up again," Moz blurted out before he fully processed what Kurosaki had said. "Wait, what do you mean 'up until'?"

"I can't go back. Especially not there... not when you're here."

Moz sank down onto the end of the unmade bed, staring at Kurosaki in awe. The serious set in Kurosaki's voice when he answered left him struck.

"You really meant it, didn't you?"

Kurosaki didn't answer him right away. He nudged himself in the space between Moz's knees, still standing when he pulled Moz into a hug. Fingers curled in his hair and tucked him into the warmth of Kurosaki's sternum. Moz held his waist and couldn't help but laugh; it felt strange being held in the same way his wife would hold him but by someone his own size.

"I mean it," Kurosaki said. "I'm here for as long as you want me. Maybe longer."

Moz looked up at his face and with his thumb and forefinger, Kurosaki pushed the corners of his mouth up into a smile.

"For me," Kurosaki added, "it was always you. It was always going to be you."

INTERLUDE

Papa?

Darling?

What does it take? To kill a man.

    Brute strength and either a faulty heart or a heart that is ironclad. Forged in the fire of injustice. You must never run in the middle of the road, and I know which one you are.

Why not just a touch? A touch can be a thing so light, so gentle. And they'd never see it coming. The small spider is far more venomous than the one that may only rely on his unwieldy limbs.

    That is still brute strength, *mi liejv*. A strength in restraint practiced in compassion when what you truly desire is violence. A snap of the neck and the silence that follows. The glitter of gore, like the confetti bomb at your sixth birthday party. Isn't that what you really want?

What I really want? I think I would like roses.

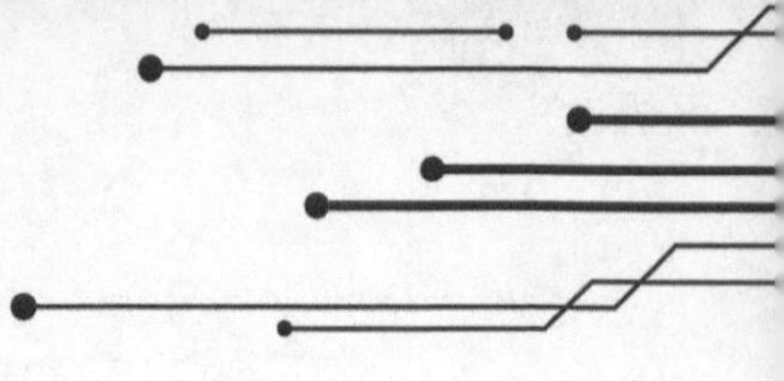

CHAPTER TWENTY-NINE
GRIFFIN

H E KNEW IMMEDIATELY THAT he was dreaming — this place was different, but familiar all the same. Griffin stood in a mirror image of Brightloch that glowed under a green neon sky. The light cast warped buildings in a sickly haze and he looked down at the flesh of his hands with spread fingers. No, he always looked like this.

Griffin glanced up at the glowing clocktower with winding hands of radial bones spinning wildly.

He looked down at his feet and saw the snake weaving through the grooves of wet cobble. His instinct was to jump back, but self-preservation failed him and he remained frozen.

"She is cannibalizing herself," The Snake hissed, a rolling and rattling sound in his ears.

"Cannibal men for cannibal gods, wrought upon the world to devour cannibal kingdoms."

Griffin didn't have the faintest idea what The Snake meant and felt a fool for it. He should have known already and the shame he felt for staying in the dark shoved with oppressive force on his shoulders.

The Snake coiled around his leg, enveloping him in scales as its girth grew heavier and heavier around his bones. Up his thigh, around his waist. Tighter. And tighter. Griffin couldn't move even though he *knew he should. Just a frightened mouse who had ignored the innate danger of a snapping spine passed down from his ancestors until it was he who shrank smaller and smaller under a serpentine squeeze.*

"My son, my star. My moon, my life," *The Snake said and Griffin's stomach pitched down to his feet. Mama's words shoved into the fangs of a beast. Serpents were not ones to sing, it seemed.*

A tall, looming figure watched from the shadows. Though it was unmoving, Griffin felt the heavy weight of its eyes on him. He wasn't sure if it even had eyes at all. Before he could sharpen his focus to seek them out, The Snake finished its coil around his shoulders and rose its head to look at Griffin.

The Snake's tongue flicked like a blood red flag in the gales of a battlefield. It watched him with unblinking beads of black that he couldn't pry his gaze from. He should have wriggled and writhed to work himself free of the grip that still tightened, but Griffin just waited. He knew he was to die.

"Cannibal son with cannibal blood."

The Snake lurched at him with bared fangs and Griffin felt the sharp burn of a bite on his cheek. Bones crushed inside him as the force tightened fast and mercilessly.

The world should have gone black.

He should have woken up.

He hung suspended in glittering scales of emerald and topaz. A distant voice spoke to him, but it was not The Snake:

"Has it been so long since you have feasted? Sit at my table and never again shall you go hungry."

Time passed in silence. The dream would not let him go. Griffin was certain that this time he had died.

Griffin rocked back into the world of the waking in slow, lapping waves on the shoreline. He came to and familiarity pieced together in the form of his slate blue bedroom walls and the grey light that filtered in through golden glass. It snowed through the night marching into the winter solstice, bleeding the days together so that it hardly felt like Iverne to Griffin. He shook off the dream and stared at the plastic stars above his head.

Another one without Mama.

Maya roused from her sprawl on the floor, shoving her head into Griffin's nest of blue blankets to nudge his cheek with her wet nose. He flinched before he laughed.

"Okay, okay, let's go."

Griffin pulled on the charcoal sweater draped across the back of his desk chair, but remained in his green flannel pajama pants. Maya circled him as he walked out of his bedroom door, slamming him into the door frame as she excitedly passed him to trot down the hall. Halfway down, she stopped and turned to him with a wagging tail to make sure he was still following.

"Show me where the kitchen is," he said to the dog.

Though she didn't understand the words, she knew the cue in his tone and their predictable placement in their routine. Maya barked and trotted out of view to run down the stairs. Griffin followed at a far more apathetic pace.

He walked into the kitchen, rubbing the last bit of sleepy sand away from his eyes. Griffin dropped his hand when he saw that he was not the first to arrive; his father and Kurosaki were sitting at two stools pulled up together at the island and their hushed tones silenced when they watched him walk in. They were sitting bizarrely close. His father seemed to watch Kurosaki's mouth forming low words.

Moz stood up from his stool, slow and not at all like someone who had been caught doing something they weren't supposed to.

"Merry Solstice," he greeted Griffin. "Is Mimi up yet?"

Griffin couldn't answer him; he just stared at Kurosaki past his shoulder. *What the fuck?* He snapped out of the spell when Maya barked and he remembered why he had been there at all. His father was the one who went for the dry food in the cabinet, undoubtedly eager to remove himself from Griffin's dumbfounded look.

"I didn't see her," Griffin finally said, "I can go get her if you need."

Moz dumped the dog food into a metal bowl and replaced it on the mat tucked beside the cabinet end. Maya bullied her way past him and began chomping in loud crunches as he straightened up.

"Sure, the plan is to go into town for the festival. We have security detail on standby if she wants to come, they just need to know."

A security detail to celebrate the holiday. Griffin despised it and felt a pang of guilt when he found himself hoping that the Queen would decline. It wasn't Mimi's fault; and it certainly wasn't safe for her without it. Trouble was farther and fewer between when Mama was there.

Griffin walked down the hallway, but not at all in a hurry.

"I'm sure it's fine," he heard his father's hushed voice just before Griffin fell out of earshot.

He frowned hard. *What the fuck was with those two?*

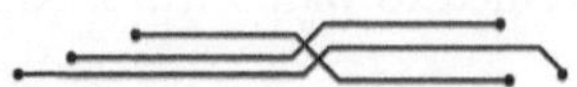

While Annabel finished trimming the tall solstice pine in the foyer with orange slice garlands and bells, Griffin followed his father and Kurosaki out the door.

Downtown was flooded with people braving the cold and icy cobblestone to peruse the stalls bannered with green and gold. Ruby pomegranates and winter citrus painted Brightloch in warmth from their crates, disappearing little by little as villagers traded coins for the last of the harvest.

Griffin made a point to walk behind his father and Kurosaki as they walked carefully over the slick stone. Somebody had to keep an eye on those two. He kept catching stolen glances between them and the warm smile on his father's face looked suspiciously similar to the one he would give Mama. It was undeniably a look of love that made his stomach turn. He didn't have an issue with Kurosaki at all, but the idea that someone would be able to steal his father's affections so easily felt like maybe he was giving up. That he decided she wasn't coming back after all.

His dynamic with a man seemed different, too. If William Mosley and Avery Porter moved around each other in a waltz, he turned with Kurosaki in a well-calculated spar. They seemed too careful to be lovers, if lovers at all. They took too long to formulate their words. Their stares felt too heavy to not hold decades of meaning.

Griffin wondered if he could love another man and admittedly, the thought hadn't occurred to him before watching Moz and Kurosaki. It had always just been Jude he gravitated to no matter who else stood in the room. Had she been any other gender, he knew he would have adored her all the same. He would never just tap out on her like his father seemingly had.

They passed city workers wheatpasting notices to the sides of brickstones already slathered in layers of posters, these ones reminding Brightloch citizens to keep a watchful eye and alert the nearest city official, Sentry or Police, if anything out of the ordinary was noticed. He couldn't help but huff a chuckle; *ordinary* felt to be a rather useless word. One poster caught his eye and Griffin stopped to read the hastily sprayed message in black:

DOWN

GOES THE

CROWN

Beneath the words was a sloppy rendering of a crown, looking nothing like the one he had seen Mimi wear once or twice before. But instead shaped like the small tags of graffiti Griffin had seen on the seawall by the harbor or slapped onto the iron of gaslamp posts. He had thought nothing of the previous sprays before, but seeing it underneath the chilling phrase gave him pause.

He followed his father and Kurosaki through the overwhelming blurs of color, taking many second glances when a shadow felt out of place. Through it all, he searched hopefully for any sign of Jude's face up until the moment they put their backs to the festival as they climbed up the castle hill with market bags in tow. Just seeing her face would have made Griffin's holiday worth waking up for.

Griffin thought of the shape of her smile when he sat on the floor of the stuffy living room, listening to his parents talk to Kurosaki while he absently tugged a toy with Maya. His stare looked blank when they sat at the dinner table around a roasted turkey and salad speckled with tart goat cheese and pomegranate arils; but his mind's eye saw hers.

It was getting far more difficult to simply not pay attention to how it made Griffin feel when he saw two people dancing around the feeling.

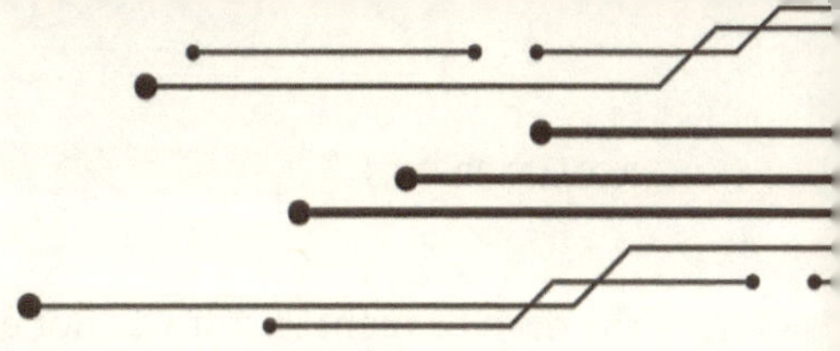

CHAPTER THIRTY
YUMI

*T*HEY WERE ALONE ON *the sand and the heat of sunshine warmed Yumi's skin. Avery sat, leaning back on her propped arms and looked from the sea to Yumi. She didn't question why Avery wore her full Scout uniform to the beach, she was just so happy to see her. Her smile turned with the small flick of the cocksure attitude that Yumi adored as she approached.*

Yumi straddled her lap and Avery's thumbs absently traced her inner thighs through her gauze shroud as she kissed her. Her mouth trailed down Yumi's jaw and nipped sweetly at her neck. Warmth ran across the ink on Yumi's sternum and she rocked into the touch when Avery's hand traced up her side to knead her breast.

Avery pushed open the dipping neckline of Yumi's thin dress and flicked her tongue over her stiffening nipple. The heat of her breath ran down Yumi's spine and pooled between her legs. Avery turned her gaze up to Yumi's face, watching her through a lovestruck haze before she spoke:

"Yumi... Yumes... Baby, you've got to wake up."

When she opened her eyes, it wasn't her wife speaking to her. The man leaned over her bed, bent at the waist with his hands shoved deep into his trouser pockets. He wore rounded black sunglasses in

235

the dead of night, but it was not enough to shield the charred half of his face from the illumination of the moonlight that poured in through the stained glass window in Yumi's chamber. He grinned just as Yumi's olfactory senses caught the sickly scent of burnt flesh.

"Rise and shine, Ink Queen. Do you remember me?"

She had only met him once when the Reapers were storming Eyon at the sacrificial grounds, but the vitriol both Moz and Jack held for him after the fact were strong enough to make the impression last.

"Hello, Todd," she said gently as she sat upright, leaning against the upholstered headboard as she wiped sleep away from her eyes. "What are you doing here?"

"You've likely noticed by now we're easier to spot. Something about the Iverne moon shining brighter through the veil. Don't ask me, I'm not a Priestess, I don't know. But I thought since I'm here, I would use this opportunity to warn you."

"Warn me? About what?"

Todd pulled his hands out of his pockets, leaning forward and planting his hands down on the bed. As Yumi watched him, she noticed the surface give under his splayed fingers. He had corporeal mass.

Definitely alarming.

"About Izaya. I fear he has something terrible planned. You know of his relationship with William, yes?"

"Moz. Yes, I do."

"I am sorry to say this, because I really, truly have no qualms with your wife whatsoever and I feel guilty that this is happening because of the man I am responsible for," Todd explained, but Yumi didn't detect an ounce of genuine remorse. "Izaya is sabotaging Avery's case. He wants her out of the picture so he can keep William for himself."

"No, that can't be right. Avery is his friend, he would never."

"Then you don't know him like I do. Izaya would do anything for that man. Like for instance, kill me."

Yumi studied him, trying to read the expression in the remainder of his face but it was void of any affect that would give away his intentions. She didn't want it to be true, but it was her wife.

"If that were true, why did he come all this way to help find her?"

"Bah!" Todd stood up straight again and looked away as though he found the question too ridiculous to even entertain. He turned back to her when he answered, "To be his knight in shining fucking armor, ironically enough. Wouldn't you feel more inclined to turn to someone if they were helping you in your darkest hour? It doesn't matter now the psychology of it because the plan is already there and it has to be you that removes that variable in the equation. Will won't do it, why would he? Izaya has to die or your wife won't be coming back."

And there it is.

Yumi threw off the covers and bolted across the opposite side of the bed, stumbling before she sprinted for her chamber door. Todd rounded the bed fast and closed a hand around her wrist with such lifelike force that she would have sworn he were living if it weren't for his seared appearance. She jolted under his grip and reached for the door with her free hand, swinging at empty air until she closed her fingers around the handle. With the new leverage, she wrestled herself free before she threw open the door and lurched through.

She felt grateful she had traded her tower sanctuary for a chamber on the second floor after her father died; Yumi wasn't sure if anyone would have been able to hear her shouts outside of its narrow echo chamber of a stairwell.

"Ooh, I love this game!"

Todd followed her out into the hallway, but his voice felt far behind her as Yumi ran. She looked over her shoulder and the revenant watched her from the open door frame of her chamber. He lifted his arms, a conductor for an orchestra of the dead, and glass splintered as the stained windows and mirrors in the hall exploded in unison.

Yumi shrieked, shielding her face as best she could with her arms as she ran and fixed her gaze downward to avoid stepping on pebbles of broken glass with her bare feet. The chill of the winter air flooded the corridor and swirled around her in frigid horror.

"WAKE UP!" She shouted.

If there was one thing Todd told the truth about, it was the new-found ability for him to move about the land of the living with ease. With power. Until the moon waned, the safest place for Kurosaki to be was in the seance parlor under the protection of a salt circle.

Yumi ran as fast as her legs would carry her and she buckled with pain radiating from the glass shards she couldn't avoid. She was thankful it was long after the staff had gone home for the night but wished the guards posted outside would hear the commotion.

"MOZ!" She yelled again.

She turned a corner and the top of the grand staircase came into view. Across from it, the first doors in the opposite wing were visible. Just as she thought she slipped out of Todd's sights, the gilded mirror at her left shoulder exploded. Yumi screamed; she wasn't going to have time to rouse her family from their beds. She had to get to the seance parlor for her exorcism kit *now*.

Yumi rounded the corner to fly down the stairs when she saw a door open from the periphery of her vision. Moz and Kurosaki came thundering out before they saw the kaleidoscope of mirrors shattered across the ornamental rugs. Both were in pajamas, though Kurosaki lacked a shirt entirely.

"Fucking hell, what happened Yumes? I–"

"*Zaya,*" Todd cut Moz off when he rounded the corner from the wing Yumi had just fled. She froze on the stairs, looking back to see the top of the revenant's maroon head of hair just over the railing. The blood drained from Kurosaki's face and his careful tiptoe around the broken glass turned to a sprint to follow her downstairs. Moz caught up quickly with his long strides, skipping steps three at a time to catch up to her.

"Did you just come out of the same bedroom?"

"Yumes, I hardly think now is the time for this!"

She ran faster on the stairs when she felt confident that she was free from the hazard of broken glass in her skin.

"We have to get to the parlor," she explained between her paced breaths. "He wants Kuro, but I think at this point he'll settle for any of us."

Moz fell behind when he jolted to a stop. Yumi looked over her shoulder to see he was heading back up the stairs, towards Todd.

"Get him to the parlor! I'm going back for Griff!"

"Don't be a fucking idiot," Kurosaki huffed, but turned to follow him.

Yumi hesitated. She was certain that of the three of them, she was the one Todd felt least eager to kill. Unsure if she would be enough to shield Moz and Kurosaki, she followed them back upstairs.

Moz moved too fast for Todd to close his fingers around as he lurched with open hands, but Kurosaki wasn't so lucky when the revenant blocked the top of the landing. Yumi caught up to him when he slowed and she grabbed him by the arm.

"Stay back, he singled you out," she warned quietly. She ran past him at full speed when she let go, barreling towards Todd at full speed. Yumi wasn't sure what would happen, but was pleasantly surprised when he stumbled off his feet, arms tangling around her to pull her down with him. He had lifelike weight to him that meant he could harm her, and she prayed that meant she could harm him right back. Even if only enough to keep him diverted.

"Go! Catch up to him!" She shouted at Kurosaki.

He didn't hesitate to run and he disappeared around the corner to catch up to Moz. Yumi turned her attention back to the dead man she wrestled on the floor and she pushed all five fingers of her right hand deep into the burned muscle of his face. Todd howled in pain, but did not slow when he tossed her aside with blunt force.

Yumi crashed to the floor and felt pebbles of glass press into her skin through her nightshirt, breaking flesh in some places. She heard a door slam from downstairs and feet running on the marble floor.

"Yumi!"

Jack's voice came from the foot of the stairs before he came pounding up them to help her. Maya trailed behind him, barking loud in alarm.

"No! Go to the parlor and get the kit! I've got this!"

He hesitated, unsure at first if he should listen. But Jack turned to run in the other direction.

"Kit," he repeated to himself. "You got it!"

Yumi rose to her feet and hissed through her gritted teeth when the glass shifted with her weight. Todd rose to meet her, lurching to shove her hard into the wall. She lifted her arms and locked her fingers around his elbows to twist his torso away.

Using her body from her hip to her shoulder, she barreled at him as hard as she could. Todd fell hard onto the glass and laughed with sick delight.

"You into some kinky shit now, Princess?"

Yumi lurched for a shard of mirror, cutting into her own palm as she gripped it to keep a strong hold as she plunged it into Todd's ankle. The revenant howled.

"Shit, ow, bitch, you fucking cunt– that *hurt!*"

Yumi turned around, ready to run to the seance parlor after Jack when she wasn't sure how long Todd would stay on the ground. Moz and Kurosaki came running back around the corner, but it was still only them. Yumi's eyes widened with horror.

"Where's Griffin?"

"Not there," Moz said through huffed breaths, his sprint slowed now that he wasn't chasing for their son. "Likely at Jude's. I'm glad he's not here, but man, are we going to have a talk about giving a heads-up."

They fled down the stairs and Maya had bowed at the foot of the stairs to bark wildly, likely yelling at Moz to run from danger.

"Yes, thank you, dog-ter! I know!" Moz answered her as their feet hit the first floor.

Above them, Todd roared wildly and Yumi heard the crash of a large piece of glass. She looked over her shoulder before they rounded the corner into the lower west wing and she saw the revenant thundering down the steps after them.

"The.. fuck does ... he want?" Moz managed between breaths and the strides of his long legs staggered on cut feet.

Yumi felt the burning blood on her own as she hurried alongside Maya. "He wants Kuro," she said again.

She couldn't see Kurosaki's expression on the other side of Moz, but she felt the heavy fear in his silence.

Yumi sprinted when the open doors of the seance parlor came into view and Jack's silhouette stood in the frame and hurried them on with a wave of his hand.

"C'mon, hurry it up!"

"*It's meeeeeeee*," Todd's voice taunted from the other end of the hall just before the large mirror on the wall exploded in splintered shards.

Glass shattered and Moz swore, holding up his arms to shield his face. Maya yelped and backpedaled to avoid the shards on the ground. He turned back, scooping the large dog up as best he could in his arms to keep her from walking across it and injuring her paws.

They hurried into the parlor and Moz dropped Maya back down

onto the clean marble floor. She postured defensively with raised hackles, looking into the hall as she barked madly.

"In the circle, now!"

Moz pushed Kurosaki into the copper ring in the middle of the darkened parlor, too frantic to be gentle. Kurosaki stumbled backwards and fell onto his palms. But he was inside; that's what mattered.

"You too, Moz," Yumi instructed without turning around. But he hadn't listened and instead came up to her side, throwing open drawers in the bureau to help her look for the salt. She wanted to yell at him to just fucking listen to her, but didn't when he pulled out the glass container with a cork rimmed in clumps of salt.

"Got it!"

He ran back, stomping on the switch that would open the metal track that ran the circle. Moz began pouring the salt, shaking it out as hurriedly as he could while still forming a solid boundary around Kurosaki. The footsteps approached just as the circle closed with Moz still on the outside.

"Salt? That's adorable."

Yumi looked to the doorway where Todd stood, grinning wickedly.

"I've always hated your ugly mug," Todd taunted Moz in a voice lined thick with murder. "Congrats on aging, Limp Dick. You were the greatest monster to ever roam this earth, and now look at you. A domestic bitch on a leash."

"Kind of weird to talk about my dick and then liken me to a monster, don't you think? If you've got something you need off your chest, you can just-"

Todd lurched for Moz and when Yumi expected impact, the revenant was knocked off his feet when a shadow of a figure darted in from the periphery. He careened onto his back, sliding across the slick floor and his sunglasses clattered across the marble when they fell off his singed face. Todd looked at the figure who faced him and shock spread across his face.

The woman looked young with two buns of pale lilac hair piled on either side of her head. Yumi recognized the energy about her, but she couldn't quite place it in her memory. She tugged down the sleeves of her purple sweatshirt, the zipper drawn all the way up to her neckline, and she smiled over her shoulder in Moz's direction.

"Hi, Mozzarella."

Todd finally broke his surprised silence to laugh as he replaced the sunglasses on his nose. "Are you fucking kidding me right now, Al? Really?"

The name clicked the recognition into place for Yumi: the young woman who had possessed her the very same day she had met Avery and Moz for the first time. She remembered the sheer terror from the discovery that she could even be used as a vessel in that way. Though she felt friendly enough, the memory still made her shudder.

Alice rolled her head over her shoulder to glare at Todd. "Don't you ever get fucking sick of this? Being both ringleader and monkey in your own damn circus that nobody would pay to watch? It's fucking sad, Todd. You're making me sad."

"*Sad?* He's responsible for both of our deaths, I am not just being *sad.* Aren't you fucking angry?"

The blood drained from Kurosaki's face and Yumi was concerned for a moment that he may faint. But she had to work fast while Todd remained distracted. Todd lurched at Alice and they grappled arms, fighting to overpower the other sibling.

"Where is it... where is it...," Yumi dug through the drawers again

"Do you know why I even fucking bothered with you, Todd? You are an amalgamation of all of the worst things about Moz. All of the poison, none of the redemption. I didn't have to feel guilty with you because I knew you were a million times worse. But that shit got so old, so fast. I literally outgrew you. I was done long before that last swing," Kurosaki couldn't throw physical punches from behind the safety of the circle, but he could certainly still throw verbal ones. Yumi smirked as she listened - *good on him.*

"Wow, somebody put their big boy pants on today! Do you feel better giving the guy you had killed a piece of your mind?"

"I didn't tell Jack to do that. Believe it or not, you're just that fuckin' unlikable."

Moz turned to Jack, but his former familiar slid the purple bottle he had pocketed into Yumi's hands just as she was about ready to give up looking, "You killed him?"

Jack shrugged, turning in his direction. "Was I wrong?"

Yumi took the purple bottle of glass from Jack, fumbling it with the clumsiness of fear. Todd was overpowering Alice with his arm pinning her shoulders to the floor and would soon be headed their way. The cork popped off to her relief and she began to pour its blessed contents onto Jack's outstretched hands.

"Yumes, hurry!"

He had looked over his shoulder to see Todd had carelessly tossed his revenant sister aside and sprinted across the seance parlor towards them. When Yumi began to dump the holy water onto her own hands, Jack fumbled with his lighter in wet fingers, grunting with frustration until the flint finally caught more than useless sparks.

Out of the corner of her vision she saw the tall silhouette. Its eyes glowed a bright white in a humanoid void from the threshold of the seance parlor, unnoticed by all but Yumi. She recognized the shape of hair tucked into a leather hair tie and the form of a beard around where its chin should have been. At its gut, flesh flapped around the steaming gore of a wound. Its bottom jaw came unhinged and the slack mouth struggled to form words but no sound came. Yumi froze.

Jack's wet hands ignited just as Yumi remembered the words to the exorcism rite.

"I call on Mona, Hands of Her Heart!"

Jack ignited her own hands and she watched the lick of the flames dance across the skin, but felt no burn when their colors shifted to an otherworldly green. She looked to the silhouette, but it had stopped trying to speak.

"Lend me the touch of Od, accept me as your harbinger!"

The flames erupted just as Alice found her footing again and kicked Todd hard in the back of the knees just as he was almost upon Yumi and Jack.

Jack lowered his hands, illuminated green with the borrowed fires of Od as he turned around. When he looked down at Todd laid out on the marble floor, he grinned. Sinister, toothy, and unlike anything Yumi had ever seen on the face of the man she knew once to be just sunshine of a boy who loved his friend. She knew better now; that love sometimes meant warped metal and spilled gasoline without so much as a flicker of his hesitation.

"I'll waste your ass in every life."

Todd's eyes widened in horror, enough for Yumi to see even beyond the round frames of his sunglasses. It was the look of a man who had just come to regret every piss-poor decision he had ever made in a life ill-spent. Jack bent at the waist, holding his flaming hands on the side of Todd's face. Though Yumi felt not even warmth in the supernatural fires, Todd screamed and writhed in searing pain under Jack's grip.

"The words, Yumi! Now!"

"*Th.. the shining light behind the Veil guides thou home! Rest, weary spirit! Rest and leave life to the living! The flame of Her beacon sends for thee!*"

Yumi struggled to remember the words as she stared down at her own hands. *The last line, fuck, what is the last line?*

"*Go with love and go with peace! If thou has none in thy soul, may thou only return when thou is whole!*"

Todd wailed, thrashing as hard as he could; his afterlife was depending on it. Jack looked on in a furious smirk as the flames wrapping around his fingers snaked across Todd's face. They danced over his charred half, rained down his neck, and caught on his singed clothing.

Borrowed Od fire swallowed him whole, casting the seance parlor in an eerie chartreuse until they died in an ashless flicker at

Jack's feet. The flames on both Yumi and Jack's hands extinguished of their own accord and they were left in darkness. It was a long moment of silence broken only by heavy, staggered breathing and the complaining creak of old copper when Moz finally dislodged the metal ring in the floor to let the salt ring scatter.

"Well, that's a new trick," he said, too lighthearted for Yumi to agree.

Her eyes adjusted to the darkness as she watched Moz extend his hand to help Kurosaki off the floor. She corked the bottle and walked to him instead of the cabinet to shelf it again. Yumi laid a gentle hand on Kurosaki's arm, goosefleshed with fear.

"Are you okay?"

He didn't answer out loud but she caught the faint and entirely unconvincing nod of his head. Yumi gave his arm the smallest squeeze before she turned up to look at Moz.

"Help him to bed and make sure he bundles up, okay? It's frightfully cold," she said. "We'll take care of this mess in the morning."

Moz nodded, putting a hand on Kurosaki's back to ease him forward gently when Yumi let go. "Watch out for the glass, okay?"

As they were leaving the parlor, he paused to look at Alice. There was a quiet sorrow in the expression on her small face, but Yumi felt she missed the story behind it.

"Thanks, Al," Moz said. "You continue to amaze us, every day."

Alice snorted a laugh. "Every day from the grave, huh? Pretty damn impressive, I think."

Moz smiled and turned to follow Kurosaki out the parlor doors.

"Oh hey, Mozzarella?"

"Hm?"

"Thanks for taking care of Kuro," she answered, with a warmth to her voice. "You always have, but I'm glad that it's different now. I love you both. Even if you're wrinkly old men now."

"I love you too, Al," Moz answered softly, and he abandoned Kurosaki's dazed side just long enough for him to wrap his arms around Aice and squeeze her in a tight hug. She looked so real to Yumi, so alive even from beyond.

"Thank you, for everything," she caught Moz murmuring before he let go.

They parted and Moz followed Kurosaki's sullen form down the hall, back to Kurosaki's guest room that they evidently shared now. Yumi stood in silence, looking from Alice to Jack as he stared at the spot Todd had been.

"I love you Alice, but fuck your brother," he finally said.

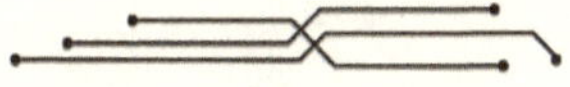

Moz,

I am bold writing this letter. If you should wake up and see me looking from the letter to you (thank you, for not burrowing into a book blanket this time), you would undoubtedly snatch it from me. And I don't want that. I want to say things that I will never speak about.

I didn't realize the decision I made that day when I stopped you from killing Todd. If I knew what would come, that I would lose your love, I would have had zero hesitation in my aim so that you would shoulder none of the guilt. I should have recognized a beautiful gift from the gods when not even a grave could hold him down.

I want to unravel you, with loving hands and longing teeth. I'll take you apart and put you back together because I have studied for years where each piece has a home in you. I could do it with my eyes closed and in my sleep. Maybe I already do.

I didn't know what you were going to be like when I came back here for the first time in over a decade, but it would seem that you have only made me love you more. There's no going back from that, and that's fine with me.

I adore you, William Mosley. And I think now I am content with the prospect of being alone forever if it means I avoid pretending I could ever feel for anyone else the way I feel about you. I am maddeningly, heartbreakingly in love with you. Still. Always.

Yours forever,
Izaya Kurosaki

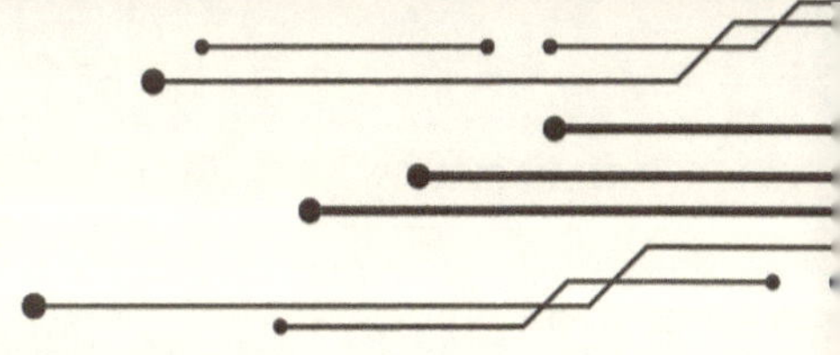

CHAPTER THIRTY-ONE
MOZ

MOZ EASED KUROSAKI BACK onto the bed of his guest room and carefully swung his legs onto the mattress. On his way to the attached bathroom, he flicked on a bedside lantern and they both winced at the light.

"I know," Moz said softly, but Kurosaki still hadn't spoken. "Hang tight for a second and I'll get that glass out."

Moz washed his hands aggressively in the basin and then a second time for good measure. He fetched a pair of tweezers and cotton pads from the kit of spare toiletries and when he returned, Moz knelt at the bedside. There were three bleeding points of flesh in the bottom of Kurosaki's feet from the shattered glass on the floor and Moz felt surprised that he hadn't limped as much as he would have expected.

"You have three bits," Moz explained. "I'm gonna count from one for you to inhale, and on three you'll exhale. Can you do that for me?"

Kurosaki nodded silently.

Moz positioned the teeth of the tweezers around the shard of glass buried in Kurosaki's heel.

"Okay. One..."

Kurosaki inhaled deeply, his shoulders rising to his ears.

"Two…"

Moz clamped down, angling one side of the tweezer head from below to ensure he could pry it free on the first try.

"Three."

As Kurosaki exhaled sharply, Moz quickly pulled the glass from the skin. Kurosaki flinched under the sharp pain, nearly kicking Moz in the face. Blood welled in the space it left and Moz applied pressure with the cotton to staunch the flow.

"Good job," he said. "Just two more."

The second shard did land him a reflexive kick in the collarbone and it nearly knocked the wind out of Moz. He coughed and sputtered as he got back up from the floor, deciding to get the final pebble of glass out as quickly as he could.

He yanked out the last of the glass and Kurosaki finally spoke:

"What, no praise that time?"

His voice was raspy and weary; jarring after how long his heavy silence had endured. Moz kept his pressure on the small wound firm. He frowned when a thought struck him sour:

"Has no one been taking care of you?"

"I don't get it, what do you mean?"

"Obviously not Todd," Moz continued like he hadn't asked the question. "Which I have some follow-up questions about that we'll circle back to later. But what about Andrew? I'm under the impression that someone caring for you without expecting anything in return isn't as familiar a happening as it should be."

Kurosaki averted his gaze and looked down at his knees.

"And frankly, darling, it worries me," Moz added.

"Jack knew it was happening."

Moz quieted. He held the tweezers in his hand as he rose from the floor and sat silently on the bed. Far away enough so to not overwhelm Kurosaki, but near enough to try to be a grounding presence. He said nothing and let Kurosaki continue at his own pace.

Kurosaki inhaled deeply, shaking more than he had when Moz was about to tenderly rip glass out of his flesh.

"In one of my letters," Kurosaki stared down as he continued, "I finally told him that the fights had escalated. And that bouncing back wasn't so easy anymore. I think he had enough of sitting and waiting for me to put an end to it. And so he offered to come solve it for me. I didn't know what he meant until a few days later but by then he was already on the ferry. Avery knew and she didn't peep a word to anyone but me."

Kurosaki looked up from his knees and his pained tears bore holes into Moz's heart.

"He jammed the locks in Todd's car and torched it while he was inside. I saw the whole thing and did nothing to stop it. Didn't lift a finger. And I felt *safe*. I thought he could never hurt me again and I told Jack that I owe him my life. He said 'no, it's because I love you and nothing more.' I told Avery what happened and in her next letter, she said she lost mine and carried on like normal but signed with more love. And I know that was her way of protecting me. Your *wife* protected me and my thanks to her was getting involved with her husband. So yeah, Moz. I do know what it feels like when someone cares for me and wants for nothing back. The problem has been that they've all been here. But I'm home now. And that might take some adjustment because I have done nothing but screw them over."

By the time he finished, tears came down Moz's cheeks as well. The knowledge that he had lived in such fear and loneliness struck him with a deep burn of regret for the words he had foolishly said. But he also felt a grateful pride in both his wife and Jack for going to such lengths to keep Kurosaki safe. Sure, Moz would have liked to be in the loop, but just having Kurosaki alive and breathing before him was the greatest gift.

He leaned forward and took Kurosaki into his arms. The man was too limp with weariness to resist him and Moz helped him back into the safety of blankets with care. Moz laid beside him and pulled Kurosaki into an embrace, holding his head against his chest. He kissed his hair and wondered when it started feeling natural again to think of him as *darling*.

"You're safe," Moz murmured, but something about those words racked heaving sobs out of Kurosaki.

He did his best to keep quiet and just stay present; to let Kurosaki come down in his own time. Izaya never came apart like this.

Kurosaki clung to him like a lifeline and his fingers absently scratched gentle patterns into Moz's shoulder blades as he cried. Moz stroked his hair, kissed his forehead; *anything* to show that Todd was a past that would never be repeated.

The tears slowed, as did the absent movement of his fingers on the back of Kurosaki's head. He had fallen into silence and the warm exhales into Moz's chest took a lighter rhythm.

"You are so loved," Moz said, barely above a tear-cracked whisper and Kurosaki only answered with the quiet rise and fall of his breath.

Moz fought the temptation to look down at Kurosaki. He thought the sight was well worth the risk of waking him again, but the moment felt fragile. How many times had he prayed for just a scrap of vulnerability from Kurosaki while they were young and untouchable? It was trusted to him now and Moz intended to keep it. To keep him.

So loved. By so many people. By me. I love you so.

He couldn't say it. His family was still shattered. Avery was still missing. His wife, with all her love and all her fury. It was remarkable to Moz how someone who vanished into thin air could still hold him in a tight grip of presence.

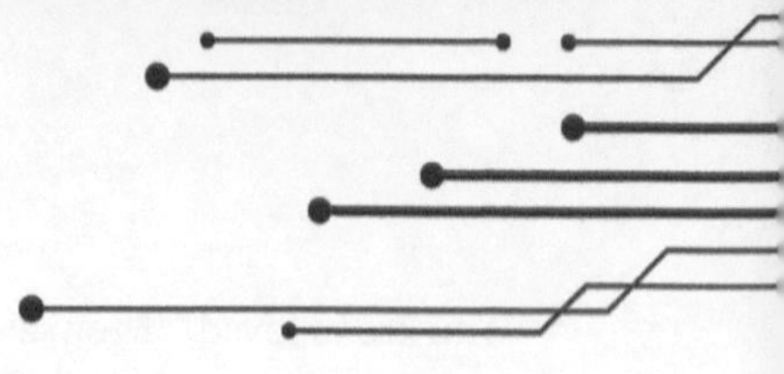

CHAPTER THIRTY-TWO
GRIFFIN

G RIFFIN DIDN'T WANT TO fall asleep. Not when Jude's room felt so comforting and he knew that his nightmares were occurring on a regular basis now. He decided it was far more preferable to stay awake beside her outside the covers. He stared for a long while at her halo of curls in the crack of solstice moonlight and the sharp lines of her shoulder.

Metal tapped from the perch and Creak's judging stare felt heavy on Griffin's back even from across the room. He held his breath for a moment before he felt brave enough to drape his arm over Jude's waist. A small and tired sigh fell from her lips as she shifted in her sleep, but she did not turn.

Griffin thought he had gone unnoticed in a long moment of silence until she mumbled:

"Get in the blanket, dummy. You'll catch a cold."

He hesitated before he fumbled to peel back the blankets far enough to climb inside, but not so much that Jude would feel even the slight bite of cold. Griffin settled again under the floral sheets, placing his arm again on Jude's side before he could find the time to second guess his actions. She backed closer into him, her long legs tucked up in front of her halfway to a fetal position and her shoulders nestled into him. Jude didn't speak again before she drifted further into sleep.

Griffin decided that risking night terrors might not have been the worst thing if it meant he could have this.

Her. It was Jude's face he would see whenever he heard the word; simple in all the ways she was not. His best friend perplexed him, challenged him, and now at times terrified him. Griffin didn't know what it would mean to be the hands of death. But it was Jude. He'd hold them regardless.

Griffin awoke with a startle when something slapped against his back with a hard thud. He turned to see Shank standing in the open doorway and his cheeks flushed furiously. Shank wore one slipper and the other had fallen to the floor after it struck Griffin.

"Get your ass up," they said. "There's been a problem at the castle."

Griffin shot upright immediately, pushing himself head-first out of sleep. He stumbled out of Jude's bed, struggling to slide on his boots again.

"What kind of problem?"

Jude stirred behind him, pushing the blankets down. "What's going on?"

"Just c'mon," they answered before disappearing down the hall and added with a shout, "we'll talk about this later."

Griffin and Jude piled into her parent's truck, one of the Department of Forest Management vehicles that they avoided utilizing for personal use unless in a case of emergency. Panic flared in his stomach when Griffin sat down in the back seat. What was so important that they wouldn't say, but dire enough to take the truck?

As they wound up the hill towards the castle, Griffin caught sight of the tall lancet windows that flanked both the upper and lower west wing. The glass had been punched out, leaving dark iron frames behind. He could see the vague shades of the tapestry and paintings on the walls opposite them. Like a bone jutting out when it should have stayed beneath the skin.

Shank was the one who spoke, "good gods."

They parked the truck outside the gate and ran through the frozen garden. Griffin shoved past Shank and Jude to push open the tall front doors.

Glass glittered across the rugs in blues and golds. Griffin's eyes widened as he looked down at them, careful with his footsteps as he walked down the lower west wing. The soles of his boots were thick enough to protect him from the punctures of shards but the sight alone made him wary. Repair crews carried ladders from one lancet window to the next after the empty frames leaking cold air were covered with boards nailed into the walls. Darkness gnawed deeper and deeper into the meat of Brightloch Castle with every pound of a hammer that left Griffin deeply unsettled.

"What happened here?"

He called out to no one in particular, so no one answered him. Shank and Jude were still in the foyer, talking in low voices and he knew they were trying to piece together the events on their own like his home was their damned puzzle. The leftmost door to the Great Hall opened and Yumi's head poked out. When she caught his eye, she stepped fully out with her hands on her hips.

"Griffin Porter-Mosley, where have you been? Do you realize the trouble we went through last night because we didn't know you weren't home?"

"No, because nobody has told me what happened."

The Ink Queen frowned and Griffin immediately regretted the attitude that drew her ire. He all but saw the angered steam rolling off her shoulders until she took a sharp inhale. *As you breathe in through your nose, contemplate if the words you are holding now are words you will have later,* he knew that she was running her own meditative advice through her mind as she took the breath. Griffin wondered if she began to regret her own platitudes.

But her demeanor did soften and she stood a little taller when she said, "there was a spiritual attack in the castle last night. A revenant named Todd set his sights on Kurosaki. He has been taken care of, but we were fearful that you were in danger until we realized that you were not home."

Griffin frowned. "Why did he want Kurosaki?"

"It is a very long and very complicated story," she answered truthfully. "If he wants to tell you himself, he will. But for now, it is not my business to share."

"Fair enough."

"Yumi, is everyone okay?"

Shank and Jude approached them. She looked past Griffin's

shoulder when she answered:

"We're all okay. Kuro is pretty shaken though, I haven't seen him yet this morning."

"Kurosaki's here? Would you like me to go find him for you?"

"No, I, uh, think it's probably fine."

Griffin had turned to look back at Jude's parent, but threw a bewildered look to Mimi. The stumble in her words was not like her at all.

"Griffin! I-" His father began his lecture as he hurried down the stairs above their heads.

Yumi's gaze slid up in his direction when she cut him off. "You're gonna have to be faster than that, Dad. We've already talked."

When Moz reached them, he held his hands on his hips in his posturing of authority that made Griffin roll his eyes every time. Moz had stopped paying mind to it long ago. He looked from Mimi to Griffin.

"There's still responsibility in adulthood, bud. Tell us where you're going next time. Especially nowadays, you know better than that."

"It was just to Jude's house. I've been there and back a million times, nothing ever happens."

"*Especially. Nowadays,*" Moz punctuated his point. "Shouldn't you be in class?"

"No, it's our off day." Truth be told, Griffin skipped class more and more frequently. More important matters had taken the form of cadavers and dreams that foretold them.

"Me and Griffin are just going to study since I'm here already,"

Jude quickly intervened. "Is that okay?"

Shank lifted an eyebrow. "Are your textbooks here?"

"Yes, a whole library, even."

"You study here and then you come home before sundown, understand?"

"Yes, Pa," Jude answered

Griffin followed Jude into the library. In one of the shelves closest to the wall of painted lancet windows, she had stashed copies of her textbooks so that she would always have some easily available to her when she spent time at Brightloch Castle. She was often quick to join Griffin in frowning at the lavishness expected of him only due to his bonus parent being the Queen, but this was the one luxury she would relish in time and time again: the books.

"I can't deal with these chairs right now, let's just go to the study," she said, clutching the textbooks to her chest. He looked back at the navy blue wingback chairs that flanked both lengths of a table in the middle of the library's nave.

"These are perfectly fine," he mumbled, but followed her anyway.

Jude sprawled across the floor of the study with her textbooks spread out around her like some strange halo of academia and one of the throw pillows from the couch stuffed hastily under her chest to support her. She lazily twirled a pen in her hand, the other propping up her head.

Griffin flinched when the phone suddenly rang. He heard the fast footfalls of his father striding down the hall, caught a glimpse of his tall shadow through the door frame, and the shrill noise stopped.

Moz spoke to the caller in low murmurs and Griffin wasn't sure if he intentionally tried to mask his half of the conversation from eavesdroppers. Shortly after, he heard the clack of the phone on the cradle and his father came back quickly in the doorframe.

"I need to go see your Aunt Maria," he said. "Stay put, okay?"

"At the coroner's office? Why?"

"She wouldn't say," Moz disappeared from the doorframe, seeking out his coat as he called out, "and I mean it. Stay home."

When he was out of earshot, Jude looked from the door to Griffin.

"We're not listening to him, are we?"

"Why start now," Griffin answered, already putting on his coat.

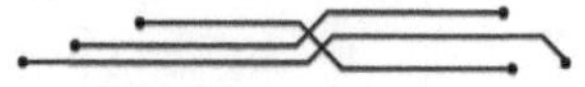

Tris,

Congratulations on retirement! I consider us a lucky world every time an exorcist gets to hang up the robe for good, but I'll count myself as particularly lucky that this time it is a dear friend.

And yet the sentiment feels silly, because I know the work will never truly be over for you. Because you are a good man who does good things, and sometimes that means putting a demon fucker down. I'll make my deposit to the Swear Jar next time I'm over, I promise.

I know they'll miss your special kind of magic at the Temple and I hope you find little ways to keep it every day. Take it easy, Big Guy.

Love,
Ave

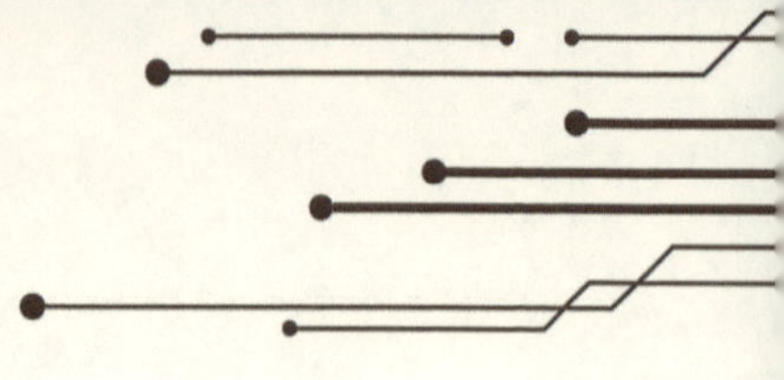

CHAPTER THIRTY-THREE
MOZ

"THANKS FOR RUSHING DOWN here," Maria said. She closed the door to the office and slid the latch lock. Immediately alarm bells went off in Moz's brain.

When she turned to face him, her back pressed against the door and she said in a hushed voice, "this was too sensitive of information for the phone."

"Holy shit, have I been tapped?"

Maria shook her head and rounded the desk before sitting down.

"No, don't be ridiculous."

She reached under her desk and unlocked the lowest drawer. She withdrew a manila file folder and smoothed her hands over it carefully with finely cut fingernails. Her lips pursed as she carefully chose her next words:

"I found something on the bones."

Moz perked up immediately, straightening in his chair before he leaned forward.

"What is it?"

She pulled out a photographic print and slid it across the desk to him. Moz gingerly took it in his hands, confused as to what he was looking at. He studied it until he found the shape of the top of a femur. He followed its curve downward, unsure what was so special about it. Just above the point where the bone would articulate with the patella plate, he found a series of scratches. They were faint and he held it closer to his face until he saw the letters:

B AB Y

His hand trembled when he looked up at Maria, watching him with a patient stare while she waited for his reaction.

"It's her... that's why you brought me here, that's what you're thinking, isn't it?"

"What do you think it means," she asked instead of answering.

"That's the name Riko gave her when she was bait at the soul harvesting operation. That's not common knowledge," he said and jabbed a finger into the paper to emphasize his point. "*This* is Avery sending a message she wants only us to understand. She knew this cadaver would go to you, she knew I would understand her message. Maria, it has to be her."

Maria remained quiet, not relenting to any infectious optimism he may have been giving off.

"How did this person die, did Avery kill them?"

Maria shook her head. "This woman died of exposure. There was no evidence of foul play at all. It is likely that Avery was the one who found and then moved the body somewhere it could be more easily found. If it was Avery at all, keep in mind."

If. He refused to accept that; it was her. And what kind of trouble was she in that she needed to send a message on a corpse, of all things?

"Who do you think she was trying to hide the message from? The police? The press?"

She paused for a thoughtful moment, spinning her ballpoint pen nimbly around her fingers. "Your guess is as good as mine. But I fear that this is another instance of your fearsome wife knowing something we don't."

The casual remark made it sink in for him. Someone who was dead couldn't take such drastic measures to stay one step ahead. And Maria wouldn't talk beyond hypotheticals if she believed that same someone to be dead.

"Maria... she's alive. Avery is fucking *alive!*"

"Now, wait a minute–"

He jumped out of the chair, pointing at her as he pushed back with, "No. This is it. This is what we've been waiting for! She's alive and when she's back, she's going to make all these fuckers' lives a living hell. Deservedly so."

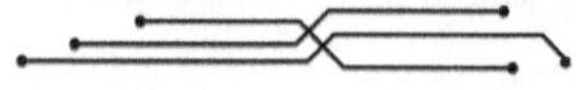

Soren,

Thank you so much for allowing me to be at the service today. I am very sorry for your loss and I admittedly don't know what the right things to say to comfort you are.

~~Harrison~~ Dad was in your life for so much longer than he was in mine and I wish I had a funny thing about him to remind you of. But I bet you have plenty of stories. Will you come visit your nephew and tell them to us? Only when you are feeling up to company, of course.

Love,
Avery

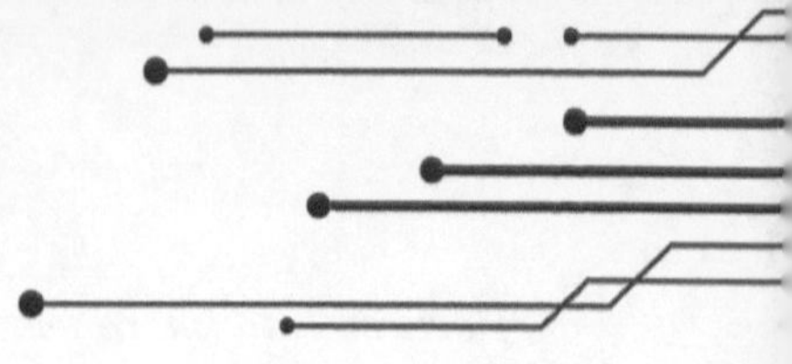

CHAPTER THIRTY-FOUR
GRIFFIN

His father emerged from the front door of the city's morgue and when Moz saw him sitting next to Jude on a sidewalk bench, he put his hands on his waist and turned his face to redirect his swearing elsewhere.

"Do you not hear me when I say to stay home?"

Griffin shrugged and narrowly avoided giving his father a shit-eating grin. "Thought I was hallucinating it. *Oops.*"

His father frowned deeply at him. Griffin knew he was going to pay for that comment later, somehow. Was there even a point to grounding if he could jump through portals with just a quick call to the Sills household?

"C'mon, we'll talk about this at home."

Griffin rolled his eyes, but rose to follow his father. He looked back over his shoulder to make sure Jude followed and she had opened her mouth like she was about to protest, but changed her mind. Jude trailed after him without a word.

As they made their way back towards the castle on the hill, a familiar face passed through the crowd of people. Moz stopped when Kurosaki caught sight of them and he stopped, changing his course altogether to walk towards his father.

"Where have you been?"

"An exorcist," Kurosaki answered like it was the simplest explanation and that Moz should have known better. His father frowned, the marred eyebrow lifted.

"With a gun?"

Kurosaki waved him off that time without answering.

His father opened his mouth to respond to Kurosaki's dismissal, but astonished gasps bubbled in the crowd around them before he could speak. They turned to seek out the source behind Griffin. Confusion washed over him when he saw a head rise above the crowd, slowly at first. Panic froze him in pins and needles when he saw the faded rose gold of her hair, framing her face in blunt lines that fell to her jaw.

The dream.

The woman launched into the air, hanging suspended ten feet above the tallest heads in the crowd. Screams turned Griffin's stomach as he watched in horror– *this is happening.*

She didn't scream, didn't fight– just hung frozen before her white sweater bloomed red at her torso. Blood dribbled over her lip and poured down her neck with frightening speed.

"CASSIE!"

His nerves ran cold when he realized this was someone his father recognized. Moz fought against the fleeing crowd to get to her and Griffin trailed close behind, unlatching the blades in his modified staff.

Cassie's body jerked, pulled forward from her center with a sickening crack, and her limp weight fell the great distance back to the ground with a wet thud.

His father froze at the edge of the cleared area and Griffin immediately understood why when he finally reached his side.

"Every forty-eight hours," his father murmured. Griffin counted backwards on his fingers: *Cassie, Theirrin, Tristan.*

He was right.

Around Cassie's mangled corpse were the same concentric circles, sigils wedged in between them in black smears across the cobblestones. Jude gasped when she caught up to them and threw her hand over her mouth.

Griffin stared at Cassie and Cassie's brown eyes stared blankly at the sky. He felt selfish for already thinking about how her unmoving freckled face would captivate his waking nightmares for the rest of his life. His father urged the crowd away and swatted at people who heartlessly gawked at the macabre scene.

So much blood...

Griffin barely caught sight of it through the shoulders of people passing in a frightened flurry: a warped rabbit mask watching him right back. He gripped his father's arm, trying to push him to look in the right direction.

"Dad, over there! That's it!"

Moz quickly drew his holstered gun and he bolted after the Rabbit. Without hesitation, Griffin followed his father through the crowd. Jude ran close behind with a squawking Creak overhead.

"Wait, Griffin!" She called out. "Stop!"

"Griffin, stay here!"

Moz shouted over his shoulder after Jude's plea tipped him off, but Griffin knew that he was in no position to hold firm when he had a suspect to tail. He chased after his father weaving in and out of foot traffic, ricocheting off shoulders of people who hadn't bothered to get out of his way.

He caught up to Moz, who was more angered than grateful for his presence.

"I said *stay back!*"

They both caught sight of the Rabbit at the same time, just as they dropped down through one of the many metal doors in the city leading down to the underground tunnel system.

"Shit," Moz swore, but didn't slow down.

They hurried to the door left open and Griffin peered into the gaping darkness in the street just as Moz began climbing down the rungs of the ladder that dropped down.

"Does this not feel like a trap to you?"

Moz looked up at him, both questioning and uneasy.

"Why would they want to trap anyone?"

Griffin shrugged and began climbing down after him.

"I said no, Griffin."

"You're gonna lose him," Griffin reminded his father. Moz grunted with frustration as his feet hit the wet stone floor of the tunnel. Griffin was shortly behind and held the swaying metal ladder as steady as he could for Jude when she descended after them.

"Your parents are gonna fuckin' kill me for letting you down here," his father lamented. But instead of pressing the fear any further, he pulled out the small flashlight that he kept in the same holster as his gun. He held up his gun in his right hand, the flashlight in his left crossed underneath the muzzle to shine a narrow beam of light into the damp passageway.

"We'll never catch up to them this way," Jude said quietly. "What if we go to the other end of the tunnel and cut them off that way?"

"It branches off in a few places," his father answered. "It would be a gamble, but we can try."

Jude nodded and split the air. The beam from Moz's flashlight fell square in the center of the portal and ended abruptly, reflecting none of the light back at them. Griffin watched in awe, remembering how the light had once been accidentally shone in his face and he saw floating spots in his vision for an hour after the fact.

Moz started towards the wound in space, but Jude stopped him. "You're gonna want to follow me on this one."

They followed Jude into the portal and the sound of dripping water was replaced with the pounding of blood in his ears. The silence made his body feel so loud and he still wasn't used to such a thing when there was constant chattering in his mind. He felt better when his father remained silent, like even the Sentinel was unnerved by the void.

Griffin followed them out of the portal, but when he stepped back into the damp air, he stood alone in the darkness. He whirled around, looking in what little light leaked into the tunnel through the seams of the metal manhole above his head. Water dripped from the snowy slush on the street above and the droplets struck the water around his feet in an eerie melody.

"Hello? Dad? Jude?"

No one.

Panic bloomed in his throat.

"HELLO?!"

Nothing.

"Shit, shit, shit, shit, shit."

-Oh, my-

"Oh, fuck off, you clown!"

He felt far less concerned about responding to the disembodied voices when there was no one else around to strike off the behavior as being bizarre. Griffin already knew it was and therefore he gave himself the permission. In a way it felt easier to keep his panic from running wild when he had somebody - *nobody?* - to redirect his frustration to.

Griffin had no way of finding out where the portal had spat him out. He had only been in the tunnels once before. It was on a dare from some of the boys in his grade eleven cohort, which didn't pay off in friendships like he had hoped at the time because he could not even recall their names or how many of them there had been. But if he remembered correctly, there were signs down below to designate what street names were up above.

He started walking forward and tried not to think about what might have been in the water he heard splashing beneath his boots.

Please don't be piss, please don't be piss, I'll be a good guy but please *do not let that be piss.*

Griffin stopped when he heard the whistling. He couldn't tell whether or not it echoed off the rounded stone walls around him. Straining his eyes, he saw the vague darkness that suggested where the tunnel headed deeper and deeper, but he couldn't make out anything else.

One.

He could just count it down.

Two.

Then things would be fine.

Three.

It couldn't be much longer before he found his father and Jude, right?

Four.

Is this how it felt to be the legendary elslith? Trapped in a dark cavern with only sound to find your bearings? Was he the monster or the disembodied tune?

Five.

But the whistling didn't fall into silence like he had expected. It echoed, taking up the same space in the collective reality that he did.

"Fuck," he swore.

-Hello.-

He did not answer his hallucination that time and froze when he heard the distinct sound of splashes in the probably-piss-water getting louder and louder. Whoever it was, they were moving towards him.

Griffin stepped carefully to dampen his splashes as he pressed his back against the nearest wall of the tunnel. He had nowhere to run to, but if he was lucky, he could make himself scarcely visible and pray that it gave him even a sliver of an advantage. His fingers tightened around the center of his staff and he was grateful this time that the metal blades were already engaged, leaving no need to give himself away with the small *shink* of sliding steel.

Before he had the chance to truly prepare himself, he saw the white shape of the Rabbit mask in the dark.

Fuck, fuck, fuck, fuck, fuck.

Despite the fear, he bolstered his posture by widening his shoulders before he dove at them with a swinging staff. But the splashes gave him away before he could land contact and their focus zeroed in on him, dodging the trajectory of his weapon.

Fighting in the small crack of light filtering in from the metal manhole above, Griffin struggled to land his blows. To his dismay, the darkness did not falter his opponent and they landed strike after strike on his staff with cracking blows from their steel shortsword. He began to panic. Griffin would be pissed if he died here; *probably literally.*

A hard swing came at him unexpectedly and the force of the jolt knocked his staff out of his hands. He stumbled backwards, trying to put as much space between him and the Rabbit as he could but it only put him further away from where his staff laid useless in the tunnel's waters. He fell onto his hands, skittering backwards in the murky water to pull him away as fast as he could go.

Griffin shouted in knee-jerk fear when the Rabbit dove for him and his staff was out of reach. He braced himself to the slash of the shortsword and squeezed his eyes shut.

Loud cracks of gunfire echoed in the tunnel and Griffin saw the bright flashes of light through his eyelids, stunning him in bright yellows. Blistering sound rang in his eardrums and left him in a numb sensory daze. The heavy weight of a body splashed in front of him and the impact he had expected never came.

Griffin opened his eyes, one before the other in caution. Light fell on the figure emerging from the mouth of the adjoining tunnel. Kurosaki lowered his rifle, dropping a hand to extend and help Griffin to his feet.

"Are you okay? Where's your dad?"

Griffin pulled himself up with the help, flinging mud off his fingers in disgust as Kurosaki wiped his own on his coat.

"We got separated when we came out of Jude's portal, I don't know where either of them are. What are you doing here?"

He watched Kurosaki adjust the strap of his rifle, swinging it onto his back after he had engaged the safety. Kurosaki lifted the flashlight that Griffin hadn't noticed had been dangling at his side, tied to a loop on his trousers and left illuminated.

"Remember how you were shouting not too long ago? We actually heard you up there."

"Where's 'up there'?"

"You're just a little bit south of the town square, the crowd dispersed a little bit to let the cops in. Now whether or not that's where you all entered the tunnels, I don't know. I lost sight of you three."

"I think we ran east, but I'm not really sure."

Before Kurosaki could respond, a split in the air spit out Moz and Jude further down the tunnel. The flashlight beam from his father backlit Kurosaki before he turned around. As Griffin lifted a hand to shield his face from the sudden light in the darkness, Moz lowered his gun.

"Fuckin' hell, what happened? Are you okay?"

Griffin looked from his father to the Rabbit's corpse at their feet. Moz sucked in a breath.

"Was hoping to take this one alive," he mumbled. "But at least we all saw what we're dealing with: humans. To at least some extent."

"Does that mean it's going to fall to the police?"

"The fuck it will," Moz answered Kurosaki sharply. "After what we just saw up there with Cassie? No, that's going to be the Sentry working overtime."

Griffin reached out a boot slowly to nudge the body with his toes, but Kurosaki held up a hand to stop him.

"Don't touch them," he said. "Moz, take them to the surface. I'll stay with the body while you alert the cops."

Moz frowned. "Sure, *love* dealing with those guys."

Despite the protest, he strode towards the metal ladder behind where the faulty portal had spat out Griffin. He gave it a shake, testing its stability. When it screeched under the jostle, he added:

"Up we go, Jude."

Griffin followed her up the ladder, letting her climb most of the way before he challenged the whining metal with his weight.

"Hey, Dad?"

Moz sucked in a breath when he climbed back to the surface after them. He wiped tunnel grime off his palms and onto his coat with a scowl.

"Yeah, bud?"

"That's not the same guy from Theirrin's house."

Moz dropped his hands and stared at Griffin. Maybe he first

waited for Griffin to explain how the weapons used were different, or that this Rabbit was much shorter than the first. But he didn't.

"*Fuck*," Moz turned his head in the opposite direction to look back at the entry to the tunnel.

His father was quick to flag down an officer, however begrudgingly he might have done so, and it wasn't long before the tunnels below were swarming with uniforms and yellow cordoning tape.

Griffin watched with Jude from a distance. Creak swooped and landed on her shoulder and she kept still, the sudden close of his talons around her limbs no longer startling her. The raven garbled a laugh at the grim scene.

"*My, my! This is getting fun!*"

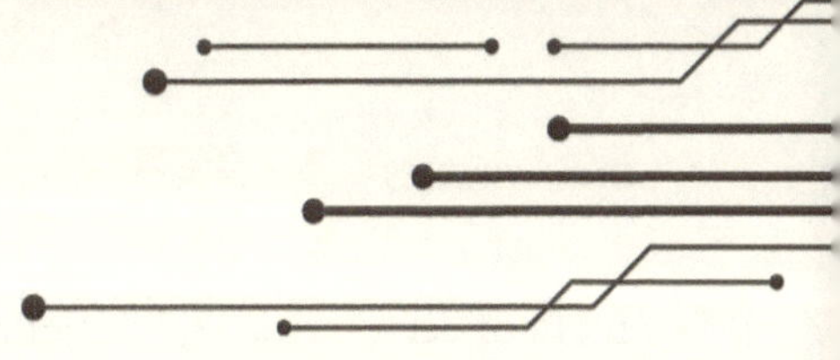

CHAPTER THIRTY-FIVE
GRIFFIN

GRIFFIN HAD NO REASON at all to be at the press conference, but he understood that there were unspoken expectations of him put in place by the Queen's advisory staff and whoever else might have been in attendance. Chairs were packed tightly in the west wing Great Hall and filled with stiff pressed suits and crisp notepads.

Mimi stood at a podium, on her feet and off the ceremonial throne. Moz flanked her on the left, his arms tucked behind his back and a serious stare under his glasses as his gaze slid from face to face before him.

"The Sentry will be working in cooperation with the Brightloch Police Department," the Queen continued to address the press before her. "With three victims in a window of only a week, I ask for the people of Brightloch to please allow them the space to investigate until we can bring justice to the perpetrator."

"How can we expect you to capture the perpetrator when you couldn't even bring justice to your own missing wife, presumed dead?"

Yumi froze.

"You have been so worried about aid to Westfall and their onslaught of demon attacks," the journalist continued, "that you have turned a blind eye to the happenings in your own kingdom. Will you even act when people are dying?"

Griffin rose in his seat. Anger burned red on the edges of his vision and faces turned to look at him as he was gathering the words to shout at the reporter.

Instead, his father spoke with a loud clarity to settle the room again: "Griffin, please sit down."

He hesitated, but Griffin finally sank back down into his seat. When faces turned forward and off of him, Moz gently nudged his way behind the podium. His father was not attempting to speak for Yumi because he felt she was incapable of answering the question, but he recognized when a nerve had been mercilessly struck too deep.

Mama was always that nerve.

"Need I remind you," Moz spoke with a slowness that built intimidation, "that it was a decision made by the Cabinet, against the wishes both of Her Majesty and Her Diplomatic Advisor. Constituents such as yourself were incredibly vocal about re-allocating resources and withdrawing from the investigation of Avery Porter's disappearance. Has two years been so long for you that you have forgotten? Because I promise you, it has been much longer for our family."

An uncomfortable silence settled over the Great Hall.

Moz looked down at Yumi, saying something quiet that wasn't meant for anyone's ears but hers. Griffin saw her nod and Moz shrank back, letting Mimi resume her place at the podium.

"The perpetrators have been described as wearing black clothing and concealed their face using a white plastic mask of a rabbit's head. We know of two incidents fitting this profile, however, officials suspect there may be more in a manner of organized attacks. If you encounter anyone matching this description, please do not engage and alert the nearest possible official. Thank you for your time."

The Great Hall erupted with reporters flinging questions left and right, but the Queen answered none of them as she hurried from the Hall with Sentinel Mosley trailing behind her dutifully.

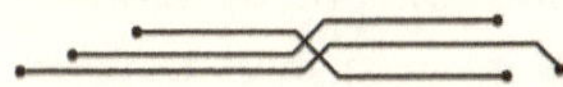

"Jude, will you go to the beach with me? I can't sleep and I just really want to sketch."

Static popped on the other end of the line and Griffin knew Jude was probably staring at her own bedroom wall incredulously in his stead.

"Are you fucking kidding me?"

"I just want one more night of normal," he said into the phone.

There was a pause and faint crackle on the quiet line.

"Griff... you were there today, it's not safe," Jude said softly.

"If anything happens, we'll just portal right out. It's not a big deal."

Jude was quiet.

"Please?" He heard the small huff of her considering before he added: "One sketch and we're out. Okay?"

"Fine," she finally relented. "One sketch."

The line went dead and he smiled. No sooner than it took for him to put the phone back on its receiver, the air behind him began to churn ice cold.

Jude brushed off her trousers as she stepped through, noticeably missing a corvid.

"I was already getting drowsy," she said, "but that certainly didn't help. You owe me."

"I'll add it to my tab."

She grimaced at him and gave his shoulder a playful shove. Griffin followed her back into the portal, staring at her right hand as she guided him through the pitched dark.

There's no harm in just reaching out and–

On the other side, the moonlight shone so brightly that he could have sworn he felt it burn on his cheeks. The lapping waves of the Stillmaw Sea glittered as they broke on the shore, tempered down in size by the rock jetty that jutted out of the harbor.

He followed her down to the seawall, stepping over to take a seat atop the sarsen bricks.

"How's this?"

Griffin tried to not let his gaze wander to her when he answered, "picturesque."

Jude sat beside him once she was sure that he wasn't going to change his mind and scout out another spot to sit. He flicked his gaze around to make sure they were alone and scanned for an errant rabbit mask. The only thing he found was the gnarled shape of a tree, jutting out of the hillside where he knew it didn't belong.

"I'll keep an eye out for you, I've got my, what are you laughing at?"

Jude stopped when he laughed at the misplaced hallucination.

"Brains," he said and turned back to the water, opening his sketchbook and withdrawing the new willow charcoals from his birthday. Griffin let the stick hover over the toothy page as he contemplated. His gaze flicked up to the water, over to the jetty beyond Jude, and the moon. Only one of those felt worthwhile.

He turned to face Jude's direction, straddling the seawall and began to sketch. Jude looked at him incredulously and he decided he wasn't going to bother lying to her about the artistic quality of a heap of beach rocks beyond her shoulder. When the look faded, she gazed out on the water and sat in the quiet with him with a sweet patience.

His cheeks flushed warm when he sensed her eyes flick down in his direction but he made a great mental effort to not look up unless he absolutely needed to reference the shape of her cheekbones or the way the light of the moon illuminated her from behind. Despite the ledger, despite the portals, despite the murders, she felt so *safe* to Griffin.

Griffin stopped when he looked up and Jude had turned her head. He looked down at the charcoal sketch, trying to calculate whether or not he could complete the portrait study as she was. But her curls masked too much of her face with the way she looked up the darkened coastline and the moon wasn't hitting her quite right anymore.

He sighed, "Jude, you moved."

She flinched in her seated position on the sea wall and turned back towards him, jutting her chin out too far as she tried to resume the position she sat in when he had started to sketch.

"Sorry, is this better?"

"Not quite, could you tuck your chin in a little and turn about five degrees to the right?"

"Five degrees? At this point, just pose me where you need me if you're going to be that particular."

Griffin huffed a small laugh; his big-brained engineer friend couldn't figure out how far to turn? He set his sketchbook down on the other side of him on the sea wall ledge before he wiped his hands as best he could on his coat to prevent the charcoal from smearing on Jude's face.

When he turned back to her, she waited with the same exaggerated posture of her chin with a stifled laugh on her mouth.

"You goof," he muttered when he gently took her face in his hands.

Griffin carefully turned her face, studying the way the moon cast light on the edges of her cheeks and threw shadows on her mouth. The gesture had been purely objective, just for the sake of finishing what he had started.

But she threw the gaze of her brown eyes back at him and Griffin froze, still holding her face with care. The look had made him nervous before, but he had never felt the way his heart pounded hard enough that she could perhaps feel the nervous pulse through his fingertips. He decided that he would add the sketch to the failed attempt pile because nothing he could ever do with the nub of willow charcoal would translate the way she looked. He couldn't flatten her to spread across a page when she was so real and vibrant in his hands.

"Jude," he murmured her name.

She nodded, gingerly setting her notebook on her lap and she lifted a hand to hold around Griffin's.

He hesitated when he leaned towards her, starting and stopping twice when he half expected her to whack him across the face with the journal.

What are you doing, she would demand. *We're friends.*

But no protest came and Jude held still as he worked out the last of his hesitation and kissed her. She felt softer than a dream, warmer than sunshine. Jude kissed him with a slow tenderness that mirrored his own.

Oh fuck, I'm kissing Jude.

It was the wordless voices that floated behind him, not the thought, that pulled him back into awareness and he parted from her. Griffin didn't turn to the source of the sound; he knew he would find nothing and it was far more preferable to watch the light of awe in Jude's eyes sparking and flaming before his own.

"Did you get the pose," she whispered, her half-grin inches from his face.

Griffin laughed, small but sincere. He changed his mind about discarding the sketch into the rubbish, but he wasn't going to finish it either. This image of Jude would be his favorite.

"Yeah, I got it."

Jude laughed a small, sweet sound and kissed him again. He had known she smelled of lavender, but the scent made him weak in the knees at this close proximity when she held a hand to his cheek. Griffin's head wobbled with wooziness, his heart raced, and he felt only mostly sure it was truly happening.

When she broke the kiss, she looked at him with her hand still cradling his face as she asked, "how long were you waiting for that?"

"A minute, I think."

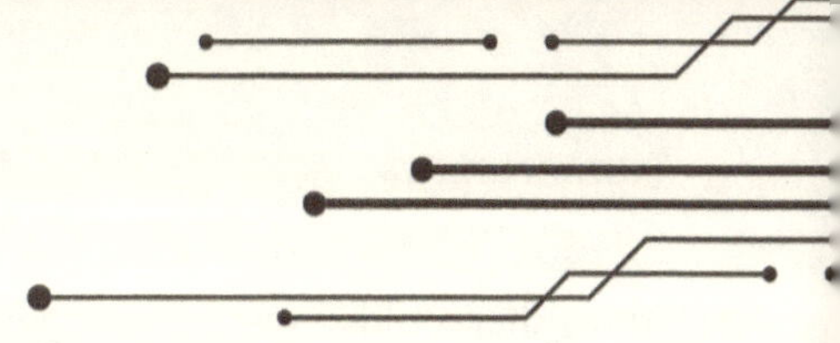

CHAPTER THIRTY-SIX
AVERY - 96 HOURS AGO

VERY WAITED WITH HELD breath under the Borrowed invisibility Mercy had taken from the young witch at the Reaper Outpost and for the first time, she hoped it wouldn't hold. Mercy stood beside her, their hand gripping her elbow, and together they watched Moz approach the corpse.

"He is very handsome," Mercy noted with dry fondness.

The cloak wouldn't mute their voices, but it did muffle them into near nothingness if their words were kept close.

She thought of the way Moz used his whole body to smile. The boyish grin would reach his evergreen eyes and set them ablaze. His shoulders would straighten out and he would lean forward like he had wanted the infection of his joy to spread quicker. Moz was a lovely and happy thing on most days, but he was a far cry from it now.

Avery watched him crouch down in front of the corpse and lay his gun down in the snow. Even from far away, she swore she saw the purple smears of fatigue under his eyes. When was the last time he had gotten a full night of sleep? His obvious restlessness was her fault and she was well aware. She would have given almost anything to smooth the worry out of his face with her fingertips, but that one thing she would never surrender was the safety granted to Griffin by keeping her head down.

"Very," she agreed softly. "You should see him when he's happy."

"You said you have a son together. Any daughters?"

Avery managed a smile and a small huff of laughter escaped her nose as she playfully nudged them with her shoulder. Mercy did not so much as sway from the shove.

"Who are those two?"

She looked to Moz's younger brother, standing back hesitantly while he fixed his gaze on the skeletal remains Avery had left for them to find. His blond hair had long ago been shaved close to the scalp and his jaw had whittled into a deceptively serious fix with age. Anyone might have been taken aback with how it had gotten there with his typical sunny demeanor, but Avery knew the truth.

"Shaved head is Jack. He was Moz's familiar and elected to stay when he was Saved. They are brothers now."

Beside her husband stood Izaya and Avery couldn't remember thinking of him as being remarkably handsome before, but it was undeniable now. His dark brows furrowed and his sharp jaw had set into a serious frown as he looked down at the bones. She wondered if he had ever sported long hair and a beard before she had known him, but strongly doubted it. This seemed to be his season of bloom.

"And that's Kurosaki. I'm quite surprised to see him, he hasn't been around in years. But he is a very good friend we've all missed terribly much."

Avery watched a man with ice blonde hair approach them, his hands shoved deep in the pockets of his peacoat unlike the uniform bombers that his officers wore. Disgust rolled up her spine and she prayed that Moz wouldn't surrender too much information to the man. He looked different from ground level than he did from her perches in the trees and Avery couldn't quite hear what he had said to Moz.

But Moz's angry voice carried well in his answer as he stood:

"No, dipshit. I don't recognize these threadbare clothes. It would have been really fucking *useful* if you idiots had found her sooner. Maybe then we'd have more to go on than this," she watched him jab a pointed finger into the man's chest. "I don't know why the fuck they put you in charge or where Woods went, but this has been utter fucking bullshit. What kind of fucking idiot asks someone to identify their wife's body and assess the scene in the same fucking go?"

Who's Woods?

"Don't touch me, Mosley. You don't want to go down that road with me."

Moz grinned, sinister and daring, and she saw Kurosaki's eyes widen like a horrified fawn.

"I paved that road, you son of a bitch."

"Get his ass, love," Avery whispered.

The man left and her boys talked in lower voices. Avery stepped closer slowly to hear them and pulled Mercy with her by the elbow. They let her without protest; Mercy knew the Cabin had left Avery rattled and that she looked to them as her lifeline. Avery was okay with that now.

Look closer - Avery urged her husband in her mind. He was standing at full height, nowhere near careful enough in his inspection to see the etching on the femur bone. She knew it would be easily found by her diligent sister-in-law, but she would have much preferred for Moz to see the message sooner rather than later.

A twig snapped behind them.

All heads, cloaked and visible, turned to the forest. Avery couldn't pick out where the sound had come from in the blanket of grey tucking the alders into the bed of winter.

"Demon," Mercy whispered.

"Don't talk about yourself that way," Avery whispered back.

Mercy shoved her hard, but kept their fingers gripped on her arm. They pulled her away from the men and assessed the trees to seek out the source.

"Moz, there!"

Avery's stomach dropped when she heard Jack's voice. She whirled around and he was pointing into the woods in the complete opposite direction from where she had walked with Mercy. Her eyes followed and no sooner than it took for her to catch sight of the antlered demon, the first pops of gunfire cracked.

"Jack, guard the body!"

"You *idiot,*" Avery shouted. She didn't care if she was heard, but no one reacted to her voice except for Mercy digging their nails through her utility jacket. "I'll find another way! You need to go!"

The beast was upon them quickly when none of their shots were landing. Avery ripped herself out of Mercy's grip and lifted her own rifle. Stealth be damned; she wasn't leaving them to the monsters when she was *right. There.*

With a thrash of the head, the demon threw Moz hard into the tree behind him. Her stomach dropped when she saw just how close he had come to being gored by bleeding antlers. Mercy shoved the barrel of her gun down.

"Don't fire," they commanded. "The unaccounted shot will only confuse them and make things worse."

Avery hesitated. But she put the gun down– just as Moz lowered his own.

"No, Stupid Hair, what are you doing?"

She had to do something, anything, to save Moz from his own stupid plan, whatever it was. Hurriedly, she reached down and grabbed a fallen branch at the base of the oak nearest where they watched. Avery slapped the tree branch with a loud *thwack!* against the frozen trunk and she watched the demon turn its head away from Moz to seek out the source of the sound. She almost expect- ed Moz to look around in confusion, but to her relief, he stayed focused. He didn't lift his gun; he was too busy looking at the lethal-sized icicles dangling precariously above his head.

"C'mon, love," she urged him in a low voice from afar. "Kill 'em dead."

In the narrow window of advantage she had created, a spear of ice soared from above and pierced through the demon. Blood splattered in inky black and her stomach sank again seeing the matter cover Moz's face. Her jaw dropped and the branch fell from her fingertips.

What just happened?

"You're telling me you did that," she heard Kurosaki's question- ing astonishment after he had approached to examine the demon's cadaver. "Without a Knight?"

"Well, fuck," Mercy was the one who swore that time.

Avery turned to them and she felt her own face twisted in a cold and fierce determination.

"We need to fix it *now*. Shit is about to hit the fan and I need to be home when it happens."

Mercy didn't turn their head away from the men, but she saw their dark eyes slide in her direction. "Just be patient a little longer. I'll take you home when it is time."

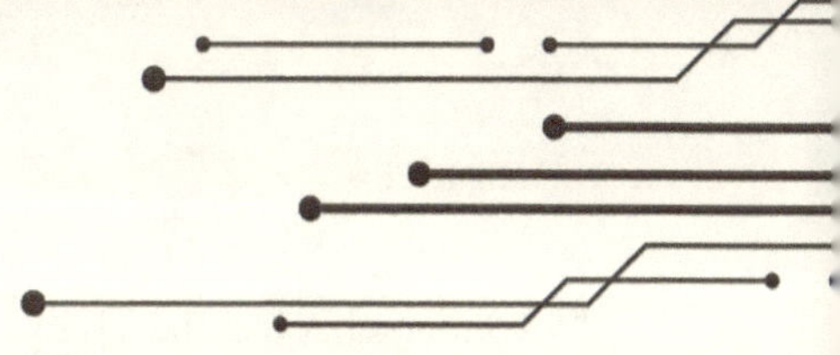

CHAPTER THIRTY-SEVEN
MORI

T HE CHILD DID NOT look up when the small shink of silver spurs announced Mori's arrival. She was far more engrossed with her game of catch for one, lying on her back across a stone bench as she tossed a ball stolen from the land of the living long ago. It made a satisfying *whack* each time Kiki caught it in her palm with ease as Mori wedged herself into the space left on the bench. Mori figured she had about ten seconds before the young girl started to whine again about being bored. She was the last to have her most recent Reaper saved, a bright-eyed girl named Ainsley, and still neither of them had been tasked with another to oversee.

Od was holding her breath. For what, Mori did not know.

Kiki caught the ball, but did not toss it again. She craned her head backwards to look at Mori behind her and stared; violet eyes cast in chartreuse.

"I'm ready to go topside," she stated, very matter-of-fact. "I miss Jack."

"You may be ready for the topside," Mori answered the child frozen in time, "but the topside isn't ready for you."

Kiki stared at her blankly, holding her for a long moment before she turned her focus back up and tossed the ball.

"I wonder what Jack-Jack is like as an old man," she said, glossing over Mori's comment completely. "He's gotta be at least a hundred by now."

Mori glanced up at the green clocktower without moving her head.

"Thirty-six."

"Same thing."

Everyone was old to a child like Kiki, no matter that she had roamed Od for just as long as Mori had. She decided that the Beldam took pity on Izaya Kurosaki and assigned the lightest demon she had on hand to the impossible weight of his burden to keep him docile and pliant.

And it had worked; Kiki was a beloved creature. The gunman Reaper had no hesitation in putting her first, even before his own true love when the sacrifice was demanded of him. Mori the Python was loved, but Alice Nielsen seemed to love martyrdom more.

"How much longer until you think that thing is full?"

That time, Mori turned around to face the wooden effigy looming in the square at the base of the Necropolis vault. At the base of the towering and featureless humanoid, three silhouetted spirits milled about aimlessly within the confines of a circular boundary in iron shackles while two sets of chains lay on the cobble. Waiting uselessly for their future captives.

She didn't think Balthazar had even seen the structure yet; the Gatekeeper was off doing whatever it was he did to avoid Keeping Gates. Mori had assumed it was striking tenuous deals with hesitant girls on behalf of Mona, but his protege seemed far more suited to the task. Mercy was a wild and clever thing who moved through any world with utmost ease. Damned, Saved, mortal — it didn't matter. They feasted on borrowed power as if they had none of their own by birthright.

It would be any moment before the next one appeared, for the first three came in a reliably timed sequence.

It started with the exorcist, Tristan Díomasaigh.

Then the witch who specialized in secrets, Theirrin Marshall.

Then the pyrokinetic one, Cassandra Glen.

Who will be next? And why?

"Next one should be any minute. The last will be within the next seventy-two hours."

A small drip of time wouldn't have even registered on the clock tower, but Mori looked anyway. No numbers, no notches. Just idle bones on a glowing green face set into black brick. She dreamed of them spinning faster and faster until they freed themselves from the gears and shattered on the stone into a million shards of old calcium. Mori longed for freedom from the dredges of time passing her by.

As she turned back to where Kiki laid on the stone bench, she saw the slinky form emerge from the glowing fog. Mori frowned.

"It's not like you to be late."

Aegis sneered at her as he approached with his clawed hands shoved deep into his trouser pockets. "I was *busy*."

"I keep telling you: if you stop licking yourself, the furballs will stop," Mori jabbed at him while studying her claws to best convey her disinterest. Kiki snorted, but Aegis was unbothered.

"That's the thing, Snake," he answered. "That's not what happens up there for us. No assignment? No fur and scales."

Mori dropped her hand and looked up at him. Aegis already watched her with golden crescent moons in place of irises and a sharp-toothed grin told her that he knew just how much this information would captivate her. She knew she threw a wrench in his carefully-planned stage directions he had worked out in his mind for this entire interaction when she looked over her shoulder to the effigy.

"The fuck is going on up there," she muttered.

"That's what I'm trying to figure out," Aegis answered, despite Mori not asking for one. "But as usual, it's coming back to Team Knight."

Mori buried her face in her clawed hands. "For fuck's sake... I should have known. Not my tomb, not my corpse."

Whack - Kiki caught the ball. "I did like them. They were fun. I liked when Mozzy painted my fingernails."

"Then you'll be delighted to hear your favorite Reaper has returned," Aegis said. Mori looked up from her hands.

Kiki bolted upright, dropping the ball, and paid it no mind when it began to roll downhill. "Kuro! Why? What's happening? Is he okay?"

"I think you should come see for yourself."

Kiki's face lit up and Mori scowled. "Aegis, I'm not playing babysitter while you galavant around like—"

"Would you rather suffer another moment of the child's boredom?"

Mori's eyes slid to Kiki. They were only just finishing up the repairs from the last time the child demon had gone mad from idleness and set the Necropolis elslith loose just to see what would happen. It worked; they certainly weren't *bored*. And the elslith wasn't hungry anymore. But Mori would have greatly preferred to avoid that again. Kiki grinned at her like she knew exactly what her elder was thinking and wanted Mori to remember that she was, in fact, capable of destruction.

Mori sighed.

"Let me tie up some ends here first."

Kiki shot up from the bench with her arms thrown in the air as she ran downhill after the ball.

"TOPSIDE!"

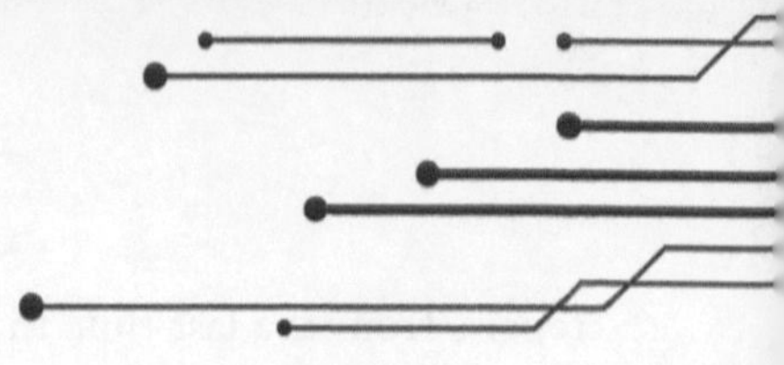

CHAPTER THIRTY-EIGHT
MOZ

MOZ RIFLED THROUGH THE papers on the floor, spread out in ways that he knew only made sense in his mind and prayed to whoever was listening that no one would step into his office and send them scattering in all directions. He searched furiously on his hands and knees, old and rough carpet biting into his palms as he scanned over the files of all of the victims. He shouldn't have to look at Tristan's face in such a disgrace.

He threw the empty manila folder and his frustration only worsened when it fluttered down unsatisfyingly. Since the attack on Yumi's capabilities at the press conference, he hadn't calmed down. He knew the hurt; Yumi wasn't the only one who was failing.

"I never have what I FUCKING NEED!"

Moz stood up, rubbing his hands on his jacket to soothe the burn in the meat of his palms. He stepped carefully over a kaleidoscope of papers to the corkboard on the wall– now completely covered with printed photographs of all the murder scenes from multiple angles.

A copy of the rendering his son had made of the concentric circles and sigils sat at its center, blown up in size so that it had an easier time mocking Moz with its mystery.

"You fucking bastard," Moz said to the arcane circle. The circle did not answer him.

He scoffed.

"Who drew you... what is that *shit* going on? Those aren't Mona's sigils, definitely not Balthazar's. So tell me... who's the bitch?"

"**You're the bitch**," the circle said finally.

"*I'm* the bitch? I didn't draw that shit! I didn't kill those kids!"

"**I did and you helped**," the circle answered.

"No, you didn't kill them either! Someone drew you for some purpose I don't fucking know and then vanished, I don't know who you belong to. Or why this is happening. So can you just tell me?"

"**No, fuck you**," the circle said.

"You fucking—"

Moz stopped. He stared at the corkboard.

"Fucking hell, I need to sleep."

The circle said nothing.

He rubbed his face and turned his back to the corkboard, stepping carefully over papers like he danced across stones in a river to make his way to his office door. When he stepped out into the hall and shut the door slowly behind him, he found several faces staring at him.

One of them was Kurosaki, looking up from a folder spread across the coffee table in the break area. His eyebrow arched in something resembling concern.

"You okay? We all heard you shouting."

Enraged embarrassment bubbled in Moz's blood and instead of answering Kurosaki, he stormed down the hall towards the front door. He heard footsteps following him just before he burst out onto the snowy front stairs of the Sentry.

He felt unsure where he had planned on going, maybe nowhere at all. But he needed to feel the cold bite of the snow on his face to help soothe the hot shame he felt in his cheeks. The door behind him kicked open and he heard the crunch of boots on snow approaching him.

"Hey, are you okay," Kurosaki asked him gently.

He felt the soft weight of Kurosaki's fingers just above his elbow, again a warm anchor for Moz to hold onto in his washing tide of anger. But it wasn't comforting this time and felt more like a gesture intended to placate an agitated child. He was burning his candle at both ends and all Kurosaki had to offer was backhanded commentary.

Moz spun around. "What the fuck was that in there? Is this funny to you? I'm busting my ass in there trying to get this shit worked out, I'm not a fucking animal in a cage for you to gawk at for entertainment."

"I'm sorry, I wasn't meaning to imply this was entertaining for me, it's just that every one of us heard you—"

"Oh fuck off with that, I'm not going to—"

"No Moz, *you* fuck off with that," Kurosaki's face was pulled into a fierce frown and the soft brown in his eyes had darkened as he glared at Moz. "I'm not going to let you say shit to me just because you need to work off your frustration. Come find me when you're done."

With that, Kurosaki yanked open the door and disappeared inside again. Moz watched him through the narrow window in the door until he vanished from his line of sight. When he did, he turned forward and looked up at the falling snow before he shut his eyes.

He took a deep breath.

"Fuck."

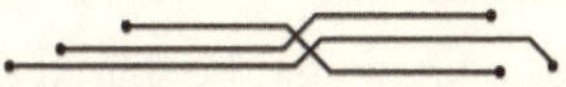

Moz woke up with his face on his desk for the second time in a row. When had he fallen asleep again?

It was quiet in the office and even without windows, Moz decided it must have been in the early hours of the morning if none of his reports had arrived yet. Bless them all, none of them knew how to move quietly if stealth wasn't of utmost importance.

He rose from his chair, nearly falling when the wheels rolled a little too fast from underneath him, and carefully stepped over his scattered papers on the floor to make his way to the bathroom. When he opened the door his feet kicked something small on his first step through the threshold of his office. Moz looked down and saw the wooden lunch container and knocked over metal vacuum flask at his feet.

Puzzled, he bent down to pick them up and looked around. His office looked out across an empty hallway and into the break room. A coffee table was decorated with a clear glass vase and an arrangement of juniper berries and pine for the Iverne season. Several leather chairs were set around it with a couch pushed against the wall. On that couch, a figure laid with their face towards the back of the couch frame and a black jacket draped over them from the neck to knee like a makeshift blanket.

Moz sighed quietly and put the food Kurosaki had left for him back in his office.

He knew he didn't deserve the kindness after the way he had treated Kurosaki. Moz wanted to blame his outburst on The Thing– or its absence– but he knew that he shared the blame with no one. That was all him.

Still he was impressed that Kurosaki snapped right back and Moz *prayed* that he had shown the same bite of tenacity dealing with Todd. Hoped he hadn't taken that shit lying down.

Thinking about his own poor behavior so shortly before Todd's, Moz knew he had to make things right. If that meant Kurosaki leaving and never speaking to him again, so be it.

Sure, it'd hurt like a bitch but I'd deserve it a thousand times over. Kurosaki didn't deserve a single ounce of unkindness in his life ever again.

When Moz came back from the bathroom, he took a detour into the break room, and knelt down next to the couch. He put a gentle hand on Kurosaki's arm and he stirred, mostly asleep still.

"Hey," Moz said in a soft murmur. "You should go home and get some sleep in a real bed."

Kurosaki stretched out his long legs but didn't even open his eyes when he answered back in a mumbled, "no."

"How does you hurting your back sleeping on a couch help Tristan?"

Kurosaki stirred again, rolled onto his back, and rubbed his eyes.

"It helps if I make sure you stay fed and functioning. It doesn't help him if you whittle yourself down to nothing or burn at both ends for days."

"You're not my personal chef nor my caretaker, I'm sure there's a million other things you could do to—"

"Would you just shut the fuck up and let somebody care about you?"

Moz was still when Kurosaki lowered his hand to glare at him. It wasn't antagonistic, but the glare of someone who was fully aware that they had won an argument without possibility of rebuttal. The jab had been sharp but meant to defend something soft.

"I'm sorry about earlier," Moz said quietly. "When I snapped at you. You didn't deserve that."

"No, I didn't," Kurosaki agreed and Moz felt the hot bite of shame again in the blood of his cheeks. "And thank you, I forgive you."

Moz smiled small at him and they sat in a moment of quiet. Like they were testing the comfort of silence again to make sure that nothing between them had been damaged beyond repair.

Kurosaki didn't fuss; didn't look away. Just watched him with brown eyes that had only just begun to blink away sleep. Moz brushed two fingers across his cheek, pushing away a lock of hair that clung to his short beard. He returned the small, sleepy grin.

Everything was still intact.

"What's in the lunchbox," Moz finally asked instead of blurting out the words perched on the tip of his tongue.

"I did my best with the pancakes," Kurosaki answered and Moz leaned back to give him space as he shifted to sit upright. "Bacon and fruit, too. If you need more I can run back, I don't know when the last time you ate in there was. There's coffee in the flask."

Moz stood from his knees and kissed the crown of Kurosaki's head on the way up. "Thank you."

"Of course. Go eat so you can do what you gotta do."

Moz nodded and he turned to walk back into his office as Kurosaki shrugged his jacket back on.

"Oh, where did you say I should go? I was half asleep."

"Home?" Moz answered with a question but without turning around.

"Yeah, that's what I thought you said."

Moz shrugged it off, finding the question just on the other side of bizarre. It wasn't until he stood in the open door frame that he stopped, realizing the weight of the word he had chosen without giving it deep thought.

Home.

Moz turned to look back at Kurosaki, but he wasn't there. He peered down the hall to catch him heading to the exit, coffee in one hand and his tin of cigarettes undoubtedly in the other.

"Idiot," Moz mumbled with fondness before he shut his office door behind him.

He began rearranging the files spread about on the floor. If he was going to solve this, everything needed to be viewed at all angles. Even if that just meant swapping what he pinned to the corkboard with what had been strewn about his office floor.

Moz took the victims' files and pinned them to the corkboard after he had cleared it of the crime scene photographs, but left the replica of Griffin's charcoal drawing at its center.

When it was all swapped, he shoved his hands in his trouser pockets and stepped backwards, careful to not trample any photographs. He sighed in frustration.

No epiphanies yet.

Moz stared hard at the board, looking from Tristan's face, to Theirrin, and to Cassie. There had to be some sort of connection - *but what*? One beloved friend and two people he knew only briefly died in the same pattern. How well did they know each other? Moz couldn't recall Tristan ever mentioning the young women in passing, but Tristan knew a lot of people. It wouldn't have been completely out of the ordinary for them to have been friends with a link he couldn't see on the surface. If Avery were there, she would have recognized it instantly.

He froze and recalled his son's voice from only days ago when discussing the possibility that the body in the woods belonged to his mother: *Do you think it's related to Uncle Tristan?*

Avery.

Moz fumbled for his wallet in his back pocket and pulled out the printed copy of a tintype. He pinned it to the board just to the left of Tristan's face so that it read in chronological order. Her face was the one that clicked everything into sharper focus for him.

Four faces stared back at him. All from people who had been at the Eyon ritual grounds that day. One had led the ritual. One had murdered a Knight.

"We've been treating these as two cases… it's just one," he murmured to himself.

Moz hurried for his files on the desk, tossing them carelessly into his briefcase because there was no time to waste.

This discovery would read as flimsy when there hadn't been a circle found anywhere near where Avery disappeared from; but he couldn't explain how he knew he was right about this. Nothing else made more sense. Before flipping off the light, he kissed two fingers and pressed them against the photograph of Avery.

"You fucking genius, love, thank you!"

With the briefcase in hand, he ran through the hall with his boots squeaking loud on the tile floor. Moz burst through the double doors into the nipping cold, flying past where Kurosaki had leaned against the stair railing with his coffee and half-finished cigarette.

"I got it, c'mon!" Moz shouted at him as he passed, not slowing in the slightest as he fished the keys to the sedan out from his coat pocket. Kurosaki hurried behind him to follow, sans cigarette, and lurched into the passenger seat.

"Why? What's going on? What did you find?"

Moz's heart raced as he tossed his briefcase into the backseat and started the car. But he didn't answer Kurosaki; he didn't want to speak to it until they were well within the stone safety of Brightloch castle.

He didn't seem to realize that Moz wasn't going to answer him until he had floored the engine halfway up the hill. Once they were inside the warmth of the castle, Moz hurried into the kitchen and swung his briefcase onto the island with a hard smack. Carelessly he threw open the latch and began scattering papers across the surface as Kurosaki watched him with a raised brow of skepticism.

Moz scrambled to find the photographs of the victims and circle but froze when he realized that in his excitement he had left them pinned to the corkboard in his office back at the Sentry. He groaned, pinching the bridge of his nose in frustration. But there was no time to run back.

"It's the same case," Moz said to Kurosaki as he planted his hands back down in front of him. "I know there was no circle at Avery's site and I don't know how I know this, I just do. There's no way else to explain how we have known all of the victims."

"It's been so long, why do you think it's the same person even after two years?"

"I don't know, maybe they needed to test the waters first. See if they would get caught."

"How did they decide who to go after?"

"I don't fucking know," Moz said, knotting his fingers in his own hair as he paced in frustration.

Kurosaki carefully thumbed through the files on the table. "So far, the only thing I can think of even connecting Theirrin and Cassie to each other is the fact that they were both there that day at the Knight exorcism. I don't even know if Theirrin was a witch on the day that this all happened."

Moz froze.

"What did you say?"

Kurosaki looked up and frowned at him.

"What?"

"That-that thing you just said, about how you don't know if—"

"If Theirrin was a witch," Kurosaki repeated for him. "Yeah, that's the only other similarity if she was. Avery, Theirrin, Cassie. Tristan is of course an outlier, but he did perform witchcraft with the Knight's exorcism rite. I don't know if that counts."

"That's it. That's the fucking pattern, they're going after the witches who were involved. They're going after Mona's daughters," Moz said. He sat down in the seat next to Kurosaki as he began flipping through the files again. "Maybe conducting the ritual was enough to put him on the hit list."

"But the ritual failed? Why would that matter?"

"I don't think they care whether or not their target succeeded, it's the principle of it. He used her spellbook to do it. And that means that, oh my gods," Moz cut himself off with realization as he slowly stood up, the last document in his hand.

"What? What is it?" Kurosaki gripped his arm, gently trying to shake an answer out of him.

He stared at the coroner's sweeping signature on the bottom of the page.

"I know who they're coming for next," he tossed the folder down carelessly back onto the table as he hurried for the door. "Get Shank, get Jack, get fuckin' anybody. They're coming for Maria and Lily."

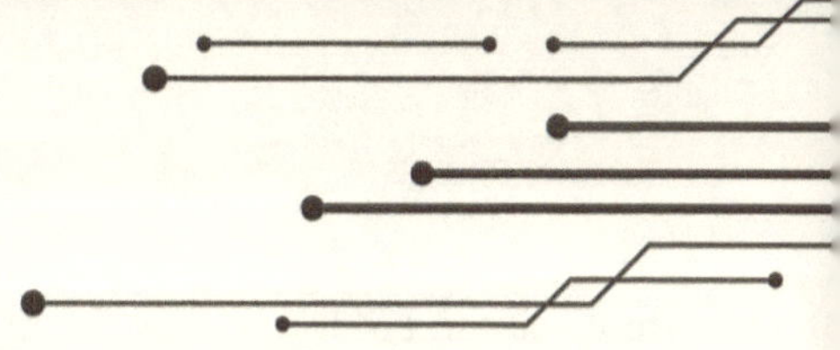

CHAPTER THIRTY-NINE
GRIFFIN

Aunt Maria answered the door and her face lit up in surprise as her eyes traveled from Moz to Kurosaki. Then they fell to the gun in Kurosaki's hands and she frowned.

"Guys... what's going on?"

"Go get Lily and pack a bag now, we'll explain on the way."

"What? Why? Where are we going?"

Moz and Kurosaki both pushed around her to enter her home, but did not answer the question. Griffin turned to look behind them before he followed, careful to make note of anyone who may have been on the street to see, but he found no one.

"We'll keep an eye out," Shank reassured him, standing at the bottom of the stoop with Jude. Had it not been for her portal magic, neither of them would have been permitted to be present at all. It was too valuable in case things went sideways, and Griffin was part of the package deal. He shut the door behind him and stood in the foyer, feeling awkward with his staff.

Aunt Lily and Maria's home was a warm place with colorful paintings of every size imaginable covering the white walls. Pothos with sprawling legs tumbled over shelves and woven pillows were thrown on the leather chaise in the sitting room to his left. Ahead of him, Lily and Maria were both already darting about in a panicked flurry in their kitchen.

Moz had followed them in and Griffin heard his father say, "they're going after the witches. Neither of you are safe and we need to keep you in the castle until we can determine if it's safe for you to stay in the city at all."

"Who the fuck is *they*, Moz?"

Silence fell when Griffin walked into the sunshine-painted kitchen. Maria had stopped her frenzied scramble to collect things and stared at Moz angrily, but he could not meet her gaze. He looked down at the floor and then at Griffin when he entered.

"I don't know," his father admitted quietly and Griffin felt the sickened shame painted on his downturned face.

Maria inhaled deeply and used both hands to push back her hair with frustration, pulling her inky bob taut against her scalp.

"Okay... okay, this is fine, I trust you," she said, sounding more like she meant to persuade herself than she was trying to convince him of her belief.

Kurosaki and Moz stepped aside to let the women run upstairs to their bedroom. They stood waiting, unsure what else to do when they heard the faint sound carrying down the hall of Maria's panicking and the soothing murmur of her wife's voice.

"You're making the right call," Kurosaki said softly to Moz and suddenly Griffin felt like he wasn't supposed to be standing there.

"I don't like constantly upending people's lives," Moz answered him.

"It's not upending their lives if you're saving their lives."

Gross.

"I'm gonna go help keep watch," Griffin finally offered. "It seems like you have this under control here."

His father hadn't answered by the time Griffin had already turned to start back down the first floor hallway. A shadow lurched at him from a cracked closet door and he yelped in startle, stumbling backwards on his heels as he crashed into the opposite wall.

Moz hurried to the kitchen door frame to investigate and looked from the hall closet to Griffin with his back pressed against the wall.

"Nothing, bud."

Griffin swung his staff at empty air in frustration. "Oh for fuck's sake," he grumbled and threw open the front door to step into the icy air.

They waited for long minutes with Jude idly swinging her scythe and kicking her legs at air until his father and Kurosaki came out the front door of the townhome, holding duffle bags for his aunts when they followed.

"Jude, you take them to the castle, okay?"

"On it," she answered Moz and held out her hands to part the space in front of her.

Nothing happened.

Frustration curled Jude's face as she held up her splayed fingers but still nothing. No portal opened. Griffin looked from her to Shank in confusion. *Has this happened before?*

"Wh...what's happening? I can't–"

"It's okay, sweetie," Shank said. "But we have to go. Get in the car."

Jude didn't argue, despite her horrified look of frustration, as Lily ushered her into the back seat of Moz's car. Maria and Lily sat on either side of her, holding their duffel bags in their laps. Griffin watched Kurosaki pull his motorcycle helmet back on and straddle the black bike before it roared to life. He frowned; he would have greatly preferred to ride passenger with him than be crammed in the sedan with five other people but it was a hard *fuck no* from his father when the lack of a second helmet was pointed out before the drive into downtown.

Crammed between his father and Shank in the front seat bench, Griffin kept as still as he could while his father began to drive back to the north end of Brightloch. They sat in a tense silence while Griffin slumped in his seat to keep out of the way of the rearview mirror until Maria finally spoke.

"Anything else you want to tell us, Moz?"

"It's all connected. Avery and whoever is killing the witches."

His father's voice was flat and low but left too much space for her to argue around.

"And how do you know this? It doesn't even sound like you know who-"

"Because I just DO!"

Griffin flinched at the shout. The sound was an unwelcome flashback to the period of time before Mama's funeral when his temper ran the shortest it had ever been. Shouting at Sentry officers, picking fights with the Queen's advisory staff, a thin patience with Griffin and Mimi before they ever had a chance to wear it down themselves. Its resurfacing made him uneasy. He felt the anger roll off Aunt Maria in waves without needing to turn to see for himself.

"Moz, you can't expect us to just drop everything and come running because of a hunch. We have lives. Ones that we worked hard for, you know this better than anyone. How long do you plan on hiding us? It doesn't make sense when we're—"

She was cut off again, this time by gunfire.

Moz lifted a hand to adjust the rearview mirror and ducked his head to get a better look behind them.

"Holy shit," he muttered breathlessly. "I need everyone to stay calm."

Naturally, nobody was calm. Lily, Jude, and Maria all huddled close as they turned around to look through the rear window and Lily shouted.

"Fucking hell! You can't be serious!"

Griffin finally gave into the urge and rose to a full seated position to twist his body to look through the rear window. Gunfire cracked again and past Jude's head he saw Kurosaki's black bike zigzag across the icy road, slipping and sliding in a way that made him anxious. His gun precariously balanced between his right hand and the throttle.

Behind him, a massive animal ran on all fours. The thing was outstandingly gargantuan with scaled legs of red beneath a frame Griffin could only compare to that of a mountain lion. It chased after Kurosaki with gnashing teeth, swinging its tri-horned head like a battering ram from hell. Viscous saliva splattered with each violent jerk and Griffin's stomach turned knots underneath his seatbelt. Kurosaki twisted around in his seat and fired twice before he had to regain control of the bike again and Griffin felt his father flinch beside him.

"He's out there on his own," he murmured. "We gotta do something."

"Moz, the kids are here," Shank warned.

"I know, I know."

Griffin turned and saw the white-knuckle grip his father had on the steering wheel and he jolted again under the gunfire. He watched Moz's eyes switch directions in the rearview mirror from the window to Maria in the backseat.

"Maria," he said her name firmly.

She turned and met the gaze through his reflection.

"I need you to try," Moz added.

Griffin looked at his aunt over his shoulder and saw her shake her head hard, flicking short black hair around her ears.

"Oh, no, no, no," she protested. "I can't do that shit anymore, Moz. Nothing good will come from that."

"Maria, I love you, but I need you to TRY," Moz's voice rose to a desperate shout and Griffin felt the anger ringing around in his eardrums with how close they were packed in the front seat bench. Before his voice could crescendo, it fell to softness: "Kurosaki is out there alone risking his life for you, please help him... Please."

The begging in his father's voice struck him hard. Griffin flicked his gaze up and saw his aunt's reflection in the rearview mirror. Maria nodded, a nervous bob shifting her throat as she swallowed. Plastic grinded as she began turning the hand crank to lower the backseat window to her right.

He looked to his father from where he crouched low again to keep his view unobstructed. The car lurched on a patch of ice and Moz steered with the shift in direction until it righted itself again. How Jude hadn't puked yet was a goddamn miracle.

Gunfire popped behind them and the motorcycle engine whined just as the beast roared out. He wanted to look behind him to see if it was closing in but he was afraid of getting in the way. Despite the danger, Maria began to hoist her torso out the open window.

"Dad, what's she doing?"

It wasn't Moz that answered, but Shank wedged against him on the right side of the bench:

"They picked the wrong witch to go first."

Griffin watched her from the side view mirror as her eyes glazed over black. Snow and wind whipped her face as she leaned out of the car's frame. She raised both her hands with her fingers splayed, palms facing the direction of the roaring beast closing in on them faster and faster.

"*To save, never to resurrect,*" Griffin heard her murmur.

She crunched her knuckles into her palm and pulled back her elbows with a hard yank and the demon-beast cried out. It stumbled, buying Kurosaki just enough time to put the gun down and throttle for more distance.

But the beast wasn't stalled for long. It came back angrier, louder, and swung clawed paws into the faces of homes as it sprinted towards its true target. Maria pulled again, rowing through air.

"I can't find it!" She cried out.

"What do you mean you can't find it?"

"I'm looking for the thread and it's just not there!"

"Dad! Dad! You gotta floor it!"

Distance closed fast and Kurosaki was forced out of the direct pathway when the demon's feet crashed down hard into cobblestone just behind them, breaking stone.

"I need more time, I just, oh gods, where did it go—"

The beast cleared the car in one leap and Maria threw her head skyward to follow it as she pulled hard with her eyes still inked over. Moz slammed on the brakes to stop from colliding into the demon's scaled legs and Jude had barely enough time to yank Maria back inside the car by her legs before she could fall out of the vehicle and crunch under the wheel wells as they skid on ice.

A shrill roar split the air and the demon titan crunched a clawed foot down into the hood. Tinted glass from the windshield shattered and the back of the sedan lifted high off the ground. Griffin's seatbelt choked against his abdomen when his center of gravity pulled him down and his feet jolted against the bottom trim of the dashboard. Steel groaned against ice as the weight reshaped the car's frame and when the frozen stage of their panic passed, every passenger in the car screamed.

Gunfire popped from behind them and Shank was the first to stop screaming. They tried the right passenger door, but it wouldn't give with how the metal had warped.

"Backseat doors! Everyone out, now!"

Maria and Lily threw open their doors and Lily dragged Jude out by the collar of her jacket. With the rear of the car perpendicular to the ground, Moz, Griffin, and Shank would have to climb up to get out.

"Kuro, you better cover our asses!" Griffin heard Lily shout.

He climbed over the top of the front seat, scrambling to get to the open doors. Another roar ripped the air and metal splintered in shards. Griffin felt the sudden jolt in his ribs like a jumpscare from a hallucination.

"DOWN!"

Griffin ducked the second his father screamed out and he nestled himself in the space between the seats. Delayed panic rose and he looked up not at the roof of the car, but a cloudy sky framed by warped beams of steel. His jaw dropped.

"Dad, the roof's gone."

"Thanks, bud! We gotta fuckin' go now!"

Moz pulled out his holstered gun as Griffin scrambled out the door. Shank followed him closely as Moz began firing off shots, louder over the rapid succession of Kurosaki's gun somewhere behind the car. Soon after Griffin's feet hit the ice, Jude's fingers closed around his elbow to pull him away from the battered car. He shrugged out of her grip just long enough to grab his staff from where it had been laid across the floor of the backseat and he followed Jude and Shank away.

They took shelter next to a storefront, crouched down low behind a covered cart to stay out of sight. Shank shoved them to the ground, holding up one finger in a stern warning.

"I swear to gods, if you don't sit your asses here and stay here," Shank's threat was only half-made before they ran back towards Moz and Maria.

Griffin peered around the corner to watch; he was far more afraid of Shank's fury than he was of his father's. Without turning his gaze, he asked Jude:

"Why do you think the portal wouldn't open?"

He expected her to snap at him for asking, but her answer sounded hurt and quiet: "I have no idea."

Kurosaki had pulled over to come between the raging demon and where Maria stood, but the bullets he fired had no visible effect other than angering the beast. His father had shifted to the side of the avenue to move towards the demon's flank, firing his own gun with much longer spaces in between the loud pops.

Moz's bullets struck scaled legs and the beast dipped in buckled blows far easier than any of the shots that Kurosaki landed on the thoracic segment in far more critical areas.

"Do you not have blessed bullets?" Moz called out between shots.

The demon roared and swung its head in a wide swipe into a storefront opposite the avenue, missing Maria and Kurosaki when he had yanked her back hard. They slid backwards on patchy ice and scrambled to get out of the way. When the demon reared Moz cracked gunfire and drew the monster away to give them ample time to regain the safety of distance.

"Where would I have gotten those," Kurosaki answered, obviously annoyed as he reloaded.

Griffin watched Aunt Lily raise her hands when her eyes clouded over with darkness. As the demon reared to charge again, the crunched car behind it rattled and quaked before the warped metal came flying at its head. He heard the crunch of bone on impact and the car soared over Kurosaki and Maria's heads, landing with screaming steel and spilled gasoline on ice.

"What the fuck was that," Jude said breathlessly behind him.

The beast was already rising to its feet from its pathetic crumple on the ground and Griffin sucked in a breath, standing as he unlatched the blades on his staff. Wings flapped as Creak soared down, this time opting for Griffin's shoulder. He grimaced under the pinching talons.

"I don't care what they said, we have to help."

"I CAN'T FUCKING FIND IT!" Maria screamed out, yanking her hands backwards with her fingers crunched back into her palms.

"What do you mean you can't find it? It's gotta be in there, right?"

"It's a trap!" Shank shouted back at Moz. "They want you distracted! Moz, get them out!"

"GOTCHA, BITCH," Maria hollered.

She pulled her arms back with great force, as if she were yanking hard on an unseen mooring line. The demon stopped in its tracks, frozen for only a second before it collapsed to the ice. A defeated whine fell from it in place of a roar.

It stilled into silence and Jude rose beside him before Griffin walked into the middle of the road to approach his aunt slowly. Maria's brown eyes returned and she neatly tucked her hair behind her ears adorned with small gold hoops. She brushed off her hands on her coat like the act had been easy, but Griffin saw her serious frown.

"What did you do to it," he asked quietly.

Aunt Maria turned to him. "There is a thread connecting each beast to Od, buried deep in their void. If you can find it, you can sever it."

-Hello.-

Griffin looked from his aunt to the carcass of the beast.

They chose the wrong witch.

He didn't know what Shank meant by it before, but he understood when Maria's small frame approached the giant mass of dead flesh and scale. She nudged it in the face with her heeled boot, an unimpressed hum falling from her mouth.

"If it's a trap, I am awfully curious to know how they got their hands on a specimen this large."

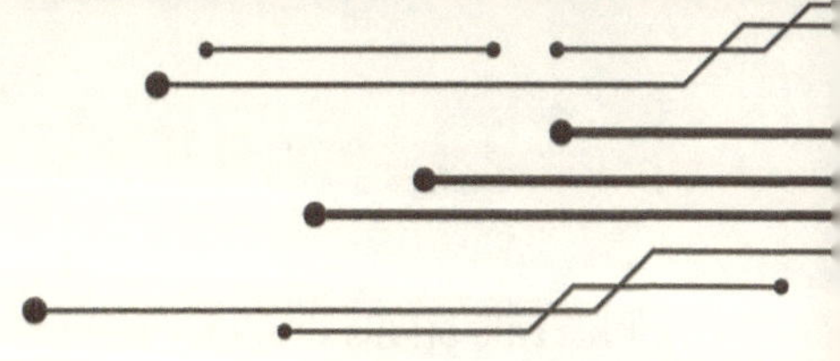

CHAPTER FORTY
KUROSAKI

When the beast had fallen, Kurosaki waited long minutes to be absolutely certain it was down for good before he peeled off his motorcycle helmet. He shook out his hair, set the helmet on his seat, and approached the others where they had regrouped in the crater-riddled street.

"Kuro, take to the rooftops and give cover to Lily and Maria. We gotta get them to the castle, but I doubt they're far behind their pet. The forty-eight hour window is closing," Moz said as he finished locking the magazine into place. He then turned to the raven perched on Jude's shoulder. "And you, Bird Brain, you're our relay. Keep an ear out for him."

Before Moz could confirm their plan, Kurosaki had already turned his back to examine the brownstone buildings that flanked the town square. He frowned; having a perch no higher than three stories above the street was less than ideal. Though he resented Eyon, at least there he had plenty of high-rise balconies to choose from.

Kurosaki dipped into the alley and his choice was made for him when he spotted the only fire escape. He looked from the three-story back to the street to check its trajectory; not perfect, but it would have to do. He patted the holster on his hip and hoisted the strap of his rifle on his shoulder before he reached under his shirt for the bullet casing on a chain.

"Be with me, Alice," he said, kissing the cold metal before stashing it back against the skin of his chest. He thought of her ghostly smile and how the light of it had only just glimmered under the surface of his haze after Todd's attack. *A wasted opportunity*– he still had so much to say to her.

He strode towards the rusting ladder. Before he could grasp the first rung, his feet were pulled out from underneath him. The world spun upside-down and Kurosaki hung suspended in empty air, staring at the cobblestone above his head.

On the dry patch of stone, black chalk streaked round lines with a subtlety he had missed when he walked over it. *Sigils*. A language he had only seen in Griffin's drawings. And he had walked right into it.

He looked ahead down the alleyway when the figures in warped rabbit masks encroached from the blanket of shadows. Their bastardized versions of Mara's face. Was it intentional?

Kurosaki laughed nervously. "This is how you got her, isn't it?"

The ladder behind him groaned under the weight of a body descending and he began to panic. As he reached for his gun, he heard the loud flap of feathered wings and a scraping squawk.

"Creak, my guy, you better fucking go now!"

The attack had been quiet and he was tucked away out of sight from the others. If Jude's familiar failed, he was a goner.

The raven left him as soon as Kurosaki swung his aim blindly behind him and fired, praying to gods and praying to Alice that he would not miss. He heard the body crumple but saw only the serrated machete fall to the ground when it landed in the circle of sigils below him.

A wash of water ran underneath Kurosaki and ruined the circle of sigils. He dropped from the air and fell to the ground in a heap. Kurosaki's heart raced and he gathered himself with staggered breath. He raised his gun, and fired quick cracks of gunfire into the chests of the other assailants who were closing in on him and the rescuer he had yet to turn to.

When the last body fell silent, Kurosaki exhaled sharply and rose from his knelt position.

"Thanks man, they really—" he turned to thank Moz but froze in shock to find that it wasn't Moz at all.

Griffin's shoulders bobbed in deep breaths and a bead of blood bloomed under his left nostril.

"Oh, no," Kurosaki murmured.

Griffin didn't respond as he wiped the blood with the back of his hand, smearing it across his face when he had meant to clean himself of it. Like father, like son— *in the worst possible way*.

Griffin turned to hurry back to the street, but Kurosaki was frozen in place. He couldn't make sense of what he had just witnessed. He'd get over the attempt on his life, that felt normal enough; but *Griffin*? Kurosaki doubted there was an explanation that had nothing to do with the Knight of Water.

He heard the faint carry of Griffin's voice, and the sharp yell of his father's "What?!"

Undoubtedly, Griffin had told him what happened and how he

was almost the latest victim. Moz and Griffin rushed back into the alley just as Kurosaki retrieved his gun from where it landed from his fall. Before they approached, Moz stopped Griffin with his arm held up and said "No, go back and tell them we're coming."

Griffin nodded diligently and ran back to the street. Kurosaki watched, unsure how Moz had missed the telltale signs of Griffin's nosebleed. He thought about speaking up until Moz closed in on him, his hand closing around his bicep to guide him back towards the alley. Kurosaki stumbled behind his angry steps, confused by his reaction.

"Where were they? Show me."

"Moz, they—"

Moz suddenly spun and pushed Kurosaki's back into the brick wall. He flinched and the force jolted him, but not nearly as hard as the way Moz left his large hand pressed flat into his chest as he spoke:

"Don't you ever scare me like that again."

It wasn't anger that made his voice shake as he looked down at Kurosaki's face; it was fear. He saw it in the wet glaze over his evergreen eyes and in the trembling flex of his jaw when he swallowed. No matter how many times he had ground at Moz's nerves when they were young, it had never once escalated to trading the same blows that came with the rage of Todd Nielsen. He hadn't then; he wouldn't start now. With his free hand, Kurosaki lifted his fingers to his chest to coax Moz to soften but he held fast.

"You don't have to worry about me," he said, low to the frightened animal in the shape of William Mosley. "I'm a grown man, I can fend for myself."

"If that was the end all, be all, we wouldn't be here right now."

Fair. Kurosaki threaded his fingers through Moz's and held them at his heart when he said:

"I'll worry about keeping the body in one piece. You just worry about the heart."

Moz looked down at his own hands and his expression split in horrified confusion, like he had awoken in the middle of sleepwalking miles from his bed. He dropped his hands and took a step back, giving Kurosaki a wide berth.

"Izaya, I'm so sorry. I, I don't know what that was but it won't happen again."

"Thank you, I know it won't. I know you didn't mean it."

"I can't lose you too," Moz murmured.

The words shattered a delicate place somewhere inside of Kurosaki's chest and he thought immediately of the sorrowful resignation in Moz's voice before— *it shouldn't have been her.*

An ache to comfort him overcame Kurosaki and he reached out his free hand to close his ringed fingers gently around Moz's elbow. His pull was gentle when he drew him closer and let the peace he found in his towering frame anchor him. Kurosaki was careful not to overwhelm Moz further and kissed only the underside of his jaw before he responded:

"You won't, I promise."

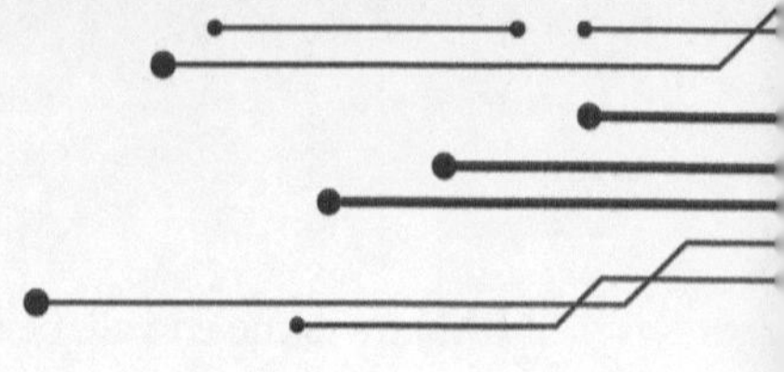

CHAPTER FORTY-ONE
GRIFFIN

W HEN GRIFFIN AND CREAK returned, Jude's tensed shoulders dropped with relief and she let the arm holding her scythe go slack.

"*I told the big dummy that the old love bird was in trouble—*"

"Excuse me?" Jude frowned at Creak. "You didn't think to mention that he could hear you?"

"*I didn't know he wasn't supposed to!*"

She then turned her confused look to Griffin. "How can you hear him? *Why* can you hear him?"

"Trust me, when I figure it out, you'll be the first person to know."

His father and Kurosaki rejoined their group. Panic radiated from his father as he whirled around in all directions, looking for any other Rabbits that would have accompanied the ones who had made a move on Kurosaki's life.

"What's going on," Shank asked, looking around with him.

"We're out of time, they're already here. Splitting up isn't going to work, they almost wasted Kuro."

"What?!" Maria interjected. "He's not a witch! What happened to that criteria?"

"They must want you real bad."

A small streak of orange against the grey slush pooling on the sidewalk caught Griffin's eye and he turned towards the off-shooting street to his right. Before it disappeared from view, the bright fur of a fox slunk low as it trotted with a flicking tail. When it was gone, he turned to Jude.

"Did you see that?"

She only paid him half of her attention when Jude answered, "I didn't, sorry."

Griffin frowned; he hadn't even specified what he meant. But he let it go.

They were the only ones on the street. Even without the demon tearing up the town in a rampage, people had made themselves scarce ever since the Queen's address after Cassie's murder.

It made the groan of metal behind them all the more unsettling.

Griffin followed his father's lead when he spun around towards the sound. Darkened figures emerged; creeping and quiet. Blood pounded in his ears when Griffin caught sight of the first warped mask.

The Rabbits appeared one after another from the shadows of the falling sun along the main street. No features could distinguish them behind their warped masks other than their varying heights and weapons; black clothed them from hooded head to booted toes.

"Fuck, " he heard his father swear, low and breathless.

The distinct shift of steel clicked as Kurosaki lifted his rifle, bent at the knees as he swiveled with assessing eyes.

"Dead or alive," he asked with flat objectivity.

"What?"

"Do you want them alive for questioning," Kurosaki clarified, "or are we sending them?"

"If they give us the choice, I would like them alive."

"I hardly think we're going to get that choice," Shank replied. To Maria and Lily they said, "come with me."

"No," Lily refused firmly. "You're not doing this without us. We're targets, not cowards."

"Damn, you got me there."

The lighthearted comment should have made Griffin feel more at ease if they were willing to crack a joke with such confidence, but the fear burned in the pit of his stomach when the Rabbits just kept coming; one after another.

"I'm gonna check you on that answer, Moz," Kurosaki called out. He turned carefully on nimble feet, determining which direction he should fire in first before chaos would fall.

When Moz lifted his own gun, he replied, "They killed Tristan, pop 'em."

The words had barely left his father's mouth before the first three shots cracked from Kurosaki's gun. His fire was returned almost immediately from above and missed shots splintered the ice around his feet. Kurosaki ducked and swung around, volleying shots at the figure on the rooftop he had once intended to claim for his own.

Moz swung his own aim in the same direction, using one arm to pull Kurosaki off to the side after the figure had ducked. "He goes first!"

"C'mon!" Griffin shouted, grabbing Jude's hand to pull her

under the cover of a shop awning.

They crouched low and Griffin looked from the sniper's rooftop to Jude's calculating face.

"I have an idea," she murmured.

"Oh no."

Jude stood up from her crouch and held both her hands open. She sucked in a breath, as hopeful as she was uneasy.

"Okay, it better work this time, I swear to gods, if it doesn't..."

She trailed off just as the black void ripped the air and her face lit up with delight. Jude turned over her shoulder to look down at Griffin.

"C'mon, I need you," she said.

Griffin flushed at the words, knowing that the way she had meant them was not the same way he had wanted to hear them. Still, he stood up and followed Jude into the portal.

In the darkness, she said, "Okay, on the count of three, get ready to swing."

"Where are we—"

"One..."

"Jude, stop for a second, where are we—"

"Two..."

"JUDE!"

"Three!"

The void spat them out and wind whipped Griffin's face hard. He quickly gathered that they were standing on the rooftop when he saw the back of a figure dressed in black, crouched at the top ledge of the building over a rifle. Jude's plan clicked together and he lurched towards them, unsheathing the blades in his staff. Bullets whizzed by their heads and Griffin tucked his limbs into himself as best as he could to reduce his surface area as a target.

"KURO, STOP!"

He heard his father shout from the ground before Griffin wrought the bladed staff down on the unsuspecting Rabbit. Flesh squished and the body toppled under the impact, but it was not satisfying enough for Griffin to know the person was dead. He ripped it out again and swung harder at the body just for good measure.

The Rabbit went still. Griffin was tempted to unmask them as he withdrew his blades, lodged deep under the flesh of their shattered neck. He sucked in a deep breath and wiped the splatters of blood from his face as best he could. When he turned to Jude, she looked at him with a delighted fascination. She had her scythe held up, ready to join in before Griffin had utterly annihilated the sniper on his own.

"Get the gun!"

His father shouted from below and Griffin reached for the fallen rifle that had clattered to the rooftop tiles.

"And the ammo," Kurosaki added.

"You get the gun," Jude said to him, "and I'll check the body."

Griffin swung the strap of the firearm onto his back just as she crouched down beside the corpse, grimacing with a *blegh* as gore squished audibly under her boot to turn it over. Carefully, she rummaged into their jacket and searched the zippered pockets tucked inside.

As she did so, Griffin reached for the strap of the rabbit mask tied around the back of their battered head. He regretted unmasking them as soon as he saw the empty blue eyes staring past him and up at the grey sky.

A dark beard had been shaved close to his sharp jaw and a splatter of gore splashed up his cheeks from the impact of blades to his neck. Blood poured out his open mouth from the last pumps of a heart and Griffin felt horrified that this man was somewhere between his age and his father's. But it was worse than that:

"Jude, this is just some *guy*. He's not a demon or anything!"

She stood up, swinging a belt of bullets onto her shoulder that she had found tucked under the bottom of their buckled vest.

"Yeah, I know," she affirmed. "We can mention that later when we get the chance, but right now we gotta get these to Kurosaki."

Griffin nodded and followed her diligently back into the void that spit them back out into the street below.

They hurried the gun and ammo to Kurosaki just as he emerged from his crouched position around the corner of a restaurant across from the dead sniper's perch. He reached out for them eagerly, taking the gun from Griffin before he swung it onto his own back. When Jude handed him the supply of ammo, he said:

"Proud of you kids, that was fuckin' fantastic."

With the sniper gone, they came back out into the street to get a better angle on the Rabbits that surrounded them at every possible escape route.

"What do we do," Jude murmured beside him.

"It's them or us," Griffin answered.

There was no time for her to come back with a witty response before the first wave of Rabbits broke their daunting stillness. Blades swung and gunfire reverberated in the air.

When a Rabbit lurched in Jude's direction, Griffin reared back his staff and cracked it hard into the side of their head. Gore splattered from beneath the crunch of bones. His movements were made with rage, flowing through his muscles with the same ease he handled the weapon with. It was just another extension of himself and he pretended not to notice Jude watching him with awed horror.

A slithering sensation of movement snaked around his skull. Warmth bloomed over his bottom lip and when Griffin wiped his face, his hand returned bloody.

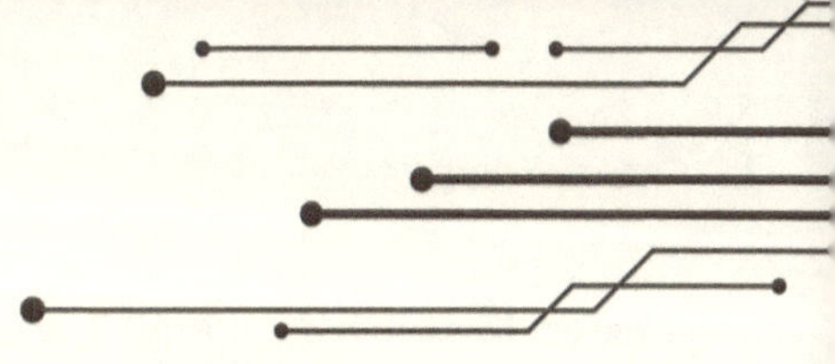

CHAPTER FORTY-TWO
JUDE

"*J*UDE, HONEY, LISTEN TO me. If you ever see Mr. Mosley with a bloody nose, I need you to book it in the other direction, okay? I don't care if you just watched him get decked in the face, I don't care what the reason is, just run. As fast as you can. Can you promise me that?*"

Jude remembered the stern instructions from her parent. She never found out why Shank had asked that of her when she was only thirteen or why they didn't let her rise from her chair at the dinner table until she swore she would heed their warning. She wished she held firm in her curiosity when Griffin looked back over his shoulder at her with a philtrum smeared in blood.

His gaze was angry and he twisted his blood-spattered staff in his palms; Creak laughed as Griffin quickly wiped the blood with the back of his hand.

"*My, my. Things just got a touch more interesting, didn't they, Little Witch?*"

Jude flinched when she turned and there was a face only a breath's distance away from hers. She let out a tiny yelp of surprise and stepped back to regain her sphere of personal space. They watched her with cat-like eyes, dark and focused. Their hair was shaved down to the scalp and they stood inches shorter than her with their fists shoved into a jacket littered with patches of red fabric.

"I need you to come with me," they said with a voice of smooth campfire smoke.

"Why would I? Who are you?"

"We haven't met before, but you have met my father. Balthazar."

Jude's tense posture eased only a fraction. "You're Mercy, aren't you?"

They stuck out their bottom lip, impressed in a smug way but did not betray any pleasure that they were recognized with a smile. They held out their open hand to her, slender with finely shaped fingernails. Mercy was nothing like the legends painted them to be; a horrible shapeshifter and the sacrilegious byproduct of a union between demon and god.

"I am," they answered. "Do you trust me?"

Jude hesitated, looking from Mercy's hand to their face. One eyebrow cocked up in interest as they awaited her reply. When she was taking too long for their liking, they added:

"I think Griffin would appreciate it if you said yes."

Griffin? Panic flared— what could they possibly have meant? Was that a thinly veiled threat? She twisted the scythe in her hands and wondered if she had what it took to kill a demigod. If such a thing was even possible.

"If you so much as..."

She trailed off when Mercy leaned forward, hand cupped around their mouth as they whispered into Jude's ear. In their hushed words that coiled around Jude, she nearly dropped her scythe. Her jaw sank, much too heavy now for her to hold. The hairs on the back of her neck rose and the heavy beating of her heart thrummed deep in the pitch of her stomach.

Then Mercy leaned back, dropping their hand slowly and awaiting Jude's answer. She looked at them first in disbelief, unable to parse at first what the words had implied. Until she finally found the words:

"Take me there. Now."

Mercy smiled, close-lipped and coy.

"After you, *mi liejv.*"

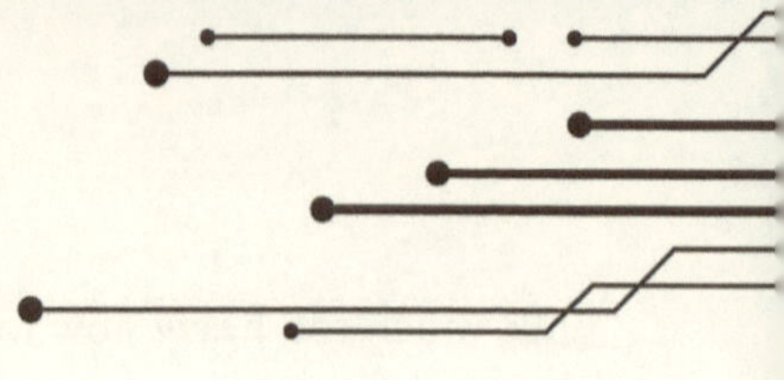

CHAPTER FORTY-THREE
GRIFFIN

JUDE DISAPPEARED WITH THE stranger and Griffin panicked. *How can she do this right now?* They needed her desperately and she was well aware of that. What could have been so important? There was no time for him to give these questions pause, so Griffin kept swinging his bladed staff wherever a Rabbit mask was in his reach.

To his left, Aunt Maria's eyes had glazed over inky black again. With her hands held at shoulder height, she crunched her knuckles to her palm, and pulled backwards like she had with the towering demon. Before her, blood and sinew dripped from under the chin of a rabbit mask and the figure fell to their knees. Wet, white lumps squished under the seam between plastic and black cowl before they thudded face-first on the ice.

"That's for setting your sights on my wife," Maria said, her voice lined thick with a scorched darkness Griffin had never seen in her before.

Griffin cracked his staff against a man's back, clearing a pathway to where he saw the black patch of cobblestone bubble and churn. The scythe rose from the ground and Jude's beautiful and haloed face followed. Her eyes were swallowed in the bright glow of witchcraft and as she emerged from the portal in the ground, he realized she had not returned alone.

The short woman rose with her, a wide brimmed hat hanging against her shoulders by a leather strap flat against her neck. Long twin braids of dark hair flanked her face fixed in a cold fury and he recognized the steel eyes peering over the barrel of a rifle instantly.

"*Surprise, bitch,*" Avery Porter's cutting voice spoke to the nearest Rabbit before she fired a crack of light and smoke.

"YEAH! THAT'S MY FUCKIN' WIFE!" Moz shouted.

Chaos erupted as they quickly closed ranks around Avery and Griffin was too panicked to feel any joy in her unexpected appearance.

Why here? Why now?

Kurosaki sprinted and was first to zero in. He dropped one hand from his gun and hooked an arm around her waist, pulling her in the direction of their rear line.

Still she held up the rifle and Griffin heard her chirp, "Hi Kuro," as happily and simply as greeting a friend after a long week before she fired two more shots.

Just when it looked like she was going to fall back into safety, her eyes met Griffin's and all hell broke loose. His mother screaming his name sent chills down his spine when he had resigned to never hearing her voice again. She thrashed like a caged animal under Kurosaki's arm and he had no choice but to let her go with both of their safety switches disengaged.

"GRIFFIN!"

"Avery, don't!"

Moz lunged for her and Avery almost evaded his reach until his fingers closed around the collar of her jacket. "Fuck off, Moz! What is our *son* doing here?"

Griffin swung his bladed staff into the torso of a Rabbit as his parents argued, yanking it back with a sickly squish of gore before the body dropped into the grey slush.

"Just look at him!" His father was definitely crying, but he let Avery go. "Did you see what he just did? That's *your* son and I couldn't keep him out of this if I tied an anvil to his ankle and left him at home."

A bullet fired from Avery's gun, splintering in the skull of another Rabbit approaching Griffin. He flinched hard and the proximity of it rattled him; too confident for comfort.

"Avery, you're out!" Kurosaki shouted. He had been counting her bullets and sure enough, her next pull of the rifle trigger came up empty. She grunted with frustration and swung the gun strap onto her back.

"What've you got, Kuro?"

"Not that one."

Avery groaned in loud and exaggerated frustration.

"Guess we got no choice, motherfuckers!"

She raised her left arm and rolled back the cuff of her green Scout utility jacket. Griffin watched her bite down on her own wrist just above the thick leather of her old woven bracelet. A hand closed around the hood of his coat and yanked him backwards.

"Fuck, fuck, fuck, fuck," he heard his father swear behind him before Griffin could react to the grabbing hand with a swinging staff.

Griffin felt the hot bead of blood running down his philtrum and over his upper lip. He looked up, about to wipe the mess off his face before the taste of iron could seep into his mouth when he caught the gaze of his father staring at him. Though Griffin heard no sound as he dragged his coat sleeve across his mouth, he read the fearful shapes of the words:

"Oh no."

"You're fucking fools for drawing the ire of the Berserker Witch under this moon," Avery called out. She lifted her hands, her left bleeding, and shadows crawled up from beneath the cobblestone. The heels of her boots lifted and her eyes glazed over black with the same clouding of the sclera that had overcome Maria and Lily. The shadows twisted into humanoid shapes, surrounding both Griffin's family and the Rabbits.

"Short leash, Avery!" His father shouted. "Kids are here!"

His mother grinned and bones cracked when the first wave of revenants swarmed. Limbs of Rabbits snapped out of place, dropping them one by one when the clouded spirits tore at them with ghostly hands.

Griffin noticed the ravenous heads of the Rabbits were turning far more frequently in Jude's direction when she dove in and out of portals, weaving around bodies that she cut down from behind just as they had done with the sniper on the roof. He felt the stirring sensation that occupied the space between his brain and his skull, shaping into sound that became a low rumble of laughter where he would hear Creak's croaking words when he dared acknowledge his presence.

"They're setting sights on Our Witch, Babs."

This voice was different. Ancient and hungry in the draw of its growl. Its presence under his skin should have frightened Griffin, but it was as familiar as the sound of his own voice and the way it reverberated within the shape of his skull. His skin itched and he imagined thousands of scarab beetles scurrying under the surface to flock to the source of the sound.

A ripping black void flashed behind a Rabbit and Jude emerged with glossed over eyes, slashing her scythe across the throat of the masked person she ambushed as they had tried to backpedal away from the wall of revenants quickly closing in. But she had failed to notice the one behind her, lurching for her with a fast flash of metal.

"DECK!" Griffin shouted as he dove with a swinging staff. Jude ducked instantly, backing carefully on her toes so she could fall backwards into her open portal.

The blades on his modified staff punctured the Rabbit mask, splintering the pieces into a kaleidoscope of plastic and bone shards. Hooked around the maxilla bone, Griffin's pull to return his staff yanked a mess of gore with the steel teeth and ribbons of blood painted the air in watercolor streaks. When the body fell into a heap, he shook as much of the flesh off his staff as time would allow. With every jostle of his staff, the splatters of blood ran up his bare hands and onto his clothing. He should have felt afraid, betrayed some sort of affect. But he didn't.

He was hungry.

A third Rabbit ran at them and he readied himself to swing again. Soft hands closed around his shoulders and Jude pulled him backwards with her into the portal, just as the shadowy form of a revenant encircled the Rabbit. Their limbs bent with snapping bones under ghostly hands until the Berserker Witch's revenant dropped the body to the ground. He heard his father shout:

"Avery! What the fuck are you—"

The void silenced his voice. When he stood in the nothingness with Jude, he clearly heard his exerted breathing in place of all else.

"I thought it was just a myth," he said to Jude. "I thought *she* was just a myth."

"It's okay, Griff, we have to hurry!"

She pulled him fast, deeper into the darkness. Her void spat them out back into the fray, but further back so that they were behind the line at the front formed by Avery and Kurosaki.

"I THINK THE FUCK NOT!"

Avery shouted when the last three Rabbits standing turned to flee. Revenants dove with clawing hands and pulled at their limbs, dislocating bone from sockets.

"Leave these ones, Ave!"

Griffin's mother turned to look back at Moz, a pleased grin spread on her blood-freckled face.

"Sure thing," she agreed. The revenants dropped the Rabbits with hard force. Their forms bobbed over the panicked Rabbits in a silent threat to withdraw their mercy if they so much as breathed wrong.

One of them sobbed; a man with a voice as broken as his right arm. When Avery dropped her hands to approach the neutralized assailants, Griffin followed her close with his staff ready.

His mother didn't shrug him off like his father would have. Didn't beg him to retreat to the safety of home. Avery wiped her own congealed blood onto her black pant leg when she stopped and looked down at the Rabbits at her feet.

"Bet you thought you were done with me, didn't you?"

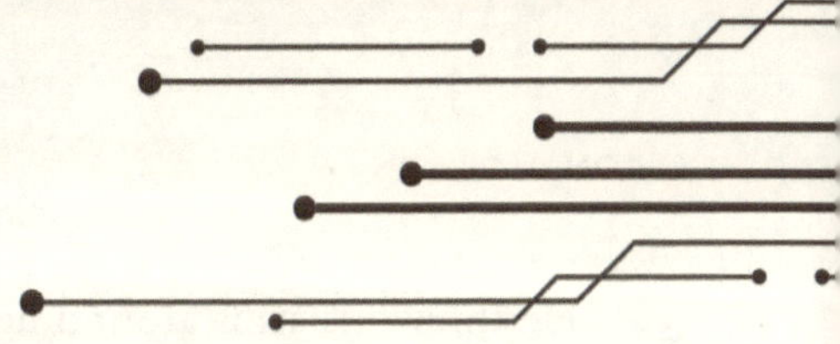

CHAPTER FORTY-FOUR
MOZ

T HE SENTRY FLOCKED FAST to the town square after Jude vanished and reappeared, having sounded the alarm before she took Shank home with her to the safety of her mother. Moz felt grateful that his team was closer to the body-littered square than the police department further east; anything to delay having to deal with Cain was a plus in his mind.

He holstered his gun just as Avery let her hold go on the last of the revenants and they faded into a dark, shapeless mist before they disappeared. She whistled a low sound, placed her brimmed hat on her head, and backed away from the Sentry officers who clasped chain bindings around the wrists of the unmasked Rabbits to whom she had demonstrated mercy. Two men and one woman, unremarkable in appearance once their looks of fear were unveiled.

Avery turned, looking back at everyone with a blood-splattered smile. Her chest heaved in exertion for air and she shifted her weight on her feet, stretching the strong muscles of her calves. Sweat glittered on her grimy and bruised face cut thin with hunger. He had never seen his wife look so utterly *alive*.

"Fucking hell," he heard Maria swear beside him.

But he paid her no mind and ran for his wife.

He threw his arms around her waist, leaning back with her weight to hold her up in a high embrace. Avery winced with a small and pained hiss, but she didn't shrug away. Her arms locked around his neck and the freeze of her cheek against his burned him so fiercely that he knew he would never need to yearn for her warmth again.

Moz carefully set her back onto her feet and held his forehead to Avery's with her cheek cradled in his hand. Her fingers wrapped around his wrist tenderly and he felt the cold surface of the leather straps on the sculpted cap.

"Hey you," he murmured with a small laughter of relief, tears building in his eyes and blurring the fringes of his vision. Moz had thought of a million and one things he could have said to his wife when he saw her again, but they all went out the window when she was finally in his hands.

"Hey, Stupid Hair," she answered with a soft and sweet voice.

Moz laughed a small sound before he ducked his head and kissed her. She felt weak against his touch when she kissed him back, her bright ferocity worn down to just a flicker in the dark. His fearsome wife was a breakable thing in his arms that ached his heart and he left a small kiss on her cold bottom lip before he parted from her.

"My brave little witch," he said. "I love you endlessly."

Their son dropped his staff to the ground with a loud clatter on slush slathered cobblestone. Griffin wedged himself into the space between Moz and Avery. Big, wet tears rolled down his cheeks and Moz felt an additional layer of relief to see the affect in his face swung so far. Any direction would have sufficed for Moz, but he was grateful that it was joy.

Griffin held his mother tight and Moz kept his arms wrapped as far around them as he could, his reach ending at Avery's waist. He squeezed them tight and he felt he held the whole world in his embrace.

"Where have you been, Mama?"

"Oh, you know. Around."

They held each other for long moments and tears faded into cold sniffles. Moz was hesitant to part from Avery and let her go inch by inch when she looked to the faces of her hand-built family. Lily ran to her first as soon as there was an opening and Avery cried all over again as her sister cradled the back of her head in her strong hand.

Tears started rolling again on Moz's face when he heard Lily sob, "I thought you were gone."

Avery leaned back, holding Lily's face in her hands. She wiped the falling tears but laughed.

"You're not that lucky yet," Avery joked.

Lily squeezed Avery tight before her wife took her place. Her reunion with Maria was equally weepy and they wiped the other's tears as they spoke:

"The bones? You insane fucking genius."

"I didn't have a notepad."

Maria laughed through tears and let her go. Avery's gaze fell to Kurosaki next and Moz felt the tension in his muscles tighten unexpectedly. He thought of Kurosaki's body heat in his lap and how he had to tell Avery. No, he *gets* to tell Avery. She was alive and could give him whatever teasing shit she thought he needed for it and Moz would take it with a smile.

Kurosaki took Avery into an embrace, tucking her head against his chest and held her close. Their reunion was wordless but profound when Kurosaki looked over her head at Moz, his watering eyes meeting his gaze. Moz let himself remain ensnared in his stare; one of his returned loves holding another. A sob began to bubble in his throat and he held a hand to his mouth to collect the sound before it could fully form.

A long moment passed before Kurosaki broke the loaded eye contact and Moz watched the shapes of the words he said low to only Avery's ears. He wasn't a skilled lip reader by any means and itched to know what was said to make Avery let go of Kurosaki and smile up at him with a radiant sunshine.

Avery turned and to Moz she declared, "I miss my wife. I'd really like to see her if that's okay."

He saw the vehicles coming down the road just beyond Kurosaki and Avery. He swore under his breath.

Moz nodded feverishly, "Yeah, yeah, go on ahead. I'll handle this and I'll be right behind you. Take Griff with you."

Confused, Avery looked from the cars, back to Moz's face before she held out her uncut hand to Griffin. Their son took her hand and together they started back to the waiting bones of Brightloch Castle.

When they had disappeared and fallen out of earshot, Kurosaki edged carefully towards Moz without taking his eyes off the police vehicles that pulled up just before reaching the body of the fallen demon.

"I've got a bad feeling about this," he murmured. Moz didn't answer.

Cain, of course, was the first out of the car. He strode by the heap of crumpled flesh and scale, eyeing it through his nose as if unimpressed by the kill. His officers flooded the scene with guns drawn, as though Moz's Sentry had failed to secure the entire scene and he found the act outrageously insulting as Cain strode towards him.

"Stay here," Moz murmured to Kurosaki as he walked to meet Cain.

"Okay, but can you please talk loud enough for me to hear?"

Moz would have loved to laugh at Kurosaki's quip back. But instead, he had to respond to the police posturing.

"The Sentry has this handled," Moz stated, not wanting to give Cain a single inch of room to wiggle his way in.

"I dare say, Mosley," he swept a hand, gesturing to the unmasked Rabbits, "wouldn't you agree that they look rather human?"

"Sure," Moz said, angry that he had to concede even the slightest. "But how did they manage to get their hands on *that*?"

He pointed over Cain's shoulder towards the demon carcass, but Cain didn't turn.

"Besides," Moz added, "they're already in custody. You're just going to fuck it up trying to switch now. We're goddamn lucky we got three of them alive and I won't have you screwing with the case just because you wanted to piss your pants about it."

"Mosley. This is clearly my jurisdiction," Cain said, his voice lowered with the threat of anger. "My road, if you will."

That sent Moz over the edge. "Listen, you son of a bitch–"

Cain turned his back and walked away. Moz only felt more enraged that he hadn't managed to get a rise out of the police captain.

"We'll sweep the scene and leave. Keep an eye out for that deposition subpoena," Cain called out.

The empty space in his head thrummed but the voice he heard was not the one he was expecting. Not a Knight, but *Todd*, of all people:

A domestic bitch on a leash.

"And you're so goddamn lucky," Moz spat the vitriol out loud.

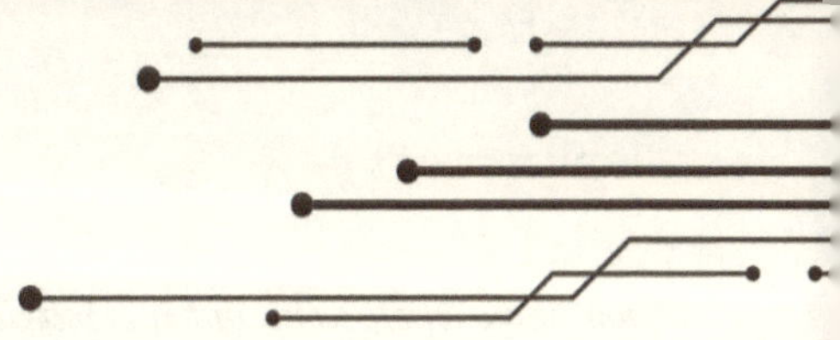

CHAPTER FORTY-FIVE

T HE FOX WAS EASY to spot in their peripheral vision even with their gaze turned downward into the weathered pages of the ledger. A bright smear of citrine was hard to miss when the rest of Brightloch was dull and lifeless in a winter slumber around them. The familiar said nothing, but they laid the ledger down in their lap as they waited for the report back.

"Well?"

The demon sat down, white belly turned away to come between the iron bench and the cobbled road sprawled out before them. It was sweet how they carried their animal body in a way that suggested they needed to be protected. What could the demon have done if they did? Once it had been insulting, but they overcame that feeling long ago. Now it was a comforting beast that curled up with them in bed on long Iverne nights.

"It is worse than I feared."

They tensed and their fingers curled tightly around the deckled edges of the book.

"How so?"

"The Knight is bubbling back to the surface, just like you said. The Berserker Witch has returned, this time carrying the stink of Od. I do

not know whose scent, but it is putrid and rotten. But we have drawn out the puppeteer and her pack of wild dogs. She is alive, but they will be waiting for more."

They huffed something resembling a sigh and frowned. Absently, their fingers smoothed over the leather cover and the texture of the pebbles held an odd comfort that they couldn't quite place. Small shapes of power, perhaps.

"Thank you, Dmitri. Were you spotted?"

"Yes. By your pet."

Their hands stilled. Looking down, they saw Dmitri's prey-driven stare over the patient set of their black-socked paws.

"Disappointing, but not surprising," they said. "I hardly think they will draw any alarming connections and I find it unlikely that anyone could believe them if they somehow did."

Contents of the book whispered in their ear, looping and hushed on the wind.

"What would you like to do about it, Reaper?"

"Nothing has changed," they answered quickly. Maybe nervous. Definitely rushed. "It was only the first of many monsters to clear the path for him. And if things have changed, I am confident we can adapt. We are quick on our feet, you and I and Papa. Still they will never see it coming."

Dmitri left them in silence, slinking back into shadow on quick legs until the crooked alleyways of Brightloch swallowed the fox whole. They opened the ledger and looked at the sole name on the first page. A fantastical first, two drawn together with a violent slash.

"Sorry, pet," they said to the page.

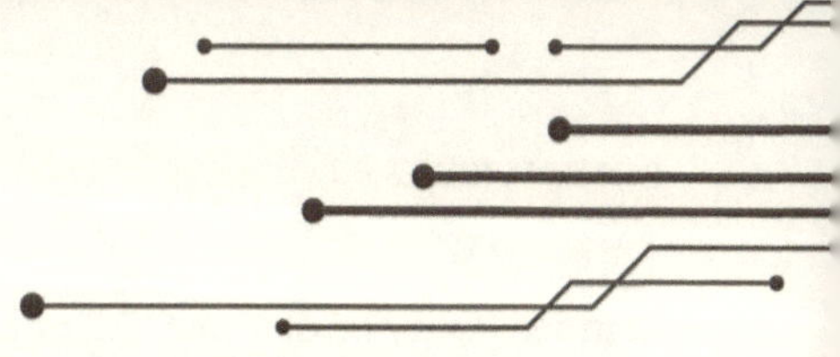

CHAPTER FORTY-SIX
YUMI

"I F WESTFALL IS NOT keeping up with the onslaught, then it shouldn't be an issue to send out Sentry officers on a rotation. No more than a week per officer and I will delegate the coordination of missions to Sentinel Mosley. It wouldn't be right to leave them to the wolves when we have more than enough resources to defend ourselves from Lost Ones," Yumi did her best to ignore the heaviness of her own eyelids as she spoke. The topic at hand was important, life-saving even, but she couldn't remember the last time she slept through the night. "I also wish to renegotiate with Eyon to discuss their participation in munitions aid."

"Your Highness, Westfall has been in contact with Eyon directly and there's not been a single—"

Her advisor was cut off when the heavy door to the meeting hall burst open. The crack of wood startled Yumi and she sat straighter to maintain her air of authority for whoever was walking in. She saw Moz's tall form easily, Griffin's behind him. The third figure brought Yumi to her feet.

"Fucking hell," Yumi swore as she stumbled to get out of her chair, sending papers and documents sliding off the table and she didn't have a single ounce of concern for the mess. Diplomacy be damned. Duty be damned. All of it, all of them.

Yumi ran to her wife.

She nearly tripped as she caught Avery's pink and freezing cheeks in her hands, turning her face to make sure it wasn't a trick. The freckles were in the right places. The light in her eyes caught the glow of chandeliers in all the correct ways. The dimple on the left side of her smile was exactly where she had left it.

"Oh gods, it *is* you," Yumi heaved through sobs.

Avery's fingers held one of Yumi's hands and she smiled, her chin tucking down to look through her dark eyelashes when she said, "Hi, baby."

Yumi pulled her into a kiss, holding her locked between her palms like she was a paper lantern on the verge of disappearing in the wind. Avery's kiss was staggered and afraid; she felt the transfer of exhaustion and Yumi let her go to cry. She pulled Avery into a tight embrace and over her shoulder she saw Moz watching them with a tear-streaked smile.

Lean arms encircled Yumi and Avery when Griffin nestled into their hug. Both his mothers looped an arm around his back and he nestled into the space, tucking Avery's head into his shoulder. Yumi silently waved Moz over and he was quick to wrap his arms around as many of them as he could, a wall of warmth at Avery's back keeping them all together. She felt Avery slacken in her arms, all of her muscles unlocking their tense hold.

They were whole again.

Yumi cradled Avery's face in her hands and pulled back her head to take a hard look at her face. It was coated in a layer of dirt and grime, flecked with blood, but still Avery smiled at her.

She laughed through her tears. "You are absolutely filthy, my beloved."

Her wife sputtered a laugh and nodded. Yumi stroked her thumbs gently across her cheeks but looked up at Moz.

"Will you make sure she gets upstairs and cleaned up? I'll finish up here and come find you."

"Of course, Yumes."

She watched her family walk out the doors and Yumi stood in place, the fat tears rolling off her jaw. Her advisors had been silent the entire reunion and when she turned to the group of mostly men, they lifted their heads to return the gazes they had uncomfortably averted.

"We are adjourning," Yumi stated firmly but smiled. "My fucking wife has returned."

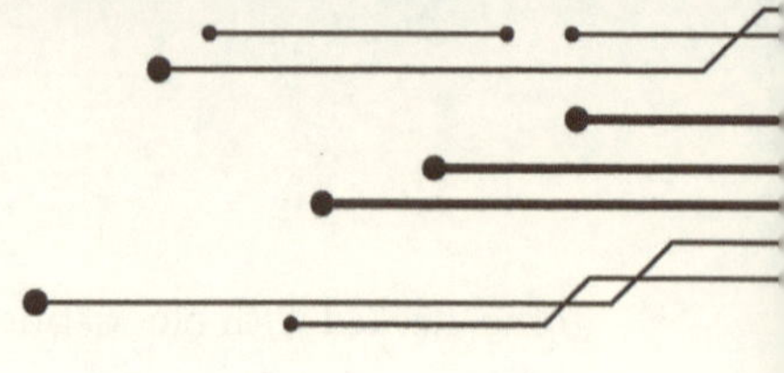

CHAPTER FORTY-SEVEN
MOZ

OZ HEARD THE SHOWER running in their adjoining bath when he cracked open the door. Humidity fogged the vanity mirror and the glass door behind which Avery's small silhouette stood in the stream. The water was almost certainly at scalding temperature— just the way she liked it.

"Love, can I come in?"

He heard no immediate answer after he called through the door, but there was a small and delayed hum from inside the steam. He set the glass of water he had fetched for her on the grey-veined marble countertop of the vanity.

Moz took off his glasses, already fogging in the wet heat, and stripped off his clothes. He cracked open the glass door, slowly to give Avery time to change her mind about company. She stood with her back to the heavy stream of water, thick sections of her dark hair clung to her shoulders and neck. Rivulets of water ran across bruises, easier to see now that the thick grime of the woods was cut through. A bloom of violent earthen green wrapped around her hip bone and met the faded cracks of purple lightning that sat low on her belly.

Seeing her whole and bare, thin and beaten, she was still the most treasured sight to see.

"Can I help you?" He asked softly.

The exhaustion swayed her on her feet as she stood and Avery nodded. Moz closed the glass door behind him as he stepped inside. He reached for Avery and winced under the water; he had assumed correctly.

He eased himself in and out again until he could tolerate the searing temperature. With a gentle touch, he pushed thick tendrils of wet hair off Avery's cheeks. Avery leaned her head forward, resting the weight of it against Moz's chest.

He cupped his hand behind her head, planting a wet kiss on her crown before he said, "I've missed you so much, Avery. More than you could ever know."

"I missed you," she echoed back, small and quiet.

He reached carefully for the bottle of shampoo on the ledge and tried to disturb her as little as possible when he hooked his other arm behind her to pour it into his open palm. Moz worked the soap into her hair and scrubbed it into foamy, dirty bubbles while she held still against his heart.

"I love you," he said softly as he reached up to detach the head of the shower to rinse out the suds without pushing her backwards into the stream.

As he reverently tended to his returned wife, he added: "I love your bravery... I love your heart... I love your joy... I love your well-placed fury... I love every part of you that you pick apart relentlessly... thank you for coming home."

He wasn't sure what reaction he expected from Avery, but it was definitely not the splatter from her small laugh against his wet skin.

"No problem... any time," she answered him.

Moz grinned. There she was.

"My funny, funny wife. I love you."

"I love you too, Mozzy."

He helped her wash in nothing but sincere care, gentle on her back in the places she was too sore to even attempt reaching on her own. She hovered like his shadow when he scrubbed himself and Moz did not voice it when he came to the conclusion that the prospect of being alone again terrified her. He bundled her up in a towel when they stepped out and helped her drag a comb through her waist length hair, taking longer than usual with the gnarled tangles in some places.

"You need a haircut, my love," he commented softly before he rinsed the comb in the sink.

"I know, I'll tell Yumi and she'll take care of me."

"Of course she will. She loves you and you're her queen. And you still haven't mastered scissors with your left hand, I'm willing to bet."

Avery watched him in the mirror with a pout on her face as she held up her right hand and lifted up her no-longer-the-middle finger.

"I've never been so happy to see someone flip me the bird," he said with a small laugh.

He locked eyes with her reflection as the fog slowly cleared from the mirror. Moz couldn't pry his gaze away from her small dream of a smile and that dimple in the left corner. It didn't feel enough to say that he loved her.

Moz kissed the crown of her head before reaching for his glasses on the counter. She studied him with a curious tilt to her square chin as he wiped condensation off the lenses with the towel around his waist.

"You're greyer than I remember," she commented.

"After all the stress you put me through?"

He watched his wife's face fall in her reflection. Her throat shifted like she was swallowing down tears and she looked at her bare feet on the mosaic tile floor.

"I'm sorry," she started, small and hushed. "I didn't—"

"Hey, hey, hey," he stopped Avery and wrapped her into an embrace with both arms, tucking her under his chin. "It's okay. I got you now. I'm sorry, I was teasing. Nobody is mad at you."

She began to cry and the sound broke him in a sharpening blade of guilt. Moz stroked her hair and kissed her damp forehead as he rocked her gently in his arms. The fog had cleared enough for him to see his own reflection in his peripheral vision even when his head had tucked down into her hair to hold her. Memories of dripping blood struck him, flashing white hot across his nerve endings.

That boy is a carbon copy of you.

This wasn't the time nor the place to address his discovery.

"It's okay," he said instead. "You're home now. Griffin's mama is back."

The small whimpers stopped.

"You wanna go see him?"

Avery pushed herself out of his hold and wiped tears from her face with the back of her hand, recomposing herself quickly.

"Yeah... yes, please."

Moz helped Avery into clean clothes and pretended not to be over the moon in delight when she opted to take one of his sweaters instead of her own. The green hem fell nearly to the knees of her black pants and he waited patiently on the end of their bed while she braided her hair. She placed the leather cap onto her right hand and looped the straps shut, tugging the sleeve of the sweater over the section that wrapped around her wrist.

"Needs to be washed, fuckin' hell," she mumbled to herself after she sniffed the cap and pulled a sour face. He just smiled.

Before Moz could ask her if she was ready, Avery had already thrown open the door of their bedroom. He followed her into the hallway and down towards the top floor landing of the grand staircase. They didn't quite make it before Moz heard the distinct clack of nails on stone.

"Incoming," he warned.

The hall rang with loud barks and the sound of paws quickened when the dog ran full speed from the upper east wing entry. Avery dropped down to her knees, arms thrown open.

"MAYA!"

Maya jumped into Avery's arms, knocking her off the careful balance on the balls of her feet and she fell onto her backside. The shepherd dog wagged her tail furiously and shoved her snout into every nook and cranny in Avery's neck, picking up as much of her scent as she could get.

"Hi baby girl! I missed you!" Avery cooed, shaking the sides of Maya's furry head with both of her hands.

Moz smiled and his gaze floated up to the oil painting above their heads. The steel eyes in Avery's portrait felt warmer with the radiant life of its subject so close again, laughter lacing around excited barks.

The heart of Brightloch Castle had returned to its yearning bones.

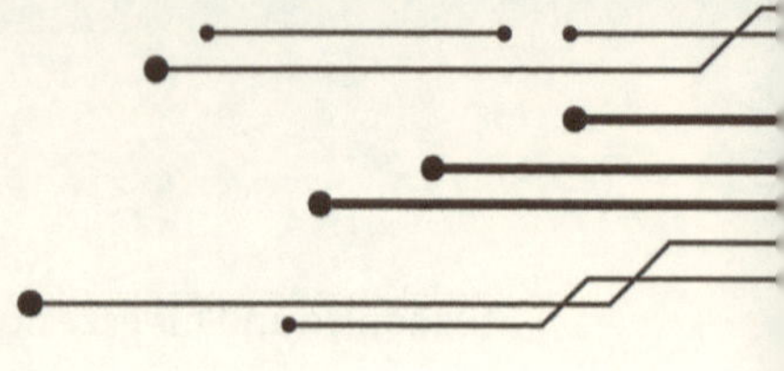

CHAPTER FORTY-EIGHT
GRIFFIN

THIS FAMILY MEETING FELT more crowded than most with both Mama and Aunt Lily there. Griffin understood why, but it was hard not to notice the awkward avoidance from most of his family members to stare while Aunt Lily explained the mechanisms of schizophrenia to Avery. It had onset while she was missing, so there was quite a lot to catch her up to speed on with regards to how her only child had changed during her absence. Mama wasn't worried about staring; she watched him like he might catch on fire at any moment and she wound her anxious hold around his hand as she nodded, listening intently.

"Like many things," Lily said to her, "it will take some adjustment. From an outside perspective, I believe he has been coping quite well both through his own work and the support from his loved ones. Griffin, if you have anything to add or correct that I've said, please feel free to at your comfort level."

Griffin shook his head. The symptoms explanation sounded routine and the accommodations Aunt Lily outlined almost perfectly echoed what his father had told Kurosaki not too long ago.

"And this all happened because I was gone," Avery murmured, her voice heavy and saddened.

"Woah, time out," Yumi interrupted. "Avery, this isn't your fault. You weren't gone by your own choice, and even if you were, that didn't cause this. Tell her, Lily."

"She's right," Lily shifted her gaze across the table from Yumi back to Avery. "Griffin's doctor has said that he was likely showing symptoms earlier than two years ago when you… they were just more subtle in the prodromal phase. A traumatic event can expedite the onset, but it's not the cause. Does that make sense?"

"Yeah, it does."

Mama let go of Griffin's hand, only to wrap him into a hug and tuck his head under her chin. It strained his neck with how much shorter she was, but he let her.

He had cried many times before when he missed these moments with his mother, but couldn't bring himself to cry now. His relief was a quiet thing and he didn't want to drown out the sound of her gentle voice with his sobbing. It could come when the feeling of missing her finally left him in peace.

"I am so sorry I wasn't here, Griff," she said softly. "I'm not going anywhere. You're my number one always and I am so proud of the young man you've become."

He held his breath and his tears, wondering why the feeling of flatness wouldn't break even for Mama.

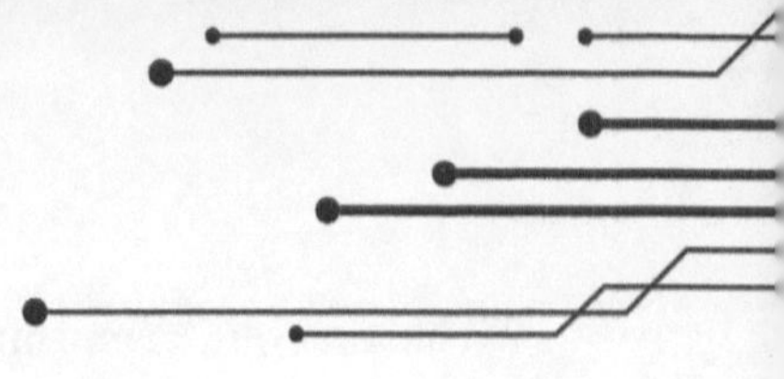

CHAPTER FORTY-NINE
MOZ

AFTER MARIA AND LILY had retired to their temporary guest room and Griffin had gone to bed, as far as he claimed, they sat around the kitchen with a mood of heaviness. Moz had expected the jubilance of Avery's return to last for months, but the daunting question of what was to come next hung over all of their heads.

"They're targeting all of the witches who were present at the ritual grounds twenty years ago," Moz stated again, the weight of their situation still feeling unreal to him. "We're not sure yet who they are."

With a mouthful of half-stale sourdough, Avery raised her hand. Moz furrowed his brows but smiled.

"Um, yes?"

"That's easy," Avery said, dropping her hand and swallowing. "The Cult of Paion."

Everyone stared at her.

"Are you fucking kidding me? You just know this offhand?" Kurosaki was the one who questioned; both Yumi and Moz were flabbergasted into silence.

Avery shrugged, but didn't turn to face where he was leaning against the counter with his arms folded. "I wasn't just sitting with my thumbs in my ass for two years."

That time, Moz did frown. "I wouldn't exactly say we were either, my love."

Avery patted him on the shoulder as she stood up, taking her empty plate to the sink, and dropped it inside without washing. *Yup, that's her.* She sat back down before she said:

"No, I know. I had some help figuring it out. It's a political faction that's cropped up in the last fifteen or so years. I saw a bunch of people come and go from the scene, and putting together that Paion never showed his ass when—"

"Wait, the scene? You were right there, that entire time?"

Avery looked from Moz to Yumi across from her, but turned to Kurosaki when she said, "not always. But I saw you when you came with them, Kuro. I thought it was important that I saw who came back. And two people always did: Gaspard and another man I don't recognize."

"Gaspard? Like the Scout?"

Avery nodded, wiping bread crumbs off the island counter with her sleeve. "That's the bitch."

Moz took off his glasses and put his head in his hands. The kitchen wobbled around him and he needed to steady himself as he gathered his thoughts.

A Scout was in on it. Someone who was there that day, no less. What about Wilson and Lind? The only person there that he trusted to not have made an attempt on his wife's life was Shank.

"This is getting a little deep for me," he muttered, rubbing his palms down flat on his face as he exhaled. "We need to catalog everything you know, everything I know, and then compare the two."

"I just really need to rest," Avery said, her voice worn and ragged around the edges. He knew she was going to sleep for the majority of the next day but couldn't blame her for it. "I want to stand in the shower again for two hours and then I want to rest."

"Sure," he agreed as he put his glasses back on. "Rest up and we'll get everything together in the morning when you have a rested mind."

"I think I should get to stay with Avery tonight since Moz...," Yumi started to say, and then trailed off as soon as she appeared to realize where her sentence was going and that this was *not* a discussion Moz had begun yet.

He froze but tried to gesture with his raised eyebrows so that Yumi could see she had fucked up. Avery looked from Yumi, to Moz, and then back at her wife.

"I *really* think you should finish that sentence, Yumes," Avery urged quietly.

Moz's stomach dropped and he reached his hand under his glasses, pinching the bridge of his nose between his thumb and index finger.

"Yumi, Kurosaki, can you please give us a minute."

Kurosaki hesitated, but Moz had never seen Yumi flee a room so fast. When they were alone, Moz readjusted his glasses, put his hand back on the ledge of the kitchen island, and turned on his stool to face Avery head-on.

She watched him with a studying gaze, the dark bags under her eyes tired. Moz felt absolutely sick that this was coming up in a way he hadn't planned or prepared for. The words he thought he wanted to say had been churning in his brain ever since he had first kissed Kurosaki, but he hadn't landed on any of them for sure. The moment was here and there was no putting this bastard cat back in the rucksack.

"Avery, my love," he spoke the words sweetly, but they had the opposite of its intended effect when she went rigid and sat up tall on her stool. He continued anyway:

"You know we have talked before about the polyamorous dynamics of our relationship. And I had always been open with you and honest when I checked in and said 'hey, I'm good on my side.' We agreed to talk about it if things ever changed because that is due respect. While you were gone, things changed. Not until very recently, but they did change after Kurosaki came to help."

Avery reeled back with a look of hurt. "While I was *gone*? Moz, I was fighting tooth and nail out there to come home! If you even knew what I... Were you even trying at all to find me or were you just holed up here with Kurosaki biding time?"

He blinked in disbelief and waited for her words to settle around him like river stones. But he could only think of long nights bent over case folder after case folder. Of catching the mocking whispers of people around him day after day and never seemed to give his family's horrible situation any grace. Moz still woke up every morning and *tried*.

The accusation was hurtful and he tried to not let it sour his words when he reached forward, cradling her face in his hands. "Avery. I looked for you day and night. I exhausted every avenue possible, even the ones that didn't make sense and painted me as a madman. I let them bury an empty coffin with your name on it because I knew that whoever it was, they would slip up. You are the sun in my sky and still I looked for you in the darkest hours. Do you want to hear that I was suffering? Because I was. Those were another two years of my life spent without you that I can never get back."

He stared at her face between his palms in the long moment she was quiet.

"If I am the sun, what is he?"

Her voice was the softest melody, one he thought he was doomed to hear only in his dreams until he met his Reaper in his final hour.

"Well, he would obviously be the moon. A light I would never see had I not first learned to love the sun. I never would have slept these two years and been driven to insanity had he not convinced me to just sleep. To try again in the morning."

She watched him, the blue eyes he had missed so terribly flitted across his face before she asked, "why now? Why after all these years?"

"That's just what happens sometimes, Ave," he answered truthfully and brushed the back of his fingers across her cheek to retrain a fallen lock of hair. "When we were younger, we weren't ready. We were more concerned about hurting everyone around us and not being concerned at all that we were hurting each other as a consequence. But with age, we learned. It was the wrong time, wrong person before, so to speak. But times change and so do people."

Avery put her gentle hand on his knee, looking down at it as she considered his words in silence. When she said nothing, he added:

"He really did help us, by the way. He was looking for you, hard. And I don't think we would have gotten to Maria and Lily in time without him. We both felt guilty for not being able to just talk to you right away. I'm grateful you're home and that we are now."

Avery stood up into the space between his knees and wrapped her arms around his shoulders, drawing him into the safety of her embrace. When Moz locked his arms around her waist, she felt smaller to him than she ever had before. Worn down by whatever had happened to her out there in the wilderness. She was silent when her hand snaked up his neck, stroking his hair on the back of his head with three fingers.

"Do you want to talk about what happened to you?" He murmured into her shoulder.

"No," she said simply.

Moz tightened his hold on her so she would never disappear again and they stood in silence for a long moment, alone in the dim kitchen. Nothing had ever felt more real and solid in his life than his wife returning to his atmosphere and he wanted nothing more than to cry. He felt the bite of an old habit that told him to hold onto the tears, that she didn't need them right now. But that wasn't his voice anymore, so he let them fall.

He cried, knuckling the back of Avery's sweater in his grip. Avery's hand stilled but she drew him as close to her as space would allow.

"No... please don't stop, I've missed that so much, Ave," he begged her through sobs. She didn't hesitate when her fingers raked through his hair again and she kissed his temple.

"I know, love," she whispered. "It's okay… I'm okay, we're okay. I love you."

Moz held Avery for the longest time and her fingers smoothed out his tears until they lulled into a quiet. They stopped falling, but his eyes were still wet when he lifted his head to look at her face.

The tender skin under her eyes was sunken and shadowed grey with cumulative exhaustion. Cheekbones that softened during the years since birthing their son had sharpened again, gaunt with hunger. Avery herself looked to be one of the revenants she had once commanded. Even so, the softest facet of her nature was exactly where she had left it. Her hands lifted from his neck and she used her thumbs to gently wipe under the frame of his glasses where it hit his tear streaked cheeks.

"I love you," he whispered.

"I love you, too," Avery said again. She kissed his forehead and held her lips against it when she added, "my saint, my hero."

He held his hand over the bumps of her spine when he lifted his head to kiss Avery. Still she felt fearful on his mouth and the affection she returned was timid. Moz feared what he would learn if she ever decided to divulge the events of the past two years to him.

She parted from him and she stroked his cheek with the thumb she still held to his face. His wife looked down at him with her home of a smile, dimple in the left corner, when she asked softly:

"Do you love him?"

"Yeah, I do," he answered. "I think I'm ready this time."

Avery smiled small and her fingers trailed down from his cheek so that she could squeeze his hand. "Please only accept the love you deserve. I can't stand by and watch someone hurt you."

His eyes widened with the realization of what she was saying. All of the fear, all of the shame; glossed over in the tide of her compassion.

"Yeah?"

"Yeah."

Moz squeezed her in a tight hug and Avery coughed, choking under the sudden pressure. She tapped his leg with her three fingers, still holding his to signal him to ease off.

"If you find Kurosaki, can you send him my way?" She asked.

"Avery, don't–"

"Don't worry, I have nothing unkind to say to him."

Moz let go of his embrace around her and stood up. "I'll go find him, I'm sure he's pissing himself over it and would like to get it past him."

Her chin cocked to the side as she smiled up at him. Small, but so familiar and so welcomed.

"Thank you, love," she said softly.

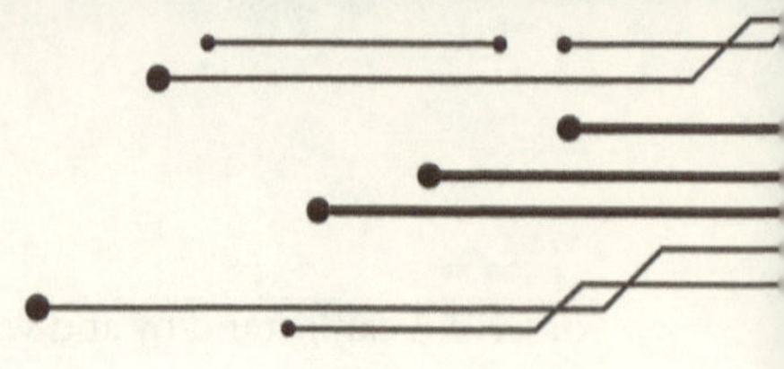

CHAPTER FIFTY
KUROSAKI

K UROSAKI VERGED ON PACING grooves into the stone floor of his bedroom. He dreaded the conversation that Moz and Avery were undoubtedly having at that very moment because he knew that if she was against it, Kurosaki would be the one to go. Moz would never drop the mother of his child if he felt forced to choose; hell, it's what he expected and hoped for if a choice had to be made. Guilt racked him hard enough for his feelings of yearning for a married man and there was no way he could live through tearing a family apart after they had just been reunited.

The knock on the door froze him in his anxious circuit until the door pushed open and Moz stepped into the teal guest bedroom. He must have seen the sheer terror on Kurosaki's face before he pulled him into a hug. Grief swelled in the pit of Kurosaki's stomach.

This can't be the last one. Please, I can't–

"Hey, hey, hey," Moz shushed him before Kurosaki even realized that the small bubbles of sobs were beginning to form at the bottom of his throat. "It's okay, we're good."

Kurosaki threw his head up, nearly knocking Moz square in the chin.

"Are you serious?"

"Yeah, she said–"

Kurosaki cut him off abruptly when he locked his fingers around the collar of Moz's black jumper and pulled him into a deep kiss. A small hum of surprise vibrated across his lips before Moz returned it, the sweet taste of clove and candied orange on his mouth. Moz held Kurosaki's face in both hands and the anchor steadied him when his feet still buzzed with the panic of his pacing. Moz's body heat felt electrified against Kurosaki as his brain only echoed one word: *mine.*

Moz let him go, just far enough to say softly: "We're good... But she does want to speak with you."

His stomach dropped. A classic Avery Porter intimidation tactic if he had ever seen one. Moz detected the clear dread on his face before he added:

"She promised not to rough house. You tell me if she breaks it, okay?"

Kurosaki opened his mouth to speak but found no words. The mere idea that Moz would have taken a side with him over Avery stunned him when he had spent so long believing he didn't have a side at all.

"Yeah.. yeah, okay. I'll do that."

Kurosaki's feet felt heavier with every step down the grand foyer staircase and he froze in the doorway when he found Avery in the kitchen, like the rest of her family tended to gravitate to. He decided it was because the room felt the least like part of a castle. If he ignored the tall lancet windows looking out into particularly manicured gardens, it was just an ordinary heart of an ordinary home.

She had a newspaper spread out on the island counter where she sat at a stool. Kurosaki didn't want to interrupt her, but also did not want to make her hunt him down a second time. So he sat down at one of the chairs across the kitchen and waited.

And waited.

And waited.

The pit in his stomach grew heavy until finally she looked up and folded the paper, neatly setting it in the center of the butcher block. Avery stood, scraped her stool across the floor, and approached him faster than he could find the time to back out.

Avery trapped him with both of her hands planted on the chair's armrests on either side of him.

"My husband, Kuro?"

His mouth went dry. He struggled to speak but found no words.

"This is the first and last time we will talk about this, Kuro. Because if you hurt him again... if you hurt my husband, the father of my son, the best friend of my wife, there will be no talking about this because you will have picked a fight with me. So I am telling you now: if you are going to run, this is your last chance. You can walk out that door right now and you will be forgiven, but any time after this I will not abide. Do you understand me?"

Every previous time Kurosaki believed Avery Porter to be a fearsome woman paled in comparison to who stood before him, hands locking him in his chair and bent to look him in the eye. This was every animal of prey with even the faintest sense of maternal instinct, all rolled into one pint-sized package. The serious flicker of her steel eyes was a far cry from the painting that had watched his every move from the grand hall foyer since the moment he had first arrived. This was not a happy newlywed; she fought the grave and won.

"I'm not running away this time, Ave."

"Do you swear it?"

"I'll swear my life on it. Every time."

She watched him for a long moment before she let go of the chair, standing up straight and seeming satisfied with his answer.

"I believe you," she decided. "Thank you for your word."

Kurosaki hadn't realized he had tensed his body until he let his shoulders drop.

"I'm going to bed," she announced as she turned to walk away from him. "As you can probably imagine, I'm tired as all fuck and we have had a lot of big conversations today. I'm glad you came, Kuro. Thank you."

"Welcome home, Ave," he said softly. She smiled over her shoulder at him and then Avery was gone again.

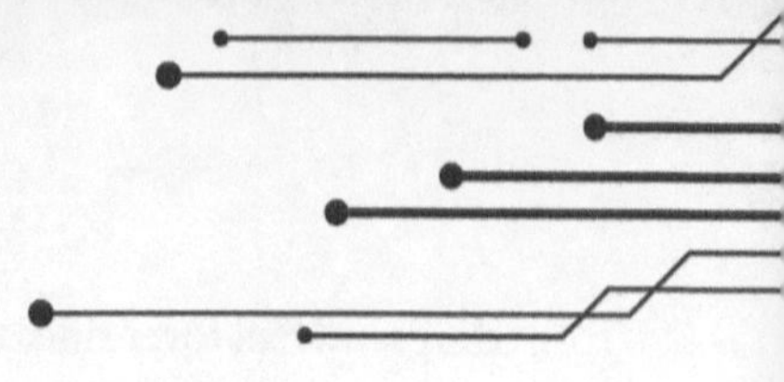

CHAPTER FIFTY-ONE
MOZ

OZ SAT ON THE third step of the grand foyer staircase as he waited for Kurosaki. Avery had already passed him by, running a hand over his shoulder as she said, "just wait for him. Let him have his own company."

"What the fuck did you say to him, Ave?"

"I wasn't unkind, I promise. But regardless of that, it's a lot."

She had bent down, planting a kiss on his head to go with their "love you" before she disappeared up the stairs towards Yumi's chamber in the upper west wing.

Moz wasn't sure how long he sat waiting and at several points he considered ignoring his wife's advice to go check on Kurosaki. Where was the line drawn between the space to breathe and the failure to help? He felt incapable of finding it as of lately.

Finally, Kurosaki emerged from the hall, his arm held up as he rubbed the back of his head. Moz frowned; Avery wouldn't have actually fought with him, would she?

"You okay?" Moz asked as he stood up. "I hope she wasn't too hard on you."

Kurosaki shook his head. "No, she was fine. Very reasonable, actually."

He widened his eyes, bewildered. "My wife? Reasonable?"

"*Ha.* No, I mean it. We're all good."

"I'm glad," Moz answered softly.

They hung in an awkward silence, standing an even more awkward distance apart from each other at the foot of the stairs.

"So, I uh—" Moz started.

"C'mon, Idiot," Kurosaki said, the name holding more endearment than insult, and he passed him to head up the stairs. Moz grinned and followed.

There was an intimacy in the act of following Kurosaki to his room and knowing that secrecy didn't matter anymore. They were together, just as they should have always been.

He shut the door to Kurosaki's room behind him just as Kurosaki flicked on the lamp at the nightstand. Moz felt a fleeting moment of bizarre shyness watching Kurosaki in the warm, dim light when he turned around to face him and a soft glow illuminated his hard edges. *Good gods* - he was handsome.

Closing the distance before Kurosaki could speak, Moz wrapped his arms around him. He held the shorter man close and relished the rise and fall of his breathing against his own rib cage. Kurosaki tucked his arms up behind Moz's back, holding both his shoulder blades in his ringed hands. Moz tilted his head down and pressed his forehead to Kurosaki's. Brown eyes swallowed his field of vision before they flicked down and watched his mouth, leaving Moz with an undeniable feeling of hunger. He knew every shape of that mouth just as well as he recalled every insult it once slung as avoidant endearments. And drawing forth the taste of it once again...

"We don't need to do this right now," Kurosaki murmured. "She just got home and I'm sure you're feeling a lot of things."

"I am," Moz admitted. "But they're all things I'm going to be feeling for a very long time. It's okay."

Kurosaki's fingers lifted from his shoulder blade and cradled the back of Moz's neck with a gentleness that he had been convinced for the longest time didn't exist in them.

Moz fumbled at first with the top buttons of Kurosaki's shirt with their foreheads pressed together, but had their placement figured out by the time he loosened the third. Kurosaki's mouth lingered just out of reach of his own like they were playing a game of chicken to see who would crash first. But the anticipation thrilled Moz and he loved the way it dragged out the moment. He wanted to be sure he remembered this forever.

When the last button was undone, Moz helped Kurosaki out of the shirt and his fingertips ran down the plane of his back, ridged with the smooth streaks of scarred skin.

"I want to be something we were never brave enough to be before," Moz murmured, his breath rushing past Kurosaki's ear and he felt the shift of bare goose flesh under his fingers.

"What's that?"

"Tender."

The ghosts of Kurosaki's scars were a map to home that Moz could read blindfolded. A puckered smear across his bicep; *road rash*. A faint comet cutting into his waist; *stabbing*. A crescent hooked in the hollow of his collarbone; *the things he won't talk about*. The lateral lines underneath his pectoral muscles; *my violently beautiful, self-made man.*

"It used to scare me," Kurosaki murmured. He didn't finish his thought with words, but turned his head towards where Moz had leaned over his shoulder to meet him again. Moz watched the handsome face that again filled his vision. The flicker of his late autumn eyes across his face. The shadows under his soft eyelashes. The anticipatory parting of his lips and small draw of his breath. It was art, it was music, it was *him.*

A second chance bloomed in the safety of relief and Moz refused to let it go to waste. Honesty this time; nothing less.

"Kurosaki, I love you."

"I love you... I love you... I have always loved you," Kurosaki dragged out the words when he closed the space and kissed him, gentle and deep. Honey warmth spread from his cheeks, dripped down his spine, and pooled low in his belly. Moz couldn't tell if it was the words or the hand sliding under the back of his sweater that made his heart thrum against his ribs. The other man pulled away just far enough to add, "You have shattered me and filled the cracks with gold."

Moz lifted his arms above his head and Kurosaki pulled off the sweater before they collided again. He held the face of the shorter man and eased him into backwards steps without letting their kiss falter. Kurosaki sank backwards onto the bed of messed blankets and Moz followed diligently.

With his arms planted on either side of Kurosaki's shoulders and his feet still on the floor, he broke the kiss to look down at him and say, "no, my darling, you have always been golden."

He meant it even more with Kurosaki splayed underneath him, a soft halo of black hair around his home of a face. His hands reached out to Moz's temples and he gently pulled the wire frame of his glasses free. Kurosaki carefully folded them and rolled onto his side to gingerly set the glasses on the nightstand. Moz watched the entire act even when the edges in his vision became a little too soft; the way Kurosaki moved was deliberate and thoughtful. Enchanting to let his eyes rest on. When he turned back, Moz leaned down into a kiss.

Kurosaki's heat sparked and crackled from below when his fingers ran up Moz's arms, across his back to press his palms against his shoulder blades. The pressure coaxed Moz down until he felt his growing stiffness nestled between Kurosaki's thighs. His soft tongue swiped across Moz's lip and Moz tugged at him with gentle teeth– loving through devouring.

Moz's mouth broke free and trailed down the short beard on Kurosaki's chin, down his neck, and settled in the hollow of his collarbone next to the ghostly crescent.

"Can I touch you?" He murmured into his bones.

Kurosaki nodded, threading his slender fingers into Moz's curls. "Fingers. No mouth."

Moz hummed a simple acceptance into his soft skin, taking a small inhale of eucalyptus before he eased back onto his knees. When they were young, Kurosaki's sexual goalposts changed every time; sometimes mid-fuck. He felt grateful that their clunky communication got easier over time and their hard-earned rhythm kept its tune after so many years of distance.

His fingers ran down Kurosaki's center with a slow reverence and over his black pants, tracing over the waistband before he unnotched the button. Kurosaki lifted his hips to help Moz pull them down and the small laugh when he struggled to get them free from Kurosaki's ankles was music to his ears. When he was finally free from the last of his clothes, Moz froze.

Kurosaki laid bare for him for the first time in decades. His skin was unknown to him, but somehow still just as he remembered. Hard lines of him had softened and the trail of hair creeping up to his navel had darkened.

"What's wrong?" Kurosaki looked at him with concern.

Moz didn't answer at first. He ducked down again and kissed him with far more fervor. Kurosaki's fingers spread across his chest and held him by the heart. His kisses trailed around the curve of his chin until Moz lifted himself to balance on his knees.

"You are a man made of the stars," he murmured and he grinned when a sweet flush crept across Kurosaki's cheeks.

Moz was careful to keep his mouth at a distance as he traced his fingers down the middle of his chest. Fluttered down his stomach. *Oh gods* - he wished he could take a taste.

He hovered between his thighs and dragged his tongue over two of his fingers before he skimmed them over his folds. Kurosaki bucked under the touch and Moz immediately lifted his hand.

"Are you okay?"

Kurosaki just laughed, a warm and heady sound with his neck thrown back on the pillow. "Don't chicken out on me now."

Moz smirked. Every time those little taunts bubbled back to

the surface, he felt young again. Like he was forever twenty-six and fucked like death was just a word in a language he would never understand. He knew it now, just as he understood the thrum of life underneath his fingers. In the writhing of Kurosaki's muscles and rush of blood to his cheeks when he worked him in careful strokes. Nestled into every note from the chorus of his moans.

"I love you," Moz said again, his face tucked against the soft flesh of Kurosaki's inner thigh.

"Come here."

He followed Kurosaki's beckon up to his face. Ringed fingers cradled his neck with a light touch when Moz kissed him with a deep burn.

Kurosaki gently pushed Moz onto his back, thrilling him with the shift in control.

"Hey now, I wasn't trying to get rough with you."

Kurosaki's gaze rolled up just as he was sliding down. He murmured, "You and I both know well enough that this isn't rough."

He helped peel off Moz's pants, far more agile in the act than Moz had been. Kurosaki didn't stop to look at their bare skin tangling together on the bed. His fingers ran down Moz's ribs as he sank down towards his waist. He would have normally requested that the silver rings come off, but the bite of metal felt like a burning reminder: *it's him.*

"You're a goddamn wet dream," Kurosaki murmured against his navel.

Moz almost managed out a laugh but gasped when Kurosaki's tongue trailed down and over his hip bones. Fingers encompassed the base of him and the flat of Kurosaki's tongue ran under his full length, over the leaking slit before he was completely taken by wet heat. He grunted at the pull on his cock between hollowed cheeks.

Kurosaki looked up at him with heady and half-lidded eyes. He took him deeper into his throat and a soft hum vibrated around Moz's length. Moz groaned and his hips bucked on reflex to push himself deeper into Kurosaki's face, taking fistfuls of his hair into his hands. He laid his free hand on Moz's hip bone and pushed down, settling him back on the mattress before his soft tongue swirled around him. Moz laughed a strained sound, half-annoyed.

"You still give head like a god," he commented, breathy and nearing half-spent. His only answer was faster bobs of his head and Moz threw back his head to steady himself.

Kurosaki sucked harder, sloppy sounds passing through his mouth when he raised his head slowly off. He held Moz's eyes as he ran his flattened tongue up his thick length and Moz felt the small twitch in his groin watching the thread of spit that followed his bottom lip. The whole sight made him *much. Goddamn. Hornier.*

When Kurosaki lifted himself, Moz sat upright to gently push him over and onto his side. They laid facing each other with tangled ankles that crashed together when one of them would shudder under a moan. He rubbed hungry pressure with wet fingers on Kurosaki, who was stroking deep and languid motions on his cock.

Their kisses were sloppy and desperate, broken by sharp sighs of pleasure. *Gods*– to think about how long he had been without was painful.

"*Moz.*"

His own name wrapped around Kurosaki's moan in his ear sent shivers rippling up his spine. The fingers wrapped around his length pulled deeper and the heat pooling in his groin burned brighter.

"I'm gettin'… real fuckin' close," Moz warned between heavy pants under the cut of Kurosaki's sharp jawbone. He tried to remember the last time he made a mess of his beautiful face.

Kurosaki's jerking eased as he said, "No you're not. Not until you're inside me."

Fuck.

But Moz grinned and they turned again in a dance long remembered. Kurosaki splayed beneath him as Moz sat back on his knees, licking a streak again on his index and middle fingers. He was slower, deliberate with tasting the other man on his skin.

Moz pushed him with one finger in the only place Kurosaki would grant him entry, slowly so he had time to relax around the penetration. Kurosaki took a deep breath and shifted his hips.

"You okay?" Moz was soft with his check-in.

Kurosaki nodded small, with focused pulls of his shoulders in each breath. Moz's finger stilled.

"Hey, can you please answer me? Are you okay?"

He hadn't expected the breathy laugh from Kurosaki and froze, unsure of what to do.

"Moz, I swear if you don't fuck me well past the point of coherence, I'm biting your dick off."

Moz's jaw dropped.

"Damn, if you missed me, just say that!"

Kurosaki flicked his gaze to Moz's eyes and a seriousness settled over their knotted limbs. The taunt didn't match the soft wanting in the parted fix of his mouth, turned up in the slightest smile. A darkness burned at its edges that could have only come from wanting what was unholy.

"I've missed you. Unbearably so."

Fire spread and Moz had never cared less about sin. The gods never cared about him. Kurosaki did; time and time again. And Moz would pray to him in skin and sweat and song and moans until he was a gilded deity to live forever.

He pushed a second finger slowly, flicking his gaze up to Kurosaki's face to find any non-verbal cues that this was no longer okay. His head threw back as he sighed out an exhale, breathing into the initial discomfort when Moz worked him carefully with a slow scissoring of his fingers before adding a third.

When it became easier to move and Kurosaki's calculated breathing eased, Moz slowed.

"Do you still want it," he murmured. "Do you want me to fuck you?"

"No, I came all this way to edge you and leave."

Moz paused and looked down at Kurosaki incredulously before he broke into a stifled laughter. Kurosaki lifted an eyebrow with an amorous turn of his smile as he watched his face. He felt every inch of warmth from the look and believed every word Kurosaki had spoken of adoration.

His laughter softened when he said again, "I love you."

"I love you," Kurosaki echoed, the shapes of the words quiet on his mouth.

Moz fished for the bottle he knew would be in the nightstand drawer. He slicked himself before he repositioned his balance on his knees and pushed the wet head of his length into his tight hole. Kurosaki moaned, every bit as untamed as he had remembered but the sound racked him with chills as if it had been new. A perfect, heavenly sigh.

The dip of his hips was calculated and he moved cautiously to pump again slowly. Deeper and deeper, little by little until Kurosaki could take the thick length. He grunted a pleased sound at Kurosaki's warmth around his cock and gripped his hips to keep him anchored and safe.

"*Yeah,*" Kurosaki managed a sigh between pushes and Moz recognized his cue to pick up the pace.

His thrusts quickened to the tune of sweaty skin colliding in carnal slaps. Moz's hands ran down the backside of his thighs to brace his bent knees as he drove his hips into Kurosaki's ass. Their moans laced around each other in a song he hadn't heard in ages but still knew the words by heart.

Moz drove into him hard, letting go of one knee so he could lean farther and kiss him deeply. Kurosaki moaned onto his tongue and Moz fucked the sounds into small, submissive whimpers. Kurosaki: masculine and tough, sharp and reserved, biting and honest. And he came undone around Moz's cock.

Kurosaki's tongue flicked across his lip before he parted from the kiss. His cheek brushed across Moz's when he tilted his mouth towards his ear to say:

"I missed this...," his own moan cut him off and the sound in

Moz's ear in time with the thrust boiled his bones. "I missed us."

Kurosaki's fingers knotted in his hair and Moz lifted himself only as high as was necessary to see the yearning look that never left his face and where he buried himself inside.

"Gods... you're so fucking beautiful."

Moz's fingers ghosted across Kurosaki's neck, nothing more than a light touch at first until slowly he let the weight settle. He wasn't going to press down the way he knew Kurosaki liked, but left it as a reminder of what kind of play could come next time if he just said the word. Moz almost regretted his own tease when he felt Kurosaki arch beneath him.

He dropped down to lay behind him, lifting Kurosaki's knee gently to slip back inside. Moz grinned wickedly at the groan that spilled from his lips and the greedy push back onto his cock. He peppered his neck in kisses and settled into the rock of his hips against his ass.

Moz's arm wrapped around Kurosaki's shoulders and his fingers spread across his chest to pin him close as he thrusted from behind. With his other hand, his fingers knotted in black hair and Moz pulled with a yank just sharp enough to elicit a small gasp. He licked a long stroke up Kurosaki's jugular and the man bucked with a loud moan in his arms.

"You're not gonna fuckin' bite me, are you?"

Moz managed out a laugh between labored pants and he paused his thrusting just long enough to take the back of Kurosaki's neck in his teeth, taking care to avoid the thread of silver chain. But it was no more than a playful nibble, no pulling blood to the surface like he had before to mark what was rightfully his. Something inside him wanted nothing more than to be gentle to Kurosaki to make up for everything.

Pressure built in Moz's muscles and his hand ran down Kurosaki's sweat-glistened stomach to reach for his dick; to take him along with him when he saw the stars. Kurosaki writhed under his fervent strokes, clenching tight around his throbbing cock until he came apart in bucking hips and gasping moans. *Gods,* he always made the most heavenly sounds.

"Good boy," Moz's praise was only half-joking, and his fingers never lifted from his heavy strokes. Moz pounded his hips faster and the spaces between his unhindered moans became shorter when he felt the throbbing burst of heat.

He emptied hot ropes into Kurosaki just as he kissed his slick neck hard, grunting loudly into salty skin. Their heavy breathing synced and Kurosaki's strong shoulders heaved into the safety of his own. Panting, he pushed slower final thrusts until they stilled.

Moz would have loved to hold him there forever while he planted kisses on Kurosaki's flushed cheeks. They laid entangled still for long moments until his erection settled inside Kurosaki.

Moz hated overly saccharine phrases like "making love", but he didn't know what else to call it. He had fucked Izaya Kurosaki before, but it had always been to show that he should have been the one that he chose. It was always a performance of who could take a beating better, who could get off their knees quicker. But *this*?

No, this was love.

This love didn't have the cut of teeth solely for the purpose of claiming what belonged to it. It didn't shove with brute force to avoid cradling close. Didn't mock or deal verbal lashings to fight for dominance when it had the same three words so eagerly ready on both their tongues: *I love you, I love you, I love you.*

He'd tolerate using the dumb phrase if it meant everything it entailed belonged to them.

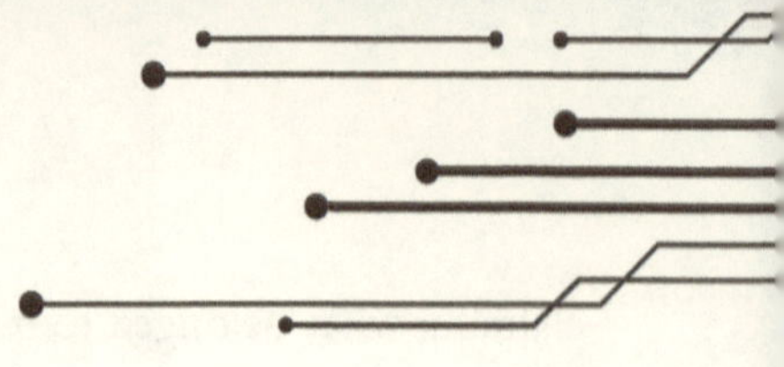

CHAPTER FIFTY-TWO
KUROSAKI

KUROSAKI SLIPPED IN AND out of sleep cradled into the warm body at his back. A gentle heartbeat thrummed slow and steady against his shoulder blade. Painted light of the early morning scattered him in teals until the peace would lull him back into slumber again. The sleep that had wrapped him since coming to Brightloch was a contentment that he could only recall feeling when he had only first began to fall in love with Moz all those years ago.

The next time he awoke, the nest of skin enveloping him had vanished. He blinked his eyes hard with determination to not let sleep claim him again.

His body ached and yet it was not accompanied with the deep-seated regret he had grown to expect after sex. The bedroom came into focus and Moz's back was to him as he pulled on a jumper over his head. Kurosaki watched the heavenly figure of eyes and wings tattooed on his back disappear under the wool just before Moz turned.

Moz smiled at Kurosaki, bent down over the side of the bed, and kissed his cheek before he murmured softly against the curve of his face, "I need to go check on everyone, take your time."

No, come back.

He yearned for the warmth of his clove and orange scented skin before it had fully left him. A sleepy grunt came from him in place of a lover's plea and he heard the small music of Moz's laugh in response.

Kurosaki felt certain he could have stayed bundled up all day long if Moz had stayed, but the warmth of the blankets lost a little of its comfort when he closed the door behind him. He sat up, rubbed the last of the sleepy sand out of his eyes, and swung his feet over the edge of the bed to stand on the cold floor.

He rifled through his backpack, mumbling to himself that he would eventually have to just put everything in the bureau drawers. He'd get to it when he ran out of clothes and had to wash them all in one go in procrastinator's folly.

Before he would dress, he fished out the black protective case for his sharps and hormones. As he unzipped it, a piece of folded paper slipped out and floated to the floor. He frowned, puzzled as he bent to pick it up. Kurosaki unfolded it and there was the neat handwriting he had spent over a decade growing excited over:

Kuro,

I don't remember how often you inject, so you getting this will be just as much of a surprise for you as it is for me!

I got so used to talking to you in writing and maybe some things are just easier to say in earnest that way still. For you, I'll get better at using my words.

I just wanted to say thank you. Firstly because, she's home because of you. We couldn't have done this without you. Your intelligence and quick wit amaze me every day, but this was something else. And thank you for keeping me together. I know I got a little scary at the end there, but still you showed up. I can always count on you, and I hope you can count on me too.

You brought me happiness in a time I thought there was none to be found — thank you. I love you, my moon.

Yours,
Idiot

P.S. Are you ever going to tell me where those other letters are? I'm doing a book report.

Tears ran down his cheeks halfway through reading, but Kurosaki openly wept at *my moon*. He didn't know what Moz meant by the endearment one bit, but it was plain that it had been chosen for him with love.

He wiped his face and folded the letter again, but this time placed it into the back pocket of his notebook with the others. Kurosaki had saved them all; not just from Moz. He saved Jack's directionless ramblings, Avery's aggressive encouragement, Shank's long-winded musings, Maria's jokes that took two pages to set the scene for. The written messages had a magic to them that he could revisit any time he needed and he hoped that none of them stopped writing to him now that he was home.

Kurosaki thought of holding Avery in an embrace the day before. "Welcome home," he had said to her and she answered with the biggest smile. She said nothing about how it should have been *her* welcoming him back to Brightloch.

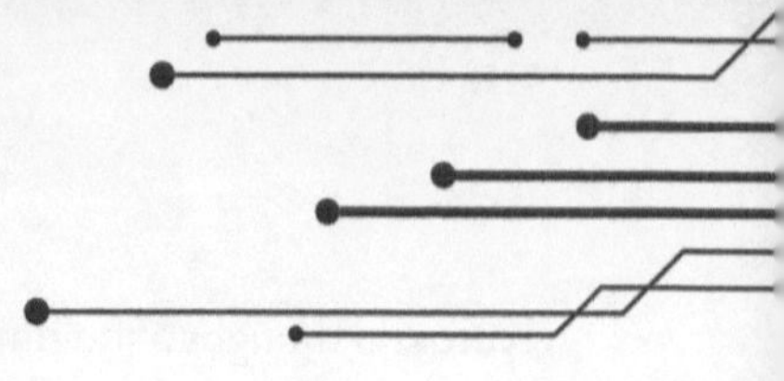

CHAPTER FIFTY-THREE
MOZ

WHEN MOZ CAME DOWNSTAIRS his son and his wife were sitting next to each other at the island. They talked over bowls of cinnamon dusted cereal and without disturbing them from their conversation, Moz planted a kiss on Avery's crown, plucked a stray black feather from the collar of her shirt, and ruffled Griffin's hair. He shifted under Moz's hand in a playful dodge but did not fight him.

He crossed the warmly lit kitchen and sat down at the table, next to where Yumi sat with her arms folded. Her face was fixed in a serious stare, watching over her wife as though she could disappear again at any moment. Sleek black hair was pulled back into a low ponytail and the strands left framing her face were threaded with faint shimmers of silver gossamer. The wide cowl of Yumi's black tunic was pulled up high just under the serious set of her round jaw.

"How was she," Moz murmured. He didn't want Avery to overhear her spouses discussing her state and risk leaving her feeling infantilized.

"Understandably fragile," Yumi answered. "I helped her get cleaned up in the shower again and got some arnica ointment on those nasty bruises. She cried an awful lot when I finally got her into bed. She cried for you and for Griffin and I had to keep telling her you would be here in the morning. That *I* would be here in the morning. It's like she's fine for a moment and then she's gone again."

The mental image of his wife sobbing in Yumi's arms punched him in the heart. He thought of how abruptly Avery's face changed in the fogged vanity from a goofy smile to biting back tears.

"How are you feeling… are you okay?"

Yumi's wet stare traveled from Avery across the room to him, her arms still folded at her chest.

"No," she answered truthfully with a wobbling threat of tears in her voice. "She's everything to me. You're all everything to me. And to see her like this? I think she was our glue this whole time, all these years. She came back. But did she?"

Moz took a deep breath and rubbed his eyes under the frame of his glasses.

"I'm sorry about last night, by the way," she added. "I didn't know you hadn't talked to her yet about him."

"It's okay, I'm not mad."

"Are you sure?"

He didn't answer her verbally, but tucked Yumi into an embrace and hugged her close. They sat silent between the two of them but listened to the sound of their wife trying to muffle her laughter as Griffin talked to her in a low voice. Avery snickered again, dropping her spoon against the ceramic bowl with a loud clatter.

"*Nooo* you're kidding me, he did that?"

The traded gossip was likely at his expense, but Moz didn't care. The walls of Brightloch Castle were already beginning to hum again with rowdy life. Halls would latch onto the sound of laughter and echo them back. She was home and their wounds would heal.

"You're my best friend, Yumes," he finally said.

"You say everyone is your best friend."

Her voice was muffled against his shoulder, held still in the hug. He wanted to laugh but didn't feel like he could. Bones felt too heavy when he wanted to be light.

"Maybe. But I mean it every time."

She huffed a small laugh when she sat upright and the beginnings of a smile appeared on her face.

"I'm guessing everything is okay then," she said. "With you and her and Kurosaki."

"Yeah, we all talked. Which by the way, you never explained why you were so privy to it so fast. And if you say it was a ghost, we're having another banishment."

Yumi turned to him and the smile had fully formed into a grin. "He's a good one. Kuro."

Moz didn't know why that had been her response, but it yanked at his swollen heart anyway.

"Yeah. Yeah, he is. And I love him for it."

Avery crossed the kitchen and poured herself another cup of coffee from the press. She leaned against the counter, watching Moz and Yumi. Her hair had been cut to a normal length for her liking, braids ending just at the bottom of her ribs. A maroon and black plaid flannel shirt hung open over a grey tunic and her black pants had been cuffed neatly just above her scuffed leather boots. In the presence of her comfortable and masculine energy again, Moz would have believed it if she hadn't been absent for a single day.

That wasn't the case and he remembered when her gaze shifted and she suddenly looked a million miles away again. Moz stood up from his chair with a scrape against the floor before he headed for the door of the kitchen.

"Where are you going?"

Avery didn't give him time to answer before she followed him out into the foyer; his shadow made of sunshine.

"If people on the inside are in on this, I need to take my case files and board home from the office. I think the Sentry itself is secure, but the police and Scouts are in and out constantly."

Avery shook her head. "Don't do that. Make a new one here and make your own copies of everything. Let them believe that you're stuck in the same place."

He grinned at her as she tipped her coffee cup to her face. If she wasn't careful, the dangerous levels of caffeine she was consuming to catch up on the past two years would leave her blood vibrating for the next two.

"My beloved, you are again a genius."

She smiled sweetly at Moz. "Don't forget it."

"Come with me," he said as he turned to trail down the lower east wing towards the Green Study. He didn't have all of his case files from his office, but he knew he could at least begin the collaboration with his wife. Avery followed diligently, saying nothing as she kept sipping her coffee.

"If you don't slow down, you're going to shit your pants," he teased her.

"I'll go faster and shit yours."

"I am so glad you spent the last two years practicing your comedy routine," he answered her as he entered the darkened Green Study. Avery passed him through the doorway, swatting his ass with the hand half-covered with a leather cap. He rubbed the burning spot with his palm and frowned at her pointedly.

"Um, *ouch*?"

Avery didn't answer as she turned the dial on the lamp and warm light bloomed in the room. She turned and looked at the empty cork board perched above a bookcase.

"Do you think that's big enough?"

It certainly was nowhere near the real estate his papers had taken up on his office floor, but it would have to do. He walked to the desk tucked into the back of the study and rifled through the drawer. Empty folders, a box of pins, loose pens, clips. As he rummaged around, he saw the shape of the figure in his periphery enter the study and stand next to Avery's shorter frame. Griffin; there hardly felt like there was any point to shooing him out of the study while they discussed. No matter how much Moz did not want their only child involved, it was beyond prevention now.

Not after the tell-tale nosebleed.

He found a notebook and plucked it out along with one of the pens. Moz ripped out a page and scrawled across it, scribbling hard at first to coax the ink out of the cartridge. He fished out a pin and strode to the corkboard. After he pinned it to the center of the corkboard, he stepped back to stand next to Avery and Griffin with his arms folded.

CULT OF
PAION

"Nowhere near enough," he answered his wife. "But it's a start."

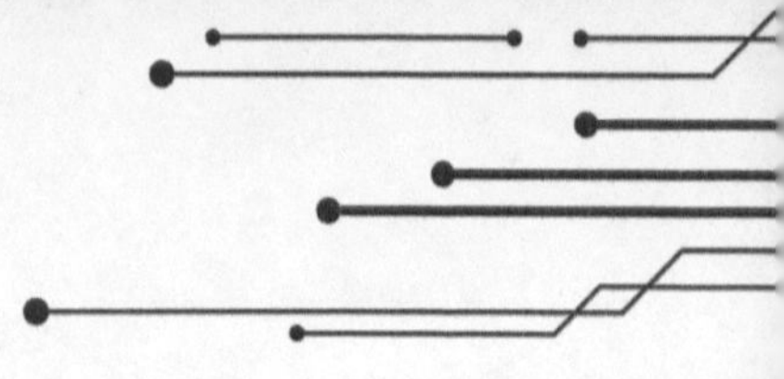

CHAPTER FIFTY-FOUR
GRIFFIN

G RIFFIN'S MOTHER INSISTED ON seeing her own grave. And memorial statue. He would have found it deeply vain if they had not been erected so hastily or if Avery Porter wasn't as nearly a hilarious woman as she was.

"And they just... put this statue up the day after the funeral? The same funeral where my coffin was empty?"

Moz nodded, arms folded and unamused on the other side of Griffin. "That's the one."

Avery snorted, gesturing towards the bronze statue with the hand holding her coffee cup. "Why did they make me twenty again? Did they forget the part about me aging again? Also, why the fuck is Aegis there? Love that he's covered in bird shit, but he hasn't been around in decades."

"Oh, haven't I?"

Avery screamed at the low voice tucked between her and Griffin's shoulders and she threw her coffee cup hard at the head as she twisted around. Griffin whirled and looked up at the towering man, eyes widening then he saw the rings of gold in inky black sclera.

My hallucination? No, his father told him this one had been real.

Mama shoved the man hard in the chest with both hands. He

stumbled backwards, colliding into Yumi and Kurosaki from where they had stood behind them. Kurosaki pushed him back into Avery's direction like he was in on some unspoken but aggressive game of ping-pong.

"What the FUCK, Aegis," Avery snapped as she bent down to retrieve her thrown coffee cup.

Griffin looked down at the bronze cat to the eerie man with clawed fingers. Aegis watched his mother with the same wondrous amusement that she kept reserved for a babbling child.

"Somebody had to watch over your kid," Aegis chided. "Some father Bone Brain is, did you know he's just been letting them run amuck?"

"If you've been watching me, why haven't you been helping," Griffin asked with his face pulled into a hard frown.

Aegis slid his eerie stare to Griffin and he regretted the complaint immediately.

"Believe it or not, kiddo, not everyone's burning purpose in life is to help you," Aegis snapped back. He added, mumbling to himself, "just like your mother, I swear."

"Aegis, please just let me be for just one morning," Mama pleaded. "Give me one morning with my family and then you can settle up whatever score it is that you have with me still."

"Oh, I don't have a score to settle with *you*. I have one with someone else. Some guy named Woods."

Griffin saw his father's posture stiffen.

"Ethan Woods? The deputy?"

"That's the guy. Why?"

"He's missing."

A smile spread on Aegis' face. "Oh, how interesting. I think I *will* depart, then. I'll come looking for you soon. Mr. Kurosaki, don't stray too far."

"What the fuck does that mean," Kurosaki snapped back at him, but was left unanswered. Aegis sauntered off, much like a cat who had found a focus far more interesting than whatever prey it had previously stalked. When he vanished around the corner, Moz turned to Avery.

"You never happened to see a guy in blues about my height out there, did you? Short red-blonde hair, kind of a square face?"

Avery shook her head. "Never."

"Fuck, okay. I know we said a walk to the water and we're already halfway there, but let's not delay terribly long. Alright?"

"They're probably regrouping right now, as we speak," Yumi interjected, a dark and grave tone to her voice.

Avery wiped the splashed coffee that speckled her hand onto her jacket.

"That's okay, Yumes," she answered. "We are too."

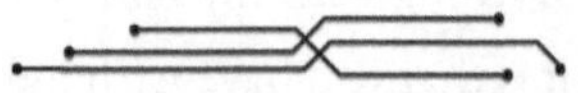

"SCOUT!" Avery shouted from the bottom of the Sills' front stoop.

Shank threw open the door wider, hurrying to slide into the nearest pair of shoes in the foyer. They ran down the steps wearing their daughter's slippers with their heels hanging over the back edge.

"SCOUT!" They shouted back before yanking her hard into a hug. Avery wobbled on her feet and put clear faith in Shank to hold her up when she knuckled the sides of their robe.

"Oh, fuckin' hell," they swore, glasses fogging before they kissed her cheek, and turned her head a little too sharply to peck the other. Shank tucked her head under their chin and hugged Avery in a tight squeeze. "If you ever do that again, I'm killing you myself. Jot that down for the record."

Griffin watched Jude enter the open door frame behind them and even the cold blue of the bruise blooming on her cheek warmed in her smile.

"That's the friendship I never saw coming," he overheard Kurosaki behind him.

"Would you believe me if I said she had a crush for the first five minutes of meeting each other," his father answered and Griffin's face flushed hard. "But she got over that real quick when they kept catching her acting dumb."

Griffin whirled around. "What?!"

"Your mother," Moz lifted the marred brow. "What did you think I meant?"

After slipping into her boots, Jude bounded down the steps of the front porch and threw her arms around Griffin. He swayed with the impact that stung the slash across his torso, but he smiled.

"I'm so glad you're okay," Jude said softly over his shoulder.

"We're going to the beach," Avery said to Shank. "Would you all like to come with us?"

Shank shook their head. "Angela understandably had the shit scared out of her yesterday, so we're spending some time at home as a family. We'll catch up with all of you later, though."

Avery patted both their shoulders. "Understood. We'll see ya."

Their families parted and Griffin followed his three parents - and Kurosaki - down the south hill towards the harbor, where he not too long ago had kissed Jude for the first time.

He followed his mother and father down the jagged stone steps that ended at the rocky shore. Just as he heard the first crunch of pebbles under his boots, Avery took in a deep inhale.

"I can't remember the last time I saw the sea."

Something inside Griffin pulled him to the shoreline where the land became the cold waters of the Stillmaw Sea. It slithered in the back of his brain in the same place he would hear the squawk of Creak's voice. He wrote it off as only in mind when he stepped towards the waves lapping and licking at the stones of the beach, until he found his father beside him.

"You feel it, don't you?"

Griffin looked up at Moz. How did he know about this new voice? But the soft way his father asked the question left room for Griffin's faith that he would somehow understand.

"What is it?"

His father looked out at the waves, drawn to a single point but Griffin was afraid to look anywhere but the serious fix of his face.

"The Knight of Sea," Moz finally said after a long moment of silence. "I understand it now. Your mother murdered one, but we failed to exorcise the others. It was mine and I carried it when I should have kept trying. And because you are my son, it is yours now too."

He turned to look at Griffin, tears welling in his eyes. "I am so sorry. We all fucked up and now it's yours."

"Is it going to hurt us?"

"I don't think so," Moz admitted, but the lack of certainty was anything but comforting to Griffin. "If it wished to, it would have by now."

They said nothing for a long moment until Moz clapped a hand around Griffin's shoulder with a small squeeze. His father left him standing alone at the shoreline, like he couldn't bear to look at the frigid waves any longer.

He wasn't lonely for long before his mother took Moz's place.

"It's pretty, isn't it?"

Griffin didn't answer, but looked down at her beside him. Mama's distant gaze lost its unsettling feeling when she had the whole expanse of the water before them to watch.

"You never went to Eyon while I was gone, did you?"

"No, why?"

She huffed a small laugh. "It's a weird place."

"I would imagine so, if that's how we end up with people like Kurosaki. Too many guns. I think Dad has a crush on him."

Avery let out a sharp, unexpected laugh and Griffin again smiled at the sound of his mother.

"Something like that," she said and he fixed his gaze back on the glittering water.

It was peaceful standing there with Mama. What she had done

the day before with bone-snapping revenants frightened him, as did the sight of her fogged eyes that burned into the backs of his eyelids before he fell into a dreamless sleep. But she was still Mama.

Griffin understood the fear of her a little better, but fear was nothing new to him. It came for him daily in hands knocking on walls and shadowy bodies for his eyes only. He could be better than fearful. He could be brave for Mama, even if it was only he who refused to run away.

A shadow rose over the waves slowly and Griffin squinted his eyes as he tried to sharpen his vision. Waves churned with whitecaps until their peaks grew higher and higher, slapping in opposite directions. A cut formed in the water, leading from where Griffin and his mother stood to where the shadow slowly took a humanoid shape.

The waves dredged water from the floor of the ocean, leaving behind a carpet of beached kelp and slick stone. He realized that whatever waited on the other end of the pathway, it was beckoning to him.

He couldn't resist the pull on his feet drawing him out over the wet rocks. Griffin carefully treaded towards the figure awaiting him at the other end of the parted sea.

"MacNonnan," he heard Avery behind him. Griffin rarely heard utterance of the sea god's name, but he recognized its strange shape in an instant. The god was cast in the shades of summer sea and tangles of aquatic vegetation looped through his long hair beneath a crown of bony spears.

His mother followed him out to sea, treading carefully in the space between the parted water towards the large, jagged stone that lay at MacNonnan's barnacle-freckled feet. Griffin stepped on shifting, wet stones and every pace he took towards the towering god rattled his nerves.

As he drew closer, he saw that the shape on the stone looked to have a long sheath and a brown handle. Both were dotted with large barnacles hat watched him right back with gaping white eyes as he approached. He jumped when he felt his mother's hand close on his shoulder.

"Oh my gods," she said breathlessly, holding him in place. Griffin turned to look at her, but Avery watched the face of the sea god. "You had it... this whole time."

"What? What is it?"

Griffin looked back down and his eyes widened. It was a sword.

"Hemlock," his mother said.

Avery let go of him, stepping around Griffin to approach the sea logged weapon before MacNonnan held up a large hand to stop her.

"Not you," he boomed and Avery flinched in surprise. "It has tasted much of your blood. It will react to you and he will know. Paion waits. You must protect it."

"But I used... oh gods, they wanted me to use the bracelet, didn't they?"

The god did not reply, but Griffin found her answer in the silence. Avery turned over her shoulder to look at Griffin.

"It has to be you, bud."

He carefully stepped past his mother, sliding uneasily on the ocean rocks never meant to be exposed to air. Griffin took the heavy longsword in his hands and upon contact, something vibrated in every nerve ending and resonated into the weaving channels of his bloodstream. His eyes widened in gaping horror and he looked from the arcane weapon to MacNonnan towering above him. The god shifted, dislodging splashes of water that fell at Griffin's feet.

"The shadow of the Knight remains in you, but be not afraid, my child. You are not a blight, not a curse, never reduced to an unholy tool. You are a gift. A boy the monsters made when they learned the meaning of the word 'hope'. Be not afraid and *run.*"

Griffin Porter-Mosley

COMING SOON

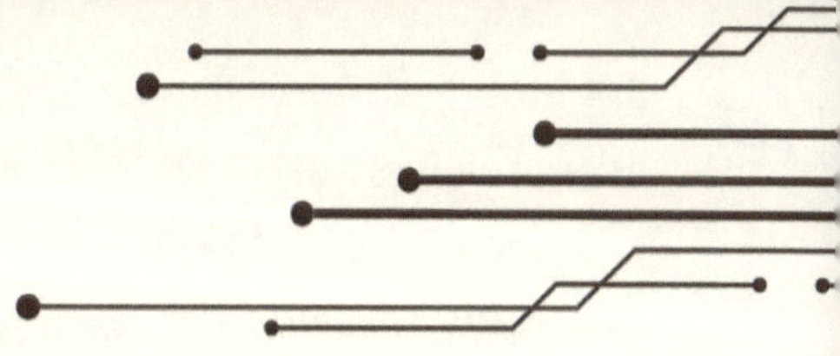

COMING SOON

"*T*HE *MEN HAVE BEEN of the foolish belief that you are the spitting replication of your father. They are wrong, Babs.*"

Griffin looked from the bleeding nose in the mirror to the dripping faucet. His face was mottled yellow with early bruising under the sockets of his tired eyes. *Exhausted* — how had he still slept so little even with Mama's return? He longed for a quiet place to curl up into himself and sleep for days. Instead, the Knight continued:

"*Your father refused his hunger. His insides had decayed in a place yours have been left untouched. You never Reaped because you had to. You killed because you desired it.*"

"That's not true. I didn't want to kill any of those Rabbits, but they would have hurt my family if I didn't. They could have killed Jude."

"*Our Witch would not fall so easily.*"

Griffin scowled at his reflection and wondered if the demon saw through his eyes.

"You keep saying 'our'. What makes you think I am eager to share?"

"*What is yours is mine. What is mine is yours. Your psychosis belongs to me. Your dreams. Your fears. The sound of your name from your mother's mouth. The absent place where most would keep their faith. Son of man, you are mine."*

Boy made by monsters according to MacNonnan, son of man according to the Knight. What difference did it make anymore? Griffin wasn't sure if he had ever belonged to himself. How long had this thing lurked in him, twisting and manipulating anything the warping in his brain had left untouched?

Sometimes he had to tell himself who he was when he felt his sense of self waver: *Griffin Porter-Mosley, son of Scout Avery Porter and Sentinel William Mosley. Refusing Heir to Queen Yumi Harthmoor. Forensic Psychology student at Brightloch University and mediocre charcoal artist. My dog is named Maya and my best friend is named Jude.* Did any of it ever matter?

"If my name is yours, yours is mine. What is it?"

"I am a thing of Od older than human speech. But you may give me one if you feel that gives you some level ground."

Five nameless Knights, all but one gone. Does destruction deserve an anchor for familiarity? Griffin didn't like the hook of a name sunk into his flesh if he couldn't cast his own out to sea. It didn't have to be a thing of endearment; just a word to call the slithering in the gap between his brain and his skull.

"You are called Six."

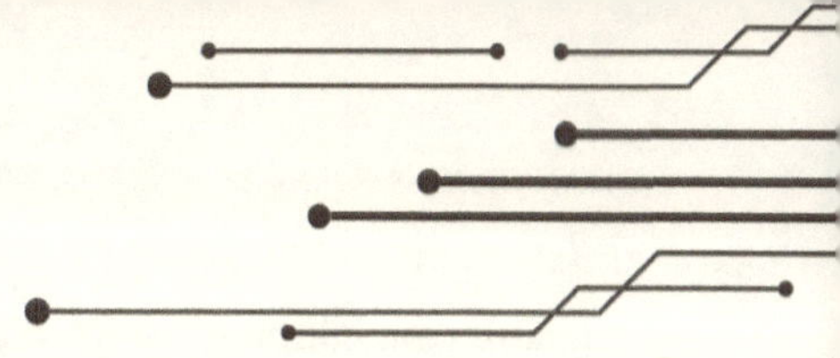

ACKNOWLEDGEMENTS

Thank you, T — for telling me I could kill my cake and eat it too. This book would have had way more uncalled for suckerpunches without you.

Thank you, Clank — for reminding me that when it gets hard to write, it's time to read. Delightfully and unashamedly; that's truly what this is all about.

Thank you, Morgan — for being so quick to love Griffin. When I wasn't sure if I should keep going, you reminded me that his voice was one worth hearing.

Thank you, Harper — for affirming that it was okay to give a story space to breathe and that things can be done just as it demands of me.

Thank you, Kalina — when this shit sucked and I felt like I was going through the meat grinder for no reason, your enthusiasm made it all fun again.

Thank you, clipping. — for making me ask what happened to the guy who ran the city once. Turns out he was working on himself and finally learned how to drive.

Thank you everyone in Congregation for your support and contagious excitement. I became a plotter and multi-WIP writer because of y'all and I will never forgive you for it (with love).

Thank you to the wonderful people at Monster Manor. Because of your hard work and enthusiasm about indie books, I (and many others) have found community. It's been a long year, pass the old man— [*gunshots*]

Thank you to my squad — for being my tether back to the real world and understanding that I came and went whenever the fancy struck. You know how hard this one was and I felt your love all the way through.

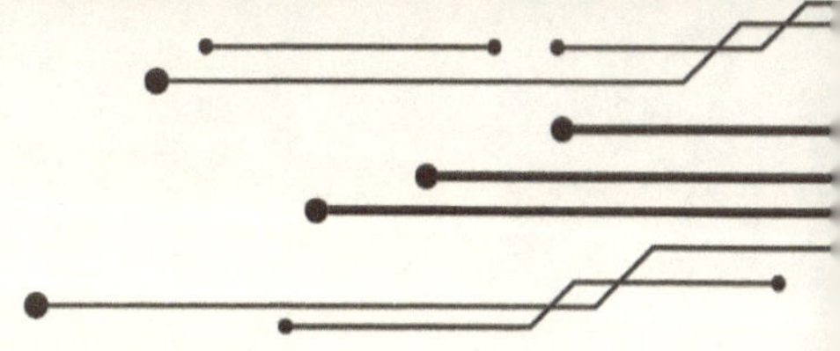

ABOUT THE AUTHOR

R ONAN GRAVES (THEY/FR: IEL) is from the Seattle area and began writing *The Shintori Chronicles* under the pen name Elle Samhain while earning their Bachelor of Fine Arts at Washington State University. They are active in the pagan and queer communities, which have impacted both their writing and visual arts.

If they're not writing or illustrating, they're probably binge watching *The X-Files*, repairing a motorcycle, or talking to cats in sing-song.

Ronan can be found on Twitter at b0dy_snatchers or on Instagram at ronan.graves